D1348714

30131 05836509 6

LONDON BOROUGH OF BARNET

Praise for

KATE RHODES

'Beautifully written and expertly plotted;
this is a masterclass'
GUARDIAN

'Gripping, clever and impossible to put down'
ERIN KELLY

'Clever, atmospheric and compelling, it's
another masterclass in plotting'
WOMAN'S WEEKLY

'Rhodes is a published poet
and every one of her sentences sings'
FINANCIAL TIMES

'A vividly realised protagonist whose complex and
harrowing history rivals the central crime storyline'
SOPHIE HANNAH

'An absolute master of pace, plotting and character'
ELLY GRIFFITHS

'Kate Rhodes has cleverly blended a tense plot with a
vivid sense of the raw, beautiful landscape of the Scilly
Isles, and every character is a colourful creation'
RACHEL ABBOTT

'Kate Rhodes directs her cast of suspects with consummate
skill, keeping us guessing right to the heart-breaking end'
LOUISE CANDLISH

'One of the most absorbing books I've read
in a long time – perfectly thrilling'
MEL SHERRATT

'Fast paced and harrowing, this gripping novel
will leave you guessing until the end'
BELLA

Also by Kate Rhodes

The Locked-Island Mysteries

Hell Bay
Ruin Beach
Burnt Island
Pulpit Rock
Devil's Table

Alice Quentin series

Crossbone's Yard
A Killing of Angels
The Winter Foundlings
River of Souls
Blood Symmetry
Fatal Harmony

KATE RHODES

THE BRUTAL TIDE

**SIMON &
SCHUSTER**

London · New York · Sydney · Toronto · New Delhi

First published in Great Britain by Simon & Schuster UK Ltd, 2022

Copyright © Kate Rhodes, 2022

The right of Kate Rhodes to be identified as author of
this work has been asserted in accordance with the
Copyright, Designs and Patents Act, 1988.

1 3 5 7 9 10 8 6 4 2

Simon & Schuster UK Ltd
1st Floor
222 Gray's Inn Road
London WC1X 8HB

Simon & Schuster Australia, Sydney
Simon & Schuster India, New Delhi

www.simonandschuster.co.uk
www.simonandschuster.com.au
www.simonandschuster.co.in

A CIP catalogue record for this book
is available from the British Library

Hardback ISBN: 978-1-3985-1031-9
Ebook ISBN: 978-1-3985-1032-6
Audio ISBN: 978-1-3985-1318-11

This book is a work of fiction. Names, characters, places
and incidents are either a product of the author's imagination or
are used fictitiously. Any resemblance to actual people living
or dead, events or locales is entirely coincidental.

Typeset in Sabon by M Rules
Printed and bound by CPI Group (UK) Ltd, Croydon, CR0 4YY

MIX
Paper from
responsible sources
FSC® C171272
FSC
www.fsc.org

For my three brilliant stepsons,
Jack, Matt and Frank Pescod

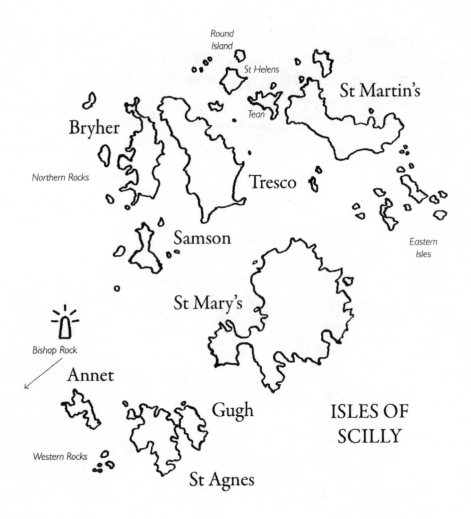

Round
Island

St Helens

St Martin's

Bryher

Tean

Northern Rocks

Tresco

Samson

Eastern
Isles

St Mary's

Bishop Rock

Annet

Gugh

ISLES OF
SCILLY

Western Rocks

St Agnes

Bryher

Tresco

Shipman Head

Badplace Hill

Louis Hayle's house

Site of activities centre

Hell Bay Hotel

New Grimsby Sound

Hell Bay

Shipman Head Down

Hangman Island

Ben's house

The Rock Pub

Porthcawls' Cottage

Lucy Boston's shop

The Town

Arthur Penwithick's house

Boatyard

Gweal Hill

Church Quay

Trenwiths' Cottage

Green Bay

Nathan Kernow's house

Penny Cadgwith's house

Samson Hill

Rushy Bay

'*Unexpressed emotions will never die. They are buried alive and will come forth later in uglier ways.*'

SIGMUND FREUD

Thursday 1 May

It's late afternoon when Ruby Travis sets off on her weekly visit to the only man she's ever loved. This could be her last opportunity to see her father, so she's determined to treasure each minute. The Tube feels airless and unforgiving while she thinks about him. Craig Travis raised her alone, and never let her down, yet the tabloids' version of his chiselled face haunts a million nightmares. She prefers to remember his smile when he collected her from school. He was the best dad ever, making up for her mother's absence, with endless gifts and surprises. He made her feel invincible, until the police stole him from her. News reporters call him a monster, but she knows different. Six of Ruby's nineteen years have been spent apart from him, yet her father remains her biggest influence. He taught her everything she knows.

Crowthorne High Security Psychiatric Hospital lies straight ahead once she leaves the Tube station. The building resembles a fortified castle, its facade blackened by a hundred and fifty London winters. She hesitates before going inside. Her father

1

trained her to be emotionless, but her feelings are too strong to ignore. She hates seeing him losing his power, yet still longs for his company. She hands over her bag and jacket before being body-searched. The man behind the counter exchanges her coat and bag for a token, then gives the same sympathetic smile he wears each week, before stowing her belongings in a locker. Ruby can't tell if he pities her because her father is dying, or because society considers him evil.

Crowthorne's sterile smell hits her as a warden guides her through corridors stinking of bleach, stale coffee and panic. Every metal door is locked, and a man's voice echoes from the walls, screaming to be set free.

A nurse speaks to Ruby in the infirmary, her voice slow, like she's explaining something complex to a child. 'Your dad wants to see you, but he's struggling to stay awake.'

'Is he in pain?'

'The morphine's helping.' Her hand settles on Ruby's shoulder. 'I'm sorry, but there's nothing more we can do.'

'Can we be alone, just this once, to say goodbye?'

'I'm sorry, love. You know the rules.'

Ruby makes her voice soft and childlike, allowing a tear to roll down her cheek. 'Please, it would mean the world to me.'

The nurse considers her request, then gives a slow nod. 'It might get me in trouble, but you can have ten minutes.'

Ruby smiles when she turns away; manipulation is the greatest skill her father ever shared. If she plays the victim, she can unlock any door, but no trick or strategy can reduce her father's suffering now. Craig Travis is lying in a hospital bed, his right hand manacled to the side rail, a last act of cruelty by the prison regime. Ruby barely recognises his gaunt face, until his eyes flick open, so dark they seem all pupil. His gaze feels deep enough to read her soul. His voice is a raw whisper when he beckons her closer.

'Come into the light, princess, where I can see you.' His fingers close around her wrist, the pain instant. His dying grip is as strong as a vice. 'It's time. Follow the plan, Ruby. I'm counting on you.'

'Let me stay in London, please. I can't leave you like this, Dad.'

'I won't rest till you begin. Remember to stick to my plan.'

'I've memorised it. Your friends helped me with everything, but it can wait.'

'Start today, Ruby. Get the bastards that put me away; nothing else matters. If you struggle, take their families. Blaze a trail so no one forgets us.'

'I promise not to let you down.'

'Don't lose your nerve. We're better than them, sweetheart. Never forget it, will you?'

'How could I? You taught me that no one else matters.'

'We're the moon and stars, looking down on those idiots.'

The light in his eyes is dwindling. It breaks her heart, but she knows his mental strength is so powerful he could linger for days, until his last wishes are honoured.

Ruby repeats the plan in her mind; it will end on a tiny island, with DI Ben Kitto, who destroyed her father's empire. She can still picture the man who worked as her dad's driver for over a year, built like a giant, with a face that gave nothing away. Kitto wormed his way into her father's confidence, then betrayed all his secrets. He deserves to suffer most of all. She's determined to work fast so her dad can follow her progress through the radio at his bedside. She stays until the nurse makes her leave, hoping for more words of love, but Travis is only semi-conscious when she kisses him goodbye.

Ruby feels stronger when she's spat back onto the pavement, with her father's dream of vengeance quickening her pulse. She walks back to the station on autopilot, her mind no longer her own.

PART ONE

1

My working day has been spent on tedious police paperwork, so it's a relief to take a stroll across my native island to see a brand-new building project. I've been summoned by the architect for reasons unknown, but she's an old friend, so I've got no complaints. A walk on Bryher is always a pleasure in early summer. The island unfolds before me as I head north from the Town, through a network of small fields where goats bleat for food, more in hope than expectation. I take my favourite path over Shipman Head Down. The site was once a Neolithic burial ground, but the only sign that I'm standing on ancient graves is a scattering of cairns rising from the moss, heather and ferns that lie underfoot.

Badplace Hill fills the sky, where Maeve Trenwith stands near the top, waving her arms in a vigorous greeting. Her long black hair is striking even from a distance. Maeve looked different at school; she was head girl back then, a brainy geek with frizzy curls and braces on her teeth. She was born on Bryher a couple of years before me, but her career has taken a different path. Maeve is a ground-breaking architect now, with her own TV show. She has designed glittering apartment blocks in Dubai, a prize-winning theatre in LA and hideaways for billionaires worldwide, but her latest project is small-scale. She and her husband are devoting six months to building an outdoor activities centre on Bryher. It's mainly self-funded, yet it's caused huge anger in the community. Many are afraid it will spoil an area of outstanding natural beauty. The Trenwiths only managed to get planning permission by stressing that a hundred per cent of the profits will be ploughed back into the island's infrastructure.

Maeve's appearance may be sophisticated, but up close her eyes sparkle with naive pleasure. She appears to be dancing on the spot, shifting her weight from foot to foot. The excitement on her face reminds me of a kid at Christmas. Maeve looks the same when she presents her architecture programme on TV. Her strong features are highlighted by crimson lipstick, and she's dressed head to toe in black despite the day's warmth.

'Thanks for climbing up here, Ben. Come and see our progress.'

'How are the foundations going?'

'Great so far, but it's complex work. The building will project from the cliffs like it's floating on air. It'll look like a cascade of glass running down to the shore.'

'If it matches your drawings, it'll be impressive.'

'The TV team are coming back tomorrow to film the next stage. You'll have design nerds flocking here all year round.'

'I can't wait for my island's peace to be shattered.'

She grins at me. 'No sarcasm, please. This project means a lot to me and Danny.'

'Is that why you called my police number to get me here?'

'The building will affect everyone on Bryher. I need your help to persuade the doubters.'

'Why? You've got planning permission, you can go full steam ahead.'

'It doesn't work like that here, as you well know. People can refuse to work for us, and block our supplies. We need everyone on board.'

'That won't happen overnight. Your plans only scraped through when the island council voted.'

'Don't they remember the hotel chain that wanted to build on the same spot? We moved heaven and earth to stop them dumping tons of concrete here.'

'People don't like change, that's all.'

'It irritates the hell out of me. Our team will learn precision building skills, the community gets the profits, and six islanders will have full-time jobs when the centre opens. What more do they want?' She musters her widest smile. 'Everyone trusts the deputy commander of the island police. If you support us, they'll follow suit.'

'I'm not that influential.'

'They respect you, Ben. Your opinion matters.'

'You brought me here to twist my arm?'

'Come and see our work. I promise you'll be blown away.'

Maeve enthuses about her project as we approach the cliff edge, but most of her words pass me by while I enjoy the scenery. The island is only two miles long and half a mile wide, yet the landscape never bores me, because it's ever changing. We're standing on Bryher's northernmost tip, where sunshine bleaches the stones underfoot as pale as chalk. When we reach the building site, there's only one house looking down from the peak of the hill. Retired businessman Louis Hayle lives in the imposing granite property; it's three storeys high, commanding a bird's-eye view of the entire island. His home is situated just fifty metres above Maeve's building site. Shipman Head lies directly beyond it, the open land littered with boulders. It's the island's last piece of solid terrain before the Atlantic takes over.

Danny Trenwith stands inland, consulting a clipboard. His appearance is the opposite of his wife's glamour. His clothes look grubby, his padded jacket and jeans spattered with mud. He was born here too, but unlike Maeve, he's still recognisable from our school days, when his uniform was always messy. Evidence of the builders' hard work lies everywhere I look. Giant moles appear to have left a trail of devastation across the downs, with earth heaped in huge piles, a mechanical digger parked near the cliff edge.

The ocean can play cruel tricks at this time of year, with storms rising from water that seems unnaturally calm, but there's no breeze today, the gulls wheeling overhead in slow circles. It's peak breeding season for the island's birds, and no one can visit Shipman Head until the fledglings depart in mid-August. Sabine's gulls and shearwaters are nest-building on the cliffs, dozens of them hovering over the dark green Atlantic Ocean.

It's only when I look over my shoulder that the scale of Maeve's project hits home. Huge steel pylons jut out from the rock like the prongs of a forklift truck.

'How do you stop the whole thing tumbling into the sea?'

'Computer modelling, and tough materials. The place will last for centuries, despite tidal erosion, thanks to reinforced steel. Those supports penetrate eight metres into the rock. You could drop the Houses of Parliament on them and they still wouldn't buckle.'

'Pity. Most politicians deserve a good dousing.'

'Our site beats all their ecology targets. The design's carbon neutral, there'll be nothing like it anywhere in the world.'

'I voted for it, remember? Save your breath for the diehards.'

She releases a slow laugh. 'Sorry, it's my new obsession. Can Danny and I buy you and Nina dinner at the Rock tonight? I want Zoe to come too, I haven't seen her for ages.'

'You're charming everyone with free meals so we stay loyal?'

'That could be a tiny part of it,' she admits, grinning. 'I'll text Zoe and see if she's free.'

Zoe Morrow was my closest friend when I was growing up, but her life's in India now. She's only home for a short break.

'I promise not to rant about the build tonight, Ben.'

'Why do I feel like I'm being recruited?'

'Because you are. Can't you see it's exciting? Don't you feel like rolling up your sleeves and getting involved?'

'I'd sooner relax with a book.'

'We'll change your mind tonight. Is eight okay?'

'That should work.'

I'm already waving goodbye. My cottage lies half a mile away, a ten-minute walk from the hotel owned by Zoe's parents. Hell Bay Hotel has expanded over the years to accommodate guests that flock here each summer to birdwatch, walk, or dive the local shipwrecks. I feel a pang of guilt for not rushing over to greet Zoe and her husband Dev when they arrived from India two days ago, but tonight's dinner will make up for my neglect. It's lucky that Zoe's always been hard to offend.

The coastline opens out when I reach the path down to the beach, and the reason for Hell Bay's name becomes obvious. The shoreline is guarded by a dozen jagged outcrops that vanish underwater at high tide, causing many ships to founder over the centuries. I'm about to head home when a man's cultured voice calls out my name.

'Benesek Kitto, I thought it was you. Can I have a word?'

Louis Hayle must have marched down from his hilltop property. His reputation as one of the island's wealthiest benefactors is long established, even though he's only lived here full-time for the past few years. He was a big presence in the days when he only summered here, investing heavily in the local economy and setting up a mentoring scheme for local kids. He made his millions from haulage, with vans, lorries and planes travelling all over the world. I remember the huge yacht he owned when I was small, and the helicopter he flew down to Bryher. He looked like a movie star back then, tall and athletic, with a wife who avoided the limelight. He's in his seventies now, but still well groomed. His expensive windcheater is zipped up to his chin, despite the mild weather, his grey monobrow giving him a look of permanent fury.

'How can I help, Mr Hayle?'

'I saw you talking to Maeve Trenwith; I hope you're not taking her side. Her husband was a protégé of mine, years ago, but now he's tormenting me.'

'Meaning what, exactly?'

'I've warned them to move their wretched building away from my property. If they don't, I'll sue their company.'

'Your case won't succeed, I'm afraid. The council approved the build.'

'I objected then and I object now. My view will be ruined, and the islanders who claim to be spiritual will be horrified.'

'Why's that?'

'Ancient settlers climbed up Badplace Hill for rituals, and to bury their dead. We're standing on thousands of graves.'

'I know it was a burial site, but the Archaeology Council says that's well away from the cliff edge. They agreed the designs.'

'It's pushing the margins, don't you think? Graveyards should be respected no matter how old. I've even heard a folk tale about the perils of digging on Badplace Hill.'

'That's news to me.'

'I'm no great believer in myths, but the story goes that disturbing sacred ground here brings bad luck. The Trenwiths will live to regret their actions if there's any justice in the world.'

He marches away before I can say goodbye. His manner was just as arrogant when I was a kid, which is why I only attended one of his summer schools. He expected every child to follow his edicts slavishly. I preferred the clear rules of rugby and boxing, or to spend my weekends running wild around the island with Zoe. Something's changed, though. I don't remember him being so angry back then. His complaints are a reminder that the building divides my community down the middle, between passionate supporters and those who resist change. Maeve Trenwith may have plenty of charisma, but she's been away too long to command much loyalty. She's forgotten how determined the islanders can be. If her building fails to win them over, their outcry will wake the dead, without any need to dig up the ground.

2

Ruby feels a new sense of purpose when she enters her one-bedroom bungalow. The rented place has been her home since leaving care three years ago at sixteen, after drifting from one foster home to the next, without making any deep connections. Social workers tried to break her loyalty and stop her prison visits. They said her father was evil; he was the worst gang overlord ever seen in London. Ruby hated them for it. Her dad was just taking care of business. He hired killers for hits, ran extortion gangs and organised cyber-crime on a massive scale. The people he had killed were the scum of the earth; he did it to protect the empire he'd built for her.

She's ignored most of the social workers' advice – apart from using an assumed name and maintaining a low profile. That fitted the plan her dad taught her years ago, in case he ever got caught. The police agreed that she must avoid the prying eyes of journalists. Her home is shabby and little bigger than a caravan, but it's been her sanctuary. It's a far cry from the mansion she lived in with her dad as a child, where her playroom was filled with every imaginable toy.

Ruby has spent many solitary evenings here, drawing in her sketchbook, or reading. But she's also kept busy, researching how to achieve her dad's wishes. She's carried out many visits over the past three years, and taken evening classes in combat judo, to be fully prepared. Her existence has gone unnoticed in this anonymous south London suburb, where she's held down a job in the kitchen of a local café without making a single friend. She has no concerns about abandoning her routine at last, to get even for her father's incarceration.

She scans the pages of notes he wrote years ago, remembering every word, before going into the bathroom to complete the first step. Ruby applies the hair dye she bought months ago. She peers through the net curtains as the colour develops. There's no one in sight; it's lucky the house is surrounded by high privet hedges, which hide it from view. One of the biggest lessons her father taught her is to trust no one, except his closest allies. A handful of his gang members remain loyal, but many have abandoned him now he's no longer in command.

A stranger peers back from the mirror once the bleach is rinsed off. Ruby's dark hair has been replaced by blonde tresses that fall to her shoulders in soft waves. She normally wears mascara, lipstick and foundation, but not anymore. The girl she's become looks younger and more vulnerable.

Ruby sifts through a shoebox full of documents to find her old passport and driving licence, and the ones bearing her new name. She places the old letters, books and personal items on the sofa, keeping one photo of her dad in her purse with her new ID. Now all that's needed is to wipe away every trace of his plan and her own involvement. She empties a can of paraffin on the worn carpet, then strikes a match. Fire dances across the floor in moments. Soon the hallway is full of flames that leap higher, making paint blister from the walls.

She throws one more match before stepping outside, with her backpack slung over her shoulder. It's 7 p.m. and the neighbourhood is quiet. Ruby has reached the end of the road before there's an explosion and the sound of glass shattering. She glances back at her home going up in smoke, with no regrets. Safety is a state of mind, her dad says; you must adapt fast wherever you land. There's excitement on Ruby's face when she hears a siren blaring in the distance. Her pace is rapid as she begins her new journey.

3

My dog is on the doorstep when I get home. He gives a single bark of greeting, but not his usual ecstatic welcome. Shadow has had divided allegiances since Nina moved into my house. The wolfdog became her loyal follower the minute she unpacked her suitcase, unwilling to leave her side.

'Are you going to let me indoors?' I ask.

His pale eyes assess me before he finally retreats. I can locate Nina from the sound of a hammer beating on metal, which is an everyday occurrence. I'm still surprised that she finally agreed to give up her independence and move in with me, after endless discussions, but her pregnancy clinched the deal. It's working fine, on a practical level. I like the way we share the chores without argument, and how she's made herself at home. The only things that bug me are her obsessive tidiness and her need to keep busy, even when she should be resting. I get the sense that she's withholding judgement on cohabiting until our baby's here, because she never raises the subject.

I can't complain about the DIY miracles she's been performing every day. She seems to get a thrill from renovating the place. The single-storey house my grandfather built has never looked more prosperous, the kitchen's quarry tiles gleaming with fresh varnish. Nina is in the bathroom, humming to herself while she sorts through tools. She's removed the sink from the wall. I can see a U-bend, screws and pieces of copper pipe lying in neat piles.

'What are you dismantling now?' I ask.

'I'm replacing the tap. I can clear the blockage at the same time.'

'Why not take a siesta? The nurse said your blood pressure was up.'

'It was just a blip. When she came back today, it was fine.'

'That's good news. What kind of reward do you want for all this hard labour?'

She glances up at me. 'You could say you love me now and then.'

'Isn't that meant to be spontaneous?'

'You emotionless brute.' I know she's teasing me, but it's a fair a point. I can't explain why the words stick in my throat when I've spent the past year trying to convince her to marry me.

'How did it go at the building site?' she asks.

'It's pretty impressive. They've driven these huge metal rods into the cliff face.'

'Why do men always love big machines?'

'Too much Lego as kids. Don't overdo it, okay?'

She pretends not to hear, too immersed in her work to care about health advice. Her chocolate-brown hair is tucked behind her ears as she studies notes printed from the internet. I still fancy her so much, even though she's eight and a half months pregnant. Her tall silhouette hasn't changed, apart from her abdomen, which curves in a neat bump. It's her expression that undoes me. She's trained as a counsellor, yet she's giving her plumbing task one hundred per cent focus, like a new apprentice, biting her lip in concentration. Nina applies single-mindedness to everything she does, from arranging my hundreds of novels in alphabetical order to binning half my clothes, claiming they were shabby. I'm certain she's been trying to fix my personal flaws ever since we got together, using the same stringent approach.

It still bothers me that she got hurt four months ago, thanks to a case I was leading, almost losing the sight in her left eye. There's no visible sign of it now, except a scar on her temple that's already faded. It's a piece of history she chooses to ignore, but my guilt surfaces whenever I see it. I'd like to wrap her in cotton wool until the baby arrives, and Shadow appears to feel the same, yet she's having none of it.

'Don't stand there gawping at me, Ben. I'm dying of thirst.'

'I'll put the kettle on.'

'By the way, someone called Sarah Goldman rang

earlier; she wants you to Skype her urgently. Is it about work?'

'She's my old boss from London. It's probably nothing; I'll make us a drink first.'

I know immediately that something's wrong. Commander Goldman is a typical senior officer, overseeing four hundred front-line police, including London's biggest undercover network, from a suite of offices at the Met. She doesn't have time for social calls to former employees. My old job fills my mind while the kettle boils and I gaze out of the kitchen window. The sea beyond looks unnaturally calm. When I return to the bathroom, Nina is flat on her back, with screwdriver in hand, too busy to notice the mug of tea I place on the lino.

It takes me several minutes to get a Skype connection, which is a feature of island life. The signal in Scilly is unpredictable, and often non-existent in winter, casting us back to a time before the internet ruled the world. Commander Goldman looks older when her face finally appears on my computer screen. She's on a task force trying to root out institutional racism and sexism in the Met, which could be a tall order. Her hair is white, as if London's crimes rest on her conscience alone.

'I'm hearing good things, Kitto. DCI Madron says you're a fine deputy.'

'That's a surprise, ma'am. He's not big on praise.'

'Strike while the iron's hot.' Her deadpan face cracks into a smile. 'Ask for a pay grade review.'

'How are things at headquarters?'

'Hectic, but that's not why I called. I've got some information. Do you remember the Travis case?'

'It's hard to forget.'

Craig Travis ran a massive gang network that I helped to break six years ago, in my last undercover job for the murder squad. I worked alongside two colleagues, Annie Hardwick and Steve Pullen, to enter his inner circle, and the man took a shine to me. I was his minder for a year, before becoming his driver. He treated me gently at first, keeping me away from the sickening violence that kept him in power for so long. Some of his gang members pretended to be hard men to impress their boss, but Travis was the genuine article. He had no conscience at all, killing anyone who crossed him, with no sign of regret. When I finally caught him in action, he had hundreds of employees, from professional hit men and racketeers to hackers and drug traffickers, his complex empire extending to every London postcode.

'I wanted to keep you informed of developments, given the scale of his network. Travis is dying of cancer in Crowthorne, but we believe he's still a threat.'

'How do you mean, ma'am?'

'A nurse heard him rambling about getting even with police who put him away, and it sounded credible. He's still got contacts. Old loyalties run deep in gangland, as you know.'

'I'm a three-hour ferry ride from the mainland. No one can reach me here, ma'am.'

'Don't underestimate him.'

'Most of his cronies are dead or locked away. How would he find us?'

'Maybe he's bought the information from someone at Crowthorne.'

'If it's taken him this long, it's out of date.'

'I want you to treat it seriously. He might just be an ailing psychopath who got what he deserved, but we still need to be cautious. Steve Pullen knows the situation, but I need to inform Annie Hardwick. Are you still in contact?'

'I called her a few times, but she'd changed her number. She had this plan to move down to the West Country and live off grid on a smallholding after she left the force.'

'She's vanished completely, which is a concern. I can't offer her protection if things escalate.'

'Annie can look after herself; she's as tough as they come.'

'Not if she's unprepared.'

'Thanks for letting me know, ma'am.'

'Stay alert, Kitto, until we speak again.' Commander Goldman's face dissolves into a blur of pixels.

I remember Craig Travis's casual delight in hurting anyone who questioned his authority, but it's his daughter I pity most. I got to know Ruby during my time working for her father; the kid was only twelve or thirteen when his empire crumbled. She was his princess, the only person he showed any tenderness. The girl must have been totally unprepared for life outside her ivory tower. Travis seemed like a typical devoted dad when he fussed over her, yet his lack of empathy for the rest of humanity was terrifying.

Suddenly the house is so quiet you could hear a pin drop. I developed hypervigilance when I worked on the case, but it only returns when I'm under pressure; it's like a sixth sense, warning me of potential danger. Nina has stopped hammering, and the only thing I can see in the window opposite is my own reflection. I'm hunched over my computer like a giant trapped inside a doll's house, with messy black hair, my expression mystified.

4

London lies in darkness as Ruby Travis follows the river path through Greenwich. She knows this area like the back of her hand. She grew up in Southwark before her father's operation took them from a council flat in Bermondsey to a mansion in Blackheath. He told her stories about how royalty used to exercise their horses in the park, and promised that she would live like a princess too, for the rest of her days. She believed they would always be together, yet he was snatched away, and her life has been on hold ever since. Now she must honour her promises.

Fear and excitement make her heart rate quicken as she comes to a halt, then places her hands on the rail, gazing across the Thames to Canary Wharf. The buildings gleam with money, scattering gold coins of light on the slow-moving river. The walkway is empty apart from a few couples taking an evening stroll, too absorbed in each other to notice the slim blonde teenager who appears to be waiting for somebody. No one sees her descend the steps, taking care not to slip on the dark green algae. Her dad brought her mudlarking here as a kid, looking for clay pipes and old glass bottles. The river's odour reminds her of afternoons spent gazing down at the silt, going home with pockets full of history, his arm around her shoulders. The Thames smells the same as ever, of spices, salt and effluent. It will carry away every trace of her old existence, apart from her devotion to her father.

Ruby glances up at the walkway again before undoing her backpack. She takes out a jacket, shoes, her old passport and a folded sheet of paper, then places them on the steps, weighed down by a stone, just above the high-water mark. She takes a final look at her face stamped on the passport. Leaving her belongings by the river is a little too neat for her liking, but the police love simple solutions. They will believe that she took her own life. From now on, she will be Chloe Moore, a budding art student from Brighton.

When a man's heavy footsteps pass overhead, she keeps her back pressed to the wall until the sound dies away. Once the pathway empties, she hurries back up the steps, abandoning her former existence like a butterfly shedding its chrysalis.

5

Exercise is a fact of life on Bryher, and tonight it feels good to let off steam after my tense conversation with Goldman. The island boasts a few jeeps and tractors, golf buggies and bikes, but most people walk to their chosen destination. There's only one tarmacked road, which runs from Hell Bay Hotel on the west coast up to Kitchen Porth in the east, where my godmother, Maggie Nancarrow, has run the island's only pub for forty years. Nina and I make the short journey to the Rock on foot, following a path I know so well I could sprint along it with eyes closed.

We're in no hurry tonight, which suits me fine. The pace of life is one of the things that drew me home from London years ago, and Nina has adjusted to it well. She doesn't bother making conversation as we walk, too busy admiring the poppies and agapanthus blooming between cracks in the dry-stone walls around the fields. She enjoys silence, but I'd like to know more about how she's feeling. She seems to be taking pregnancy in her stride, but she's a stoic, rarely complaining about anything, and I might not guess if she was hating every minute. The nurse has warned her to rest. It concerns me that she ignores the advice, even though I'd probably do the same. She hates following orders, which is a trait we share.

'Have you thought any more about baby names?' she asks.

'Not again, please.' It's the one issue we can't resolve; I can't face revisiting it tonight. 'Let's decide when he's here.'

'We need to be ready.'

'Engelbert, maybe?'

'God, you're annoying. What if it's a girl?'

'Veronica? Or Delilah?'

'We'll come back to the name issue, Ben. It's not going away.'

'I can handle a daughter so long as she's not the needlework type.'

Nina releases a slow laugh. 'And if she is? I enjoy a bit of craft now and again.'

'I'll cope, but I'd prefer a kid who likes outdoor stuff.'

'We'll get what we're given, Ben. Right now, they know we're talking about them. Our kid wants your undivided attention.'

She takes my hand and places it on her bump. I can feel the steady kick of our child's feet pulsing through her linen top, dancing to a rhythm we can't hear.

'He's doing a workout.'

'I love feeling it,' she says. 'But I want my body back, soon. I could murder a vodka and lime.'

I recognise almost everyone in the Rock when we join the crowd. Maggie's inn has overlooked New Grimsby Sound for two centuries; it was a drinking den for smugglers back then, with low ceilings and a huge inglenook fireplace. Some old fishermen are passing the time of day in the corner. Maggie is behind the bar, chatting on the phone, her expression animated. She's a powerhouse, even though she's only five feet tall and well into her sixties. Her appearance hasn't changed much since I was a kid. Her petite build is still trim, grey hair worn in a mass of ringlets, her eyes shielded by round-framed glasses.

Billy Reese serves us, without raising a smile. Maggie's partner should be collecting his pension too, but he's dressed like a biker, with grey hair and a long beard, *Guns N' Roses* emblazoned across his T-shirt. It doesn't take him long to broach the island's hottest topic as he pours our drinks.

'Where do you two stand on this building nonsense?' he asks. 'Surely we get enough visitors without a bloody outdoor activities centre?'

'Locals will use it too,' Nina says.

'Can't people birdwatch without an expert holding their hand? It's Louis Hayle I pity; it'll be right under his nose.'

'At least the Trenwiths are funding it,' I reply. 'Our economy could do with a boost.'

Billy's weather-beaten face forms a scowl. 'They've brainwashed you, mate. Have you visited Louis' place lately?'

'Not for twenty years, but we had a chat earlier. He thinks I've sided with the enemy.'

'I play chess with him sometimes, and it's getting him down. How would you feel if someone parked a monstrosity in your front garden when you retired?'

'Talk to Maeve, Billy. She'll be here soon with Danny.'

'Those two don't care. They'll bugger off once the place is up.'

'Ignore him,' Maggie says, once her call ends. 'His kitchen hand resigned today; he's been a nightmare ever since.'

Billy gives a sigh. 'The lad's found some flash job on the mainland without giving me notice. I can't find a replacement, and that building project's a thorn in my side.'

'Get over it,' Maggie tells him. 'Let's move with the times.'

'It'll be a bloody eyesore.'

'Stay in your kitchen till you cheer up.' She gives us a long-suffering smile. 'Find a table, you two, I'll get you some grub.'

'We'll wait for Danny and Maeve, if that's okay?'

'No problem. I'll bring it over when they get here.'

'Perfect.'

She gives a cheery wave before serving her next punter. My godmother loves plying us with food and

31

drink; she rarely gives us a choice, but I'm not complaining. Her default reaction in good times and bad is to feed the whole community, keeping the pub open in winter, when the population dwindles. I suspect that her relationship with Billy only lasts because of the kindness that runs through her like the letters in a stick of rock.

Nina and I find a table in the corner, beside some computer-generated images of the building plans displayed on the wall. It's a shrewd move on Maeve's part. Everyone on the island has seen the drawings, because the pub serves as a village hall, with music nights every week, as well as yoga classes and birthday parties. They show a structure that looks too fragile to survive a gale. It's a miracle of glass and steel that appears to be held together by confidence alone, which is a hallmark of Maeve's work. I've seen photos of her most famous apartment block online. It looks as fragile as tissue paper, with panels reflecting the intense sun of Dubai.

I scan the crowded room as we sit down, looking for Zoe, but there's no sign of her and Dev yet. My friend has kept a low profile since flying back from India. She hasn't answered my texts either, which is unusual. My gaze falls on a woman sitting alone in a corner; she's around sixty, attractive, with high cheekbones and carefully styled dark hair. Sandra Trescothick spends her weekdays at the town hall on St Mary's. It's her job to register births, marriages and deaths, so she knows every detail about local families. Her body language interests me. She's watching the world go by as she sips her wine. It's unusual to see anyone quite so relaxed in a public place, without feeling the need to read a book or check their phone.

The pub falls quiet when the Trenwiths arrive, as if everyone has been gossiping behind their backs, but the volume soon returns to normal once they join our table. They still strike me as an unlikely couple. Maeve looks like a rock chick in her leather jacket and jeans, black hair tumbling over her shoulders in loose waves. Danny's appearance is more low-key. He's in his forties, wearing a shabby corduroy jacket, and baggy jeans. He peers at us through glasses so thick his eyes look like wet chips of slate.

'Sorry we're late,' he says. 'DCI Madron called about indemnity insurance. He wants me to sail over to St Mary's tomorrow with our forms.'

'My boss loves paperwork. You've been warned.'

'Thank God he's not my problem,' says Maeve. 'People like that drive me nuts.'

Their roles appear clearly defined. Maeve enjoys the spotlight, while Danny is happy to project manage and stay out of the public eye, orchestrating every practical detail. I barely remember him from school, but he attended one of Louis Hayle's summer camps with me and my brother when I was around twelve. He seemed to love sailing on Hayle's boat, and building kites on the beach. He appears much less upbeat now, as if hard work has drained his *joie de vivre*.

I listen while Maeve quizzes Nina about what drew her to Bryher; I can see she's intrigued by the twisting path that brought her here. My girlfriend had to choose between training as a doctor or going to music school to study violin. She opted for medical training, but withdrew after her first husband died. Then she trained as a chiropractor, finally pursuing counselling as her career. She's secured a part-time job at St Mary's Hospital, to begin once her maternity leave ends. Nina falls silent once all the questions are answered, happier to listen than talk, like Danny. He sits back while Maeve shares anecdotes, her smile burning at full strength.

The evening passes easily, with a few beers and some excellent seafood risotto, which is one of the Rock's specialities. My gaze lands on Maeve's hands as we eat. Heavy silver rings adorn each of her fingers; some are set with stones, the others bearing symbols or letters.

'That's unusual jewellery,' I comment.

'Ugly, you mean?' Maeve says, smiling. 'I made the rings myself; each one has its own meaning. Silversmithing keeps my creativity flowing between building projects.'

'Ben's terrified our baby might be artistic,' Nina says, laughing.

'He's keeping his own skills quiet,' Maeve replies. 'Ben was top of the class in English. If he wasn't playing rugby, or boxing at the gym, he was reading some big American novel.'

The conversation keeps returning to the couple's

architectural work. It sounds like they've been on a roller-coaster ride, with mishaps as well as victories. Our talk only returns to the activities centre as we finish our coffee.

'Why did you come back?' Nina asks. 'You could be building palaces for the super-rich in some exotic city.'

'We couldn't let a hideous four-storey hotel get built on Bryher,' says Maeve. 'It's personal too. We had to leave the islands because there was no decent work. The activities centre means we can help some of the local kids stay here into the future.'

'The building's legacy doesn't bother me as much,' Danny says, his face tense. 'I just want it up and running. Our next project is a huge conference centre in Madrid, but Maeve won't rest till her precious activities centre is finished.' He ends his speech with a frown. It's the first time the couple have seemed out of step.

Maeve prods his arm. 'It was your idea, remember? We've been lucky, so why not pay it forwards? Leaving Scilly broke my heart. I dreamed about the islands for years; the big skies and cairns shaped my imagination.'

'It's odd that Louis Hayle objects so strongly. I know it will affect his view, but his reaction's pretty extreme. Your building's way better than a hotel complex,' I say. 'He told me about mentoring you years ago, Danny.'

'He helped Maeve too, but Louis was a hero of mine as a kid,' he replies. 'I keep trying to win him over, but he's having none of it, which is a pity. He seemed like James Bond back in the day, with his helicopter and that ocean-going yacht. You were here, Ben, you must remember his glamour.'

'My brother and I only joined one summer camp. It was fun for a few days, but his rules were too strict for us. I preferred running wild with Zoe. You two spent weeks up there, didn't you?'

'He taught us to sail. It's sad when old role models let you down,' Danny replies, his voice solemn. 'Louis can't see that we're doing something positive. Everyone on Bryher will benefit, but his bloody view is his only concern.'

'Maybe's he's used to getting his way,' Nina says. 'We all lose power as we age, and he must still be grieving for his wife.'

'We'd never do anything to spoil this place. I want to live here again one day,' Maeve says. 'We're keeping my parents' old cottage as our holiday home.'

'It's good to have a base here.' Danny lifts his gaze to mine. 'How come Zoe never showed up tonight?'

'I don't know, but you'll see her before she flies back to India, I'm sure. They're here for ten days.'

'She's another one that had to leave Bryher to achieve her potential,' says Maeve.

The couple look thoughtful as we say goodnight, as if discussing the past hit a raw nerve. We're heading for the door when my godmother scurries over, clutching a carrier bag. She rises onto her toes to kiss Nina's cheek then mine, telling us to open the present when we get home. Maggie rushes away before either of us can thank her, leaving a trail of energy fizzing in her wake. When I glance at Sandra Trescothick's table, my uncle is keeping her company, which surprises me. Ray is famously solitary, a boatbuilder who avoids small talk like the plague, yet he appears relaxed tonight. Sandra's smiling like he's told a first-class joke. Ray's oilskin is draped across a chair, proving that he intends to stay for a while. I've never seen him drinking with a woman before. I file the idea away to tease him about later.

It's eleven o'clock when we finally get outside. My eyes struggle to adjust from the pub's brightness to complete dark; there's hardly any light pollution in Scilly, with nothing to detract from the night sky. I'm not prepared when a wave of panic suddenly hits me. The darkness is so complete, anyone could be watching us from the shadows, and Goldman's warning rings in my ears. A memory arrives before I can stop it, of driving Craig Travis to a meeting in some abandoned flats at night, before I understood the scale of his violence. I could only see shapes in the dark, but the sound will stay with me for ever. Once you've heard a man screaming for his life, it's hard to forget. The cries lasted a long time. Two of Travis's thugs were wielding machetes; it looked like they were slicing him apart.

'Are you okay, Ben? You seem preoccupied.' Nina's question jerks me back into the present.

'It's just an old memory.'

'You're anxious about the baby coming, aren't you?

I feel the same. It'll change everything. Some days it scares the shit out of me.'

'I'm looking forward to it.'

She looks amused. 'The same old Ben, showing no sign of human weakness.'

'I've got plenty, but I want a family with you more than anything. I'm prepared to make sacrifices.'

'That's a good answer. Maybe it's just my hormones running riot.'

We come to a halt when we reach the first stile, tipping our heads back to watch the constellations, her hand in mine. My eyes fix on the North Star. It's easily the brightest thing in the sky, neon white against a glittering backdrop. The immensity of the view is humbling, yet my head's full of tension. There's still no breeze rising from the sea. I'm happier with Nina than I've ever been, but scared to exhale, in case the fragile bridge we've built between us collapses without warning.

6

Ruby has spent her evening in a cinema, watching action movies, to kill time. It's after midnight when she reaches Soho and heads for a private members' club that stays open late into the night, to keep watch. The evening crowd is thinner as she buys a coffee from a stall that's just closing. People are flagging down taxis or waiting for night buses when she positions herself outside the bar's main entrance. She takes a few breaths to steady herself, hoping that the man she's seeking is ready to go home.

When he comes barrelling down the steps ten minutes later, she walks into his path with calm deliberation. He blunders into her so hard she almost falls, and coffee splashes her jacket. Ruby feels a quick pulse of hatred as she gazes up at one of her dad's old henchmen. She hasn't seen Malcolm Pierce in years, and it's clear he doesn't recognise her. He was a powerful member of her dad's gang, but now he's just a middle-aged drunk in a cheap suit, the fabric shiny with wear.

'Sorry, love, I've had a few beers. Are you okay?'

'I'll survive.' She puts on the Eastern European accent she's practised many times, in case anyone's listening. 'Have you been celebrating?'

'Drowning my sorrows more like. I spend too much time in that damn place.' His gaze focuses on her again. 'You're too pretty to be out this late.'

'I'm going home from work.'

'Take some cash to replace your jacket first.' He takes a step closer, fumbling for his wallet.

'No need, it'll come clean in the wash.' Her smile is forgiving.

'At least let me buy you a drink.'

'I should be on my way.'

'Just a quick one, please. Don't make me beg.'

Ruby can see misery in his eyes. She remembers her father saying that he often slipped into self-pity. 'One coffee, that's all.'

He beams in reply. 'I knew you were an angel the minute I saw you.'

Pierce leans on Ruby's shoulder as she leads him inside a fast-food café that stinks of bacon and cooking fat. The guy has shared all his sorrows before their drinks arrive. He messed up a crucial decision and now his friends have cut him adrift; his life's been in free fall ever since. It's even cost him his marriage. He sees his kids once in a blue moon.

'Poor them. Children need their fathers,' she whispers.

'You've got a lovely voice. Where are you from exactly?'

'Riga, but I had to leave. I came to London for a better chance.'

'You'll get it, love, with looks like yours.'

'That's very sweet.'

Ruby focuses on the next step, now that she's reeled him in. She prepares to leave, saying that her room in a shared flat is only a few streets away. Pierce protests loudly, his speech still slurred.

'Let me walk you there, love,' he says. 'You're not safe at this time of night.'

She makes a show of refusing, then finally agrees. He's still telling her his woes when she leads him outside. They follow the road until they reach the alleyway she chose months ago, on one of her research trips, with no CCTV in sight. It appears empty, apart from litter bins and boarded-up windows.

'This is the quickest way.'

Pierce rushes after her, unwilling to say goodbye. She waits until they're surrounded by darkness before coming to a halt.

'Aren't you going to kiss me?' she asks. 'That's what you want, isn't it?'

He looks happy for the first time tonight. He lunges closer, but never receives his kiss. He's still smiling when Ruby drives a blade into his chest, then withdraws it, the flick knife clutched tightly in her hand. She's done it before, as an initiation ritual for her dad, but this part always sickens her. The sound he makes is more animal than human, a guttural scream when he hits the ground, until she gives his head a vicious kick.

Thankfully he takes less than a minute to die. There's no blood on her clothes, just a coffee stain that's almost dried. Her father's pride in her success floods through her veins. Ruby pulls on latex gloves before removing Pierce's wallet, his watch and signet ring, then stows them in her bag, taking care not to dirty her shoes. Now the police will struggle to identify him. She considers cutting her father's symbol into his skin, but it's too early for calling cards. When Ruby looks down at her victim's body, all she feels is hatred. Pierce was the first to squeal, giving names to the police; he was instrumental in condemning her father to a lifetime behind bars. Her dad's knife is filthy with blood, so she wipes it clean on Pierce's jacket, then walks away.

Ruby waits in the darkness for the right moment. Now that the night-time crowd has disappeared, Soho is deserted. When she finally steps out from the alleyway, streetlights beat down on her face, which appears just as fresh and innocent as before.

7

Friday 2 May

I wake at dawn with a half-forgotten nightmare filling my head. I stare at the ceiling to clear the images, but they return whenever my eyes close. I can still picture Craig Travis's thugs knifing an enemy outside a warehouse in Lambeth, the man's body thrown into the Thames while he was still protesting his innocence. The victim died in my place, which haunted me for years. Travis knew his operation was in danger. Someone was ratting on him, yet he never doubted me, even though I was a relative newcomer. I've never understood why even psychopaths like Travis trust me so easily. Maybe my size provides camouflage. I look big and heavy as a carthorse, with a raw-boned face that must conceal my fear.

The bed is empty when I reach out, so I put on my dressing gown and go looking for Nina. It crosses my mind to tell her about Travis and his sick fantasies, but she looks so serene, I'd hate to give her stress. She's sitting at the kitchen table, drinking tea and studying the ocean with Shadow at her side. It's a clear morning, with no clouds to spoil the horizon, the water still tinged pink.

'Couldn't you sleep?'

'Junior's doing somersaults again,' she says, patting her bump.

When I lay my hand on her stomach, I can feel the same steady kick under her skin, as if our baby hates being cooped up, like me.

'The kid'll be a footballer.'

She smiles at me. 'He normally sleeps through the night. It was you that woke us, tossing and turning. Are you worried about something?'

'Fatherhood maybe, like you said. It's a whole new world.'

'There's something else, I can see you're worried.' Nina's expression changes suddenly, her face convulsing with pain, eyes screwed shut.

'What's happening, sweetheart?'

She grips my hand tight. 'Braxton fucking Hicks.'

'What the hell's that?'

'Muscle contractions in late pregnancy. Jesus, that hurts.'

'I'll call the doctor.'

'No, it'll pass,' she replies, dragging in breaths. 'This is nothing compared to labour. I'll be screaming for gas and air.'

'Me too, at this rate.'

'Thank God, they're fading already.'

The colour soon returns to her cheeks, and I make an effort to look relaxed. She's got enough to deal with right now; I can't tell her that a madman I put away might be seeking revenge. My eyes catch on Maggie's present, still wrapped in its carrier bag.

'Why not open it?' I say.

When Nina upends the bag onto the table, a flood of baby clothes spills out, putting the smile back on her face. Maggie must have spent her last trip to the mainland stocking up on vests, hats and romper suits. I pick up a T-shirt that's smaller than the span of my hand. It hits me for the first time that our lives have a different purpose now. I can't forecast what effect the baby will have on our relationship.

Nina's calm again, her amber gaze meeting mine with the force of a laser. 'We really need to pick the names.'

'I still think it'll be easier when he's born.'

'Listen to me, Ben, please.' She hesitates before speaking again. 'If it's a boy, I'd like his middle name to be Simon.'

'So you keep telling me.'

I should agree immediately. There's nothing wrong with the name, except that it belonged to Nina's late husband, who died in his twenties from an aneurysm no surgeon could mend. It's a part of her life we rarely discuss, even though it's shaped our relationship from the start. She ran away from the islands soon after we met, still faithful to his memory. It took her another year's grieving to fly back and find me again. I used to resent Simon for that unshakeable loyalty, but there's no point in envying a dead man.

'We can call him Elvis if you agree to marry me.'

Nina frowns. 'That's emotional bribery. Why does a wedding mean so much to you?'

'Maybe I'm a traditionalist. We're having a kid, so let's do it properly.'

'We'll still be a family, married or not.'

'What if it's a girl?'

'One of her names could be Simone.'

'I'm sick of this debate going round in circles.'

I'm too annoyed to argue, so I stomp away to get dressed. Simon is an indelible part of Nina's history. I should act like a grown-up and accept how much she loved him, yet it still bothers me; if I try to erase him, it will only leave another scar.

Nina has disappeared into the bathroom by the time I emerge in tracksuit and trainers. I don't want to act like a spoilt child when she needs my support, but exercise will clear my head, leaving me even-tempered for the rest of my day off. Shadow chases ahead as I leave the house, then jog uphill to Shipman Head Down, slowly hitting my stride. There's no sign yet of Maeve and her team as I pass Great Rock and head for Church Quay, with the dog leading the way. The island is still asleep, a *Closed* sign in the grocery shop window. I feel better after my ten-minute sprint, but keen to burn off more adrenaline.

My uncle Ray is the island's earliest riser, which could be a throwback to his days at sea. He's sitting on a bench outside his boatyard, smoking a needle-thin roll-up, dressed in oil-stained overalls. I used to marvel at his work ethic, but I realise now that he labours seven days a week purely for the love of it. He looks like an older version of me, over six feet tall, poker-faced, with wide shoulders, his hair steel grey. He wears his privacy like a badge of honour. I can't resist teasing him, even though I'm still out of breath.

'You were enjoying the registrar's company last night.'

He takes a drag from his cigarette. 'Sandra's an old friend, that's all.'

'Talking to a pretty woman isn't a crime.' There's no response, his face impassive. 'Give me a mindless job, Ray. I'm sick of thinking.'

'That pile of new timber needs shifting indoors, but keep Shadow outside. The dinghy's been varnished. I don't want his paws on it.'

I fling my arms wide to tell my dog he's free to roam, then cart strakes of ash and weathered oak inside. It's a better workout than any gym, the muscles in my shoulders and arms burning as I carry each load. Ray is busy lining a dinghy with sheets of spruce when I go back outside, so I collect a nail gun to help him finish the job. It almost makes me wish I'd accepted his offer of work twenty years ago, instead of running off to London; the wood's smooth texture is a pleasure to handle, though I lack the patience to do it every day.

I'm still enjoying myself when my phone rings. I expect it to be Nina complaining about my abrupt exit, but Maeve Trenwith's number appears on the screen. Her words are too garbled to understand.

'Repeat that, can you? The line's bad.'

'There's a problem, Ben. Come to the site, please, as fast as you can.'

The line goes dead without warning. It could be due to a weak signal, or the panic resonating in her voice.

8

I say a hasty goodbye to Ray, then head north by the quickest route with Shadow chasing my heels. The path takes me along the island's eastern shore, past Church Quay beach, where the ebb tide has exposed acres of white sand. I'm almost level with Maggie's pub when Hangman Island rises from New Grimsby Sound. The island's name comes from the executions carried out there during the English Civil War, but there's no sign of danger today. The sea is flat calm as I pass the huge boulders littered across the beach by Small Boat Carn. I'm level with Horse Point when the metal structure of the new building spikes out from the rock face. Maeve is on the clifftop above, witch-like hair streaming as she beckons me up the path.

It's clear that something's wrong, so I give Shadow a stern warning to stay back. He obeys me for once, settling himself on a patch of long grass. The building team has downed tools. I can see half a dozen men in high-vis jackets standing in a gaggle, faces downcast, as Maeve rushes over to greet me. She looks nothing like the high-spirited woman I saw last night, her skin unnaturally pale.

'What have you found?'

'Come and see for yourself.'

She leads me towards a trench in the ground, near the cliff edge. It's four feet deep, the mud clawed into grooves by the digger's prongs.

'Is this where the foundations are going?' I ask.

'That was the plan, until our foreman spotted something from the digger.'

I catch sight of Jamie Porthcawl, a local builder I've known since birth. He's talking to Danny, their heads bowed. They've chosen a man with a good professional reputation; Jamie is also one of the most laid-back characters on Bryher, but there's tension in his hunched shoulders today. Maeve points at something in the trench below, glinting white against the mud. I jump down into the trench for a closer look and my suspicions are confirmed. A human skull lies exposed, making me catch my breath. It's mottled with dirt, the jaw gagged open, as if the victim died screaming. I'll need to make sure the area is protected from the elements, and from prying eyes, until expert help arrives.

Two male voices sound in my ears while I stare at it. When I turn round, Danny is trying to keep Louis Hayle away, but the old man barges past, his frown deeper than ever. There's something threatening in his manner, even though he's a spent force. He gasps when he peers down at the skull, then releases a torrent of words.

'What did I tell you, Kitto? Those bones are probably Bronze Age. I'll sue the Archaeology Council for this travesty.'

'Step back, Mr Hayle. This whole area's a crime scene; I'm about to cordon it off.'

'That poor creature's rest shouldn't be disturbed.'

'I have to find out if the death was recent. Go home, please, you're obstructing police business.'

'I don't trust any of you. I'll stay here and make sure no harm's done.'

I rise to my feet then eyeball him. 'Leave the site now, before I issue a formal warning.'

He tries to stare me down. 'This is on your conscience, not mine.'

Hayle struts away, towards his house perched on the hilltop. When I bend down to study the skull again, it looks like a broken eggshell. I can't tell whether the passage of time or injury has made it shatter. Instinct makes me scan the ground, for more remains, but there's only a bare expanse of earth. If this burial is part of an ancient grave site, the body was laid far from its community.

Maeve's face is still pinched with shock when I step back onto the grass. I can see Danny ten metres away, gabbling into his phone, while Jamie Porthcawl stands by himself. The builder's frown could be due to uncovering the skull, or knowing that the project will be interrupted, leaving his workers unpaid.

'Send your team home, Maeve. This is a crime scene now. There'll be no more digging till we know what happened.'

The tension on her face triggers my sympathy. Danny will have calculated the exact cost of the build; any delay could jeopardise a project that's close to her heart. She hurries over to her team, and I watch disappointment spread across their faces. Work is scarce in a place this small. It feels uncomfortable putting the project on hold, but I've got no choice. My first responsibility lies with the nameless victim whose skull lies in white fragments embedded in the ground.

9

Ruby orders a sandwich in a café at Paddington station, but soon pushes it away. She's running on adrenaline after walking from Soho last night, avoiding street cameras and staying in the shadows. She hid in a doorway nearby with her baseball cap pulled over her face but got little sleep. People march past the window as she sips her Coke. They come from all walks of life: commuters, students, and pensioners. Each one has tasks to complete, just like her, although theirs look innocent. She sees a teenage couple arm in arm, laughing at some joke. The sight makes her feel lonely. She's only had a few meaningless flings, and now a real relationship is out of reach, but her dad taught her that regrets are a waste of time.

Ruby takes her notebook from her backpack and gazes down at an address scribbled in biro. She's visited the area many times. The house is in Royal Oak, only a short distance away. Suddenly the muscles in her chest feel too tight to breathe. The weight of her dad's expectations rest heavily on her shoulders; it's taken years to organise every stage. She's determined to get it right.

She leaves a tip beside her plate, smiling at the waitress like any well-mannered tourist, and replaces her cap before returning to the concourse. Ruby keeps her face averted to cheat the security cameras gazing down from every corner. It's easier to breathe once she's left the station, even though the streets are full of sightseers. She knows the area well, from visiting her father in Wormwood Scrubs, before the prison's shrink insisted he was a menace to other inmates. That led to her dad's transfer to Crowthorne, where his life grew harder. She used to wander the streets close by, wishing they could be together. It feels good that they're united in purpose now, even though he's dying. If she can deliver his plan to the letter, they'll share her success, no matter what happens next.

Ruby follows the Westway for ten minutes. The wheels of juggernauts grind overhead, the air reeking of petrol fumes, until she turns left down Porchester Road, into a neighbourhood she's visited by day and at night. It's full of Victorian houses, the streets sprinkled with modern buildings that sprouted from old bombsites decades ago.

Number 7 Sutherland Place looks well maintained, the front door shiny with new paint. Detective Inspector Steve Pullen must be house-proud, with money to spare on window boxes full of miniature roses. She could wait on the street corner for the next man on her list, but he might not return for days, and it's too risky – residents could be watching from behind net curtains – so she walks straight to the house opposite. There's a bed-and-breakfast sign displayed in the window. It's another property she's been monitoring, so she feels confident when the landlady answers the doorbell. The old woman studies her through watery blue eyes.

'I'm Chloe Moore, Mrs Caston. I called yesterday to book a room.'

'Call me Iris, dear, I've been expecting you,' the landlady says. 'I've got two vacancies; you can take your pick.'

'Could I have one facing the street, if possible? I'm an art student. I love Victorian buildings; I want to sketch the local architecture while I'm in London,' Ruby says, as the woman leads her upstairs.

'Does this one suit you? It's south-facing, so it gets plenty of light.'

'Perfect. Shall I pay now for the first night?'

'Let's settle up when you leave. Breakfast is from seven to nine.'

'Thanks so much, I feel at home already.'

Ruby's fake smile vanishes once she's alone in the genteel room, with a direct view of her target's house. She perches on the window seat with a sketchbook on her lap, but she's too distracted to draw. Her attention is fixed on the property opposite, watching to see who enters or leaves.

10

It's midday by the time Shadow loses patience with the slow pace of police work in Scilly. He trots in the direction of home, returning to Nina, which is just as well. I can see the police launch arriving at Church Quay, from my high vantage point on Badplace Hill. My deputy, Sergeant Eddie Nickell, is escorting the island's only qualified pathologist, Gareth Keillor, to the crime scene. The pair could be father and son as they march uphill, but their personalities couldn't be more different. Eddie is in his late twenties, still excited by his job, treating every day as a new challenge. His fresh face makes him look like a teenager, even though his daughter is already at playschool. Keillor is retirement age, with thinning salt-and-pepper hair, dressed in golfing trousers, giving nothing away. I thought he was a dry old stick at first, but he's got a decent sense of humour, and he's an excellent golf coach. I'd rather we were out on the fairway today than gazing down at a human skull, but there's no avoiding it.

'Your timing's lousy,' Keillor mutters. 'If you must unearth skeletons, do it later in the day, please. I was at the driving range, improving my swing.'

'Sorry, Gareth. I couldn't just leave it in the ground.'

'What do you need to know?'

'When it was buried would be a good start.'

The pathologist grimaces before lowering himself into the trench. Eddie's reaction is more enthusiastic; he offers me a broad smile, as if unearthing human bones is his ideal form of entertainment. Keillor circles the fragmented skull at a slow pace, then leans down to take a photograph, before pulling on surgical gloves. His expression is solemn when he steps back onto the grass.

'Do you want the bad news first, Ben?'

'Good, please. I'm a born optimist.'

'I can give you some facts about the victim. The skull's from a male. It's possible that it's still attached to the spinal column but you'll need expert help uncovering it. I don't think we're looking at prehistoric remains. When Halangy village was excavated on St Mary's, they didn't find a single bone, due to the soil's acid ratio. It'll be the same here on Bryher. Bones dissolve within fifty years under such acidic conditions – the oxygen content does them no good at all – and that skull's in good condition. No hair, so I assume the victim was bald.'

'And the bad news?'

'He was murdered, with this weapon.' Keillor holds

out a shard of rusted metal, around six inches long. When I produce an evidence bag, he drops it inside.

'What is it?'

'No idea, but I can see what happened.' We kneel by the bone fragments. 'The killer drove this spike through the parietal bone. It went in through the crown of the victim's head, straight through his brain, probably piercing the roof of his mouth.'

'Jesus.'

'An unpleasant way to go, certainly. Let's hope the victim was already unconscious, or maybe someone held him down.'

'Would it have been quick?'

'Instantaneous, and whoever did it had strength, to cause that much damage. You need a bone specialist for the rest. I know plenty about flesh and blood, but little about skeletons, I'm afraid. Contact the forensics lab and see who they recommend. An expert should be able to prove my theory from metal residue left behind.'

'How can you be sure it's male?'

'Men's skulls are bigger than women's, with thicker bone. The areas of muscle attachment are more heavily defined.'

'Can you guess his age?'

'You'll need a lab with a mass spectrometer to tell you how old he was at point of death. The attack was brutal, that's the main point. Whoever drove that spike through his head wasn't afraid of blood.' Keillor looks apologetic. 'Bring the skull over to the hospital if you want more detail.'

'No need, thanks. I'll invite Liz Gannick over from the mainland.'

'Wise plan, she'll give you chapter and verse. The woman's terrifying, but she's the best in her field.'

The pathologist knows Dr Liz Gannick better than I do, even though she allows few people close. Her abrasive style bothers me less than in the early days. Cornwall's chief forensics officer never minces her words, but she's helped me on several cases. I thank Keillor again, then he pats my shoulder and sets off to wait for the next ferry back to St Mary's.

Eddie looks dumbfounded, which isn't surprising. We've had a domestic murder on Bryher in recent history, after a family turned toxic, but nothing to equal this kind of violence. He helps me to rig a plastic awning over the skull when a familiar figure appears in the distance. DCI Madron is a small, stiff-looking man, wearing full uniform as he marches across the moor, then ducks under the yellow crime-scene cordon. I'm surprised he bothered to make the journey; he generally remains behind his desk in Hugh Town. Our egos have clashed so often over the past three years, I'm braced to deflect his criticism. His grey hair is slicked into place with so much Brylcreem even the twenty-minute ferry ride has failed to disturb it. He listens in silence while I explain the situation. It's a surprise when he keeps his temper in check for once.

'I assume you've suspended the build indefinitely, Kitto?'

'Of course, sir.'

'At least there's a local expert on hand. Do you know Penny Cadgwith?'

'I know everyone on Bryher.'

'She spent years in war-stricken countries, exhuming bodies from battle zones, so they could have proper burials.'

'Penny gave that up a while ago, didn't she?'

'But her knowledge is still first class. Get her to make an assessment. Is there anything else I should know?'

'A TV crew's coming over tomorrow to film the next stage of the Trenwiths' build, and Louis Hayle's furious. He thinks we're ransacking the island's version of Stonehenge. He's wrong, according to Keillor. The bones have only been there a few decades, or they'd have dissolved in the acid soil. I'm treating this as a crime scene.'

'Get Danny to cancel the TV people, and I'll deal with Mr Hayle. I want this site guarded in daylight hours, but there's no need to be here 24/7. No one walks up Badplace Hill at midnight unless they're hunting for ghosts.'

'We'll keep it secure all day, boss.'

'Make sure you get that expert verdict.'

The DCI straightens his tie before setting off uphill to confront the island's biggest complainer, leaving me amazed. Madron has remained calm in the face of adversity for once. Maybe that's because our victim was attacked years ago, the brutality of his death diluted by time. When I peer into the hole again, the skull's jaw is still twisted open, the long roots of its teeth exposed. It looks like he's trying to share his murderer's name, if only someone would listen.

11

Ruby is working on her laptop. She set up an email address for her new identity months ago, giving Chloe Moore Facebook and Instagram accounts, but her online presence needs to be more convincing. She checks herself in the mirror, running a comb through her blonde hair. It's still a shock to witness her transformation. There's no trace now of the dark-haired girl she was, with eyes circled by black eyeliner. No one will recognise her as Craig Travis's daughter.

She takes a few selfies, then posts them, slowly fleshing out her new persona. Ruby has never used social media before, because the police warned her against it, and dating sites were out of the question. Her father said that a relationship would be a mistake, so she's never pursued one. Social media appears full of pointless rubbish. People upload hundreds of pictures of their clothes and pets, even their meals, as if every boring detail matters.

She scrolls through a London news site until she finds her actions reported. *MAN STABBED IN WEST END ALLEY*. Police are appealing for witnesses; they assume last night's killing was a mugging gone wrong, because the man's pockets were empty, leaving his identity a mystery. She's willing to bet Malcolm Pierce was so friendless no one's reported him missing. Her father would be proud, but she'd rather forget her victim's agonised screams.

Ruby notices some new movement on the street. A middle-aged woman has emerged from the house opposite, her hair pinned back from her face. Ruby recognises her from photos she's seen. Her name is Fiona Pullen; she's a tall, curvy redhead with a relaxed smile, her skin shiny with health. She spends a few minutes fussing over her window boxes, then retreats inside. Another hour passes before a teenage boy appears, clutching a shopping bag from Sports Direct; Ruby can imagine him showing his mum the brand-new trainers he's bought, after trying on dozens of pairs.

She leans back in her chair. Patience isn't her best trait, but it will be essential to complete her mission. If DI Steve Pullen is working away, it could be days before he returns home. It's almost 2 p.m., and she ought to go out before the landlady wonders why she's skulking indoors on a sunny day. She decides to pick up food from a local shop to keep her energy high during her vigil.

The front door of number 7 swings open just as she's leaving the B&B. Fiona Pullen gives her a smile, like she's welcoming a new neighbour, then sets off with a gym bag slung over her shoulder. Ruby's heart is beating with excitement as she follows in her wake, dodging street cameras and leaving a wide gap between them. She learnt years ago how to become invisible.

12

Eddie stays behind to guard the skull. It's possible that a runner or dog walker might stumble across it, if we leave it unattended. I scan the down for Shadow's pale grey fur, but there's no sign of him. He's probably glued to Nina's side, but his independent spirit means he also enjoys solitary adventures. He's an opportunist, hanging around people's houses begging for scraps, but I learnt long ago that leaving him indoors alone is a mistake. He once destroyed my living room furniture in half an hour, chewing the carpet and scratching every wall.

It's no surprise when his distinctive howl greets me as I head south across open land. He bounds towards me, always keen to join the action, but I'm still processing the macabre discovery. I assumed that the skull was an ancient relic at first. Smugglers were often buried alongside drowned sailors on the island's downs and beaches after their ships foundered. There was no other choice, with the island's churchyard already full, but

Keillor sounded certain that the man's remains are far more recent.

Penny Cadgwith's house lies a fifteen minute walk away, above Great Par beach. I've always known that she was employed by the United Nations, visiting war-torn countries, but not the exact nature of her work. Nina has become friendly with her over the past year, and she seems too gentle for such tough work.

My walk takes me through the Town, with Shadow bounding down the lane, his high spirits out of step with my mood. Some locals are chatting in the street, casting curious glances in my direction. The news of our grim discovery will already be common knowledge. I have little chance of keeping it secret on an island with fewer than a hundred permanent residents, where most families are interrelated. News spreads by osmosis, whether or not it's true.

I notice how isolated the Cadgwiths' home is when I drop down South Hill. The detached property looks as humble as mine, built from grey local stone. It's the view that provides its appeal. It's the only property on the bay, overlooking Merrick Island and Illiswilgig in the distance. There's no escaping the island's history here, with Great Carn standing tall on the hillside above. The conical stack of rocks is one of Bryher's many ancient landmarks. No one knows why the island's early settlers piled stones into towers, two or three metres high, leaving their signatures all over the landscape. The Cadgwiths' property appears built to withstand the centuries, just like the relics. Its walls have been polished smooth by the Atlantic wind, shuttered front windows set in recesses to protect them from gales.

No one answers when I ring the doorbell, so I walk round to the back with Shadow at my side, into a profusion of flowers. Penny is doubled over a beehive at the end of the garden. She looks startled when I call her name, before beckoning me closer.

'It's okay, Ben, the bees are drowsy today.'

'Shall I leave Shadow on the lane?'

'He's fine here, don't worry. They won't hurt him.'

She's a small woman in her forties. Her dark hair is untouched by grey, apart from a wide silver streak running through her fringe. Her face is angular, giving her a bird-like appearance. She's dressed simply in dungarees and a T-shirt. Her only protection from the bees crawling over her fingers is a thin pair of gardening gloves.

'Don't you ever get stung?'

'Rarely,' she says, smiling. 'And only if I do something stupid. I can tell if they're angry from listening to the hive. The sound tells me if they'll accept visitors. Do you mind if I check the last frame?'

'Go ahead.'

Several people on Bryher keep bees, but I had no idea it was Penny's hobby. My family have known hers since I was born, and she's a returner like me, coming back to the house where she was born to raise her kids. I watch her deft movements as she extracts another frame from the hive, glistening with honey and crawling with worker bees. They don't seem to mind being exposed to the open air, only a few flying away, while the rest continue their labour.

'This is the tricky bit,' Penny says. 'Getting the frame back inside has to be done gently. I can't risk upsetting the queen, or the whole lot will swarm.'

She takes her time slotting the wooden square into place, while a dozen bees hover overhead before returning to the hive.

'You make it look easy.'

'Nina should try. She's got the right calm temperament.'

'That counts me out; impatience is my middle name. Can we have a chat inside?'

Penny walks slowly as she leads me back to the property, her voice breathless. I follow her through flower beds rioting with spring colour: purple agapanthus, jonquils and blue heather. The profusion of blossoms must provide the ideal diet for her bees. Shadow gives an odd reaction, just as I'm about to walk through the back door. He sits on his haunches and releases a howl of protest.

'You're a nightmare,' I tell him. 'Stop that racket right now.'

The creature pays no attention, trying to prevent me entering by blocking the doorway, until I have to push him aside. His barking continues, so I shut the door to drown out the noise. I can see no obvious reason for his agitation once I'm standing in Penny's hallway. The atmosphere is serene, her sitting room shabby but pleasant, with furniture that's worn from long use. I see pictures of her kids as teenagers on the wall; both are at college now, living on the mainland. The most recent photos are of Penny and her husband standing on a sunlit beach, their expressions content.

'I hope you're not after Bryan. He's in Penzance all week, training some shop managers on their new IT system.'

'It's you I need, but it's bit sensitive. It's linked to your old job.'

'Sorry, I'm not following you.'

'A human skull has been found near Shipman Head. I thought you might be able to help us. You've got experience of identifying human remains, haven't you?'

She stares up at me. 'I quit my job three years ago.'

'How did you get involved?'

'The UN recruited me when I was working for the Science Council. My master's degree is in osteology.'

'What's that?'

'The study of skeletons, to find out why people died. Bones contain loads of information about diet, illnesses and genetic mutations. You can tell a lot from a tiny scrap. My job was to identify victims of genocide, often in mass graves.'

'Would you be prepared to examine the skull?'

'I'm out of practice, Ben. It might not help.'

'Anything you can tell us would be useful.'

She shakes her head. 'Pretty determined, aren't you?'

'Just keen to know why a man died on our island.'

'Today?'

'If that's okay. It's on Badplace Hill.'

She rises to her feet slowly. 'We'll need to take my golf buggy. My asthma's playing up, so walking would take ages, with me wheezing all the way.'

'Does the pollen make it worse?'

'Ironic, isn't it? My bees adore spring flowers and so do I, but my lungs can't cope.'

Shadow has stopped making his infernal row when we get back outside. He's behaving himself again, following Penny's buggy at a respectful distance. The air still feels oddly calm as we make the journey north, to find Eddie gabbling into his phone when we reach the site. Penny hesitates before stepping out of the golf buggy, clutching a leather bag. When we step down into the trench, her breath rattles in her chest. She takes a puff from an inhaler, then gazes down at the skull. She's rocking on her feet, like the first gust of wind could blow her over.

'Are you okay, Penny?'

'It brings back memories, that's all.'

Her manner becomes business-like once she pulls on latex gloves, then crouches down to examine the bone fragments. Her kitbag is full of trowels, spades and brushes. She uses a circular motion to dust earth from the skull. Soon I can see the first couple of vertebrae as she scrapes dirt away.

'This could be a complete skeleton,' she says. 'Do you want me to find out?'

'How long will that take?'

'Two hours, with luck.'

'Thanks, it would help us a lot. Do you mind?'

She shakes her head. 'This is what I trained for, and I'm curious to know why he died.'

My phone buzzes while I watch her work. She's removing earth with a wooden spatula, her methods painstaking. When I look at the screen, it's another Skype call from Sarah Goldman, so I leave Eddie standing guard. The commander's face is expressionless when it appears on my screen.

'I've got an update about Travis, Kitto. His daughter Ruby committed suicide last night.'

'That's sad news.'

'Did you spend much time with her?'

'Plenty over my two years in Travis's operation. He let me wait inside his house, if I was driving him somewhere. The kid seemed lonely, rattling around in that huge place, even though he spoiled her rotten. He called her his princess. She was his only soft spot, but he exposed her to things no child should see.'

'How do you mean?'

'He had this screwed-up idea that she'd run his gang after he'd gone. She saw men being tortured for disloyalty, or executed. God knows what he made her do behind my back.'

'She was only nineteen. A psychiatrist had diagnosed

her with a borderline personality disorder two years ago; she couldn't form close relationships, except with her dad. The authorities tried to shield her, but that bastard got her in the end.'

'What happened, exactly?'

'Ruby torched her house, then threw herself into the Thames, leaving a suicide note.'

'She didn't have much luck. Her mum died in childbirth, and a dad like Travis would leave anyone traumatised.'

'He's still hanging on in Crowthorne's infirmary. Apparently he didn't react to the news of Ruby's death, the man's a true psychopath.'

The DCI's comment surprises me. If anyone could find a chink in Travis's emotional armour, it was his daughter, but maybe he's protecting his macho image even now. He'd hate any of the prison wardens to see him vulnerable.

Craig Travis's victims often ended up in the Thames, so there's poetic justice in the girl's suicide, but it still seems tragic. What hope was there for a child who never knew her mother, with a father who expected her to be impressed by horrifying violence? Maybe the toxic words he whispered in her ear tipped the balance. When I google her name on my phone, there's just one photo of her, at fifteen, emerging from Wormwood Scrubs after visiting her dad, flanked by social workers. The kid looks like a Victorian street urchin. She's got dark hair, a small build and a face built for sorrow, with heavy black make-up shadowing her eyes.

I put my phone away, still rocked by the news, and turn back to the crime scene. Penny Cadgwith's expertise shows in her work. Half of the man's spine is already exposed, the discs of his vertebrae curving at an odd angle. The thing that unsettles me most is that I can't tell whether the murderer is still on Bryher after several decades, convinced they've got away with it. They must have no conscience at all to drive a spike through a man's brain. I don't need a medical degree to see that the victim was thrown into his shallow grave like a piece of rubbish, without care or ceremony.

13

Ruby is sitting in a pub on Westbourne Park Road, pretending to read a magazine. She only glances outside occasionally. The neighbourhood has become gentrified in recent years, with three-storey Regency buildings standing in proud terraces, their ironwork fences painted black. Fiona Pullen is inside the health club opposite, doing yoga or Pilates. Ruby drinks two glasses of orange juice before Pullen finally emerges an hour and a half later, auburn hair still wet from her shower.

Ruby slips outside without attracting attention, keeping her face averted so the camera over the pub's door won't catch her profile. Pullen is moving slower now, as if exercise has left her too relaxed to rush. There are only a few people around once they leave the main street, lugging shopping bags or dawdling home from lunch with friends. Ruby's father told her to kill family members if the main targets are out of reach, and this could be a perfect opportunity.

Twenty metres of pavement separates the two women, and Ruby senses her chance when Steve Pullen's wife turns down an alleyway. She'll make it as quick as last night's attack, leaving the woman's body by the bins, tucked out of sight. Her fingers close around the knife in her pocket, but she's disturbed by her phone making a series of loud bleeps, forcing her to duck behind a wall. It's a text from Denny Lang, her dad's oldest friend, answering her request to meet up later to discuss the plan one last time. He's the only person who knows how to contact her, since she threw her old phone into the Thames.

Ruby has missed her opportunity thanks to Lang's interruption. The alleyway stands empty, apart from a mange-ridden cat hunting for its dinner. She heads back to the main street to buy energy drinks for tonight's vigil with a sense of frustration. Killing the bastards who hurt her father should be a pleasure, but the need for success is so powerful, she's getting impatient. When she sees her image in a shop window, she does a double take. Ruby would prefer to hide behind a shield of make-up, but naked skin is the best camouflage of all. It makes her look like a schoolgirl, with absolutely nothing to hide.

14

Eddie has worked hard on his phone while I've been with Penny, persuading Liz Gannick to fly over and help us. He deserves a break from sentry duty, so I send him on home visits, to reassure people that the remains could be decades old. It's a pity Gannick can't get here immediately, but nothing happens fast in Scilly, and Penny Cadgwith is a good substitute. I'll have to accept that the crime scene's chain of evidence will be compromised by her excavation, but the case deserves the same urgency as a recent killing, with full forensic support.

It's almost 4 p.m. when Maggie Nancarrow arrives; my godmother was bound to appear sooner or later. She has an uncanny ability to sense the exact moment when hunger strikes. I haven't eaten since breakfast, so she's a welcome sight hurrying uphill from the bay. She's dressed in her usual no-nonsense garb: jeans, walking boots and a bright red windcheater. She travels everywhere fast, as if time-wasting is a capital offence.

She observes the tent over the human remains with open curiosity.

'I've brought sandwiches, snacks and coffee.' She tips her head back to inspect me, nut-brown eyes looking for clues. 'Spill the beans then. What have you found?'

'A skeleton. It may have been there ages.'

She nods rapidly. 'This place is called Badplace Hill for a reason. Nothing good happens up here, that's why. Smugglers killed customs and excise men here in the old days, then left them in unmarked graves.'

'It looks much more recent, but I need a professional opinion. Penny Cadgwith's working on it for me. She should be able to say how long the bones were underground.'

Maggie's eyes widen. 'I'm surprised she's volunteered. Didn't you ever see her on the news?'

'Not that I remember.'

'Her team were heroes, working in terrible conditions, exhuming bodies in searing heat. When I looked her up on the internet, it turns out she's a world authority. She's worked in Rwanda, the Congo and Iraq.'

'Why did she stop?'

'Exhaustion, I think. She quit a couple of years ago and hasn't worked since.'

'Maybe I pushed too hard to bring her here.'

'Penny's no walkover. She looks frail, with her asthma and so on, but she's tough. She's survived witnessing terrible things.' Maggie scans my face again. 'If the bones are from an islander, why the hell didn't any of us notice them going missing?'

'All we know for sure is that it was a male. Gareth Keillor's certain we're not looking at an ancient grave, but don't share that, will you, Maggie?'

'Have I ever broken a secret?'

'No, thank God. I'll give out more details at a public meeting. Have you got somewhere at the pub we can use as an incident room?'

'The party room's free, if you can stand the decor. You can hold your meeting in the bar.'

'Great, and thanks for the baby clothes, by the way. Nina loves them.'

Maggie's too distracted to listen. 'I still can't believe a lad got killed quarter of a mile from my pub and no one knew.'

'We'll find out what happened, don't worry.'

My godmother's phone rings, summoning her away. She bounces onto her toes to kiss my cheek, then sets off downhill, trailing positivity like a comet's tail. It's not surprising she's so well liked. Maggie doesn't just run the island's pub, she's also the selling agent for local fishermen, fighting to get high prices for every catch. It's her industry that binds Bryher's community together, although she rarely accepts praise. If anyone tries to thank her, she shrugs it off, as if helping people is second nature.

Penny emerges from the tent to collect more tools, her expression grave. I can see it's the wrong time to offer her food, even though Maggie's supply could support a small army. Shadow appears as I take my first bite from a ham sandwich. The creature's ability to sniff out grub is even keener than Maggie's nose for gossip. He's too proud to whine, but watches me so keenly I feel obliged to chuck him a sausage roll. He swallows it in one, then looks at me expectantly.

'That's your lot,' I tell him. 'No one likes a scrounger.'

His behaviour changes in a blink. Suddenly he's lost interest in my picnic, his ears pricked as he scans the horizon, giving a single loud bark. A man's tall form is approaching, with a German shepherd racing ahead. Shadow leaves my side to greet the dog, and I recognise its owner immediately.

Nathan Kernow has lived in the Town all his life, but I don't know him well, even though we're around the same age. He went to a boarding school on the mainland, so our paths rarely crossed. He's a familiar presence in the pub, accepted by everyone despite his eccentricity. His clothes taste is unpredictable, and today it looks like he's raided a dressing-up box; his raincoat hangs open, revealing high-waisted trousers, a crisp white shirt and a bow tie, his blonde hair cut in an Eton crop. Most of my contemporaries are lifeboat volunteers, like me, or members of the gig racing team, but Nathan never gets involved. The guy doesn't seem interested in the sea, even though it's our closest neighbour.

He offers a cautious smile, before pointing at the

tent ten metres away, circled by crime-scene tape. 'That looks like something from *Line of Duty*.'

'Nothing so glamorous, I'm afraid.'

'I hear you've found some human bones. Is that true?'

'The building team uncovered them this morning.'

He stares back at me. 'Shouldn't we hold some kind of ceremony?'

'I'm more concerned about keeping the site secure right now.'

'I bet the builders are fed up. It'll stall their plans, won't it?'

'That's for sure. Where are you heading, Nathan?'

'To see the hatchlings over on the headland.' He pulls binoculars from his pocket to prove his point.

'You're a twitcher?'

'It gets me outdoors; I spend too long staring at my computer.'

'Have you always worked from home?'

'It's not exactly a career.' He gives a slow laugh. 'I design computer games. You could say I make my living from being a world-class geek.'

'I never played as a kid. My parents refused to buy a TV, and our computer was too ancient.'

'Lucky you. I wasted my adolescence on *Final Fantasy*.' His gaze fixes on me again. 'What will happen to the skeleton now?'

'I'm getting a specialist opinion. Everyone must keep away from the crime scene in the meantime.'

Shadow is bounding across the grass with the

German shepherd, but his manner changes again when he spots my companion. He gives a vicious snarl, jaws snapping when Nathan reaches down to pet him, forcing me to grab his collar. God knows why he's taken a sudden dislike to the guy. His bark sends the games designer into retreat. I can see his hands shaking as he clips the lead back onto his dog's collar.

'Sorry about that,' I say. 'He's got no manners.'

Nathan sets off before I can say goodbye, long arms swinging as he lopes back to the Town. Shadow's behaviour is docile again now his adversary has departed. It seems odd that I know so little about Kernow, even though we're contemporaries. He lived with his mother for several years until she died, but the rest of his life is a mystery. I'm still thinking about him when Penny re-emerges.

'I've found something, Ben.' She points at the bare earth inside the tent. I can see a groove in its surface where she's cleared the soil away. There's a tattered piece of fabric overlapping the skeleton's right hand.

'Do you know what it is?'

'Some kind of bag, made of cotton or canvas.'

'Filled with something?'

She looks puzzled. 'Bits of rusted metal. Can you see those orange stains from oxidisation? The corpse must have been buried naked, otherwise his clothes would be intact too. Fabric survives for centuries underground.'

'Could you put it in an evidence bag, please? The forensics officer can check what's inside.'

'I'll try and lift it in one piece.'

I'm still absorbing the idea. Why would an adult male's naked corpse be buried on a hilltop, after a fatal head injury, with a bag of metal scraps in his hand?

When I look at Penny again, a tear is rolling down her cheek.

'Sorry if this is upsetting you,' I say.

She dabs her eyes with a hankie. 'It's a lonely death, that's all, and I'm out of practice. You have to keep your humanity doing this kind of work. Every unmarked grave deserves a few tears.'

The whole skeleton is visible now. The man must have landed with legs akimbo, one arm flung above his head. Someone dropped his corpse into a pit, placed the bag in his right hand, then covered the grave and sauntered away.

'What can you tell me about him?'

'He was healthy when he died. I can't be accurate about how long ago it happened, but he was definitely young.'

'Why are you so certain?'

She points at the skeleton's pelvic bone. 'Children have cartilage at the top of their thigh bones, which calcifies after they stop growing, between the ages of seventeen and twenty-five. His bones haven't fused fully; I'd say he was in his late teens.' She looks up at me again. 'That's another odd thing. His head was shaved just before he died.'

'How do you know?'

'Look through my magnifying glass. There's stubble, just a millimetre or two long.'

When I crouch down, I can make out patches of mid-brown fuzz still adhering to fragments of bone.

'Isn't it an old wives' tale that hair keeps growing after death?'

'You're right, it stops immediately. It needs oxygen to survive, but hair follicles are subcutaneous; the roots are exposed once the skin decomposes.'

My confusion lingers. It's quite rare for teenage boys to shave their heads; it would have made him conspicuous on the island. The killer might have done it and kept his hair as a trophy.

'Thanks for your help, Penny.'

'I'd like to carry on, but the light's going.'

'You've finished, haven't you?'

'I can get the bag out for you now, but I should excavate for a metre around the body, to see if anything else was left in the grave. It's the best way to find a victim's identity. I could take casts of his teeth tomorrow, if that helps.'

'We've got a forensics officer coming over later in the day, but getting casts done early would be great. There's one more thing. Can you estimate how long he's been in the ground?'

'The lab will need to run tests, but I'd guess between twenty and thirty years, from the colour and condition of the bones.'

She stoops down again, so focused on lifting the

scraps of cloth into an evidence bag she seems to forget my presence.

'You've really helped us, Penny, thanks so much. Let's meet back here tomorrow morning. Is eight o'clock okay?'

She appears unwilling to leave, despite her initial reluctance to help. It looks like she'd prefer to work all night to discover the victim's name, now that she's begun. She loads her tools back into her kitbag with the same measured grace as when she handles her bees, but her face looks drawn when we say goodnight. I'd probably feel the same after spending a long afternoon excavating a young man's grave.

I go back into the tent to take a last set of photos, even though the light's poor. Then I lay plastic sheeting over the skeleton, weighing it down with stones, in case a fox passes this way tonight. Instinct tells me to guard the site, despite Madron's advice, but I push the thought aside. I need to catch up with Zoe, and no one's likely to come up here in the dark, hunting for lost souls.

Night has arrived suddenly when I get back outside. Darkness falls in a heartbeat on Bryher, and there's no illumination anywhere, except when I look south. Bishop's Rock lighthouse flickers on the horizon, three miles away, sending out needle-thin pulses of light. It's stood there for a hundred and fifty years. It's still preserving sailors' lives, despite becoming automated. I gaze down at the photos on my phone. They're grainy and unclear, but the man's broken skull is fixed in my mind. If Penny's right about how long ago he died, I would have been somewhere between nine and nineteen when the murder happened, yet I don't remember anyone going missing. I can't guess where he came from either, but someone on Bryher must have an ugly secret to share.

15

Ruby continues her watch over the house opposite. There's still no sign of Steve Pullen, and it looks like his wife and son have settled down for a cosy evening. The house glows like a beacon, the curtains open in the upstairs windows, revealing details of their lives. There's a big wooden-framed bed in the master bedroom. Ruby's heart hardens. It's a travesty that the couple have slept there peacefully while her father endured years of broken nights on a lumpy prison mattress. The downstairs curtains remain closed, but shadows flicker behind the fabric, adding to her frustration. That bitch and her son remain safe inside, enjoying each other's company.

When she checks her watch, it's almost time to meet Denny Lang. Ruby feels uncomfortable as she puts on her jacket, because she'd rather not go, even though she gave the invitation. Any error could bring the police running if they guess that she's still alive.

Ruby slips out of the B&B unnoticed. Flagging down a taxi, she tells the driver to take her to Tobacco Dock. He keeps up a flow of chat about football and politics. She responds with monosyllables as the city flicks past, keeping her head down so he won't remember her face. Oxford Street is a glitter of shop windows, the pavements empty until tomorrow's fashion victims arrive. She feels better once the taxi reaches Victoria Embankment. The river was her biggest consolation after her dad was caught. She drew solace from watching London's great artery pulsing with activity, barges and clippers plying between wharves. It was a reminder that she was alive too, despite feeling dead inside.

She arrives at the wharf five minutes early. It's in a neglected part of Shadwell, with warehouses crumbling from disuse, stagnant water lying in the dock's basin, stinking to high heaven. She waits in the shadows until a BMW pulls into the car park and the passenger door swings open. Denny looks older than before, his face carved with deep lines, as if his conscience is troubling him at last.

They sit together in his car, gazing at the lighters ploughing west and the water gleaming in the dark. Denny says nothing for a while, then turns to stare at her.

'Why are we here, Ruby? It's not safe.'

'This is my last chance to run over the plan. I'll never see you again now that I'm Chloe Moore. You helped me so much; I wanted to thank you in person.'

'I just followed your dad's wishes, sweetheart, but I'm glad it's almost over. My time with him still bothers me. I was a bog-standard accountant until he recruited me. I saw terrible things but chose to look away.'

'What are you saying, Denny?'

'Avoid doing stuff you'll regret, love. It'll be on your conscience for ever. There's still time to stop all this.'

'Dad deserves a proper tribute.'

'I know,' he says, his eyes blinking shut. 'But I have to live with my past, and so will you. Once he's gone, you can make your own decisions.'

'It sounds like you want him dead.'

'That's not what I mean.'

She inhales a long breath, assessing the guilt on Denny's face. She remembers his kindness when she was small; he often took her to the park for ice cream, but that means nothing now the truth has surfaced.

'It was you that betrayed him, not Pierce, wasn't it? I never doubted you, but a warden at Crowthorne said it was one of dad's closest friends. You blew the whistle. How else would they have known where he was hiding?'

'They're talking shit, Ruby, prison guards lie all the time, for money.' He shakes his head, but her father taught her how to watch for signs that someone's lying. 'Promise me you'll start over somewhere new. Craig shouldn't make you do his dirty work.'

'I'd never betray him, you disloyal bastard.'

Lang's face is blank with shock when she rams her knife into his ribcage; he screams for help, even though the unlit car park is empty. Her father's rage sings in her veins. She grabs his keys, and once he's locked inside, she carves a symbol on the side of his BMW: a square slashed through with vertical lines. Then she drops a lit match into the petrol tank.

She waits in the darkness while Lang claws at the windows.

Childhood memories make her shut her eyes, but it's too late for regret. He had to die, for betraying her dad, and revenge feels easier this time. When the car explodes she smiles as flames spew upwards, turning it into an inferno.

16

It's 10 p.m. when I set off from home to see Zoe. She still hasn't answered any of my texts, which means she's either sick or angry. It's a relief to escape the strained atmosphere between me and Nina. I should apologise for leaving so abruptly this morning, but the skeleton on the downs has soured my mood. I'd rather smooth things over tomorrow, and a chat with Zoe will help. My friend always tells the truth, never accepting bullshit or compromise.

Hell Bay Hotel is lit up like a beacon when I cross the beach. Shadow has stayed indoors with Nina while she reads one of her classic novels, by Dickens or Jane Austen. The sea looks peaceful, the waves flatlining while the wind holds its breath. Half a dozen container ships are ploughing west to America, their lights blinking at the vanishing point where the Atlantic meets the sky. The walk only takes me ten minutes. When I peer through the panoramic windows of the hotel bar, a solitary bartender is polishing wine glasses, while a few OAPs nurse their last drinks of the day. My friend must be upstairs with her husband, in the flat she uses when they visit the UK.

I'm about to jog up the steps when a man's cultured voice calls my name.

'Long time no see. Help me drink this coffee, will you?'

When I spin round, Zoe's husband is sitting at a table in the shadows.

It took me a while to accept Dev. Half of me was glad Zoe had found happiness, the other half unwilling to see our friendship change, but the man's charisma is irresistible. He won me over after I flew to Mumbai for their wedding. We became friends during the three-day ceremony, which included feasts, dancing and parties with hundreds of his Sikh relatives and friends in venues right across the city. He's in his early forties, with aristocratic features, an athletic build and the self-assurance that comes from a moneyed background. His parents sent him to the best private school in India, then the Royal College of Music in London, where he developed a love for composing and perfected his English. He could have drifted through life frittering his inheritance, but ten years ago, he opened a residential music school for street kids in Mumbai. He met Zoe after she took a job there teaching singing. Since then, a dozen more schools have opened, and his phone never stops ringing.

'You don't normally touch caffeine, Dev.'

'I needed a boost, to be honest. Zoe's been in bed all day.'

'Is she sick?'

'Just a bit low.' The frown on his face makes me concerned.

'Why, exactly? She's dodging my calls.'

'She'll tell you herself.' He looks away. 'I've been helping out in the restaurant while she rests. The hotel's busy for this time of year; there's a party of thirty from the British Ornithological Society, all obsessed by puffins and guillemots.'

'Zoe's usually the first to roll up her sleeves.'

'She prefers her own company right now. Tell me about this skeleton you've found. Have you discovered its name?'

'We've only just begun. The one distinguishing feature is a cloth bag clutched in his hand. I shouldn't give out details, but I know you're always discreet.'

'You'll find his secret, Ben. I admire your determination.' He rises to his feet. 'Let me fetch another cup for this coffee.'

'No need, thanks. I used to drink double espressos then sleep like a log, but not any more.'

'It'll probably give me bad dreams.' He drops back onto his seat. 'Tell me more about your work, please. I need distraction.'

'It's not very uplifting. The body was chucked into the ground like a piece of rubbish.'

He looks amazed. 'That never happens in Sikh

families like mine. If a relative dies abroad, we fly their ashes home to be scattered on the Ganges. People think the sacred river will carry their soul to heaven.'

'Do you believe that?'

'Not really, but it's a beautiful idea.'

'I envy people their faith sometimes. It must help in a crisis.'

'Zoe doesn't believe in the afterlife, which is a pity. It might help her recover.' His face suddenly clouds with worry.

'What's wrong? Tell me, Dev, or I'm going up there.'

'She hates people knowing, but you two are so close it seems crazy to keep it from you.' He rubs his hand across his jaw before speaking again. 'She had another miscarriage a few days ago, after ten weeks. It was our third cycle of IVF.'

'I had no idea. I'm so sorry.' The news makes me long to be with her, no matter what Dev says, but I can't intrude.

'Nothing I say comforts her.'

I feel a pang of guilt that Nina fell pregnant so easily. Zoe was the first person I told, before any member of my family. Dev's broken expression reminds me how lucky I am. We go on talking for another quarter of an hour, then I can see him tiring, so I rise to my feet.

'Tell Zoe I'll visit tomorrow, whether she likes it or not.'

'Thanks for your company, Ben.'

We give each other an awkward hug before he climbs

the fire escape at the slowest pace imaginable. I don't blame him; facing Zoe's sadness on top of his own can't be easy.

My mood is flatlining as I make my way home in the dark, using my pocket torch to avoid boulders littered across the beach. It's only when I reach my porch that something unexpected catches my eye. A thread of light is flickering due north. The only property on the down is Louis Hayle's place, but the light is near where the skeleton was found.

I set off at a rapid jog. There's no point in calling Eddie, because he took the last ferry home to Tresco hours ago, and this might be a wild goose chase. One of the islanders could be taking a late-night stroll. I'm hitting my stride as I reach the down, then something trips me, and I pitch forwards onto a bed of heather. My airways fill with its dry perfume, lips tinged with salt as I scramble back onto my feet. I spin round, looking for whoever toppled me, but the down appears empty. There are just thickets of gorse, and a line of sea grape bushes, moulded by the breeze. I only catch sight of a figure in the distance when I'm about to leave.

'Who's there?' I yell out.

Nathan Kernow blunders towards me carrying a flashlight. He looks older than before, his thin frame vulnerable, even though he's swaddled in an oversized coat.

'It's late for birdwatching, Nathan. Why are you here?'

'I'm holding a vigil. That poor creature shouldn't be alone now his peace has been shattered.'

'I can't believe you came back, after hearing the area was out of bounds. You're trespassing on a crime scene.'

'We have to respect the dead. Let me stay till morning, please.'

'Go home, Nathan; you're breaking the law. Vital evidence may have been destroyed.'

The games designer admits defeat with a nod, but my curiosity about his motives increases when I see that he's made himself comfortable, with a blanket spread across the heather, right by the tent we erected. Candles are burning on a makeshift altar, and I can see wildflowers lying on a fallen branch, the four points of the compass carved into the wood.

'What's all this?'

'It's a funeral of sorts. I hope someone would do the same for me.'

'We'll talk about it tomorrow.' The man's behaviour makes no sense, but at least he appears to have done no harm.

Kernow scrabbles on the ground, gathering his belongings, then hurries away. He's left a solitary candle flickering inside a jam jar, making the site look eerie. I feel unsettled by his behaviour, but his reluctance to leave seemed genuine. He must be certain that his ritual would help, to spend a night in such a lonely place. Nothing has changed when I check inside the tent. It's still protecting the skeleton from predation and the elements, the bones covered by polythene, yet my discomfort lingers. I'm so used to the Atlantic's hard gales, the early summer stillness puts me on edge, with not even a blade of grass stirring in this ghost-ridden place.

My conversations with DCI Goldman have made me imagine danger where none exists. The down is deserted when I blow out the candle and walk home. The sea's silence feels uncanny; the waves are quiet for once, keeping their secrets to themselves.

17

Saturday 3 May

Ruby rises early for breakfast, after a calm night's sleep. She sits facing the window, at a table for one. The dining room looks like a throwback to Victorian times, with floral table-cloths, lace doilies and artificial roses gathering dust on the mantelpiece. She prefers modern interiors with no clutter, but produces a smile for the landlady when she appears from the kitchen. Ruby orders a full English, then sits back to watch the street come alive. When an Ocado van blocks her view, she wills it to vanish. She needs to complete her work soon. A long delay will make her easier to trace.

'Did you have a nice time yesterday, dear?' the landlady asks.

'Great, thanks. I met up with an old friend. I've been admiring the lovely period details in your house this morning.'

'Really? It looks commonplace to me.'

'Not at all.' Ruby smiles again. 'The porch is typical of the era, like the sash windows and gables, full of style that modern homes lack. It's incredibly well preserved, Iris.'

'I'm so glad you're enjoying your stay.'

The landlady finally leaves her in peace to enjoy her eggs, sausages and fried tomatoes. Ruby is surprised by her appetite. Last night's events were unpleasant, but her dad taught her to separate feelings from facts. Denny Lang deserved to die for his disloyalty, even though he treated her like his favourite niece. She blinks away an image of his hands scrabbling at the window, unwilling to let it haunt her.

She applies herself to her meal, clearing half the plate before glancing outside again. When a brand-new Lexus pulls up outside number 7, she puts down her fork immediately. The driver is about fifty, with greying hair combed back from his tired face. Steve Pullen has probably been on another undercover job; the bastard will have lied his way into someone else's confidence.

The cop's wife is already waiting in the porch. All Ruby can see is a middle-aged man, several stones overweight, in a crumpled suit, yet Fiona Pullen looks delighted. She flings her arms round his neck before he's put down his suitcase, then the couple disappear inside.

'Bingo,' Ruby mutters. 'Welcome home, Steve.'

The landlady appears by her table. 'Did you call me, dear?'

'Just to thank you, Iris. Breakfast was delicious.'

'How about some more tea?'

'That would be great, if you don't mind.'

When the old woman scurries away, Ruby memorises the registration number of Steve Pullen's car, then relaxes in her chair. Now her chance has come, she can imagine the pleasure on her father's face.

18

Zoe is on my mind as I drop slices of bread into the toaster. Nina is at the breakfast table, still in her dressing gown, even though there was no need for her to rise early. Yesterday's row is lingering in the air. We still can't decide what to name our baby, but there's a tacit agreement not to raise the subject again until we're both ready for the final say.

Shadow stands at Nina's side like a bodyguard, unaware that she's well able to look after herself. She's sitting with hands folded over her rounded belly again, gazing out at the sea. I've never met anyone so calm. I have to swim, or run round the island to remain on an even keel, but there will be no time to exercise until the skeleton's identified. My concerns about Nina are replaced by curiosity about Nathan Kernow's odd behaviour last night. I need to find out if his vigil sprang from a sense of guilt.

Nina doesn't speak when I sit down opposite; her work as a counsellor has taught her to use silence to good effect. She eats a full slice of toast before finally voicing her thoughts.

'Something's nagging at you, isn't it? I'm getting tired of asking why.'

'I go into myself sometimes, that's all.'

'You could try letting your feelings out, instead of keeping them locked away then flying off the handle.'

'My family never had deep, meaningful chats like yours. We just got on with stuff.'

Nina nods her head. 'There wasn't much choice for me, with an Italian mother who's also a diva. She rants and raves all the time, but there must be a middle way.'

'It doesn't come naturally.'

'I know, Ray's the same. Maybe that's why he's spent most of his life alone. Our lives would be easier if you let me help you more.'

'You do, all the time. I'm grateful for it.'

'Don't thank me, please, just speak your mind. I hate having to guess what you're thinking; sometimes I'm way off the mark.'

I stare back at her, surprised. We're both so strong-minded, it takes a crisis for either of us to admit we're wrong.

'Can we talk about this later?'

'Why not get it off your chest before work?'

'I'm running late.' I swallow a deep breath before continuing. It crosses my mind again to tell her about Travis, but it's not the right time. 'Dev was upset last night. Zoe's had a miscarriage in the past few days.'

'Not again.' Tears well in Nina's eyes. 'That's her third since they started IVF.'

'You knew they were trying?'

'I guessed, last time they were here. The poor thing's having a tough time with the injections and the uncertainty. Why didn't she call me?'

'She will, when she's ready to talk. I'll go and see her today.'

Nina can seem unshakeable, but she's as sensitive as the violin she practises on every day. I hate leaving her upset, but there's no choice. I have to get to work.

Shadow noses his way through the gap once I open the front door. He bounds across the beach at top speed, chasing seagulls, then spins in wild circles. It's an object lesson in *joie de vivre*, and my own cares fade as I follow the well-trodden path through the heart of the island.

The white plastic tent is visible as I climb Badplace Hill. I'm halfway to the top when I see Eddie hurrying up from the beach, his outsized uniform flapping in the breeze. I wait for him to catch up. He must have caught the first ferry over from Tresco. His eyes burn with excitement when he greets me, as if the skeleton we've exhumed is the best thing ever. The sergeant has a talent for everyday policing, travelling between the islands, stewarding events and supporting the community, but he comes alive under pressure. He was in his element last year when he had to liaise with MI5 before Prince William and Kate Middleton made a flying visit.

This is his first chance to work on a cold case, and it's clear he's enjoying the challenge.

I watch Penny Cadgwith's buggy arriving from the Town when we reach the crime scene. I can tell her asthma is giving her trouble; she's so out of breath she has to use her inhaler before she can speak normally. I give her a minute to recover, my gaze shifting to Louis Hayle's grey-walled house above us. His face appears at a third-floor window. Maybe I'd feel the same in his situation, as if the huge seascape encircling the property was mine alone. When I turn back, our visitor appears to have recovered.

'Thanks for coming back, Penny. Are you sure you're okay to work?'

'I can't stay at home when there's a riddle to solve.' She's clutching her tool bag, her gaze steady.

'I'll shift the polythene for you.'

Eddie follows me inside the enclosure, which already feels hot and airless, the temperature higher than yesterday. I move the rocks with care, then peel back the plastic sheet. I can't believe my eyes once the task's complete. There's only a patch of bare earth. The skeleton Penny worked so hard to expose has vanished, and the thief has done a thorough job. The earth has been rubbed smooth, not a single indentation to show where the bones lay.

Eddie's face registers incredulity while my heart races. Last night's strange encounter with Nathan Kernow immediately floods my mind.

'You're certain all the bones have gone?' Penny asks, frowning.

'Everything,' I reply.

'That can't be right. Can I see?'

'Go ahead.'

She pulls on sterile gloves before entering the tent. I watch her expression turn to disbelief as she pores over the ground on hands and knees. There's a tremor in her voice when we get back outside.

'Who's crazy enough to steal a skeleton?' Shock has turned her skin even paler than before. 'It's such a clean job, I'd say they're an expert.'

'Someone's afraid of being identified. The killer thinks we'll work out who the victim was from his remains. I was banking on it, to be honest.'

She nods. 'Any science lab can extract DNA from calcified bone. If the dead man was an islander, you could have taken samples from everyone here to find a match.'

Her point makes sense. Most of Bryher's hundred-strong community are descendants of five main families, the majority of us distantly related.

'It won't stop us finding his identity. At least we've got the murder weapon, and the bag that was in his hand.' It's still wrapped in plastic, on a shelf in my living room, waiting until Liz Gannick arrives.

'This will slow you down.' Frustration shows on Penny's face. 'The dental records would have sealed it for you. I'm sorry, Ben, there's nothing more I can do.'

'There's no need to stay. I'm grateful for your help.'

'Ring me if you find anything, won't you? I'll come straight back.'

I watch her buggy trundle back down the hill, cursing under my breath. I should never have followed Madron's advice. Louis Hayle is bound to pay us a visit once the news gets out. I need to know if Nathan Kernow returned to complete his vigil; he may have seen someone else here, or even removed the bones himself. When I tell Eddie about his ritual, complete with candles and flowers, he doesn't appear surprised.

'Nathan's a true hippy. I heard he joined some weird cult in the States years ago, until his mum dragged him home.'

'He's an obvious suspect. I want to speak to Louis Hayle first, to see if he witnessed anything, then we'll talk to Nathan. But it's possible someone else wanted to stop us finding out the identity of the victim, we have to keep our minds open.' I gaze down at the site again. 'The murderer's still on the island. They've worked hard to wipe away the traces.'

'Wouldn't they just sling the bones in the sea?'

'They took trouble burying the victim in the first place. It's possible they'll do it again.'

Eddie looks sceptical. 'That's one hell of a risk, isn't it?'

'It's easier now there are just bones to carry. It's lucky Liz Gannick's flying over to St Mary's this afternoon; she'll be able to analyse the bag. I've arranged for

Lawrie Deane to ferry her over on the police launch, then I want the island locked down. No one leaves or arrives without our agreement.'

We check the ground one more time. I'm hoping for footsteps across the newly turned soil, but the only tracks appear to be mine and Penny's. It hasn't rained for days, and Maeve's digger has gouged the surrounding earth into deep furrows. It looks like someone used a fallen branch to sweep their prints away, and it strikes me again that the stunt was carefully planned. The theft of a skeleton sounds more like a joke than a policing issue, but there's no way some teenager strolled up here for a macabre dare. Every shred of evidence has been removed, leaving us with few clues to chase, apart from Nathan Kernow's presence at the scene.

I call DCI Madron as we cover the short distance to Louis Hayle's property on the summit of Badplace Hill. There's a long silence when I explain the situation, which always spells trouble. His calm manner when he assessed the scene yesterday evaporates fast. He's outraged that I failed to stand guard all night, even though he advised against policing the site round the clock. When I remind him that it was his decision, he yells so loudly, I switch off my phone with a sense of relief. Frustration makes me feel like hurling it into the sea.

Louis Hayle's home sits so near the crime scene, it's an essential visit. My deputy's people skills will come in handy, because my own bluntness rarely pacifies the general public, while Eddie is skilled at pouring oil on troubled waters. Hayle's attitude to the building project makes sense from the top of Badplace Hill. He's got a three-sixty-degree view of the islands from Bryher's highest peak, with the downs rolling away to the sea. His house is a grander version of the granite cottages that huddle in the valley below, built in Victorian times to withstand storms, turning its back on the sea's hard winds, with a slate-tiled porch that faces Tresco. The activities centre will change his surroundings for ever and bring droves of walkers flocking past his home.

I can hear classical music playing a slow waltz when Mr Hayle opens his door. His manner seems gentler on home ground. I don't expect courtesy from an old man whose charm has turned abrasive, yet he invites us inside without delay. The place is less luxurious than I remember from my childhood, despite its size, but many original details have been preserved, including the tiled floor in the hallway. It still has the stripped-down look of a holiday home, even though Hayle moved here permanently several years ago. I can see little evidence of the man's personality, with every wall painted white or pale blue, until my eye catches on a cluster of photos celebrating his achievements. He's holding a sporting trophy aloft in the biggest one, his frame lean and athletic. The next shows him in the Himalayas, surrounded by peaks glistening with snow; the man seems to enjoy standing above the rest of society, looking down on us all.

Hayle's former athleticism is missing when he leads

us into his drawing room, his tall form slightly stooped. I catch sight of a brass crucifix on the wall, and shelves packed with books, including his own on succeeding in business. I can't tell if his faith ever clashes with his belief in capitalism, but now that his anger has faded, he's just an old man, with a haunted expression. I'm certain the best way to tackle the situation is to accept responsibility before he can accuse me of negligence, even though I was following Madron's orders.

'There was an incident last night, Mr Hayle. I'm afraid the bones we found were removed from the site.'

'Are you serious?' He stares back at me, eyes wide. 'Those people have no conscience whatsoever.'

'What do you mean?'

'The Trenwiths are hell-bent on inflicting that wretched building on me, but I never thought they'd stoop that low.'

'You're accusing them of stealing human bones?'

'Daniel and his team can start again now, can't they? They'll be here tomorrow with their diggers making that infernal noise.'

'The site will be closed for weeks. A forensics expert is coming over from Penzance to check it, which always takes time.'

His scowl deepens. 'Those two will stop at nothing.'

'You seem to view the building project as a personal vendetta.'

'I used to have influence on these islands. They want to prove it's no longer the case.'

'A man died, Mr Hayle, yet you only seem concerned about your view.'

'Nonsense, I protested about graves being desecrated in the first place.'

'The Trenwiths have never expressed any personal animosity towards you, in my company at least, but let's focus on the crime. Did you see anyone on the downs last night?'

'Only Lucy Boston, around six thirty. She often walks here after closing her shop.'

'No one else?'

'How would I know? I don't spend every minute gazing out of my window. I was in bed by ten thirty, listening to Radio Three.' He jabs his index finger in my direction. 'This is an utter shambles; I've a good mind to complain to your superior officer.'

Eddie steps into the breach before a row can escalate. His voice is calm when he points out that no one could have forecast such a bizarre crime. Louis Hayle calms down after five minutes of his gentle reasoning, but he looks at me with distaste when I ask another question.

'How long did your family own this property before you moved here permanently, Mr Hayle?'

'Three generations, but surely you know that already? There are no secrets on Bryher. I spent summers here every year while I was working, doing my best to improve the local economy. My wife preferred London until she reached her fifties. We planned to spend our retirement here, but she'd have hated how the land's being abused. Bryher's beauty lies in its ancient fields and clean beaches. If that changes, this place will be ruined.'

'I understand how you feel. We have to get back to work, but thanks for your time.'

He glares at me. 'You made a serious error, Benesek, but at least you owned up. I value honesty above every other virtue.'

His words appear positive, but his tone of voice is so patronising, it sounds like he's criticising a poorly behaved child. His disdain follows me down the path, along with a blast of classical music, but he's correct about one thing. I should have followed my instinct to stand guard, despite Madron's advice. It's my duty to put it right.

I instruct Eddie to set up the vacant room at the Rock as an incident room. We need to hold a public meeting there at midday. He'll have to call round and make sure everyone attends. I want the killer to feel like we're onto him from the start. If he's under pressure, it's more likely he'll slip up. My deputy jogs back downhill with his usual enthusiasm.

My phone buzzes in my pocket before I set off to see Nathan Kernow. It's another message from my old boss in London, saying that one of Craig Travis's gang members, Denny Lang, died in a car fire last night. His body had to be identified by dental records. I remember Lang well from my time undercover; the accountant was close to Travis, but his loyalty soon melted away.

He was a quiet, grey-faced man, mumbling the names of a dozen other gang members to shorten his stretch. I can't pretend that Craig Travis is powerless any more; his influence lingers even though he lies dying in Crowthorne. The past is coming alive, with angry ghosts threatening to invade the present.

19

Ruby has spent the morning in her room at the B&B, making sketches. She dreamed of becoming an artist as a child, but that was just a fantasy. Craig Travis's daughter could never sign up for art school, and even if she had enrolled, the fees would have been crippling. She finds drawing easy, because she's learnt to be watchful. One small detail can make the difference between life and death.

When she looks out of the window again, her landlady is leaving the house, carrying a shopping bag, which means the flat downstairs is empty. She knows Mrs Caston's habits from watching the property and hiding in her back garden. She's bound to waste hours browsing round the shops, then treating herself to a coffee. Another thirty minutes pass before Steve Pullen's son exits the house opposite, dressed in his football strip, ready for practice. Ruby stares at the front door without blinking.

'Now, my lovely,' she mutters. 'Come out to play.'

Fiona Pullen must love yoga, because she emerges mid-morning with her gym bag slung over her shoulder. The redhead looks pretty and carefree, taking care to shut the door gently. Her husband is probably resting after his hard work, the bedroom curtains still closed. The plan can begin. Ruby checks her appearance in the full-length mirror. She's dressed in a dark blue T-shirt, Levi's and tennis shoes, with a small pink rucksack slung over her shoulder. She looks like any other carefree student off to meet her mates, but tension is mounting inside her ribcage. A single mistake would land her in jail for decades.

The house is quiet when she goes downstairs. Iris Caston has left her flat unlocked, the rooms smelling of old-fashioned lavender perfume. Ruby lets herself out of her kitchen door and hurries through the back yard, then down a ginnel, with no one in sight. She walks down a quiet side road, then stands in the alley behind the Pullens' property. Entering it will be harder, but she's buzzing with excitement. She pulls on gloves before scrambling over a fence. She's thankful for the thick hedge that surrounds the property, hiding her from the neighbours' view, allowing her to pull on thin plastic overalls and overshoes unwitnessed, then cover her hair with a hood. She can't afford to leave even a single strand behind.

It takes her five minutes to cut the correct wire to stop the CCTV capturing her image. She has to shimmy up a drainpipe onto the flat roof, then prise the bathroom window open with a chisel, muffling the sound with a wad of cloth. Her mind floods with relief when she clambers inside. It takes courage to tiptoe across the landing, aware that Pullen may already have detected her presence.

She waits outside the bedroom, peering through a crack

in the door. Pullen is asleep, lying on top of the duvet, still wearing his trousers and shirt, his shoes placed neatly at the foot of the bed. When Ruby's gaze lands on a framed photo of his family smiling for the camera, her anger increases. He cost her the one relative she's ever loved. She assesses the room coolly, then sets to work.

The detective must be exhausted, because he doesn't stir when she climbs onto the bed. His eyes only open when she straddles him, and by then it's too late. Her knife is five inches into his chest. He yells just once when she pulls it out, but he's already too weak to scream. Blood drips from the corner of his mouth. She used a pillow to protect herself from the spray, so her overalls are spotless. She leans down to whisper in his ear.

'Craig Travis sent me. Never forget him, will you?'

Steve Pullen is already dead when she cuts her dad's symbol into the palm of his hand, a square slashed through with three vertical lines. She wipes her knife clean on the duvet, then leaves by the same route. There's no need to rush when she reaches the garden and folds her overalls into her backpack.

Ruby's pulse rate is back to normal by the time she walks down Talbot Road, and her mood has improved. A guy on a motorbike wolf-whistles as she passes through Royal Oak. She turns to blow him a kiss before sauntering down the steps to the Underground like she has all the time in the world.

20

I go straight to see Nathan Kernow after my clash with
Louis Hayle. Shadow materialises at my side, hoping
for a new adventure as I head towards the Town, but
I remember his hostile reaction to Nathan last time. I
fling my arms wide to let him know that he's free to
roam, yet when I look over my shoulder, he's tracking
me at a distance. I can only hope he won't make a nui-
sance of himself outside Kernow's house.

It takes me ten minutes to reach the Town, where
two dozen low granite houses huddle together, protecting each other from winter's harsh winds. Kernow's
cottage lies at the eastern edge. My curiosity's rising,
because I've never been inside. I know he spent time
living inside a cult, but I don't yet know if that's connected to his ritual last night. His home is the middle
property in a small terrace; the front garden is packed
with overgrown shrubs, flourishing between stone
pavers that lead to the front door. I catch sight of
Nathan through the bay window. He's hunched over

his computer, his back turned, giving me a view of his screen. The animation he's creating looks oddly life-like, despite being a fairy tale. A man is waging war against a one-eyed monster, the Cyclops's huge eye gazing down at him.

Nathan swings round, startled, when I tap on his window. He's wearing another mismatched set of clothes: an over-sized guernsey, ancient jeans, and brogues that would look better with a suit. He inspects me from under his blonde fringe, his haircut a throwback to his days at public school. The man looks startled when I ask to come inside. His hallway is heaving with so many house plants the air feels damp against my skin; aspidistras in large pots line the walls, spider plants and ferns arranged on shelves, with a vine trailing across the ceiling. His German Shepherd emerges from the undergrowth to sniff my shoes, then retreats again.

'Sorry about all the greenery,' he says. 'I should do some pruning, but plants hate being attacked. Come to the kitchen, it's easier to move in there.'

The kitchen also contains plenty of foliage, but there's a narrow space around the table. The shelves are packed with books on spirituality and mindfulness, plus a row of vegan cookbooks. The man may look like a throwback to an earlier age, but he seems to have embraced the craze for clean living.

'I need more information about last night, please. Did you go back to the crime scene after we spoke, Nathan?'

'Of course not. I followed your advice.'

'The bones have been taken.'

He stares back at me, shocked. 'And you believe I would ransack a grave?'

'Anything's possible and you were there just before they vanished. Can you explain fully what you were doing on Badplace Hill?'

His hands waver, like he's plucking ideas from the air. 'I had a kind of premonition after we spoke the first time. I saw that poor man writhing in agony in a field of mud. I couldn't abandon him.'

'I still don't understand.'

He hesitates before speaking again. 'My faith sounds weird to some people, that's why I don't often discuss it, but I believe our souls and bodies are connected. Proper burial rites can free our spirits. People like me are called neopagans these days.'

'What does that mean?'

'It's an umbrella term for pagans, Wiccans, Druids and shamans. We see nature as our goddess and try not to harm the environment. You can tell from my clothes, can't you? They all come from charity shops in Penzance. I hate the idea of perfectly good stuff going to landfill.' He gestures at his well-worn shoes, then his gaze meets mine again. 'I hate the way the moor's being dug up; I think of it as sacred ground.'

'Louis Hayle feels the same. Have you spoken to him about it?'

His response is slow to arrive. 'I don't see much of him these days. He's not that keen on visitors. Louis

115

has changed since he ran his youth summer camps, all those years ago.'

'You attended some, did you?'

'Not many; they weren't really my cup of tea.' His gaze slips away.

His calm manner makes me assume he's telling the truth, or he's a skilful liar. 'One more thing, Nathan. The compass sign carved on your piece of wood last night – what does it mean?'

'It's a pagan funeral symbol. We ask the goddess to bless the dead with air from the east, fire from the south, water in the west and earth in the north. When a soul's been blessed by all four elements, it leaves its mortal form without regrets.'

'And you prayed for that on the hill?'

'I wanted to help him. Some spirits hate leaving, if their death's been hard. That man had a right to stay there undisturbed. It appalls me that someone tampered with his grave.'

The expression on Kernow's face is suddenly so fierce, my alarm bells ring at full volume, yet I've got no clear evidence apart from his presence at the grave site last night. He seems sincere about his spiritual outlook, even though it baffles me. I've never believed in reincarnation, but I can see the appeal; it's a pity we only get one shot at being alive.

'Did you see anyone on your way home?'

He shakes his head. 'A few ghosts, but that's to be expected.'

'Are you serious?'

'Of course not,' he replies, suddenly more relaxed. 'You probably think I'm mad, but pagans have been around since before Stonehenge.'

'I'm more interested in the here and now.' I glance around his plant-filled room. 'Tell me about your life here before your mother died.'

His shoulders flinch. 'Why's that relevant?'

'A young man suddenly went missing. Your mum took in paying guests, didn't she?'

'She needed money after Dad died, when I was eleven. She had to raise me here alone, until family members clubbed together to send me away to school.'

'Do you remember many of the people who stayed here?'

'Not really, I was still a boy. It was mainly couples wanting a B&B for a week or two in the summer. A couple of guys came over for longer stays, to work on the trawlers, but I don't remember their names.'

'You didn't come back for a while, did you?'

'After boarding school I did an arts degree in California. Mum was thrilled when I finally returned here to live. That was about six years ago. My wages meant she could stop renting out rooms. It's a pity she didn't have long to enjoy her freedom. She passed away soon after.' There's a quake in his voice, like the pain is still raw. 'Is that everything? I've got some graphics to finish.'

'Those images look really lifelike.'

'I can't claim much credit; the software's improving all the time.'

'You spent a few years with some group in America, didn't you? What was its name?'

'The Children of Nature. People called it a cult, which isn't true.' He rises to his feet abruptly. 'That's a tale for another day, I'm afraid. I have to finish that sequence.'

'Okay, but I'll be in contact again soon, when I have more information. How come you're toiling away at the weekend?'

Kernow looks uncomfortable. 'My boss expects total commitment; that's why our games win prizes.'

A fern brushes the back of my neck as he shepherds me to the front door. The guy ejects me while I still have questions to ask, but there's no hard proof he entered that tent, or that he's a hiding a violent past.

When I return to the Rock, Eddie's got his head down, making phone calls, in the party room behind the bar. It only gets used for occasional wedding receptions and meetings. The ceiling is stained yellow from nights long ago when fishermen huddled by the fire smoking pipes. The floral wallpaper is so out of date it's probably back in fashion by now. Eddie has organised the space well, with a printer linked to his laptop, and a corkboard on the wall for photos. I'd like to update him on my chat with Kernow, his wary manner, and his jungle of triffid-like plants, but Eddie's phone is still glued to his ear.

When I search for the Children of Nature online, it's described as a cult that preyed on vulnerable young people for several decades. Once they were recruited, they gave up their money and possessions, tending the land on a ranch and worshipping nature. The group was eventually broken up by the FBI, the organisers jailed for bribery and extortion. I can't imagine how the experience affected Kernow, but I sensed anger in him when he spoke about the grave on Badplace Hill being desecrated.

I'd like to search his home, but right now there's insufficient evidence to apply for a warrant. When I call one of Nathan's neighbours, she reports seeing him return home after midnight and not hearing him leave the house again. The games designer is our only suspect, despite his gentle manner. It's possible that he returned to the site last night, long after his neighbours were asleep, but I doubt he's the killer. He would have been my age when the victim was murdered, little more than a child.

News spreads fast across the islands, even when it's wrong. The lounge bar at the Rock is full when midday comes around, the place buzzing with excitement. Most people love the slow pace of life here, with one day sliding into the next, and seasonal routines dominating the calendar, but a crisis always brings the community together. They're talking at high volume, keen to know why an emergency meeting has been called, even though some of the facts are already in the public domain. I want to use this opportunity to make the killer afraid that we already have clues about his identity.

Maggie has rigged up the projector she uses on film night each month, when old movies are served up with beer and snacks, but today's images will be less entertaining. I've known most of the crowd before me since I was a boy. Ray is standing at the back of the room, his face impassive, with Sandra Trescothick close by, reminding me of them sitting together at the pub. Nina is next to Dev, but there's still no sign of Zoe. I catch sight of Lucy Boston in the front row, and remember Louis Hayle mentioning that she took an early-evening walk on Badplace Hill. She's taken over running the island's only shop recently, since the previous owners retired. Lucy is one of those women who remain girlish as they age. Her grey hair is scraped back into a ponytail, her round face permanently anxious since her brother died unexpectedly.

I catch sight of Jamie Porthcawl and his wife, Bella, as I download photos from my phone to Maggie's laptop. He looks more relaxed than yesterday morning. The couple always seem content. He enjoys his work, and she runs a successful small business making greeting cards, which are sold locally and on the mainland. The only strangers in the room are a few elderly birdwatchers from Hell Bay Hotel. They're wearing combat trousers, khaki waterproofs and stout shoes, their long-lensed cameras resting on their laps, as if a firecrest might suddenly break cover and fly across the room. Maeve and Danny Trenwith slip into seats at the front, right at the last minute. I'm about to open the meeting when Louis Hayle glares at me from under his grey monobrow. I'm not a natural public speaker, but my hefty build gives me an advantage. People always expect the biggest man in the room to take the lead, their faces expectant when I rise to my feet.

'Thanks for coming, everyone. You'll have heard that a human skeleton was unearthed yesterday during the building work on Shipman Head Down. I thought it could be part of an ancient grave at first, but the bones were placed there much more recently. It was a young man, in his late teens or early twenties, and it looks like he was buried in a shallow grave between twenty and thirty years ago. We think he suffered a violent attack that left him with a fatal head wound. I hope none of you are squeamish, because I'm about to show you exactly what we found.'

There's a collective gasp when a photo appears on the blank wall. The skeleton looks pitiful when I study the image again, with its fractured skull and jaw choked with mud.

'He was placed in the ground naked, with a cloth bag in his hand containing some rusted metal. We still need to find out exactly what the items were. Speak to me or Eddie, please, if you know anything about the victim. We already have several strong leads, so I expect a quick result. In the meantime, I'm afraid no one can leave Bryher or visit without our permission, because the skeleton was removed from the scene last night. That happened between midnight and eight this morning.'

Someone laughs, like I've told a first-rate joke. 'What kind of idiot would steal some old bones?'

'The killer must be desperate to remove DNA evidence, even though the murder happened years ago. That will help us in the long run, because they've left a trail for us to follow. If any of you saw activity on Badplace Hill late last night, please let us know. You can help us get this resolved so we can all go back to normal.'

My statement is followed by a hushed silence. I explain that I need to know exactly who was on the island last night.

'Could a holidaymaker have moved the bones?' Jamie Porthcawl asks.

'We'll check the CCTV at the hotel, but it's unlikely. In any case, whoever did it is still here. No one's left Bryher since last night. We've called a halt on local boats leaving Church Quay. I think the victim was an islander, but we'll be checking records from the pub and the hotel through the years to see if any guests suddenly disappeared.'

'What makes you so sure he was local?' Louis Hayle calls out. 'Maybe someone brought him to Bryher with a specific desire to commit murder.'

There's a low murmur of interest before I speak again.

'It would have been easier to drop the body at sea.

Someone wanted to give him a burial of sorts; I think this landscape matters deeply to the killer.'

Hayle looks unconvinced, as if I'm plucking ideas from the air. When I scan the crowd again, the initial excitement of an unsolved mystery has been replaced by discomfort. Everyone is suddenly aware that the killer could be sitting right beside them.

I throw the meeting open to questions, but the crowd disperses fast. Someone is hiding an old secret, and the islanders are famously tight-lipped. It's never a good idea to rat on a neighbour when your welfare depends on good social connections. Bryher normally welcomes newcomers, but a few people have been ousted over the years. The community's judgement can be quick and decisive. If you're violent or tell lies it's likely to cost you your job, and your circle of friends will vanish overnight.

Sandra Trescothick approaches me as the bar empties. I was planning to consult her, and her intense expression proves that she's keen to help solve the mystery. No other islander has such good knowledge of past inhabitants. She's smartly dressed today, her elegant coat matching her sleek blonde hair. If she has any romantic interest in my uncle, they'd make an unlikely couple, given that he rarely changes out of his overalls.

'This is strange, Ben. Did you see this kind of thing much in London?'

'Hardly ever.' I witnessed enough deaths to last me a lifetime, but few cold cases, so I'm not telling a lie.

'I'll go back through the records, but no one's gone

missing in recent years. Local families are accounted for in the council's archive. I can show you every birth, marriage and death since records began. There are no gaps.'

'This must be an exception.'

She looks bemused. 'People don't just disappear from the islands. You're welcome to come and see the record books any time.'

'I'll do that soon. Thanks, Sandra.'

'Good luck finding out what happened. That poor man deserves a decent burial.'

She walks away, her gait measured, which seems fitting for the holder of such a serious job. Sandra's been the archivist of island life, from cradle to grave, ever since I can remember. If she can't explain who went missing, the truth could lie out of reach.

21

It's half past one when Ruby heads back to Royal Oak. She's wearing a different outfit, and carrying shopping bags from Zara and Primark. The new clothes will erase her old image as a goth, their pale colours chosen to go unnoticed.

It's obvious before she reaches Sutherland Place that Steve Pullen's death has been discovered. Police cars are cruising past, uniformed officers going door to door, their expressions solemn. The Met never care unless the victim's one of their own. They pull out all the stops when an officer suffers, like it's a national tragedy, even though her father's basic needs have been ignored.

She takes her time returning to the B&B, observing details. The road has been cordoned off, a gaggle of locals watching the free entertainment like motorway drivers craning their necks to see carnage after a crash. Three squad cars are parked outside number 7, and officers dressed in white overalls stand on the pavement clutching boxes of equipment. When Ruby approaches the cordon, a young WPC gives her a reassuring smile.

'Can I have your name?'

'Chloe Moore. I'm staying at the B&B.'

'Wait here, please. I'm afraid there's been a fatality.'

Ruby widens her eyes. 'It's not Mrs Caston at number ten, is it? She's in her eighties.'

The young officer's tone softens. 'Don't worry, love, I'm sure she's fine.'

Ruby takes a step back once she's given her fake phone number and address, certain that her new identity will pass any test. She's checked it many times. Ten minutes go by before she's allowed to return to the B&B, where Mrs Caston is standing in the porch, fiddling with her beads. The landlady looks older than before, her expression anxious.

'Thank goodness you're back, dear. I was worried about you.'

'What on earth's happened, Iris?'

'A neighbour's been killed in broad daylight. He was such a lovely man. I can hardly believe it.'

Ruby lets her mouth drop open. 'That's awful, on such a nice street.'

'It's tragic for his family.' The old woman's face is suddenly paler than before.

'You don't look well, Iris. Let's get you back inside.'

She leads Mrs Caston down the hallway, supporting her arm. She can feel the old woman trembling. Ruby sits beside her on her faded settee, holding her hand, until colour returns to her cheeks.

'Thank you, dear, you're so kind, but don't worry about me.'

'It's fine, honestly. Rest there for a minute, I'll make you some tea.'

Ruby has bought herself time to take care of details. She wipes the back-door handle with bleach, making sure everything she's touched is scoured clean, before bringing the old lady her drink. Once she's back in her room, she takes care not to sit too near the window, so no one catches her spying. Crime-scene officers are still flooding the scene. Fiona Pullen and her son must be at the local station, broken by grief. Now that Ruby's third target is dead, she can hear her father's delight humming in her ears.

22

A breathless calm greets me when I leave the pub. A few yachts are moored in New Grimsby Sound, with dinghies floating in their wake, the sea so smooth it looks like the water's been ironed. Hangman Island almost fills the channel between Bryher and Tresco, a yardarm standing on its rocky peak as testament to a brutal past. No one knows exactly how many prisoners died there during the English Civil War, but folklore says that turncoats were left hanging for days to warn soldiers against mutiny. There's no escaping history in Scilly, which is why I voted for the activities centre. The islands have been occupied for millennia, but they need to keep on evolving or they risk becoming a museum.

Lucy Boston's shop lies fifty metres north of Ray's boatyard on Church Quay; it's been modernised since she and her brother took over. Brightly painted tables and chairs stand outside, alongside pots of flowers. The sign above the door announces that the shop's new name is The Bryher Pantry. It's empty when I arrive, and I notice that the interior is less cluttered than before. The previous owners stocked hundreds of items, but the emphasis now is on high-quality local produce. The fridge contains goat's milk from Bryher, alongside ice cream and cheeses from St Agnes. Bottles of locally brewed beer take pride of place on the shelves beside freshly baked bread.

I wait for Lucy to return, instead of ringing the bell. The shopkeeper drops an armful of newspapers on the counter when she sees me, her expression panicked. I know from experience that anxiety is her default reaction, because she used to work in the kitchen at the hotel. Zoe describes her as sweet but highly strung. Today she looks like a rabbit caught in the headlights. She's been even more jittery since her brother, Christian, died of a sudden heart attack at the age of fifty last year.

'Sorry I left the meeting early, Ben. I hate leaving the shop closed.' Her voice is strained.

'How's business going?'

'It's too soon to tell. I've been asking people for feedback. That's why I bought the coffee machine, to make hot drinks.' Her words fade into silence, as if her confidence has expired mid sentence.

'You often walk up Badplace Hill in the evenings, don't you?'

She gives a cautious nod. 'Christian used to tell me off for going there after dusk. He said it wasn't safe.'

'Really? No one's ever been attacked there.'

'He was always superstitious.'

'I wondered if you spotted anything unusual on the downs last night.'

'Just your tent. The only person I saw was Jamie Porthcawl. I thought he was allowed there because he's foreman for the build. I didn't break any laws walking past, did I?'

'Not at all, Lucy.' I point at her new coffee machine. 'Can I try one of your cappuccinos while we chat?'

The news that someone other than Nathan Kernow was seen at the site makes me watch her more closely. She appears to relax slightly with a task to complete. I take a seat at the only indoor table and scan the interior again. It's as clean as a whistle, the lino freshly scoured, the shelves painted duck-egg blue. She must have spent days smartening the place up, yet her body language remains apologetic. She perches on the seat opposite, watching me sip my coffee, visibly relieved when I give a thumbs-up.

'Did you speak to Jamie last night?'

She shakes her head. 'I don't think he noticed me. After he went into the tent, I didn't see him come out again.'

'You're certain he went inside?'

'Positive, yes. It was seven thirty-ish, just getting dark. I thought it was odd, because of all that yellow tape, but Jamie's such a decent bloke, I never questioned it.' The frightened look has returned to her face, and she's fiddling with the end of her ponytail, twisting grey hair around her fingers.

'It's okay, Lucy, I'm only gathering details. This place looks great, by the way. You'll have loads of customers in high season.'

'It was my brother's idea; he was always the confident one. It still feels weird being here alone.'

'You're doing fine. It must have cost a lot, kitting the place out so well.'

'Christian always managed our finances.'

Her eyes cloud with tears, which takes me by surprise. Her brother died a year ago, yet she's reacting like it happened yesterday. I'm not great at comforting people, too big and awkward for easy physical gestures, but I let my hand settle on her wrist until she blinks the tears away. I can tell she's embarrassed when she speaks again.

'Sorry, Ben. It stirred things up for me, seeing that skeleton. Who'd do such a terrible thing? People deserve dignity at the end. I got the undertakers to put Christian in his best suit for the cremation.'

I never imagined that a photo of human bones would cause such a personal reaction. 'Have you seen a grief counsellor at all, Lucy? You can book sessions through the health centre.'

She shakes her head. 'Everyone's supporting me, and I chat to Nina sometimes when she comes by. You've found yourself a lovely woman there, Ben.'

'I'd better get her some of those chocolates on your top shelf. She's developed a sweet tooth.'

'Have them as a gift, please. She's been so kind.'

'Charge me the going rate, Lucy. I want you to stay in business.'

I insist on paying before taking my leave, but the visit has raised fresh questions. Why did Jamie Porthcawl return to the crime scene, and how many more islanders have been shaken by the pictures of the victim?

When I ring Porthcawl, he sounds apologetic, but his tone is relaxed. He claims to have lost a compass of his father's, a family heirloom. It was preying on his mind, so he combed the building site by torchlight, believing it might have fallen from his pocket. Something about his story fails to convince me. I've known him all my life – he's even done building jobs on my cottage – but his voice is slightly off key, like an actor doing a bad audition. I'd like to see him face to face, but it'll have to wait. Liz Gannick is due at any minute, and I need to brief her about the case.

I'm waiting on Church Quay when the police motorboat finally appears at the mouth of the bay. Shadow bounds out of Ray's boatyard like he's expecting his favourite visitor. The vessel looks worse than ever, with deep scrapes along its starboard side, fluorescent paint scratched from its hull. Sergeant Lawrie Deane's expression is weary, as if the chief forensics officer has spent the half-hour journey from St Mary's offloading her woes. My colleague is in his fifties, with a shock of red hair and a stern expression that's misleading. He loosens up on his days off, buying his two grandkids ice creams in Hugh Town, or taking them crabbing.

Dr Liz Gannick, the forensics chief, looks young from a distance. The woman's so petite she could be sixteen; her short hair is dyed black, with a few orange streaks framing her face. It's only on closer inspection that her true age shows. Deep lines bracket her mouth, and her forehead is etched with a frown. She greets me in a northern voice that sounds like a foghorn. She's already poised beside her kit box as the boat moors, prepared for action.

'Send that dog home, for God's sake. He'll get in our way.'

Shadow has materialised at my feet, pawing the ground with excitement. He took a liking to Gannick on their first meeting; I know the feeling's mutual, even though she'd never admit to any form of emotion.

'I've brought the mobile lab. Fetch it for me, can you?'

She swings herself off the boat using crutches, while Lawrie lowers her wheelchair onto the quay.

'I don't need that today,' she snaps. 'It's only for emergencies.'

'Leave the chair here, please, Lawrie,' I instruct the sergeant. 'I'll collect it later.'

Gannick stares up at me, unsmiling. 'Where's the crime scene?'

'Thanks for coming over, Liz.'

'Stop being so fucking polite. Let's go, we're losing evidence all the time.'

I drag her kit box along on its castors, passing on

details as we walk. The woman's prowess on her crutches impresses me every time we meet. She covers the ground at speed, her feet barely touching the ground, but it's clear she's having a bad day. Her frown deepens as I tell her what I know about the skeleton. She looks surprised to hear that Penny believes the bones are from a teenage male, buried between two and three decades ago.

'How did she figure out the time of burial? You'd need DNA and bone density scans for a reliable date.'

'She made a judgement based on professional experience. Have you heard of Penny Cadgwith? She's an expert on war graves.'

Gannick raises her eyebrows. 'Quite a woman, by all accounts. She might be in the right ballpark, but gut instincts are useless. Results have to be measurable.'

'We'll struggle with so little to analyse. Eddie's put the murder weapon and the cloth bag in your hotel room.'

'Why the hell didn't someone guard the bones overnight?'

The scorn in her voice brings me to a halt. 'Let's agree something right now, Liz. I want your help, but not if you treat me like an idiot.'

'Can't you just admit you've screwed up big-time?'

'It was Madron's decision, not mine. And if you use that tone again, you're catching the next ferry home.'

She observes me through narrowed eyes. 'Remember I'm your senior by a long chalk.'

'It's my case, Liz. Are you staying or going?'

She pulls in a long breath. 'Show me what you've got, then I'll decide.'

The rest of our journey passes in hostile silence, apart from the castors on the kit box screaming as I haul it over rough terrain. The atmosphere only improves once my visiting expert has donned her white Tyvek suit; her tone of voice is almost civil when she asks for some large stones to weigh down the protective film she places around the crime scene. I gather lumps of granite that lie among the heather and bracken, the area full of trip hazards. When I return, Gannick has collapsed the tent to give herself room to manoeuvre, too deeply immersed to pay me any attention. The woman may be obnoxious, but her work ethic is humbling. She's already taking samples with minute tools, storing them in plastic vials, scribbling numbers on a clipboard.

Half an hour passes before she speaks again. 'Your thief's a neat freak. I bet they researched how to cover their tracks on the internet. I'll need to do soil analysis for particles of bone, as well as hair and skin cells from the culprit. There's still an outside chance of identifying him, or her, through clinical evidence.'

'Do you think the bag we found will help? Penny took a lot of care removing it.'

'Sounds like she's the only one who did a decent job.'

'My point stands. Drop the criticism, or we don't work together.'

'Stubborn as a mule, aren't you?' Her lips form a hard line. 'I never apologise to anyone.'

'Even when you're wrong?'

'That's rare.'

'I'll settle for being treated like an equal.'

'Me too.'

'So we're agreed?'

'More or less.' She withholds her smile, but there's a glint of humour in her eyes. 'Now bugger off, can you? I work better alone. Don't come back for two hours, and remember to take my chair to the hotel.'

She dismisses me with a waft of her hand, but I don't waste any time figuring her out. Gannick and I have worked on enough cases for her contrary nature to be a fact of life. It sometimes feels like a friendship's growing between us, then her hostility returns, more caustic than ever. I'm prepared to accept it for now, because she's my best chance of getting a result, but I'm curious to know why her personality is ever-changing.

Shadow stays close as I collect the wheelchair from the quay. The creature seems to have guessed that I plan to kill two birds with one stone and call on Zoe at the hotel. His intuition is unnerving; he's already charging down the track through Town, heading for Hell Bay.

Zoe's guests are ranged along the beach when we arrive, dressed in camouflage gear, like veterans from jungle warfare. They're too busy gazing through their binoculars to notice a big, ungainly man dragging a wheelchair through thickets of marram grass on the dunes. I can't tell what type of birds they're tracking. Storm petrels, gulls and puffins are all regular visitors at this time of year. None of the ornithologists are suspects, because Eddie checked the hotel's CCTV this morning, proving that no one walked up to Shipman Head last night to collect the bones. They're free to leave the island, but seem to be having too much fun.

I park the wheelchair in reception, then jog up the fire escape to Zoe's flat. She's still not answering my calls, so arriving unannounced is my only option. There's no answer when I tap on the door, but it's unlocked, so I walk inside. The living room stands empty, with miles of blue sea flatlining outside the window.

'Zoe? Are you here?'

My voice echoes from the walls, which unsettles me. We've never been out of contact for more than a week, except in Year 10, when she dated a friend of mine, despite warnings that he was only after her body. Zoe always sees the best in people instead of spotting their flaws. It's a pity that her generosity often leaves her vulnerable sometimes. There's no sign of her in the kitchen or bathroom, but when I push open the bedroom door, she's curled up under the duvet. Only her shock of Marilyn Monroe hair is visible on the pillow. I've never been great in emotional situations, but running away isn't an option this time.

'Why are you hiding from me?'

She pulls the duvet over her head. 'Go away, big man, please.'

'We help each other, remember? I'm staying put, so you may as well talk.'

Her face is grimy with tears when I peel back the covers, and it's clear that Dev was understating the situation when he said she was feeling low. She finally hauls herself to a sitting position but still won't meet my eye.

'Want some tequila to drown your sorrows, like the old days?'

'I'd need a gallon or two.'

'At least give me a proper hello.'

When she doesn't respond, I drag her into my arms. She resists for a minute, then collapses on my shoulder. Instinct makes me rub her back until the sobbing starts. Under normal circumstances I run a mile from women in distress, but Zoe's the exception. I couldn't care less that my shirt's getting soaked.

Dev appears in the doorway while she's crying loudly enough for the noise to reverberate from the walls. I give him an apologetic look, but he seems relieved. I can tell the poor sod's been waiting days for her to let go. The door clicks shut as he leaves, giving his wife time to release her sorrow. Zoe's sobbing comes to a halt ten minutes later. She's too strong to let misery dominate for long, but there's no sign now of the blonde goddess who used to leap onto a table at the pub to knock out power ballads without any sign of nerves.

'There's gunk all over your shirt,' she mutters.

'Who cares? That's why God invented washing machines.'

Her hands cover her face. 'What do I tell Mum? She's been going nuts buying toys and stuff.'

'Let Dev break the news.'

'I can't. She'll take it better from me.'

'Give yourself time then, kiddo. No need to rush.'

Zoe's story emerges in fits and starts. She and Dev found a brilliant IVF consultant in Mumbai, but each attempt has failed, every lost baby narrowing their chances. She's afraid her marriage is vulnerable too, because Dev is desperate for kids. They've talked about adoption, but it's not the same. She wants to speak to Nina, but it doesn't feel right to mention the miscarriage while Nina's heavily pregnant.

'Don't be daft, she's waiting for your call.'

Zoe's expression brightens temporarily when Shadow appears in the doorway. He jumps onto the bed and settles in the hollow I've left behind, with his muzzle resting on her knee, and soon her tear ducts are working again. He doesn't flinch when Zoe sobs into his fur, like it's his job to absorb all her woes. My respect for him rises by several notches. The dog stays put when I murmur an apology about having to get back to work, because my phone is vibrating with so many unanswered voice messages it's set to explode. I take my leave, then go down to the hotel patio to listen to them.

Madron's droning voice requests a progress report, then Eddie gives me an update. The final voicemail is from Commander Goldman. Her voice is a quiet monotone when she asks me to contact DCI Madron immediately. I'm certain there's been another death if she's getting my senior officer involved. It feels like the past is getting closer all the time.

The sea is behaving strangely when I shove my phone back into my pocket; it looks like a pool of mercury, without a single ripple. The sky is blank too, refusing to give away secrets.

23

Ruby is sitting in front of the mirror in her room with her sketchpad on her knee. She'd like to hit the road immediately, but leaving too soon might raise suspicions. Her heart rate increases when a man's voice echoes up the stairwell, informing Iris Caston that he needs to question her guests. It takes her a moment to steady her nerves. She's had years to practise her reactions in the mirror. She only has to widen her eyes and flutter her hands to look like an anxious schoolgirl.

She's still clutching her sketchbook when the landlady taps on the door. She lets it swing wide, revealing the tidy state of her room.

'Sorry to disturb you, dear. This young man needs a word.'

'It's no problem at all, Iris.'

The police officer is in his early twenties. His eyes linger on Ruby's face, then skim over her blonde hair and the new blouse she's wearing. She can always tell when men fancy her, and this one's struggling to conceal it.

'Can I take your name please, miss, for my records, and how long you're staying?'

'Chloe Moore. I'm travelling home to Brighton tomorrow.'

'Been visiting friends, have you?'

'I'm an art student, doing a project; I've spent most of my time drawing the local buildings.' She keeps her voice light. 'It's not my best skill. I have to work hard at it.'

The officer's gaze drops to the self-portrait on her sketch-pad. 'That looks pretty lifelike to me. It's obvious you've got talent.'

'I wish my tutors agreed,' she says, smiling.

'This won't take long.' The man's tone of voice suddenly becomes serious. 'You'll have heard about the fatal attack across the road.'

She nods rapidly. 'It scared me, to be honest. Do you think the area's safe now?'

'The killer will be long gone, don't worry. We're just asking people if they spotted anything unusual. Your room's well placed to see number seven.'

'I'm afraid I've hardly been here. I went shopping this morning about ten o'clock.' She gestures at the bags piled on a chair. 'When I got back, the road was cordoned off and poor Mrs Caston was in tears.'

'The whole community's reeling. The victim was a police officer.'

'That makes it even sadder,' Ruby says, her tone gentle. 'Did he have kids?'

'One teenage son.'

'I'm so sorry. Whoever did it should be locked away for good.'

'We'll find him, don't worry. If you remember anything,

please give us a call. Good luck with your studies.' The officer gives her an appreciative smile, then says goodbye.

Ruby can hear the man in the next room receiving different treatment, the conversation echoing through the thin wall. He gets a grilling, while her interview only lasted a few minutes. When she glances in the mirror again, she looks too vulnerable to hurt a fly, with waves of blonde hair framing her angelic face. Ruby's instincts are still telling her to pack up and leave while the going's good, but there's no need. Why deviate from the plan when it's going so well?

24

DCI Madron summons me to St Mary's for a meeting at 7 p.m. to discuss information he's received from Goldman. He appears to be enjoying having the upper hand; there's nothing he likes more than being in the know while I flounder. Eddie will have to look after Liz Gannick and field questions from the islanders without my help.

I give Nina a ring before setting off from Church Quay in my bowrider. There's no answer, so I leave a message saying I'll be home late. My bad mood fades once the boat enters New Grimsby Sound. The water is pewter grey and calm, the wash from my engine creating the only ripple as I motor along at top speed. My daily commute is the best perk of my job, even when I'm under pressure. I know the mile-wide stretch of the Atlantic between Bryher and St Mary's so well my gestures are automatic, giving me time to observe the birdlife. Seagulls are keeping pace overhead, mistaking me for a fisherman, waiting for scraps to be tossed into the water.

I let the peaceful atmosphere flow through me, almost managing to forget Craig Travis and the lives he stole during his brutal reign over London's underworld, but bad memories return as St Mary's fills the horizon. The man loved dealing out brutal punishments. He killed the families of those he hated. People said that he lost his conscience after his wife died in childbirth, but he struck me as a bona fide psychopath. I still can't guess how I crept under his radar, staying on the fringes of his outfit until I became his driver. It was only a matter of time before his deals were exposed. I loved working undercover, despite the risks; I was single back then, with little to lose. The excitement of existing on a knife edge fuelled me for years, but now everything's changed. I wouldn't sacrifice my life with Nina for anything.

DCI Madron is the only person at the station on Garrison Road, the reception desk empty when he beckons me into his office. He usually reacts to crises with endless criticism, but there's no sign of panic today. He's wearing dress uniform as usual, his tie almost tight enough to throttle him, black shoes polished to a mirror sheen.

'Give me an update on the Badplace Hill case, Kitto. Then we'll discuss events in London.'

My boss's stare is cool as I describe Liz Gannick's search for primary evidence at the scene. He listens intently when I explain that Eddie and I have been questioning the community about who could have been on Badplace Hill when the bones went missing. The killer tried to remove all the evidence, decades after killing the teenage boy, but I remind him that it looks like we have the murder weapon, which could yield fresh information. The only people displaying suspicious behaviour are Nathan Kernow and Jamie Porthcawl, by visiting the crime scene unauthorised.

Madron makes no comment until I finish, then immediately switches topic. 'Commander Goldman is about to give us a video call about the Travis case. She wanted me present when she shares her news. Then we'll decide how to handle the threat to you and Nina.'

'I don't want her upset this late in her pregnancy. I'm not in serious danger here while Bryher's locked down.'

'I'll be the judge of that. Shielding yourself and Nina is essential, Kitto.'

Commander Goldman's face appears on his computer screen before he can say anything else. I can tell from her expression that it's bad news.

'Denny Lang's killer was highly effective. The car was torched with him inside, leaving no evidence behind. The hit man's paying homage, it seems. Travis got even with a few of his enemies that way.' Her eyes blink shut for a moment. 'There's sad news about Steve Pullen too, Kitto. I'm afraid he was killed this morning in his own home.'

The information sends shock waves through my system. Steve was the senior officer in my team, with razor-sharp instincts. He worked right at the limits of safe practice, yet always made it home unscathed. The bloke was a decent human being too, a committed Arsenal supporter, great company in the pub, and a passionate family man, but this is the wrong time for personal grief.

'What was the MO?'

My boss glances down at her notepad. 'His son found him stabbed to death inside their home. The hit was so clinical, it has to be a contract job. Forensics are having no luck at the scene.'

'Someone must have stayed loyal, if they're paying a hit man to kill Travis's enemies,' Madron comments.

'He could persuade anyone to do anything,' I say. 'Lost souls join gangs; they're too weak to operate alone.'

Goldman stares out from the screen. 'I want you and your girlfriend in a safe house today, Kitto.'

'We can't leave yet, ma'am. Our baby's due in two weeks.'

She ignores my comment. 'You can have your pick of doctors on the mainland. There's a refuge near Land's End. Why not stay there until the killer's found?'

'Safe houses aren't always secure. What about that undercover officer who was shot outside one last year?'

'We fixed that leak; it won't happen again.'

'Another had acid thrown in her face just a few months ago. Addresses are cheap on the dark web, from police insiders.'

'Listen to me, Kitto. I'm concerned about your safety, and Annie Hardwick's too. My officers still can't track her down, despite combing information about West Country smallholdings. I think she may have foreseen something like this happening one day, given Travis's power.'

'I bet that's true, ma'am. She was always one step ahead.'

'Hardwick may already be dead; you could be the last man standing. I'm offering you armed protection.' Goldman leans forward until her face almost fills the screen. 'I've sent some encrypted photos. Take a look before you refuse point blank.'

I can still hear the concern in her voice as her image fades to a blip in the centre of the screen. The pictures she's sent will fuel my nightmares for weeks. One shows a burnt-out car, with the driver dead behind the wheel like a charcoal scarecrow, his hands reduced to blackened claws. But it's the shots of Steve Pullen that trigger my anger. My old colleague is lying on a bed, his expression agonised. The bloodstain on his chest has formed a perfect circle, like the bullseye on a dartboard. The killer used another of Travis's favourite methods: a blade straight through the heart. The next image shows a square slashed through with lines cut into Pullen's palm, and my spirits sink. I can no longer deny that I'm in trouble.

Madron leans forwards to inspect the image more closely. 'The same pattern was scratched on Denny Lang's car, according to Goldman's notes. Do you know what it means?'

'Three strikes and you're out; Travis has that symbol tattooed on his forearm. You could make two errors in his outfit, if he was feeling generous, but the third was always fatal.'

'Someone knows exactly how his mind works.'

The symbol reminds me of Maeve Trenwith's rings, even though the design is different. Madron is talking again, trying to change my mind, but I'm not running away, just because one of Craig Travis's cronies is trying to wipe his slate clean. I've got a duty to protect Nina, as well as my community. We're safest in a remote place, where you can see a storm brewing on the horizon across miles of clear ocean. My boss is still lecturing me about professional responsibility, but I keep my gaze fixed on the wall to avoid lingering on my old friend's corpse.

PART TWO

25

Sunday 4 May

I wake up before the alarm, with my head full of echoes. Nina doesn't even twitch when I ease out of bed. She's lying on her side, hands resting on her belly, protecting our baby even in sleep. Madron urged me to tell her about the threat I'm facing, but it feels wrong to worry her until I find a solution.

I carry a mug of coffee out to the bench in front of the house, still dressed in boxers and a T-shirt. The air's so warm, summer seems to have arrived early. There's still no breath of wind. When I scan the horizon, my concerns fade. Only the Atlantic's blankness lies ahead, with matchbox-sized freighters dotted along the shipping lane. The view south is less clear, the island of Gweal shrouded in early-morning mist. I'm still certain we're better off here than in a safe house. Bryher is so remote, and the community so tiny, even a practised killer would struggle to reach us without being spotted.

No can leave the island without being run through our system, and soon we may need to close all travel from the mainland, but until then Shadow is a good early-warning system. His shrill bark alerts us to visitors long before they arrive, although he's no match for a trained assassin.

I'm still thinking about the island's safety when a hand touches my shoulder, making me jump out of my skin.

'Sorry,' Nina says, observing me more closely. 'Are you okay?'

'I was in my own world, that's all.'

She's wrapped in her dressing gown, her chocolate-brown hair glinting in the sun as she joins me on the bench. 'Dreaming about what, exactly?'

I force my mind back to everyday reality. I'm not prepared to share bad news yet, but it's the right time to clear up the issue that's dogged us for months.

'I've been mulling over baby names. Do you want to hear what I think?'

'Go ahead.'

'You loved your husband, and lost him much too soon. I can handle Simon being our baby's middle name, but not Simone, if it's a girl. I wouldn't inflict that on anyone. It sounds like some crusty old French philosopher.'

Nina's face lights up. 'I knew you'd meet me halfway.'

'There's another reason why I was struggling with it.'

'What?'

'I'd like to use my dad's name, but you were so hung up on Simon, I never mentioned it.'

She remains silent for a moment. 'Mark's a classic name, and it would be lovely to keep your dad's memory alive. Mark Simon Kitto sounds good, doesn't it?' She parks herself on my lap, her arms folding round my neck. 'You deserve a kiss for finding the right solution. In fact, why don't we go back to bed?'

'Tempting, but I'm due at work. Remember that offer tonight, though.'

'I will, don't worry.'

'Tell me why you hate the idea of us getting married so much.'

Her smile stiffens. 'Isn't that obvious?'

'Not to me.'

'Don't play dumb, Ben. Look how well my first marriage turned out.'

'I won't die on you, I promise.'

'That's what they all say.' Her amber gaze is steady when she looks at me again. 'You matter as much as Simon did. I can't risk it again.'

'Do you seriously think I'll get sick if we tie the knot?'

'Fears aren't rational, or easy to control. I'm not ready for the next step, that's all.'

'But you will be one day?'

'Maybe, but there's no guarantee. Tell me why it bothers you so much.'

I gather my thoughts before explaining. My parents had a strong marriage, until dad's boat sank without a trace. Every time he came home from sea, I'd watch them embrace, their bodies so close it looked like they wanted to melt into each other's skin.

'It's permanent, how I feel about you. We're having a child. I'm ready to make promises in front of a big crowd, then throw the mother of all parties to celebrate.'

'Let's decide once the baby comes. Is that okay?'

'It'll have to be, won't it?'

Nina's eyes are glossy with tears when she kisses me then disappears back inside. I hope she's crying about her first husband, not the man who's trying so hard to become her second.

My mind swings back to the crime scene on Badplace Hill, like a compass searching for true north. Someone on the island is in the same position as me, aware that the past could soon overwhelm them, but the outcomes are different. The picture of Steve Pullen flashes into my mind. Tension presses on the back of my neck like a gathering migraine, and exercise is the only cure, so I go indoors to put on swimming shorts.

The tide is at its highest point as I cross the beach, but Shadow is taking the sensible approach, with no intention of getting wet. He waits by the tideline while I stand waist deep in mid-blue water. The cold makes me catch my breath, but exhilaration soon takes over. My hefty build helps me once I'm churning through the waves. I've swum since childhood, only bothering with a wetsuit on freezing winter days. I leave Hell

Bay at a rapid crawl and head north, with seabirds skimming overhead, monitoring my progress. Bryher's frayed coastline extends to the east, with sweeping bays guarded by granite sentinels. No wonder smugglers loved my home island most of all the Scillies, with so many caves and shelters to hide their contraband.

I see something moving when I reach Shipman Head Down. A man is up early, striding towards Anchor Carn. It's my uncle Ray, moving with uncharacteristic speed. He's got a sailor's rolling gait, but it's a surprise to see him there. Ray is such a creature of habit, I'd expect him to be in his yard by now, or on the quay smoking his first roll-up. He's following the path towards the crime scene, too focused to notice me wallowing in the sea. My eyes track him until he's too far inland to see his outline. I push my curiosity away, aware that I'm becoming paranoid, then flip onto my back and swim home, the muscles in my shoulders straining with cold energy.

I feel better after a shower, my mind focused again. Eddie rang last night to say that the Trenwiths were out when he called at their home to see if they knew why their foreman had been at the crime scene the night the skeleton disappeared. Their property is my first port of call. I want to find out if they asked Jamie Porthcawl to return to the building site, even though it was out of bounds.

It's 8.30 a.m. when I reach the cottage Maeve inherited from her family. It stands at the edge of the Town, with Broomfield Carn's rocky profile lying near the boundary fence. The house is nothing like the shimmering towers of glass that have become her trademark. It's small and humble, with windows set deep into its granite walls. When Danny appears in the doorway, he seems preoccupied. His eyes look as small as pinpricks as he scrutinises me through his thick glasses.

'It's good to see you. Come and join us for breakfast, Ben. We've got plenty.'

I sense a problem from the flatness in his voice, and the scowl on Maeve's face when we enter the kitchen. She conjures a smile, but the atmosphere is so leaden I'm certain they were having a row. The couple go through the motions of making me welcome, offering me a seat at their table. Maeve is elegant in her black garb, the only spot of colour provided by her trademark gash of crimson lipstick, her hands glittering with silver. As usual, her husband fades into the background. He's dressed in jeans and a sweatshirt, salt-and-pepper hair in need of a cut. His body language is apologetic, with shoulders hunched like he's cowering from an attack.

'I won't stay long,' I say. 'But your building site will be off limits for a while, I'm afraid.'

'We guessed,' Maeve says, attempting a smile. 'The island seems to resent us messing with its landscape. Danny's got cold feet anyway; he hates upsetting his old mentor.'

He frowns at her. 'We're needed in Spain, it's just the timing that's off.'

'The activities centre's our attempt to give something back, but the situation's tricky, Ben. We had to fight off a dozen top architects to get the Madrid project. There's a picture of my design on the wall behind you; we're calling it the Waterfall.' She points at a computerised drawing of a building that spears up from the ground like an arrow, with a river of glass rippling down one side.

'It's already in jeopardy,' Danny says. 'A French architect is desperate to take our place. Maeve ignores the emails, but they keep me awake.'

'Why do you always pretend I do less work than you?' she snaps. 'We can't just quit and walk away.'

I hold up my hand, calling time on their row. 'This is a murder investigation, remember? A man lost his life on that ground. Nothing else matters.'

'You're right, of course.' Maeve looks embarrassed. 'Sorry we're so work-obsessed, Ben.'

'I need to know if either of you saw Jamie Porthcawl at the crime scene on your way to the pub on Friday night.'

'Why would he go there?' Danny asks.

'Apparently he was looking for something, but I wondered if you'd sent him to do a recce.'

'Of course not, but Jamie's always been sensitive. Maybe uncovering that skull upset him, and he wanted to know what else you'd found.'

'Vital evidence may have been spoiled.'

Danny stares back at me. 'He's keen to work, like us.

The build's costing far more of our personal cash than we expected, and the Design Council's grant's already blown. Jamie was probably checking it could go ahead. Why not ask him yourself?'

'We already spoke on the phone, but I'll interview him in person too. Everyone's alibi has to be tested. Did he say anything about losing his dad's compass at the site?'

'Not a word.' Maeve's expression interests me more than her husband's evasion, her surprise looks too convincing to be fake.

'Someone walked into that tent later in the evening to remove the bones.'

Danny looks at me like I'm the village idiot. 'It wasn't me, if that's what you're asking. It's a crime scene to you, but it's just a building site to us. There's no point going there unless we can work.'

'We didn't leave the house after getting back from the pub,' Maeve says.

'I don't like socialising here after so much criticism of the build,' Danny adds. 'Most of the islanders are small-minded bigots. That's why I left in the first place.'

'Now who's talking rubbish?' his wife says, turning on him. 'I'd move back here in a heartbeat.'

'Keep your team away from the site, please. No one can go near it till you get the all-clear,' I say, rising to my feet.

Maeve scurries down the hallway behind me, apologising for her husband's bad mood, the frustration on her face clearer than before.

'Dan hasn't been right since we came back. The pressure's getting to him.'

'I can see that, Maeve. Thanks for the coffee. I'll keep you informed about developments affecting the site.'

Danny Trenwith appears to be paying a high price for living in his wife's shadow, but the concern in her voice proves she loves him. I still don't fully believe Jamie's reason for entering that tent, but it's possible he's desperate for the build to proceed. There's even a chance that he removed the skeleton and chucked the bones into the sea to smooth the path for the Trenwiths. I'll have to pay him a visit, but not until I've seen Liz Gannick. She's staying in a suite at Hell Bay Hotel, just below Zoe's flat.

The forensics chief takes time to answer when I knock on her door. She looks calmer when I'm finally allowed in, but the conversation could go either way. Gannick's mobile lab takes up most of the living area, a microscope standing on the dining table beside vials of coloured liquid and specimen tubes. Numbers are scrolling across her computer screen like a roll of ticker tape.

'How did you sleep, Liz?'

'Not great. Some woman's been bawling her guts out, but that ended a while back, thank God.'

'I know who that is. She's grieving for something.'

Gannick rolls her eyes. 'Tell her to do it somewhere else.' The shrill tone is absent from her voice today, leaving exhaustion in its place, as if other people's emotions drain her energy. My thoughts adjust when I spot a pill bottle on the table, the medication's name exposing her secret.

'Those are heavy-duty painkillers, Liz. I thought something was bothering you.'

A bitter smile crosses her face. 'A medic now, are you?'

'I only know they're prescribed for serious pain.'

'I rarely take them. Let's get down to work, shall we?' Her energy is reviving already. She swings across the room on her crutches to where a light shines down on fragments of green metal. 'This is the murder weapon, freshly cleaned. I looked at your photos of the skull in the ground. Your victim died fast, after having that spike driven though his brain.'

'Our pathologist agrees with you.'

The piece of metal looks sharper than before, six inches long, its copper surface glinting now that the oxide's been removed. Something shifts in my chest as I stare at it, aware that I've seen one just like it in the past.

'It could be a massive nail, or something the killer made,' Liz mutters.

'Have you found any bone fragments from the skeleton?'

She shakes her head. 'There should be particles in my soil analysis when I get to it. I've been checking what was in the skeleton's hand. Some of the metal was carbon-alloyed steel, with a low chromium content, so it's rusted away.'

'What are you saying exactly?'

'They make files, chisels and picks from it. I think he was holding a set of precision tools.'

The bag lies unrolled on a plastic sheet, and when I look more closely, my stomach contracts. I recognise its shape, and a patch of grey canvas has retained its colour despite years underground. Ray had an identical one until it went missing when I was in my teens.

'It may not help you much,' she says. 'Plenty of people have one just like it in their DIY kit.'

'I'll see what I can find out.'

She's too absorbed to notice I'm unsettled. Why would a toolkit from my uncle's yard be clutched in a dead man's hand? I can't help remembering Ray walking up Badplace Hill so purposefully this morning, like he was heading straight to the crime scene.

Gannick has moved on to her next problem, peering into her microscope at specks of earth smeared across a slide, oblivious to my concerns. Her jaw is clenched with determination; she's already forgotten I exist.

26

After I leave the hotel, I go straight to Jamie Porthcawl's home in the Town, but there's no one at home so I cut south across Shipman Head Down. I should visit Ray's boatyard to find out the truth, but I'm running late for a catch-up meeting with Eddie at the Rock. My journey takes me past All Saints' Church, where a small group of islanders and tourists are waiting for morning communion. The church was built two hundred years ago, like most of the houses on Bryher, from local materials. It's a squat granite box with a slate roof, the tower added forty years later, after the community had saved enough money for a bell.

When I scan the worshippers again, I see Sandra Trescothick and Penny Cadgwith chatting together, their faces animated. I can tell they're enjoying each other's company. Strong friendships form right across the islands, because our lives are so interlinked during the long winters, we rely on each other for support. Sandra Trescothick is famously self-sufficient, but I'm glad to see she's got close friends. She's lived alone on Bryher for a few years, since her only son left for university.

I spot the Porthcawls and head straight over; Jamie steps in my direction like he's shielding his Christian friends from our conversation, but they're already filing inside the church.

'Could we have a quick word, please, Jamie?'

He looks uncomfortable. 'The service is just starting. Can it wait for an hour?'

'Fine, I'll come to yours.'

'Any time after church. I'll be at home all day.' He does his best to smile, even though his face looks strained.

I'm surprised that such a down-to-earth man is God-fearing, but a lot of the islanders are Christians, which may be connected to living close to the sea. It's seized so many lives over the years, people rely on prayers as self-defence. I scan the queue again, expecting to see Louis Hayle, who attends church most Sundays, but he's nowhere in sight.

My godmother's pub is pulsating with music when I arrive, 'Born in the USA' spilling from the kitchen doors at ear-splitting volume. Billy looks like a diehard rocker when I step inside, with a red bandana round his head, his T-shirt proclaiming his undying loyalty to Bruce Springsteen. He turns the music down, but continues chopping onions as he gives me a brief nod of greeting. Maggie and Billy have only lived together a few years, but I've learnt how he operates. He's easily wounded by thoughtless remarks, and holds long grudges, but his loyalties are unshakeable. It's clear I'm not in his good books.

'Shadow's been scrounging again. Why not feed him, once in a while?'

'He's cunning, Billy. If you give him scraps, he'll never leave you alone.'

'It's not my fault the creature's hungry.'

'What's really bugging you?'

He narrows his eyes. 'I'm not thrilled about a skeleton appearing a few hundred metres from us, if you must know. It's like one of those horror films where people start dying for no good reason. At least that bloody activities centre won't happen now. Those two can bugger off and spoil someone else's view.'

'How come you're so against it?'

'Look what the developers did to Newquay. The council let some idiot put up a hotel on the surfing beach, then Jamie Oliver opens a sodding restaurant, and fifty more hotels pop up beside it.'

'How does Maggie stay cheerful with you around?'

'I feed her well, but I can't get a bloody kitchen hand. Clear off and let me work.' His knife is moving so fast, I'm glad to be out of reach.

Eddie has turned the pub's function room into Scotland Yard, with folders bulging with witness reports. It crosses my mind to tell him about my old colleague getting killed, but the DCI warned me not to share the news with the team, in case it reaches the wider community. My deputy looks so excited, I'd hate to take the shine off his day. His positivity keeps our working relationship strong, and explains how he talked me into becoming godfather to his three-year-old daughter, Lottie.

'I've got a feeling that bag in the skeleton's hand came from Ray's yard, Eddie.'

He gazes up at me. 'Should we get him in for questioning?'

'I need to get my facts straight first.'

'What happens next?' he asks, looking at me like I'm a world expert.

'Gannick's going back to the crime scene to take more earth samples. She thinks whoever took the bones must have left evidence. She'll send the samples for analysis to the lab today. It's possible we'll get a DNA profile of the killer within forty-eight hours.'

'Do you still think the victim was an islander, boss?'

'It's more likely than a tourist. We've got around a hundred permanent inhabitants, with our numbers doubling for a few months in summer. How would a hotel guest figure out the best place to hide a body?'

'With difficulty,' Eddie says. 'But a holidaymaker wouldn't be missed so easily, would they? The hotel staff would just assume they'd hopped on a ferry and gone home early.'

'We need to see if the pub and hotel have records going back thirty years, to cover our bases. Can you chase that down, while I focus on finding out who took the bones? Penny Cadgwith could be right about the killer fearing exposure. DNA can be extracted from bone samples now, so they had to act fast. If Gannick finds a fragment of bone from the victim, we could establish a genetic link by testing the island's whole population.'

'We still need a suspect.' Eddie's smile dims for a moment.

'I can't believe someone murdered a teenage boy then dragged his body up Badplace Hill alone. The victim was unconscious when that spike entered his skull, or another person was holding him down. I bet the killer had help, or at least confided in someone.'

'You think a local on Bryher has kept the secret that long?'

'A few people are acting strangely, like Jamie Porthcawl going back to the scene. He was twitchy just now too, when I tried to talk to him. Nathan Kernow's still a suspect as well. His mother took in paying guests decades ago; maybe our victim stayed there.'

Eddie stares at me. 'Do you think he'd have attacked one of his mum's lodgers? He was just a kid.'

'He'd have been somewhere between nine and nineteen, but it would explain why he went up to the site.'

'Out of guilt, you mean?'

'He was tense when we spoke, so we need to keep watch. Let's get to work, Eddie. See if anyone remembers a visitor suddenly disappearing years ago.'

Eddie gives a slow nod of agreement, but there's resignation on his face. Loyalty matters more than justice to many islanders, like in the old days. Smugglers still use the islands as an entry point to the UK for drugs, booze and tobacco, and people prefer setting their own rules. Our case demonstrates the islanders' aversion to the law. We've pressed the whole community for information, yet no one's willing to speak. I can't blame them entirely – I'm keeping information about Travis to myself too, even though Nina deserves the truth.

27

It's 11 a.m. when Ruby arrives in Plymouth. Her rucksack feels heavy as she steps off the train, so she goes to the public lavatories and stuffs the clothes she wore in London into a carrier bag, then dumps them in a wheelie bin behind a coffee bar, keeping her baseball cap pulled down as she leaves the concourse. The first stage of her father's plan has been achieved, but she can't slow down. It would only make her vulnerable.

It's years since she travelled outside London. This city feels much smaller, the pavements narrow, with shoppers walking at a snail's pace. Their speech is different too, when she eavesdrops on conversations. People leave pauses between sentences, content to let silence hang on the air. Ruby's senses are on high alert as she follows arrows on the pavement directing her to the bus station. She glances over her shoulder, making sure no one's following, then comes to a sudden halt when she spots something unexpected. Her face is printed on the front cover of a tabloid newspaper discarded on a bench.

The headline reads, *MONSTER'S DAUGHTER PAYS WITH HER LIFE*. Thankfully the picture was taken years ago, when her hair was dyed black, skin caked in make-up. When she picks up the paper, she sees that the journalist has portrayed her as a tragic victim: her mother died giving birth, then her father was imprisoned for heinous crimes. Ruby Travis never stood a chance; she was a psychopath just like her dad. Is it any wonder she burnt down her miserable home, then threw herself into the Thames, weeks after her nineteenth birthday?

She drops the paper into a bin. The press is making up lies; she loved being Craig Travis's daughter, and her faculties are sharper than any journalist's. An odd feeling stirs in her chest when she reaches the bus station. The terminus is crowded with couples, families, and teenagers chatting on their phones. It feels like she's the only solitary traveller as she queues for a ticket. The link with her dad felt strong while she was in London, but now it's fading. She can still hear his rasping voice saying he loves her, but the gap opening up between them is terrifying.

She reaches the front of the queue, still immersed in memories. The assistant behind the glass panel watches her fish out a credit card, her gaze patient.

'Where are you going, love?'

'Single to Bodmin, please.'

The woman smiles. 'Lucky you, the moors are beautiful this time of year.'

'I can't wait, it's a great place to hike.'

Ruby is glad to pocket her ticket. She spent months tracking her next target down, calling in favours from computer hackers and her dad's old contacts, who twisted a few high-level arms in the police, yet all that effort came to nothing. A simple trick worked in the end, enabling her to get information from one of Hardwick's relatives. She needs to stay focused, without letting distractions slow her down.

28

Jamie and Bella Porthcawl's home lies close to Nathan Kernow's, just three doors along the terrace, but it's far tidier. It boasts a few well-tended flower beds and a square of neatly cut grass. The window frames look newly painted, the brass door-knocker gleaming.

Jamie opens the door before I have time to knock. If he feels guilty about his actions at the murder site, there's no sign of it today. I've employed him several times since I came back to Bryher; he fitted a new kitchen for us only a few months ago. Tradesmen stand or fall by their craft in Scilly, where word of mouth is all-important, and Jamie prides himself on the quality of his work. I've never seen him in his Sunday best until today, his jacket worn with black jeans and brogues, his bald head shiny in the sunlight. He seems more relaxed since his visit to church, his manner easier when he invites me inside.

The house smells of air freshener and floor polish;

a grandfather clock gleams in the hallway. The place seems full of heirlooms and traditional furniture, a mirror on the wall in an ornate frame. When I'm led down the hallway, I catch sight of Bella in their living room through the open doorway. She's busy tucking packets of cards into envelopes, even though they only got back from church a short while ago. She's wearing a green dress, her strawberry-blonde hair pinned back from her face when she smiles at me.

'Fancy stuffing some envelopes for me, Ben? I've got a rush on. Would you believe some people actually buy Christmas cards in May?'

'Crazy,' I reply. 'My answer is never to send any.'

'You'll put me out of work.'

Her smile pulses more brightly, and it dawns on me that I've never seen her sad. I'm about to ask after her business, but I can hear Jamie in the kitchen making coffee. The couple's Labrador is lying in a basket when I join him there. She's so deeply asleep, she doesn't stir when Jamie leans down to stroke her fur. His gaze is still fixed on her when we sit down at his table.

'Kidney failure the vet says. She sleeps most of the day now, so it's only a matter of time. It feels wrong to put her down, after fifteen years.'

'I know what you mean. Shadow annoys the hell out of me, but I'd hate to lose him.'

Jamie goes on stroking his dog, even though she barely responds.

'Tell me about your work on the activities centre,' I say.

'It was going well till I found that skull. It's lucky I saw it from the digger, or it would have been smashed apart.'

'That doesn't explain why you went back.'

My question makes him flinch. 'Sorry, I should have got your permission. Losing Dad's compass preyed on my mind. I couldn't believe I'd dropped it; I always carry it with me.'

'Like a talisman?'

'To feel close to him, I suppose.' He shifts awkwardly in his chair. 'It's still missing.'

'I'm surprised you took on work from the Trenwiths. You've got a great reputation here, and Bella's business is going well, isn't it?'

'She needs to expand; we want to rent an industrial unit on St Mary's and employ some packers. The activities centre will help us move forwards – if it ever happens.'

'You trespassed on a crime scene, Jamie. You know that's illegal, don't you?'

'Sorry, I wasn't thinking straight. It was a stupid thing to do.'

'I'm not trying to shame you. I just need to understand.'

'Dad and I worked together, sailed together, hung out in the pub. He gave me that compass on my eighteenth birthday. It means the world to me.' His voice is measured, but he still won't meet my eye.

'You've made it harder for my team to find out who it was lying in the ground. You've made yourself a person of interest too.'

He looks shocked. 'Come on, Ben, I've never hurt anyone in my life.'

'It's odd behaviour, that's all.'

'I feel responsible, after finding the skull. I'm stuck here twiddling my thumbs, and that build may never get completed. Let me know if I can help.'

'Thanks for the offer.' I pause before speaking again. 'Are you and Bella close to Nathan Kernow?'

'Not really, to be honest. He went all New Age last year. Nathan's got a kind heart, but shamans and warlocks aren't my bag. It seems like mumbo-jumbo to me.'

'Is paganism a new thing for him?'

'He's tried Buddhism, and Scientology too. He prefers researching belief systems to practising them, I think.'

There's disappointment in Jamie's voice. When I look up, I see a small brass crucifix on the wall, beside a cluster of photos. The couple's faith seems to be a distinct strand in their lives, alongside work, family and friendships. I know they miss their kids, who both work on the mainland, but it's the wrong time to ask how they're doing.

Bella is still hard at work when I leave, with packages

heaped on the table ready to post. I walk back towards Ray's boatyard, unable to explain why Jamie's story failed to clear away my doubts.

29

Ruby boards an old-fashioned bus for the last hour of her journey. It winds through narrow lanes, across a landscape that feels too exposed. She's used to concrete and crowds, but her view now is of undulating fields of unripe wheat, livestock and few human beings. The buildings are made from crude stone blocks, a stark contrast with London's glittering skyline.

She's glad to reach Bodmin at last. The village is a sweep of cottages rising to a church on top of a hill. Once upon a time the villagers would all have worshipped there, their consciences policed by the local priest. Ruby still feels exposed as she wanders through the village looking for the pub she found online, which rents out rooms. It's called the Hole in the Wall, but she wanted to check it over before committing herself to staying there. When she finds the place, it looks ideal, with no CCTV and a basic interior. There's a dartboard on the wall, a pool table in the corner and St George's flag hanging by the door.

The landlord is bottling up behind the bar. He looks too old to be running the place, his face covered in deep wrinkles.

'What can I get you, young lady?'

'A room for tonight, please, and maybe tomorrow too.'

'We've got a vacancy.' He studies her more closely. 'You don't look like a hiker to me. They normally have all the kit and caboodle, blow-up mattresses, camping stoves and God knows what. Or are you a birdwatcher?'

'An art student. I'll be out drawing if the weather's fine.'

'You never know in the West Country, love.' His eyes glitter with amusement. 'We get all four seasons in one day on the moor.'

'I brought my waterproofs, just in case.' Ruby forces a smile, even though she'd rather end the conversation. The more time the old man spends looking at her, the more likely it is that he'll remember her face.

'Let me show you the room.' He leads her up a narrow set of steps, talking nonstop, even though he's out of breath. 'Do you know why this place is called the Hole in the Wall?'

'I can't guess.'

'Smugglers drank here in the old days. We've even got a false floor, where they hid from the lawmen.'

'That's good to know in case the police come looking for me.'

The old man laughs. 'On the run are you, like Bonnie and Clyde?'

'Not anymore. This place feels like home.'

He opens a door at the end of the corridor. The room is small and sparsely furnished, but the view is endless, the moor's lush grass full of mounds and hillocks.

'Perfect,' she says.

When the landlord looks at her again, Ruby's tension fades. His eyes are milky in the sunlight pouring through the window, cataracts blurring his vision. It's another stroke of good fortune.

'Just you tonight, is it, love?'

'That's right. I'm on my own.'

He gives another brief laugh. 'Maybe you'll find a handsome Cornishman out on the moor.'

Ruby is so glad when the landlord finally leaves, she leans against the door, and lets herself exhale. She could take a day off, but her father needs good news, so she rummages through her belongings. There's an Ordnance Survey map in her backpack, with her next location marked in red. She's brought a compass too, and a camera, like any other walker going for a hike across the moor.

She changes into denim shorts, trainers and a windcheater, even though the day is warm. Then she puts her father's knife in her inside pocket and leaves by the fire exit, with the map clutched in her hand.

30

Shadow appears from nowhere when I leave the Porthcawls' home. The creature bounces up on his hind legs, determined to lick my face.

'Faker,' I tell him. 'You'd kiss anyone for a free meal.'

He ignores my lack of faith, trotting beside me as I take the five-minute walk back to Church Quay, in search of Ray. I'm in luck. The boatyard door is open, the sound of hammering getting louder all the time. My uncle is attacking a piece of spruce with all his might, raining hammer blows on the length of wood, still one of the strongest men on the island despite his age.

'Why not put it back in the steamer?' I ask. He soaks the lapping in hot steam to make it soft enough to bend.

'It only needs to flex by another centimetre.'

'Want me to try?'

Ray seems glad to hand over his hammer, pointing at the yield spot. I beat the wood until the fibres loosen under my hand. The task is so satisfying; it's a reminder that I may have chosen the wrong career twenty years ago. I could have learnt most of my uncle's skills by now. I'd be a qualified boatwright instead of a cop haunted by a renowned psychopath.

My uncle gives me a thumbs-up, then inspects the strake, holding it at eye level to judge the curve.

'Decent work.' He puts down the piece of wood. 'Staying for lunch?'

'If you've got time. I need a word with you.'

I follow him up to his living quarters above the yard. It's one of my favourite places on Bryher, shaped by his self-sufficiency. He built most of the furniture from offcuts that would have gone to waste. I take a seat on the bench I helped him make as a kid, while he roots through the fridge. Five minutes later, he passes me a plateful of bread, cheese, tomatoes and ham. My uncle's food is like him: honest, with no frills, but always fit for purpose.

I'd like quick answers, but there's no point in talking to Ray during a meal. He maintains his silence as he sits beside me looking out to sea, taking slow mouthfuls. I watch clouds drift over Tresco's hills, beyond New Grimsby Sound. The water is so still, the yachts moored in the channel look like they've been set in dark blue resin, but my uncle's serenity eludes me. I keep remembering him marching up Badplace Hill, like a man on a mission.

'There's going to be an almighty thunderstorm soon, isn't there?'

Ray finishes his last mouthful. 'The Met Office says this calm should last three more days, which suits me fine. The humidity helps the wood.' He's still the best weather forecaster on the islands, after years in the merchant navy.

'I saw you walking on Shipman Head this morning, when I was swimming. What were you doing there?'

He gathers up our plates, setting them down in the sink with a clatter of protest. He hates being quizzed, but I've got no choice.

'Taking exercise, like you.'

'You were close to the grave site.'

'I needed some thinking space, if you must know.'

I lean back against the wall and let silence spin out between us, until he finally speaks.

'I'm considering selling the yard. It's best to stop while I've got a choice.'

'You've said that before.'

'Nothing lasts for ever. I'll be sixty-five next year.'

'So what? You're fitter than most fifty-year-olds.'

'Rubbish, I'm an old man with a hernia.' He takes his pouch of tobacco from his pocket and starts to roll a cigarette. 'You came here for something, Ben. What is it?'

'Information about the past. You know we're investigating the murder of a teenage boy, killed between twenty and thirty years ago, then buried in a shallow grave on Badplace Hill. I don't remember anyone going missing when I was a kid. How do you think it happened in a community of less than a hundred, without raising suspicions?'

Ray's sea-blue eyes assess me. 'People arrive and leave like the tides, except us natives. They try out our lifestyle, then run back to the mainland. Our winters don't suit everyone.'

'Let me show you something, Ray.' I pull my phone from my pocket and display my photos of the items from Badplace Hill. 'Do you recognise either of these?'

My uncle squints at the images. 'That's a copper clouting nail. I've got a few in the storeroom. It's been years since I worked on trawlers big enough to need them.'

'How about the other picture?'

'It's just a scrap of old cloth.'

'I think it's that canvas roll bag you lost, with compartments for hand tools.'

He studies the image again, suddenly more interested. 'You could be right. It annoyed the hell out of me; I had to replace a chisel my grandfather passed down.'

'How long ago did you lose it?'

'When you were a boy, twenty-odd years ago. What's this about anyway?'

I take my phone back from him. 'Someone used that clout for a murder weapon, and your toolkit was in the victim's hand.'

Ray stares back at me. 'Are you serious?'

'Who do you think put them there?'

'No idea.' He fixes his gaze back on the sea, collecting his thoughts. 'I went to the pub one night, leaving the yard unlocked. I only realised my tool bag had gone when I started work next morning. Maybe someone took the clout then too.'

'Who did you suspect at the time?'

'I thought it was some kid on a dare. I asked around and no one knew.'

'What year was it exactly?'

He hesitates before replying. 'You'd just finished primary school, I think.'

'Twenty-seven years ago?'

'It may have been the year before.'

'You must remember someone going missing from Bryher.'

A frown darkens his face. 'Some men deserve to end up in a shallow grave. Maybe you should let sleeping dogs lie.'

'It's my job to find out who died, no matter what he did.'

Ray hesitates for a moment. 'I had a Polish lad working in the yard for a bit. Do you remember Jakob Bazyli?'

'I don't think so.'

'Jakob was my apprentice for a year. He shoved a note under my door apologising, then left without saying goodbye. I never clapped eyes on him again.'

'Where was he staying?'

'Over at the Kernows.'

'How did he leave the island?'

Ray gives an exaggerated shrug. 'He was here one day, gone the next.'

'I'll have to track him down. Tell me everything you remember.'

'I don't keep records more than five years, but I know Jakob was from Warsaw. He was a hard worker, the honest type. I can't see him stealing my toolkit. I think he was more homesick than I realised; the lad used to sing Polish songs in the yard. He was missing some girl at home.'

'Nothing else?'

'It was decades ago.'

I'd like to go on, but I've already pushed my luck. My uncle's expression is blank, even though I can tell he's rattled. He always keeps his cards close to his chest. Irritation clouds my thoughts, until he leans over to tap me on the wrist. Physical gestures are so rare from Ray, it takes me by surprise.

'I've got something to show you, down in the yard.'

When I follow him back downstairs, he leads me to the corner where he stacks offcuts, and pulls back an old dust sheet. I'm speechless when I see what's underneath. It's a cot, made from seasoned oak, with delicate island flowers carved on each side. It's set on rockers, with spindles he's run through the lathe, and it's been polished to a shine. Ray's craftsmanship and the care he's taken knock me sideways.

'That's beautiful. Has Nina seen it yet?

'I wanted to check with you first. I can always give it to someone else.'

'It's better than anything we could buy. She'll be thrilled.'

Pleasure crosses his face, then vanishes. 'It's just odd bits of wood I threw together in no time.'

'Liar, it must have taken days.'

I stand there admiring his joinery, but Ray seems eager to get back to work. He's given me a new lead, and some background information, which I'll have to chase down. It makes me uncomfortable to record items from his yard being found at the murder scene. I'd like his advice on the Craig Travis situation too, but Ray has no experience of gangs, or grudges that last for generations, so I take my leave.

I've witnessed my uncle's softer side, which rarely surfaces, but the visit has triggered a new dilemma. I can't explain why, but I feel sure he's holding something back. He could solve the mystery for me if I can ask the right question.

31

Ruby knows the second stage of her father's plan might be challenging. It took two long years to track her next target down, until she hatched a simple plan. She pretended to be a van driver, delivering flowers to the woman's sister, asking her to confirm the sender's address after giving the name. She recited the address of a remote West Country farm in a blink, exchanging Annie Hardwick's safety for a bouquet of roses. The next stage will involve physical exertion. Ruby has never walked across open country before; her closest experience was a trip to Epping Forest with a couple who fostered her for three months, then put her back in care. They said she was too secretive, and their younger child found her frightening, even though she'd just begun to feel safe there.

She's been walking for half an hour, but still can't find the place. The farm stands near the bridleway, yet there have been no signs for it. Maybe she took the wrong turn at the last stile? The instructions she's memorised are imprinted on her mind. A successful hit has to be clinical, leaving no trace behind. She steps away from the path to sip from her bottle of water and finds herself in a glade. The dappled light sifting through high branches is beautiful, but there's no time to admire the scenery. It's only when she stands up again that she spots a building, almost hidden by trees. She takes care to stay in the shadows as she approaches, stopping frequently to check that no one's following.

Ruby comes to a halt when she reaches a boundary fence made of rusting barbed wire. A small farm building stands fifty metres away. It looks derelict, but a horse peers out from a stable door, chickens squawking in an enclosure. There's an old-fashioned well that must still be in use, with a bucket hanging from a chain. She can smell manure and creosote, but whoever lives there is using modern technology, even though the buildings are falling apart. There are solar panels on the farmhouse roof, and more on the barn. Her biggest concern is the three CCTV cameras rigged up on the barn and farmhouse walls. She'll have to tread carefully to avoid being caught on film. Rudy's still gazing at the place when a sound reaches her. It's the crackling noise of footsteps on dry undergrowth, but when she swings round, there are only densely packed trees, scenting the air with rain and decay. She waits near the boundary, hoping someone will emerge.

Ruby is ready to give up for the time being, by 3p.m. She is almost certain the farm belongs to an ex-cop. She's doing a good job of staying hidden, and the place ticks all the right boxes. Hardwick told people she wanted to live off grid, preferring to be alone. She's a survivalist too, passed her SAS training with ease, before joining the police. Maybe she knows her undercover work has left her vulnerable, even in the middle of nowhere. Ruby keeps her gaze glued to the building for another five minutes before stuffing her water bottle back into her pack. It's tempting to scramble over the fence and hide in the barn, but Hardwick might be indoors, watching.

'See you later,' she hisses under her breath.

She walks back to the pub slowly, stopping to look at the scenery. Its beauty registers but doesn't affect her deeply. The green counterpane of fields is seamed together by crumbling dry-stone walls, spotted with yellow patches of gorse. It stretches as far as the eye can see. Ruby feels too visible on this rolling grassland, to stop and admire anything for long. It's a relief to return to the pub. When she glances through the front window, the landlord is chatting to some old-timers at the bar, no other staff in sight. The man's vision is poor, and he's too stuck in his routine to remember details of her movements. She can rest easy until tonight.

32

A surprise is waiting for me when I return to the Rock for my 4 p.m. briefing with Gannick and Eddie. Madron has come over from St Mary's. He looks out of place in the neglected room, assessing the dust on every surface with a look of disgust. Eddie gives me an apologetic shrug. I know he'll have tried hard to keep him away, but our boss believes I need close supervision. Gannick is too busy staring at her tablet to notice the tense atmosphere.

'I want every protocol followed,' the DCI says. 'Let's start with a progress report from each of you, please.'

Madron believes in hierarchies, so he turns to Gannick first, due to her seniority. He gives a deferential smile, but the forensics chief hates social niceties.

'I haven't made much headway,' she announces. 'I spent hours trying to extract DNA from the items found at the scene.'

I lean forward to have my say. 'I've spoken to my uncle about the items. He says the murder weapon is a copper nail, referred to as a clout, normally used in shipyards to rivet heavy pieces of timber. The cloth and rusted metal could be the remains of a tool bag he lost over twenty years ago. I've spoken to him, and it's obvious he's not involved.'

The DCI holds up his hand like he's stopping traffic. 'Both items at the murder site came from Ray Kitto's yard?'

'It seems likely, sir. He also mentioned a young Polish man called Jakob Bazyli who worked for him twenty-seven years ago. Bazyli left suddenly, so we need to track him down. Apparently he left a note at the boatyard, but the killer could have done that.'

'Why didn't you bring Ray in for questioning?'

'If my uncle killed one of his workers, why would he tell me the young man's name, and would he leave his own possessions at the scene?'

Madron's pale grey stare lingers on my face. 'We'll talk about this after the meeting.'

Gannick describes taking soil samples from the spot where the skeleton was found, while irritation churns in my stomach, but I have to accept Madron's point. I was wrong to break protocol when interviewing a relative. My attention only returns to the meeting when the forensics chief explains that there may have been fragmentation, if the bones really were decades old. She would only need to find a minute piece for the lab to extract DNA.

'Thanks for your hard work,' Madron says.

She gives a quiet laugh. 'That's just the start. I'll have to spend tonight staring into a microscope till I find that bone.'

'Anything to add, Kitto?' Madron's smile vanishes as he studies me again.

'I've been trying to find out who could have removed the bones undetected. Jamie Porthcawl visited the site unauthorised. He entered the tent on Friday evening, even though the area was cordoned off. He claims to have dropped his dad's compass there, but I'm not convinced. Nathan Kernow was at the site later on, around midnight, before the bones were taken.'

'What in God's name was he doing trespassing on a crime scene?'

'Conducting a pagan burial ritual, complete with candles, wild flowers and a hand-made altar. He would have been a young boy at the time of the murder, but we still need to keep track of him.'

Madron frowns. 'You think he took the bones?'

'He may have removed them on a second visit, but I'll keep an eye on Danny Trenwith too. Him and Maeve have a lot to gain by getting rid of the skeleton. They're desperate to finish their build. Things seemed tense at home when I spoke to them.'

'I can see why. We can't keep them waiting indefinitely.'

'With respect, sir, this may be a cold case, but it's still a murder investigation. I want to find Jakob

Bazyli, but it could have been someone else in that shallow grave.'

'Look at the Porthcawl family, will you? The younger lad left quite suddenly, if I recall correctly. His name was Hugh. He settled on the mainland, according to hearsay, but I've never seen him come back to visit.'

'Why didn't you mention that before, sir? You know we're looking for a missing person.'

Madron tuts under his breath. 'The Porthcawls are a respectable family. No missing person was ever reported, and Hugh may simply have established a new life elsewhere. The lad struck me as a high-flyer.'

'We'll check his whereabouts, but we can't prove he left the islands; the shipping office lost most of its records recently, due to a computer virus. I'll speak to Arthur Penwithick to see if he remembers anything about visitors using his ferry.'

DCI Madron's expression warms again when he turns to Eddie. I still don't fully understand why he saves his contempt for me alone, apart from his admission years ago that I bear a physical resemblance to his oldest son. The young man was a thrill-seeker, which led to his death in a motorbike accident, and Madron views me in the same light. No matter how painstaking my approach, he always accuses me of recklessness. I wish we had a better working relationship, but it's been tense ever since I started working for him four years ago, so it seems unlikely anything will change.

Eddie finishes his report by describing his progress through the island's census, checking individuals' names at every property on Bryher. He's come across no missing persons so far. It still bothers me that Madron knew about a young man leaving the islands without any clear explanation, but at least we've got a new lead.

Gannick raises her head again. 'Whoever wound up in that grave must have been terribly isolated not to be missed.'

I nod in reply. 'No one's ever reported a relative or acquaintance disappearing, according to the registrar. I'll go over to the Town Hall on St Mary's tomorrow. Sandra Trescothick's been checking the official records for us, but she's had no results yet, so I'll take a look myself.'

'You all have defined roles in the investigation, so keep going, please. Hard work gets results,' Madron says. 'Follow me, Kitto. I want a private word.'

It's dusk when we leave the pub. My boss leads me towards the beach so we won't be overheard, marching like a platoon sergeant. A line of sweat has developed on his upper lip when he finally comes to a halt.

'What in God's name is wrong with you?' he snaps. 'Give your uncle a formal interview, and record every word, or we'll be accused of whitewashing events. Do you hear me?'

'Loud and clear, sir.'

'Why do you never exercise caution? The same goes

for the Travis case. You were instrumental in exposing that gang, and the killer's a sick individual. A graphologist has just analysed the suicide note his daughter left behind. Apparently she was under huge stress when it was written. She may have been forced to write it, then thrown into the river.'

'Why murder his daughter? I thought they were targeting the police team that put him away?'

'Maybe the killer thinks she didn't show her dad enough respect.'

'I'm still safer here than on the mainland.'

Madron's grey eyes turn icy, despite the heat. 'What does Nina have to say?'

'I shan't worry her till it's unavoidable.'

'She doesn't know?'

'I'll pick the right time to share the news.'

'Nina's smart enough to make her own choices. I insist you tell her immediately.'

'She'll want to stay here, on the islands.'

'Listen to me, Kitto. I won't tolerate another broken rule.' His frown forms a deep groove between his eyes. 'Tell her in the next twenty-four hours, or I will.' He struts away before I can argue.

It's 7 p.m. when I check my watch, and the clock's already ticking. I walk closer to the sea, then drop onto a boulder, hoping the peace and quiet will help me decide what to do next. Hangman Island lies directly ahead, the yardarm still visible in the fading light. I loved swimming out there as a boy, then racing my

196

brother to the top of that rocky mound. But the relic looks different now. It's just a monument to a forgotten war, a place of pointless bloodshed.

33

Ruby goes downstairs at 7.30 for her evening meal. The pub is crowded with locals, but few observe her closely as she settles in a corner. She wants to blend into the wallpaper, just another tourist poring over her guidebook while she eats. She takes her time, washing her lasagne down with a pint of beer, because rushing would make her stand out. People who move too fast or make too much noise draw attention to themselves. She feels uncomfortable when the landlord approaches her table, heads turning to see why she's been singled out.

'Been drawing today have you, love?' The man asks, his voice too loud.

'I did a few sketches. The light here's beautiful.'

'Wait till you see the Hurlers' Stones, or the waterfalls at Golitha. Show me your drawings tomorrow and I'll buy one off you. This place needs some decent art on the walls.'

'I'm not that good.'

He gives a braying laugh. 'Course you are. I won't take no for an answer.'

The landlord returns to the bar, but he's blown Ruby's cover. The whole room's watching her now, wondering about the budding artist in their midst. She keeps her head down while she finishes her drink, then hurries back to her room.

She waits until 9 p.m., peering out of her window to check the coast is clear, then slips out of the fire exit. It still feels like she's being watched, after suddenly becoming the centre of attention through no fault of her own. She has to walk fifty metres down the road before joining the footpath, but luckily the sky is blanketed with cloud, making her invisible. The journey is harder now, with granite shapes rearing from the dark like startled horses, the ground slippery underfoot. She uses her torch to navigate through the thick darkness.

Ruby stares at the old farmhouse once she reaches the boundary wall. Annie Hardwick must be at home, because lights blaze from the downstairs windows. She'll need to get closer to find the best access point. There's no sound as she picks her way across the farmyard, apart from chickens clucking, the birds locked in the henhouse for the night. It's a relief to find the barn doors open, the dry smell of hay filling her airways when she goes inside. She peers out at the house. The back door will be the safest way inside, if she can jemmy the lock.

Pain arrives suddenly and without warning. Someone has her in a chokehold, a hand smothering her nose and mouth.

'Who the fuck are you?' a woman's voice hisses.

'You're hurting me,' Ruby mumbles. 'I can't breathe.'

'Answer my question.'

'My name's Chloe,' she manages. 'I need a place to sleep.'

'Liar. How the fuck did you find me?'

'I ran away. I couldn't stand it there.'

It's only when Ruby pretends to cry that the woman's grip loosens a fraction. She can feel her dad's presence protecting her as she waits for her luck to turn.

34

I return to Jamie Porthcawl's house after my conversation with Madron, the man's stern warning rattling around my head. I'd rather focus for now on the bones uncovered on Badplace Hill than the violence emerging from my own past. I've tried casting my memory back to the islanders I knew as a boy, but I was too busy growing up to care about the adult world. My dealings with Jamie over the years make him seem an unlikely murderer, and he's not the type to hide his feelings easily. One of the reasons he's well liked across the islands is for wearing his heart on his sleeve, so open and honest he's rarely out of work.

The Porthcawls' house looks welcoming as dusk settles over Bryher, orange light emanating from the downstairs rooms, but when Bella answers my knock on the door, her eyes are red and puffy.

'Are you okay?'

'We've had an awful day, to be honest, Ben. Our

dog died a few hours ago. She went peacefully, thank God, but I haven't stopped crying.' She takes a step back, beckoning me inside. 'Come in, I'll put the kettle on.'

'Sorry to trouble you again, Bella. That's sad news about your dog.'

'Jamie's in a right old state. It would help him to talk to another bloke. He's hiding in his workshop.'

She leads me outside, where music is spilling from a large shed in the back garden. Jamie seems to be exorcising his grief with some classy American soul, Marvin Gaye's silky tenor explaining that he heard it through the grapevine. The builder looks startled when I tap on the door. He swings round with hammer raised, and I put up my hands.

'I come in peace, Jamie.'

His man cave is equipped with power drills, saws and hammers, his tools lining the wall in neat rows. He switches off his music straight away.

'Sorry, I didn't hear you coming.'

'Bella told me about your dog. Are you okay?'

'We knew it was coming, but it's still a shock.' He gestures at the pieces of wood lying on his workbench. 'I'm making a box to lay her in before we bury her in the garden. It's weird how they become part of the family, isn't it?'

'I know what you mean.'

Jamie's straightforward personality shows in every corner of his workspace. It's neat and orderly, the floor swept clean. I can tell he enjoys his time here. There's a chair by the workbench, and an old-fashioned radio.

'Have you got news about Badplace Hill?'

'Not yet. We're looking for evidence to help us identify the bones.'

'So you came back here?' His eyes linger on my face.

'I need information about any islanders who left Bryher suddenly, twenty or thirty years ago. Your brother Hugh moved away in that time span, didn't he?'

Jamie's body language changes immediately, his shoulders tensing. 'He's been in the States for over twenty years. We're not in contact.'

'We can talk about this tomorrow if it's easier.'

He shakes his head vehemently. 'No need, it's ancient history now.'

'Why did he leave so suddenly?'

'It was inevitable, I suppose. Bryher was too small for him. Hugh was three years younger than me, but way smarter. Everyone expected him to become a big shot one day.'

'Did you get on?'

'We had our ups and downs. He could be a pain, but I loved him anyway.' He gazes down at his workbench. 'He won a scholarship to a boarding school on the mainland. Dad thought he was lording it every time he came back, which pissed him off royally. After Hugh finished his A levels, they rowed nonstop. Dad expected him to help with building work, but Hugh refused. He wanted a gap year, even though I was busting a gut labouring for Dad full-time.'

'Was your father angry?'

'Furious. Mum got so sick of the shouting matches, she used to go out to get away from it, but I understood Hugh's position. He saw the island as a trap, thwarting his ambitions. I can't remember what sparked the biggest row between them, but it ended the relationship. Hugh walked out and never came back.'

'What happened exactly?'

Jamie scrubs his hands across his face. 'Dad said he was insulting the way of life that had supported him since childhood. There was a lot of yelling, then one of them threw a punch. Hugh packed his bag and stomped off into the night.'

'Did he leave Bryher straight away?'

'He must have cadged a lift off a boatman. Mum tried to track him down on the mainland, without any luck. Two years later, Dad threw Hugh's things out and redecorated his room, but he paid the price. I think the stress brought on his Alzheimer's, and poor Mum bottled everything inside.'

'Did Hugh ever make contact?'

'Just a few letters from the States, years later, saying he'd made a life for himself out there.' He gives an awkward shrug. 'I wrote back inviting him to Dad's funeral, but the letter bounced. Bella says I should forget it and move on. If Hugh doesn't want contact with us, why force it?'

'Did your mum keep his letters?'

'I expect they're in the attic somewhere, among the junk.'

'Can you find them for me tonight?'

His reply takes a long time to arrive. 'You think it was Hugh's skull in the ground, don't you?'

'I have to track down any young men who left Bryher unexpectedly back then. Sorry if this is uncomfortable, but I need a DNA sample from you as well. If we find any bone fragments, we can use it to check if it's your brother.'

'That skeleton can't be his. My parents were simple people, regular churchgoers. They never lied to me about anything.' His eyes glint with anger.

'I'm afraid they may have been fooled as well.'

There's an awkward moment when I produce a plastic tube from my pocket, then take a swab from his mouth, neither of us meeting the other's eye.

'I'll find those letters tonight.' His expression is calming, the bad temper I witnessed almost gone. 'What do you think of this box, Ben? I'm using teak, so it should last years.'

I glance down. 'It looks top quality to me. I'll let you finish it.'

The sound of Marvin Gaye's wistful voice follows me back to the house. Bella gives me a hopeful look when I return to the kitchen, but I'm keen to leave. I never enjoy questioning someone I like, but it goes with the territory in Scilly, where lives are so tightly connected.

It's 8 p.m. by the time I finally get back to Hell Bay. My head's still spinning with unanswered questions. Someone is sitting on the bench outside my house, his lanky form instantly recognisable. Dev hasn't adapted to island life yet, his appearance much too smart. He's dressed in expensive jeans, trainers and a well-cut jacket, putting me to shame. When I look through the kitchen window, Nina and Zoe are at the table, their heads bowed close while they talk.

'Did they kick you out?' I ask, joining him on the bench.

'More or less.'

'We could stage a protest.'

'Not yet, Zoe needs a woman's support right now.' He looks out at the sea. 'It almost broke her this time.'

'You must be feeling it too.'

'It's different for us, isn't it? The trauma happens inside their bodies, not ours.'

'She'll recover. Zoe's one of the toughest women I know.'

'The trouble is, she wants a kid so badly, the feeling never goes away.'

'She says the same about you.'

'It didn't occur to me that we'd struggle. I thought babies would arrive every few years until we drew the line.' I can hear sadness echoing in his voice. 'How about you, Ben? Are you looking forward to parenthood?'

'I'm just hoping not to screw it up.'

He gives a dry laugh. 'Zoe and I should adopt. We work with thousands of kids in India who all deserve a loving home.'

It's the yearning on his face that pulls me up short. It's a reminder that I'm thirty-eight years old, well past the point where most people start a family. My own father worked day and night at my age to support his teenage sons, but I only appreciated his sacrifices after he died. The memory is soon interrupted by a peal of laughter from inside the house, and Dev looks relieved.

'Thank God, I hate it when she cries.'

'She hardly ever did when we were young. One time she fell when we were rock-climbing and broke her ankle. Most kids would bawl their eyes out, but she just gritted her teeth and got on with it.'

'The word's "indomitable", isn't it? That crime-scene guru you brought over seems the same; I chatted with her this morning. She certainly speaks her mind.'

'Liz can be tricky, but she's brilliant at her job. I'm expecting answers soon.'

'Strange, isn't it? That young man was someone's son or brother, yet no one noticed him disappear.'

The front door swings open before I can reply. He rises to his feet when Zoe emerges, then walks straight into his arms. There's relief on his face when she finally draws away, his arm still slung around her shoulders.

'How are you doing?' I ask her.

'Better, big man, just really tired. Nina's an amazing listener. I've chewed her ear off for hours.'

'Don't I get a hug goodnight?'

I catch a glimpse of my old friend's zest for life when she jumps into my arms. She still smells of jasmine and fresh air, like the old days.

Nina looks pale when I go inside. I can tell she's absorbed some of Zoe's sadness, even though she's trained to keep her emotions separate. It must be different when a friend unloads their woes, rather than a client. She seems relieved when I tell her to put her feet up; I'll bring her camomile tea in bed. When I pour boiling water into her favourite cup, the smell of summer flowers greets me, another reminder of how much life has changed. I only drank black coffee until Nina arrived; even my food and drink choices have been revolutionised.

I look out of the window at starlight reflected on the ocean, letting the quiet slow my racing thoughts. If one of Craig Travis's cronies wants to settle old scores, I'll stand my ground, but I'll have to tell Nina tonight. The idea of anything happening to her or the baby scares me far more than getting hurt myself. It's taken me a lifetime to find what I need; there's no way I'll put it at risk.

I spend a while rehearsing how to explain the situation, ten minutes passing before I'm ready to tell the truth, but when I reach the bedroom, Nina's fast asleep. She doesn't flinch, even when I clatter around, then drop my clothes on a chair. My back feels stiff with tension as I slip under the sheets. Nina shifts towards me, her head settling on my chest. The speech I prepared lingers in my mind, its message too urgent to ignore.

35

Ruby's still weeping as Annie Hardwick drags her indoors, and it's easy to produce tears. She only has to remember her dad dying in the prison hospital alone, denied his dignity. Hardwick frogmarches her to a room with basic furniture. The table is built from old scaffold boards, with benches made from pallets, and a rusting stove in the corner. The floor is so muddy it can't have been cleaned in weeks, and Hardwick's appearance is neglected too. Her head is shaved, her black jumper full of holes, oil stains on jeans baggy with age, but Ruby can see she's got a strong physique. Ropes of muscle run down her forearms, and her gaze is laser-sharp.

'Tip your bag out on the table,' she snaps.

Ruby follows her orders. She watches as the woman rummages through her belongings, still shaken at being caught. The ex-cop peers at her fake driver's licence, and the sketchbook she uses for her alibi. Luckily her father's knife is tucked inside her jacket.

'You're a long way from home, Chloe Moore. Or is that an alias?' Hardwick says.

'I told you. I need a safe place to sleep.'

'Bullshit. I bet you're not alone. Where are the others?'

'What are you talking about?'

'Why's a girl from Brighton on Bodmin Moor?'

'I grew up in care, now I need a new start.'

'Don't give me sob stories. Tell me who sent you, for fuck's sake.' Hardwick grabs her arm, her grip tight enough to burn. 'Start talking or I'll get the police.'

'You're hurting me.' Ruby makes her voice sound even more broken. 'I left without telling anyone. The hostel they put me in wasn't safe, this bloke hung around at night. I was afraid he'd break down my door.'

Hardwick stares at her, but Ruby senses a glimmer of softness. 'When's the last time you ate?'

She squeezes out a few more tears. 'This morning, at the station.'

'Why didn't you ask for help in town?'

'I'm no beggar. I can take care of myself.'

'Is that right?'

'Let me go. If I'm in your way, I can sleep in the forest.'

Hardwick studies her again. 'We'll strike a deal. Stay one night in my barn and leave in the morning. There's a youth hostel nearby; they'll take you, till you find work.'

'I was heading there when I got lost.' Ruby glances round the kitchen again, noticing damp stains on the ceiling and tiles peeling from the wall. 'This place will be amazing. I can see why you're doing it up.'

'It's a long job, but it's coming together.'

'What should I call you?'

211

'Nothing.' The woman's posture stiffens again. 'You don't need my name. We're in the same boat, Chloe. It wasn't safe for me back home either.'

Hardwick continues speaking, but even now Ruby can see she's not fully convinced. She never turns her back or drops her defences, as she talks about the land she's renting from a farmer who doesn't ask questions. She keeps a few livestock, grows most of her food and generates her own electricity. The ex-cop is still describing her new lifestyle when she glances out of the window. Ruby seizes her chance, grabbing a cast-iron skillet from a shelf, her blow hitting Hardwick's shoulder. The woman stumbles then rebounds. She boots Ruby in the guts, her second kick sending the skillet flying from her hand.

'You little bitch. Who the fuck sent you?'

'Craig Travis, of course.'

'I knew it.'

Hardwick grips Ruby's arms at her sides, until she squirms away. She manages to grab an empty wine bottle and smashes it against the woman's temple, but even that doesn't knock her out. Hardwick doesn't fall until Ruby delivers a hard punch to her jaw. She stares down at her still body, feeling a moment of pity. The woman is tough like her, living by her own rules, but her dad's wishes must be honoured. Hardwick is so deeply unconscious she doesn't make a sound when Ruby carves his symbol into her forearm.

She drags Hardwick's inert body out into the farmyard, but the ex-cop is finally coming round, hitting out blindly with her fists. Ruby pulls out her knife, but Hardwick knocks it away, the blade slicing through Ruby's top. Pain makes her fight even harder. She aims a fierce kick at Hardwick's face, silencing her at last. Then she pulls back the wooden cover over the old well and peers at the dark water below. Hardwick is still breathing in ragged gasps when Ruby heaves her body over the edge. A loud splash follows seconds later; then a furious howl, which she ignores. It only takes a moment to replace the cover, as drops of blood drip from her wound. It's better to focus on details instead of the woman screaming out curses.

Ruby enters the barn to find Hardwick's tools. She uses a hammer and a handful of nails to batten down the well's wooden cover. Even if Hardwick manages to climb to the top, she'll still be trapped, until exhaustion makes her drop back into the water below.

She goes back inside the farmhouse, then uses Hardwick's computer to check the CCTV footage; it only takes a minute to wipe all records of the last few days, removing her image from the film. Next Ruby spends hours cleaning all evidence of her presence from the property. Hardwick must be dead by the time she's finished. No more cries come from the well, but a noise startles her when she finally leaves. It sounds like someone's approaching, with footsteps slow and heavy, but when she turns round, it's just the horse she saw before. The creature's calm gaze weighs on her as she backs away, delivering its judgement.

'What are you staring at?' Ruby snaps.

Suddenly she's desperate to leave, her torch beam etching

a line on the filthy ground as she breaks into a run. She only feels lighter once she's sprinting back through the dark woodland. Kitto will soon be dead too, and every name will have been crossed from her father's list.

36

Monday 5 May

I wake up to find the bed empty again. Panic drags me to my feet, only fading when I hear Nina moving around in the kitchen, humming to herself. I try to act normal, even though a hard conversation lies ahead of us. I need to share the news today, instead of letting Madron take charge.

Nina looks beautiful this morning, dressed in her dark blue dressing gown that almost touches the floor. She's standing by the window when I wrap my arms round her from behind, my chin resting on the top of her head. When she relaxes against my shoulder, my tension eases away.

'Say it, Ben. The words won't kill you.'

'How do you mean?'

'The world won't stop spinning if you say you love me.'

'You know I do. But we need to talk about something else.'

'Let me sit down first. This bump weighs half a ton.'

She takes the seat opposite me at the kitchen table. She's giving me her counsellor's smile, her expression calm, like nothing could disturb her equilibrium. Her face changes slowly as I explain about the Craig Travis case, and the past catching up with me; she's paler than before, which isn't surprising.

'Your old job sounds like a living hell. How did you cope with all that evil?'

'It was my duty to protect people.'

'And me, by keeping your mouth shut? Is that how you see it?'

'This last month's been hard on you, with your blood pressure going up . . .'

'Listen to me, Ben, I'm not a child. I can make my own decisions.'

'It's the wrong time to put you in danger.'

'Do I look scared to you?'

'You never do.' Her oval face is beautiful, but the anger in her eyes is hot enough to burn.

'Tell me my options, one by one.'

I explain that safe houses aren't always guaranteed. We might be more secure here, while the island's locked down, and threats are visible from a mile off.

'I'm not leaving while some madman hunts you down, but I have to be certain our baby's safe. Now go back to work and let me get my head around this mess. If you stay, I'll only scream at you.'

'Would another apology help?'

'Not in the slightest.'

The sun's shining when she gives me my marching orders, but I'm relieved the truth is out at last. Hell Bay has never looked more peaceful. The ebb tide has drawn the sea so far back from the land the Atlantic is just a pale blue ribbon stretched along the horizon. Shadow's ears prick up when he sees me leave. The creature's got a wayward streak, but at least he's loyal, standing guard in the porch. He's fought hard to defend me in the past and I know he'd do the same for Nina.

I leave a voice message for Eddie as I walk east, asking him to track down Hugh Porthcawl. If Jamie was telling the truth, his brother should be easy to find by using his passport number. Other islanders may also recall his last journey away from Bryher. I need to speak to Arthur Penwithick, the ferryman, but he's the island's shyest resident. If I bring him to the Rock to face questions, he's bound to shut down. My best option is to meet him on safe ground.

It takes me ten minutes to reach Church Quay, where my bowrider is moored, but I need to wait for the 9 a.m. ferry, which is making its way across New Grimsby Sound. Arthur Penwithick has run the ferry service to St Mary's for over thirty years. He delivered my brother and me there each morning, and still carries the island's kids to school, come rain or shine, unless there's a storm warning. His appearance hasn't changed much since then, even though he must be in his late fifties by now. He still wears a mariner's cap over hair as coarse as wire wool, his skin reddened by the Atlantic breeze, front teeth protruding rabbit-like over his lower lip. Some islanders claim he's got learning difficulties, because he struggles to hold a conversation, but I'm convinced it's just shyness. He's run a small but successful business on his own for decades.

I catch the mooring line when his ferry arrives. The boat is in good order, painted dark blue, the deck big enough for thirty passengers. People in Scilly always hope it's not raining when they make a crossing, because the wheelhouse only accommodates two or three people, the rest destined for a soaking. Penwithick waits until the stroke of nine, through force of habit, even though there will be no more passengers. The island is locked down, with no one leaving unless they have our permission. I hope I'm correct about being able to extract answers from the ferryman if we're on territory where he feels safe. I wait until we reach open water, where there's nowhere to hide. It looks like he'd rather dive overboard than join a conversation, but some of his tension seems to ease as he focuses on steering his beloved boat.

'You see people come and go, Arthur. Have you ever noticed someone disappear from Bryher without explanation? I'm talking about twenty or thirty years ago, so it's a big ask.'

'I'm no good with names.' He keeps his gaze on the sea ahead.

'Try and remember for me, please.'

He looks panicked. 'Holidaymakers sometimes divide their time between two or three islands. How would I know where they end up?'

'How about Jakob Bazyli, the lad who worked for Ray?'

'I don't remember him.'

'Or Hugh Porthcawl? He left Bryher and he's not come back since.'

His voice sounds defensive. 'I carry hundreds of people each week. Most days I don't even notice their faces.'

'I'm talking about islanders, not summer visitors.'

His voice sounds defensive. 'Many have their own boats, like you. They don't rely on my ferry.'

'You can't remember a single man who left Bryher suddenly and was never seen again?'

Penwithick shakes his head, his gaze fixed to the deck of his boat.

'It was a long shot, but thanks for trying. We all need to check our memories. Someone arrived on Bryher and ended up in a shallow grave. Contact me, please, if you remember anything.'

I'm forced to take his silence for assent. The ferryman has withdrawn inside his shell, and the green outline of St Mary's is filling the horizon. The effort of making conversation seems to have exhausted his daily supply of words. When we reach Hugh Town, I thank him for the ride. At least it hasn't been a wasted journey. I need to see Sandra Trescothick's records too.

219

The quay is busy as I head for the centre of Scilly's biggest town. Ferries are waiting to take holidaymakers to the off-islands, a queue forming for trips to St Martin's, with its wide sandy beaches. I feel a sudden pulse of guilt about Penwithick's finances. While Bryher's locked down, he can only carry passengers with my permission, his income dwindling overnight. It will impact on the pub and hotel soon too, so there's a limit to how long it can continue.

I push the thought aside as I walk down the Strand to the Town Hall. The imposing three-storey building towers over the surrounding fishermen's cottages. It's in good condition, because the place matters to the whole community. Sooner or later everyone in Scilly will come here, to register a birth, marriage or death. My last visit was eight years ago, to record my mother's death from MS. I remember Sandra Trescothick taking me through the forms, her manner gentle while she explained which boxes to tick.

The registrar's office is by the entrance, her door always open unless she's got an appointment. Sandra is busy inputting information into her computer, but rises to her feet when she finally spots me, her face brightening.

'There you are, Ben. I've got the books ready for you.' She points at a stack of leather-bound volumes. 'Want to see how they're organised?'

'Great, thanks. It may not answer my questions, but it's worth a try.'

'I'll help, don't worry, and Eddie's going through the census online. We should spot any gaps between us.'

Sandra's reassuring manner hasn't changed over the years, and neither has her image, her dark blue dress giving her a quiet elegance. She shows me the index patiently, pointing out different headings. The names are a roll call of islanders I've known, or lost. It pulls me up short to see my father's name. The entry was made twenty-four years ago: Mark Kitto, missing, presumed drowned. But I'm not here to dwell on the past.

'Is there anyone in particular you want to check?'

'Hugh Porthcawl. Do you remember him?'

'He suddenly upped and left the islands, but that was no surprise.' A frown appears on her face. 'He dated my old pal Penny Cadgwith for a year. Hugh was clever, and a bit full of himself. He seemed sweet on her, until he ran off to the mainland, to chase his dreams. She never got a single letter.'

'That's a brutal way to say goodbye.'

'Penny heard later that he'd become a big business-man abroad. I bet he wanted a clean break, to fulfil his ambitions. He'd spun her all these lies about being madly in love, promising they'd be together at uni, after his gap year. I thought he was okay at the time, but he was too cowardly to admit it was over. The bloke always put his own needs first.'

She runs her finger along the line detailing Hugh's birth and his registration at Tresco primary school.

There's nothing whatsoever to confirm how he's spent the rest of his life.

'You know every family on these islands, Sandra. Can you think of anyone else who disappeared, even if it seemed innocent at the time?'

Her calm gaze meets mine. 'People think island communities never change, but that's not true. My son Joe's a good example. He's just finished uni, so he's coming back tomorrow to work on the boats, till he finds something permanent. His name appears on the census, then disappears again.'

'It makes my job harder, that's for sure.'

'One name crossed my mind.' She fetches a scrap of paper. 'You probably remember the Polish lad who worked at Ray's boatyard, Jakob Bazyli. I don't have a formal record, because he was only visiting, but he popped in here once to ask me about applying for citizenship. It was soon after I started my job, but I still remember giving him the forms.'

'Do you know if he fell out with anyone in Scilly?'

'He was too gentle for that, but he left poor Ray in the lurch, with Louis Hayle's yacht to finish. I felt so sorry for him.' Her gaze lingers on my face. 'Hasn't he told you about me? You looked surprised to see us together at the pub.'

'Ray's not exactly an open book.'

'I liked him for years, so I took the plunge and invited him round for dinner.'

'How long ago was that, Sandra?'

'Two years this August.'

My amazement must show on my face, because she releases a peal of laughter. I struggle for a minute before finding the right words.

'I'm glad to hear it. He was alone much too long.'

'We're chalk and cheese, but it seems to work.'

Sandra applies herself again to the record books, leaving me floundering. Ray was solitary for my entire childhood. He has an uncanny ability to draw secrets out of me, yet he's kept his relationship hidden. Either he's a master of camouflage, or I'm an oblivious fool.

I push the thought aside, to focus on the records, but my thoughts soon return to Penny Cadgwith being jilted. Islanders leave Scilly for obvious reasons: a new job, a relationship, or to die in a hospital on the mainland. Those last journeys are easy to trace, but Hugh Porthcawl is an exception. What happened to him could be far darker.

37

Ruby checks her bed for signs of blood when she rises at
10 a.m. She had to wad sheets of toilet paper over her wound,
and it still hurts every time she moves. When she inspects it
in the bathroom mirror, it's a clean cut, three inches long, just
below her ribcage. She makes a tutting sound under her breath.
Why didn't she kill Hardwick straight away? The woman showed
kindness, making her forget the rules, which was a big mistake.
Her father taught her that a successful hit must be emotionless.

The bar appears empty when she goes downstairs, the
landlord's booming voice silent. She leaves by the front door,
then stops at the nearest chemist. She carries several items to
the counter along with bandage and plasters, so the assistant
won't remember what she bought, but anonymity is impossible in such a quiet place. She's the only customer, and the
middle-aged woman behind the till seems determined to chat.
Ruby keeps her head down, hoping there are no CCTV cameras
hidden on the top shelves, while the assistant recommends
local beauty spots to visit.

She finally escapes after a five-minute delay. It crosses her mind to go back to her room to bandage her wound, so blood won't stain her clothes, but the landlord always wants to chat. Every conversation makes it more likely he'll remember details, so she retreats down a deserted alleyway and stuffs a wad of bandage down her shirt. Now she's free to join the footpath to St Austell.

There are no other walkers in sight as she travels in the opposite direction from Annie Hardwick's farm. The open landscape still sets her nerves on edge; the moor has few trees, and miles of uninterrupted sky, the earth boggy underfoot. She'd like to run back to the village, but there's a last task to complete before she can leave. Ruby comes to a halt beside a towering pile of rocks. Giants appear to have wandered across the land, piling boulders on top of each other until they look certain to fall.

She sits on the grass to begin her sketch. It's important to make her fake identity seem authentic, even if it wastes time. Ruby studies the elemental landscape, and soon last night's misery is soothed away, while her pencil marks the page. She spends an hour creating the picture. It's incomplete, but it's her best attempt, so she hurries back to the pub, where the landlord is in his favourite position behind the bar.

'We missed you at breakfast, love.'

She smiles at him. 'My bed's too comfortable, that's why. It's a shame I need to go home today.'

'Let's see your sketches first.'

'I'm not proud of them.'

'Come on, love. No one goes to art school unless they're talented.'

'You can see my last one, but the rest are rubbish.'

He gives a low whistle of admiration. 'That's brilliant, love. You've caught the spirit of the place.'

Ruby considers giving him the drawing just to shut him up, but it would leave a trail for the police to find.

'I promise to come back next summer,' she says. 'My work will get better, so I'll show you then.'

'That sounds fair to me.'

He offers her a reduced rate for her room, and she accepts his generosity. It gives her a glimpse of a parallel world where people are gentle and no one ever gets hurt. She can't pin down why she feels so uncomfortable walking away, with her backpack slung over her shoulder. The sun is shining and there are no police cars in sight. Maybe it's because her next target will be the hardest of all. She remembers DI Ben Kitto when he was one of her dad's trusted employees. Thinking about him still makes her blood boil; it was his betrayal that condemned her father to a life of suffering. There's another reason too. She had a teenage crush on him. He was a giant of a man, good-looking and cool under pressure, but now he's her biggest enemy.

When she reaches the bus station, Ruby studies her map of Cornwall. The Isles of Scilly look like a handful of pebbles flung across the Atlantic Ocean, scattered far from the mainland. She shuts her eyes and concentrates, remembering her dad teaching her about self confidence; if she believes she can finish the task, nothing can slow her down. She swallows a few deep breaths, then approaches the ticket kiosk to start the last leg of her journey.

38

I realise the scale of my task halfway through the first record book. It's five hundred pages long; every typed entry about men of the same age as our victim will have to be checked against Eddie's notes. I stay until midmorning, then take my leave, thanking Sandra Trescothick for her help, still adjusting to the news about her relationship with Ray. She gives me a gentle smile before confirming that I can come back any time to complete my work.

Hugh Town is bustling when I walk back down the high street. Holidaymakers are browsing for souvenirs in the small art galleries and gift shops. When I pass the newsagent's, Avril Mumford is behind the counter, where she's stood for decades. She beckons me inside, but I smile, then shake my head. Mumford's has stood at the centre of town for a hundred and fifty years, and Avril knows every piece of island gossip. I'd go in for a chat on any other day, because she's a favourite of mine, but time's not on my side.

Isla Tremayne is the first person I see at the police station on Garrison Lane. The young PC looks bored behind the reception desk, which is a waste of her talents. She joined us less than a year ago after completing university and returning to Scilly, and she's as sharp as a tack. Madron insists on keeping her and Lawrie Deane at the station in case problems arise on the other islands. I can see his point, but Bryher is at a standstill until the mystery's solved. Isla is a typical islander, with a straightforward manner, her black hair cropped short, no make-up on her freckled skin. She's a swimmer like me, with a strong, athletic build. The frustration on her face is obvious.

'How's it going, sir?' she asks. 'I wish I could help out on Bryher.'

'We could use you. Eddie's drowning in visitor records from the pub. I'll ask the boss, but he may not agree.'

Her face lights up, and I remember feeling the same. I spent two years as a beat officer, dealing with domestic assault, burglaries and small-time drug dealers, until undercover work beckoned. My first assignment got me hooked, despite the danger. I recognise my own desire for excitement in Isla's expression, but Madron seems to enjoy turning down my requests. I ask her to make sure Jamie Porthcawl's DNA sample reaches the lab in Penzance today, and she looks pleased to be included in the murder hunt.

It's noon by the time I've persuaded the Crown

Prosecution Service in Truro to release search warrants for Nathan Kernow and Jamie Porthcawl's properties, even though both men were seen at the murder site. Porthcawl still needs to convince me that his brother is alive, and Kernow's odd behaviour on the night the skeleton vanished can't be ignored. The possibility that he attacked one of his mother's lodgers as a teenager needs to be investigated too. Eddie sounds as frustrated as me when we speak on the phone.

'I've got nothing on the missing men yet. I've asked the Polish embassy to check if Jakob Bazyli ever returned home, and there are no records of Hugh Porthcawl anywhere in the UK since he left Bryher.'

'Try the passport office again; keep ringing till someone answers. Then you can help me search Nathan Kernow's place when I get back.'

'Will do, boss.'

My deputy ends the call before I can speak again, clearly keen to return to his search. I'm not looking forward to my next conversation, but there's no avoiding it.

I take a breath before tapping on my boss's door. He's sitting behind his mahogany desk, which gleams with polish, his long-service certificate framed on the wall. The man's obsessive nature shows in every detail, with ranks of colour-coded folders arranged from A to Z, by category. His grey stare is razor-sharp when he catches my eye.

'Why are you here, Kitto?'

'I'd like to take Isla back to Bryher, please. We need more feet on the ground.'

'How would that work? I have a duty of care for St Martin's, Tresco and St Agnes too. That would leave just one officer at my disposal while you hunt for some missing bones.'

'He was still a murder victim, sir.'

'You don't have a scrap of evidence to follow.' His gaze bores into my face. 'But I'm glad you've spoken to Nina at last.'

'Who told you?'

'She called me with some requests. It's a pity you had to be forced into telling her about the threat. An intelligent woman like Nina deserves the truth.'

'Don't tell me how to run my relationship.' I choke out the words.

'Feelings are running high, so I won't discipline you for using that tone. Calm down and listen for once in your life.' My boss's stare is glacial. 'Nina wants to stay on Bryher provided it's locked down, and no more visitors come over to Scilly from the mainland until the threat has passed.'

'We need to give the *Scillonian* twenty-four hours to cancel.'

'It's done, Kitto. The Cornish force are sending backup before the last ferry sails.'

'They don't have any specialist guardsmen.'

'Six more plain clothes officers on Bryher will help keep you both safe. That's my last word on the subject.'

He gives a nod of dismissal, leaving me fuming. I'm stunned that Nina called him without telling me first, but it's a fair punishment for keeping quiet. I apologise to Isla on my way out; the DCI's decisions never change once he's made a pronouncement, even when they're wrong. If he brings officers over from the mainland, there will be little to occupy them. The Atlantic keeps us wrapped in a wide safety net. No one can enter our terrain by ship or air without registering their names.

I carry my irritation with me during a smooth crossing back to Bryher, but a surprise is waiting for me at the pub. Liz Gannick has arrived when I thought she'd be in her makeshift lab at the hotel all day. The forensics chief looks ill, her face as white as bleached linen.

'Are you okay, Liz?'

'I've spent too long peering into that sodding microscope.'

'How's the pain today?'

'Seven out of ten, if you must know.'

'I wouldn't ask otherwise. What caused it in the first place?'

'A botched operation to correct my spina bifida. They messed up so badly I've got bone pressing on a nerve in my back 24/7, but it's too risky to operate again.'

'Sue the bastards.'

'Money won't help. Work does, and vodka, but the tablets are shite.'

'Want me to visit your surgeon?'

'With a crowbar, ideally.' A grin illuminates her

face like a flash of lightning. 'But I have news. Take a guess what's in here, Ben.' She waves an empty plastic tube at me.

'Fresh air?'

'Look closer.'

There's a white speck lying at the bottom, no thicker than the tip of a needle. 'Is that bone?'

'You bet it is. My hard graft finally paid off. We need to get it over to the mainland asap. You'll have your victim's DNA in twenty-four hours.'

'Brilliant. We can start testing the islanders, now we've got something to compare.'

I'd like to share her excitement, but the answer might not be so simple. The victim may have no connection with Jamie Porthcawl's family, and Jacob Bazyli's relatives are still out of reach. We've been chasing answers for three full days, with no clear result, but a splinter of evidence is better than none.

39

Nathan Kernow is at home when Eddie and I reach his house at lunchtime, with the sun warm on our backs. His pagan identity doesn't show in his appearance today; he looks like an English lord dressed for an autumnal walk. It's only on closer inspection that the image crumbles. His corduroy trousers are worn thin, his tweed jacket a fraction too small. He hovers on the doorstep, clearly reluctant to admit us, and his German Shepherd echoes his mood. The dog sniffs the air warily before slinking inside with her tail down.

'We've got permission to search your house, Nathan. But can we talk for a minute first, please?'

Eddie looks shocked by Kernow's plant collection. I push past foliage that presses in from all sides, like we're entering a greenhouse at Kew Gardens. It's easier to move in the lounge, where two computers stand on a dining table and books on coding and games design are stacked by his chair. Kernow gestures for us to sit down, but he remains standing, arms rigid at his sides.

'Why are you singling me out?'

'We need to identify the victim,' I reply. 'You were there the night his remains went missing.'

'I told you, it felt important to honour the dead. I saw it as my duty.'

'Tell us about Jakob Bazyli, please. How well do you remember him?'

Kernow reacts like I've shoved him backwards, slumping onto a chair. 'You think it was him on the moor?'

'We're just following all lines of enquiry.'

'Jakob seemed kind. He was here all summer, but I didn't get to know him well.'

'How old were you then?'

'Around fourteen. I was home from boarding school. He was teaching himself English but hardly spoke to us. I'd hear him repeating words in his room sometimes. I got the feeling he was homesick.' Kernow's anxiety shows; his hands are trembling when his speech fades into silence.

'Did he leave any possessions behind, or a suitcase?'

'I can't remember. Mum said he took the *Scillonian* over to Penzance. I don't even know if he went back to Poland; we never heard from him again.'

'Write everything down, please. I'd like documentary evidence too. Did your mother keep a record book when she ran her B&B?'

'I threw it away.'

'That's a pity. If you remember anything, let us know. We'll start the search now.'

Eddie disappears upstairs, leaving me to tackle Kernow's indoor jungle, my head still buzzing with questions. I can understand why he got rid of his mother's records, but it makes his story impossible to check. The two young men could have had a bitter row that ended in murder.

Kernow remains in the living room while I search the kitchen. My job is made harder by the dozens of ferns ranged across the worktop and spider plants hanging from the shelving. When I look through the cupboards, I only find evidence of Nathan's veganism. His fridge contains soya mince, tofu and rennet-free cheese. There's a photo of his mother in middle age on his French dresser. She's a delicate-looking woman, with a tired smile. The picture was taken in her back garden. It must have been after her husband's death, because Nathan is at her side, around twelve years old, his blonde fringe hiding his eyes. The boy's body language interests me. He's clinging to her hand, at a stage when most boys are desperate to seem grown up.

I can hear Eddie rummaging around upstairs and hope he's having more luck. It takes me half an hour to check the downstairs rooms, looking behind furniture and lifting loose floorboards. I'm hunting for a letter, or anything to show that Jakob Bazyli may have been hurt here. Nathan's bank balance comes as a surprise when I glance at his latest statement. The man's a high earner, with more than fifty grand in a savings account. He doesn't need to buy second-hand clothes, which supports his claim that he's made an ethical decision to stop any more rubbish going into landfill.

Eddie's voice is a low whisper when I go upstairs. 'He's kept all his mum's stuff, boss. It's a bit *Psycho* if you ask me; all it needs is a rocking chair.'

I get his point when I enter the room. The air smells of dried flowers and mothballs; Mrs Kernow's dressing gown is still hanging behind the door, pairs of high-heeled shoes lined up by a chair. Her make-up bag lies on the dressing table, like she might return any minute to powder her nose.

'There's nothing here except junk,' Eddie mutters.

'Let's check the loft.'

'He hasn't got a ladder. Can you give me a boost up there, boss?'

Gymnastics was his favourite subject at school. Eddie's feet touch my hand, then my shoulder for a split second before he sails through the opening, in one fluid movement. Five minutes pass before his face appears at the opening, his expression blank.

'You'd better come up here, fast.'

He's gone before I can request more details, and Nathan Kernow appears at my side.

'The loft's empty. There's nothing there of any monetary value, believe me.' He's rubbing his hands together like he's trying to remove a stain.

'We need to check anyway. Can I borrow a stepladder, please?'

He doesn't reply, and his dog is getting more agitated.

She releases a loud whine when I remove a chair from the bedroom. I try to copy Eddie's ascent, but fail in the attempt. My hulking shoulders often cause problems, especially when it comes to buying a suit, but I finally squeeze through the opening into complete darkness.

'Where's the light?' I call out.

'The bulb's gone.'

I can only see a thin trail of yellow from Eddie's torch. The roof space is twenty feet long, with hard-board laid across the joists. My deputy is crouching by a table covered in fabric, with unlit candles at either end. The home-made altar makes my breath catch in my throat. It's covered in dried heather, stones and a jam jar full of dried flowers. The last item is raised high above the rest, catching my attention when Eddie's torchlight picks it out. It's a piece of bone, three inches long, stained yellow by time.

40

Ruby is still in Bodmin, waiting for a train to Penzance. It's been delayed, but the announcement board doesn't say when it will arrive, sending her anxiety through the roof. She'll have to stay on the concourse, with a CCTV camera peering down from above. They always make her feel edgy, even with her baseball cap shading her face. She buys a cappuccino, a chocolate bar and the *Daily Mail*, then looks for a place to hide. She shelters behind a pillar, shielded at last from the camera's prying eyes. The cut on her ribcage still burns, even now it's coated in ointment, and dressed with a bandage.

She takes a bite of chocolate before opening the paper. There's no mention of Annie Hardwick, just a maudlin piece about Steve Pullen, listing the medals he won during his long police career. There's even a statement from his wife, begging for evidence to explain why her husband was killed so mercilessly. Whoever murdered such a heroic man should rot in jail, according to her. The statement sends a pulse of guilt through Ruby's system. She's not just killing the officers who sent her dad to prison. The ripple effect will hurt their families, when they've done nothing wrong, but it can't be helped. She soon puts the thought aside, remembering that her father's plan will deliver natural justice. Those officers stole the one person she loved; everyone they love is now tainted by their actions.

Ruby flicks through the pages until she's confronted by a picture of her father, his face haggard. The headline trumpets: *UK'S WORST GANGLORD CLINGS TO LIFE.* He's defying doctor's expectations by hanging on, despite his terminal diagnosis. She reads on: *Craig Travis has made a living will, to have his ashes sprinkled on the River Thames, but his victims' relatives are fighting it. Many of his victims were thrown into the Thames, their bodies never found. Is it right that a vicious killer's ashes should pollute London's great waterway? Take part in our poll below. Share your views on whether Britain's worst mass murderer should have his last wish granted.*

'Bastards, the lot of you,' Ruby mutters under her breath.

She drops the paper into the nearest bin, but the story has soured her mood. The chocolate in her mouth tastes too sweet, so she ditches the rest of the bar too. She keeps her arms folded tight across her chest as the announcement board flickers, trying to quell her nerves about killing her next target.

41

Nathan Kernow's face is blank when I show him the bone from his home-made altar, wrapped in an evidence bag. He answers my questions in monosyllables until I let Eddie take over the interview. My size and baritone voice can intimidate people, while the young sergeant's gentle style often helps to expose their secrets.

'Clear things up for us, please, Nathan,' he says. 'That's all we want.'

Kernow's body language changes when we sit at his table. He responds well to my deputy's conciliatory style, his hunched shoulders lowering. When Eddie shows him the bone again, he seems less defensive.

'I know people think I'm an oddball,' he says. 'That's why I keep my beliefs private, like I said. Nature lies at the heart of my faith. I keep my shrine to the goddess in the attic, in case visitors think it's some kind of voodoo. I often put feathers, leaves and shells there. It's a reminder that everything comes from nature, the living and the dead.'

'My sister believes the same,' Eddie says. 'She's into Buddhism. That's similar, isn't it?'

Kernow gives a rapid nod. 'Pagans like me often practise meditation too.'

'Where did you find the bone?'

'On the beach last week. It didn't come from Badplace Hill, if that's what you mean.'

Eddie scribbles in his notebook. 'Is there any way that skeleton could belong to Jakob Bazyli? Sorry to ask, but we have to know.'

Kernow shakes his head. 'I was just a kid when he stayed here. Why would I hurt him?'

'Someone else could have done,' Eddie says, leaning closer. 'Give us any details you remember about his contacts, please, Nathan.'

'Ray Kitto, but few others. Jakob preferred to be left alone when he got in from the boatyard.'

'Did he have a quick temper?'

'He seemed shy like me.' Kernow's eyelids flutter before he speaks again. 'Mum was glad when he left, but only because she preferred people to be chatty.'

'So there's no chance his relatives' DNA will match this bone, once we track them down?'

He hesitates. 'None at all.'

'You found religion a while back, didn't you?' Eddie asks. 'Can you tell us a bit more about that church you joined in America in your twenties?'

'Why's that relevant?'

'I'm just trying to understand your mindset.'

'My mother forced me to come home, but I loved it there,' Kernow replies finally, gazing down at his hands. 'Outsiders called it a cult. They said we were brainwashed, but it never felt like that to me. I only planned to stay in California a short while after I graduated, but the farm was like the Garden of Eden. I've never been quite that happy again.'

There's yearning on his face when his speech ends. I've always been intrigued by how easy it is to lose your identity. All it takes is a powerful personality, able to enslave the vulnerable by filling their minds with lies. Eddie's bringing the interview back to the events on Badplace Hill when my phone vibrates in my pocket.

I step outside to take the call, but the line's so bad I can barely hear the caller. It's Dr Ginny Tremayne, the island's chief medic, and my colleague Isla's mother. Her voice is scrambled, the words difficult to hear. The only message I pick up is that Nina is in hospital on St Mary's, then the line dies. I'm all fingers and thumbs when I try to ring back, but the call doesn't connect, so I shove my phone into my pocket and set off for Church Quay at a jog.

I'm running at full pelt by the time I reach the shore, and Shadow has materialised out of nowhere, leaping onto my boat before me. The challenge of island life hits home at times like this. Nothing happens fast enough, a mile of clear blue ocean separating me from Nina when she needs me most. The bowrider's engine rattles as I push it to top speed, the boat scudding across flat water.

I leave it beached on the sands at Hugh Town, not caring if it gets stuck there until tomorrow. Shadow is still at my side as I run past the station, then uphill to the hospital, panting for breath. Penny Cadgwith and Bella Porthcawl are together in the corridor, standing outside a treatment room. The two women look shaken, increasing my anxiety.

'Tell me what happened, please.'

'Nina fainted,' Penny says. 'Bella and I were with her when it happened. We'd brought some things for the baby, and we were drinking tea in your kitchen. She came round after a few seconds and we walked her down to the harbour. Ray brought the three of us over in his boat.'

'What's the doctor saying?'

Penny touches my arm. 'She'll be fine, Ben, honestly. If it's any comfort, I fainted three times during my first pregnancy.'

'Who's with her now?'

'Ginny Tremayne.'

'Is the baby okay?'

'You'll have answers soon, I'm sure. Ginny's a brilliant doctor.'

I collapse onto a seat, flanked by the two women, who fuss over me. Penny brings coffee from the machine, her eyes full of concern. Bella seems more relaxed, her strawberry-blonde hair clipped back from her freckled face as she chatters. This is the plus side of island life. People volunteer to help whether you've got a broken leg or your generator fails in the middle of winter.

Bella's voice sounds casual when she mentions that Jamie has found the letters Hugh sent from America, he'll bring them to me whenever I like. The news fills me with relief. I felt sure that such a laid-back bloke wouldn't attack his own brother. Bella wanders off to make a phone call, leaving me alone with Penny; I couldn't care less about the case right now, but I ask questions to keep myself distracted.

'Can you tell me about your relationship with Hugh Porthcawl, Penny?'

She looks surprised. 'Why do you ask?'

'I need to know about any men that left Bryher suddenly.'

'Hugh was my first serious boyfriend, at seventeen. He used to write me sweet letters from his boarding school. I was so naive I thought it would last for ever. He was brighter than everyone I knew, and more driven. It took me ages to get over it, but I don't blame him for running away now.'

'Didn't you hear from him again?'

'Never.'

'Was that a surprise?'

'It hurt like hell at the time. I assumed he'd met some- one else. They call it ghosting these days, don't they?'

'The skeleton was an islander who vanished. Hugh fits the profile.'

'He's not missing, Ben.' Her hands freeze in mid-air. 'His mum showed me letters he sent from America. It was our relationship he wanted to escape.'

'That may not be true.'

Penny shakes her head. 'Hugh wanted to get rich and see the world. I was fascinated by all that confidence, but he felt limited here. He was always chatting to successful islanders, finding out how they made their fortunes.'

'Who in particular?'

'Louis Hayle, mostly. He gave Hugh the dream of running his own business one day. He said you only need one brilliant idea, then all you had to do is work round the clock to make it a reality.'

'That sounds a bit simplistic to me.'

'He made it sound easy. I think Hugh believed every word.'

'I still don't see why he ran off without telling anyone.'

'It took me years to accept it, but I only learned to value the islands' peace as an adult. No one on Bryher hated Hugh enough to kill him; he was just an eighteen-year-old boy.'

'How was his relationship with his family?'

'Tricky at times. His mum loved him to bits, but he fought with his dad and Jamie, because they were so happy here. It was a clash of personalities.'

'The brothers weren't close?'

'Hugh said they argued about almost everything.'

'Sorry to push you, Penny. It can't be easy, looking back.'

'I was young enough to believe his promises about us being together for ever, like Romeo and Juliet,' Her face looks burdened by distress. 'Maybe he got sick of me following him around like a lovesick fool.'

'We'll soon know if it was him. Did I tell you Liz Gannick's found a bone sample on the moor? The lab's analysing it now.'

Penny smiles back at me, but her bird-like face is tense with strain, and she doesn't say a word.

42

The 3 p.m. ferry is about to depart when Ruby reaches Penzance harbour with five minutes to spare. The *Scillonian* towers over the quay, the ship's white hull marked by dents and scrapes, proving that its daily journeys have taken their toll. She's the last passenger to arrive, but the attendant who checks her ticket gives her a warm smile.

'Welcome on board. You're cutting it fine, young lady.'

'Sorry, my train was late.'

'You're lucky we're sailing today; crossings are cancelled from tomorrow until further notice.'

'How come?'

'There's a police situation down there.'

'That sounds intriguing.'

'Sit back and enjoy the ride.'

The woman clips Ruby's ticket, and her heart rate slows to normal. She's glad to be on the final leg of her journey, even though the last hit promises to be the hardest of all. She can't make plans without seeing the islands first.

People are milling about on deck when the ship finally

leaves harbour, gliding slowly through the water. Passengers are already disappearing into the café, but Ruby stands by the rail to watch the land recede. The sea always helps her state of mind. Her father took her to Southend when she was small, to go paddling, eat ice cream, then amble down the pier. She used to dream of moving to a coastal town, but her future now is unimaginable. All that matters is doing her duty, the weight of it keeping her in the here and now.

She's still in the same position an hour later. The land has disappeared from view, leaving a blank expanse of ocean, with seabirds keeping pace overhead. The majority of passengers appear to be OAPs. They're sitting on folding chairs and eating sandwiches from Tupperware boxes, a few old men dozing in the shade. There's just one person her own age, a young guy in well-cut jeans and a white T-shirt, glancing in her direction. It only takes one smile to bring him strolling in her direction. He's better-looking than she thought, medium height with dark hair, but it's his expression that interests her. His face appears innocent, as if he's never experienced pain in his whole life.

'We must be the only passengers under seventy,' he says.

'That's harsh. Some of them could be sixty-five.'

His dark eyes scan her face. 'A stickler for detail, are you?'

Ruby smiles. 'I notice things, that's all. What's your name?'

'Joe Trescothick, yours?'

'Chloe Moore.'

'Nice. Ever visited the islands before, Chloe?'

'It's my first time.'

'So you need a local boy like me to show you the beauty spots.'

'Pushy, aren't you?'

'I'd say friendly. It's the island way.'

'What if I refuse?'

'I'll be gutted, for the whole journey.'

'We can't have that. Which island are you from, Joe?'

'Bryher, born and raised.'

Ruby brightens her smile. 'Lucky you, it looks amazing in my guidebook – the land that time forgot. I can't wait to see it.'

'You won't be saying that when the phone signal breaks down and the internet's screwed. Let me give you the low-down over coffee.'

She considers saying no, but he comes from Bryher, which she needs to know like the back of her hand. When they head for the onboard café, their reflections in the window make her blink. She still hardly recognises the fragile blonde she's become, with a dark-haired stranger shepherding her inside.

43

I've known Dr Ginny Tremayne all my life, but her decision to keep me locked outside Nina's room irritates me beyond words. She stands in front of me blocking my way, looking much the same as when she gave me a tetanus jab at sixteen after I'd cut myself on a piece of jagged metal in Ray's yard. She's a plump woman in a white coat, clutching a clipboard, grey hair scraped back from her face.

'Nina's resting, which is what she needs. I'll check her over again soon.'

'Then she can come home?'

'Pregnant ladies faint for all kinds of reasons, Ben, some serious, some trivial. We have to be confident she's okay, so I'm sending her to the mainland. I've booked a bed for her in Penzance hospital's maternity ward.'

'She's not due for a fortnight.'

'The birth plan needs to change.' Ginny gazes down at her notes. 'Her blood pressure's fluctuating, which could mean pre-eclampsia. It's not serious right now – the foetal heart rate's fine – but there's protein in her urine too.'

'What does that mean?'

'It's a warning that her body's under strain.' Ginny puts her hand on my arm. 'We need to cover our bases. This hospital isn't equipped to help her or the baby if there's any trouble. Penzance is your best option. They've got a brilliant neonatal unit. Okay?'

'If it keeps them both safe, I'll live with it.'

'Good man.'

She hurries away before I can ask any more questions. It takes me a moment to accept the new information, but maybe it's come at the right time. I'm the one under threat, not Nina; if she keeps her distance from me on the mainland until our baby's born, she won't get caught in the crossfire.

Nina still looks pale when I'm finally allowed into her room, and I'm kicking myself. I should have stopped her decorating the house and made her rest once in a while. I was wrong to tell her about a threat that might still be far away. She seems serene, as always. All she wants from home is an overnight bag with pyjamas, toiletries, a hairbrush and fresh clothes. She's already accepted the doctor's advice about Penzance, and I'm reminded of how different we are. I resent being given orders, but Nina is more pragmatic. She'll take the fifteen-minute flight early tomorrow morning without any complaint.

My girlfriend's amber stare is impossible to avoid.

'Come with me, Ben. We'll be safer in a big community, with a police team around us.'

'It's best you keep away from me till things settle down, and I'll have the guards you forced Madron to bring over.'

'I won't apologise. Safety's all that matters right now.'

I muster a smile, determined not to increase her stress. 'I probably misjudged the level of risk.'

'Don't bullshit me. I need the truth, Ben, okay?'

'If some hit man's after me, I don't want him anywhere near you, or the baby.'

'I'll go to Penzance on one condition.'

'What's that?'

'Be there for the birth, or I'll never forgive you.'

'Of course I will. Trust me on that, Nina, please.'

'Your job always takes priority.'

'Not this time. I'd never let you down.'

'Promise me you won't get hurt. Do you hear?'

It's the tremor in her voice that shocks me. She's unflappable most days, but not now. I'd love to keep her within touching distance until our baby's here, but that's no longer an option. My past needs laying to rest, once and for all.

44

Penny Cadgwith is still waiting in the corridor when I emerge. She seems to relax when I explain that Nina will have to stay in Penzance hospital until our baby arrives.

'I had both my kids there. The staff are wonderful.'

The investigation fills my mind again. 'Can I get your professional opinion before you go?'

'Of course. Have you found something?'

I pull the bone from Nathan Kernow's loft from my pocket, wrapped in an evidence bag. 'Could this be from our skeleton?'

Penny squints down at the bag for a few seconds. 'I'm afraid not.'

'How do you know?'

'It's not human. That's from the hind leg of a fox.'

The news makes me feel like kicking a wall. I'd love the case to be open and shut, with Nathan Kernow the obvious culprit, but the games designer may have been telling the truth after all. I thank

Penny again for bringing Nina to the hospital. It's hard to focus on the case with her condition clouding my mind.

My phone rings just as I'm walking back to the harbour. It crosses my mind to ignore the call, but then I see Madron's name. I need to go to Bryher to collect Nina's things, but instinct makes me pick up anyway. The DCI sounds like an irate sergeant major, summoning me to the station immediately for an emergency team meeting. He must know about Nina's admission to hospital, because news here travels like wildfire, but that won't soften his view. Madron believes that police work trumps every other responsibility.

I arrive at the station by 4.30, to find the entire team assembled. Lawrie Deane is parked behind the reception desk, while Isla types notes into her computer. Madron has even brought Eddie and Liz Gannick over from Bryher. The DCI struts out of his office, his expression grave when he calls us inside. He sits in his throne-like chair, while the rest of us hunker on hard plastic stools.

'Let's get procedural matters out of the way first. I want to update the chief super on our progress, then one of you needs to calm Louis Hayle down. The man's been on the phone again, complaining about slow progress with that skeleton.'

'I'll visit him again, sir,' I reply.

'Do it today, Kitto. Journalists are phoning too,

now they've heard the Trenwiths' building is on hold.' Madron turns to my deputy. 'What have you been working on, Eddie?'

'Checking the census, sir. It's taking a while to track down everyone living on Bryher between twenty and thirty years ago. I've found a passport number for Jakob Bazyli, who stayed at the Kernows' house. Europol will be able to track him down, if he's still alive.'

'We still can't find current records for Hugh Porthcawl,' I add. 'We're checking with the DVLA, the passport office and HMRC. It's possible he sent letters home from the USA, but they could be fakes.'

'That's not our most pressing concern.' Madron gives me a full-on stare. 'Tell your colleagues about the personal danger you're facing, Kitto. Your old DCI thinks the threat may already have reached the islands.'

'I don't believe that, sir. The hit man's acting fast; he'd have come for me by now.'

'You can't keep everyone in the dark indefinitely. Give them the truth, before I do.'

The mood changes when I share my story. Eddie looks impressed that I spent months as Craig Travis's driver until we had enough evidence to expose every part of his operation. Lawrie Deane is round-eyed with shock, while Isla scribbles notes, as if my police career is an exam topic to learn by heart.

'I worked the case as an undercover agent with DI Steve Pullen and DS Annie Hardwick. It looks like Travis has hired a hit man, by using contacts outside to kill his old enemies. His daughter Ruby committed suicide a few days ago, but may have been coerced. Then his accountant's body was found in a burnt-out car. Steve Pullen was murdered two days ago, at his London home. He was stabbed through the heart, which was Travis's favourite way of dispatching traitors.'

DCI Madron raises his hand. 'It doesn't stop there, I'm afraid. Hardwick was found dead two hours ago. She'd bought a smallholding on Bodmin Moor and was living off grid. Her sister raised the alarm after she stopped answering her calls. I want to show you all photos from the crime scene, so you understand the threat we're facing.'

A picture appears on the wall when he touches his keyboard. It shows a farmyard with a dilapidated barn. The farmhouse looks neglected, but it would have been Annie's idea of paradise. A few chickens are pecking at the dirt, a horse peering out from its stable. She wanted an outdoor life, handling every challenge alone.

'Hardwick may have known she was under threat, but believed she could fight off any attacker,' Madron says. 'She kept in contact with her immediate family but barely spoke to her neighbours, and had no social media presence. That's why she was so hard to locate. She was thrown into that well you see in the photo. I've got another image to show you, but anyone with a weak stomach should leave the room now.'

Lawrie Deane stumbles in his haste to reach the door. The rest of us remain seated as the final image appears; it shows my old colleague's body, dressed in worn-out combat trousers and a ripped jumper, her head covered by a stubble of grey hair. She's lying on a tarpaulin, hands bloodied, with dirty water gushing from her mouth. The same symbol that was carved on Steve Pullen's hand is visible on her forearm: three vertical strokes inside a square, like someone's chalked up a score.

'She went in alive,' Gannick mutters.

'Correct,' Madron replies. 'They think she kept her head above water for a long time, until the cold finished her.'

'The sick fucker.' The words slip from my mouth unchecked.

Madron's tone sharpens. 'Cursing won't bring your friend back, Kitto. I don't want any leaks from this meeting, or people will panic. From now on you will all wear stab-proof vests and carry tasers and batons. I'm not having any officer die on my watch.'

Deane looks shocked by the instructions when he returns. He's served as a sergeant in the island force for over twenty years without ever wearing defensive gear. The other security details fly over my head. I can still see Annie's drowned body, even though it only appeared on the wall for a minute. Madron announces that he's placing all the islands on full lockdown with immediate effect. The last ferry from the mainland is on its way over now; it won't sail again until the case is solved, but Travis's paid assassin may already be here. Six plain-clothes officers will arrive in a police launch from the mainland tomorrow, to guard me round the clock. People will only be able to fly in with our authorisation, and anyone coming to Bryher will be ID-checked. Ginny Tremayne's decision to move Nina to Penzance is starting to feel like a blessing, but I can't visit her with a hit man following me. I'd only bring the danger straight to her door.

I still feel numb when I leave the station at six. Annie Hardwick was skilled in self-defence, so her assailant must have been strong, or else she was caught by surprise. When I think of all the officers I've worked with, Annie was the toughest. She'd have fought every inch of the way. The killer may have picked up an injury during the struggle, which could make them easier to spot.

When I reach Hugh Town harbour, I curse under my breath. I was in such a rush to reach Nina, I forgot about leaving my boat anchored in shallow water on a falling tide. It's beached on the sand, and destined to stay there till tomorrow morning. I'll need to beg for a ride from one of the fishermen on the quay.

St Mary's looks like a different world as I head through Hugh Town's narrow lanes. Early holiday-makers are enjoying the warm weather, sitting on benches overlooking the sea with ice creams in hand.

The Island Deli is packed with young parents, kids and prams. A group has stopped there after collecting their children from nursery, to have a cappuccino before going home. The islanders look a hundred per cent relaxed, while my own body feels like a violin string, vibrating at the wrong frequency.

I'm out of luck when I reach the quay. Arthur Penwithick's ferry is out of commission while Bryher is locked down, so my best option is to beg a ride from a local fisherman. My spirits only rise when I catch sight of my uncle's boat, with Shadow dozing on the roof. Ray is swabbing the deck with soapy water, his movements languid.

'Need a lift home?' he asks, when he catches sight of me.

'Can we talk first?'

He beckons me on board and parks himself on the wooden seat in the wheelhouse, but I prefer to stand, my body fizzing with adrenaline.

'Go on then. Get it out of your system.'

'I should have interviewed you at the station about that clout and tool bag from the murder site.'

He stares back at me. 'You think I killed him?'

'No, but I have to treat everyone the same.'

'That's not your biggest problem, is it?'

I ignore Madron's warning to keep the threat quiet. Ray never shares secrets, and I value his opinion most of all. His expression barely changes as I describe the trail of destruction wreaked by Craig Travis's follower. The killer is moving fast and leaving no evidence behind; Pullen's house was entered without triggering a single CCTV camera, even though there are dozens on the surrounding streets, and I'm willing to bet that Annie Hardwick's security devices are clean too. I've been speaking for ten minutes when Ray interrupts.

'What are you going to do about it?'

'Nina's my top priority.'

His face creases into a smile. 'She's Shadow's too, I found him howling for her outside the hospital. The nurse told me she's flying to the mainland hospital.'

'Madron's got officers coming here tomorrow to watch my back.'

'That'll help, and you can see a stranger coming from miles off on Bryher. Stay at mine till your guards arrive. If someone's looking for you, they can fight two of us, instead of one.'

'Thanks but the whole police team will stay together at the pub. No one's going to storm the place, and I promised Nina to stay safe.'

'It's lucky she's got a cool head.'

Ray seems to be taking the situation in his stride, and thank God he's not dealing out platitudes. I hate being told that everything will be fine when there's no guarantee. But I still need to know why his belongings were found at the crime scene.

'Something else is bothering me, Ray. You were

refitting Louis Hayle's yacht when your tool bag was stolen, weren't you?'

He looks away. 'The job turned into a nightmare after Jakob left. Hayle wanted a luxury finish in both cabins but argued over every penny, even though he was loaded.' My uncle's clipped tone reveals his attitude towards the man.

'Not his number one fan, are you?'

'Bullies aren't my cup of tea.'

I have a sudden memory of Hayle ordering me and my brother around, expecting the kids on his summer camps to follow his rules. Something about his confidence struck me as fake, although I couldn't explain why.

Ray's face is impassive as he speaks about Hayle. His features look like they've been chipped from a mountainside, so inscrutable I'd need Liz Gannick's microscope to determine what lies inside. His expression only softens a fraction when he glances at me.

'You look spent,' he says. 'Sit down before you keel over.'

My uncle carries on cleaning his boat while I take a seat. My eyes linger on vessels scattered across the sand like beached fish after high tide. The island's biggest lifeboat is anchored in deep water, ready for the next shout, but there's no point in raising an alarm. If the killer has arrived, they're hiding in plain sight, and the risk level is already critical. I tip my head back to study the bleached-out sky. When my gaze levels with the horizon again, the *Scillonian* is sailing towards Hugh Town, for the last time until the threat lifts.

45

Ruby and Joe are still talking at 6.30, when St Mary's comes into view. They're back on deck, feet on the rail, watching the ocean slip by. She's surprised by how easily the conversation flows, and it's been worthwhile. Her new contact has been easy to milk, giving useful information about the islands.

'What made you choose Scilly?' he asks. 'It's a hell of a long way from Brighton.'

'I need somewhere quiet to make a decision.'

'About what?'

'Whether to finish my art degree or get a job.'

'I know how you feel. My business course cost me forty grand, and it won't guarantee me a career.'

'I've saved up enough cash to stay in a hotel for a week or two, then I might look for work.'

'There's plenty right now. The hotels always need summer staff.'

'I can give them my CV.'

Joe's face grows serious. 'I'm going back to my mum's. She's great, but it'll be like turning the clock back after three years away. I want to be on Bryher, but the only job I could get is taking tourists out on a seal-watching boat.'

'Will you live at your mum's?'

'Sort of. There's a big shed in the garden, so I can misbehave.'

'What's Bryher like?'

'Beautiful, but only locals can go there right now, and people who've been vetted. Mum had to warn the police that I'm coming home. Builders found a skeleton in an unmarked grave, so they're limiting who can visit.'

Ruby widens her eyes. 'Was there a murder?'

'Decades ago apparently, but everyone's upset. The islanders rarely see that much drama.'

'I'll be so disappointed if I can't visit.'

The ferry is arriving at last, but Ruby is frustrated. The situation will make it harder to reach Ben Kitto. She pushes the thought aside as passengers gather their belongings and put on coats at a leisurely pace. Hugh Town is even prettier than it looked on Tripadvisor. It's more like a village than a town, strung along a sandy bay, with low-roofed houses facing the beach and a lifeboat house poised above the harbour. A fleet of dinghies and old-fashioned sailing boats are protected from bad weather by the quay's long arm. Ruby experiences an odd sensation rising in her chest; it feels like a homecoming, for reasons she can't explain.

'How do you like it?' Joe asks.

'I've never seen anywhere so tranquil.'

'It is most days.' He gets to his feet. 'I could ask for your number, but that would be predictable, wouldn't it?'

'Very.' It crosses her mind to give it to him so she can exploit his contacts on Bryher, but instinct tells her to take it slow.

'The Atlantic Hotel's your best bet for tonight. Tell them I sent you.' He smiles, then walks away, joining the crowd of passengers.

Ruby feels more relaxed. It's been so long since she flirted with a handsome guy, it's lifted her mood. She swings her rucksack over her shoulder and heads for the gangway, thinking about Detective Inspector Ben Kitto. She's a hundred per cent confident that he won't recognise her as the quiet, dark-haired child he sometimes played video games with, before blowing her world apart. She's in the dominant position now, with knowledge of all his weak spots, as well as the people he loves. A man with a baby on the way may fight even harder to protect himself and his family. She'll have nowhere to hide if she makes a mistake, but it's too late for doubt. Ruby gives the middle-aged cop who checks her ID her biggest smile when she disembarks.

She studies the landscape again then prepares to disembark. Fishermen's cottages are lined up beyond the quay, painted in pastel colours that reflect the sun. It's only when she looks closer that she spots her final victim. The man is poised on the deck of a small boat, his appearance matching her memory of him. He's still built on a giant scale, holding himself like a heavyweight boxer, his black hair in need of a cut. An older man steers the boat nearer, and she gets a close-up of Kitto's face as they pass, her pulse quickening, as she thinks of the crush she had on him, and her father's dying wishes. There's no conflict of interest; she feels nothing but hatred now. If she had a gun, she'd aim for his heart and watch him plunge into the sea. The cop is oblivious to her death wish, his face pale and solemn as the boat drifts past.

46

My spirits calm as we reach Church Quay on Bryher. I
felt the same way as a child when the ferry delivered me
home from school, the island's peace and beauty wiping
away the day's boredom. I scan the beach, but there's
no one in sight except Lucy Boston, carting deckchairs
back inside her shop, closing up for the day. When she
gives me a wave, the gesture is childlike, her hand flapping the air before she retreats.

Shadow seems glad to be home, already bounding up
the jetty as Ray moors. My uncle lifts his head to say
goodbye, his eyes the same mid-blue as the sea.

'I meant to say, Louis Hayle was looking for you last
night, moaning as usual.'

'About what?'

'The skeleton you found.' Ray's too busy knotting
the mooring rope to look up. 'That man spends too
much time on his hill, with only ghosts for company.'

My phone shows two calls from Hayle last night, but
the signal must have been down, his irate messages only

arriving now. I want to get back to St Mary's fast to give Nina her overnight bag, but I promised Madron to call on Hayle and listen to his latest complaints about the building project trespassing on sacred ground. Shadow runs ahead as I set off north, passing the horseshoe bay of Kitchen Porth, where we part company and he hurls himself into a mass of seaweed with joyful abandon. I'll have to hose him down later. He's got an uncanny skill for locating anything foul-smelling in a mile-wide radius.

Badplace Hill looks unchanged since the skeleton was found. The only evidence of human activity is the piles of soil littered across the moor before the land falls into the sea, the Trenwiths' digger still parked perilously close to the edge. My phone vibrates in my pocket as Louis Hayle's property comes into view. I feel certain it's him complaining again, but it's just an old voicemail from Madron urging me to keep safe. It strikes me again how impressive the granite house looks, perched above the island with a view of the ocean that seems infinite on such a clear day.

I ring the bell, but there's no reply, so I jab it a second time, giving Hayle the benefit of the doubt. I'm about to walk away when I notice that the door is open a fraction, even though he seems the type to keep his property secure. Classical music greets me when I step inside, which could explain why he didn't hear the bell.

I don't take long to locate Louis Hayle. The man is waiting in the hall, but not as I expected. He's spread-eagled on the tiles at the foot of the staircase, his head twisted at an odd angle, eyes gazing at the ceiling. I can tell his neck's broken, and shock makes me go through the motions on autopilot. When I check for a pulse, there's no heartbeat; Hayle's skin is clammy, and still slightly warm. He probably fell down the stairs in the past hour, but the facts could be more sinister. Someone could have worked hard to make it look like he tripped. His eyes are wide open, his dying gaze hard to interpret, signalling either terror or pain.

The music is still blaring through the speakers. I think it's the 'Ride of the Valkyries'. The same refrain keeps on repeating, with drums and cymbals crashing in my ears, louder than a force nine gale.

PART THREE

47

I'm still kneeling by the body when footsteps rattle outside, then a familiar voice calls Hayle's name. My godmother steps inside before I can stop her, but the smile on her face soon fades.

'Stay there, Maggie, don't come any further.'

A carrier bag drops from her hands as she observes the scene. 'Jesus, what's happened?'

'Ring the hotel, can you? I need Liz Gannick here straight away.'

She looks startled, but follows my instruction. I can hear her voice, high and urgent, as she places the call. Instinct tells me to check whether anyone forced their way inside, but Gannick will need the scene preserved. When I stare down at Hayle's face again, his final expression looks like blank-eyed surprise.

'You poor bastard,' I mutter under my breath.

There are dark swellings on his forehead and jaw, blood coagulating on the cuts, no other visible injuries. The wounds may have come from falling down the stairs, but the set-up looks unnatural. Whatever happened, it's easier to sympathise with Hayle's loneliness now that he's gone. Death is always a great leveller. Rich or poor, kind or cruel, the dead have rights, no matter how they lived. The man's complaints have been replaced by a raft of questions. I can't help remembering Ray's voice saying that he disliked Hayle, although I've never seen him lash out at anyone. Hayle could have lost his balance, but the killer may have been terrified that the old man had witnessed something incriminating from his high vantage point, and silenced him before he could tell anyone.

When I turn round, a carton of soup from Maggie's bag has spilled across the tiles by the threshold, half a dozen food packages on the floor. I could hunt for a mop in the kitchen, but that might do more harm than good, so I'll leave the mess until Gannick arrives.

Maggie is perched on a bench outside, clutching her phone, her face white with shock, despite the early-evening warmth. Shadow is sitting at her feet, ready to defend her from all comers. My godmother looks up at me, her expression puzzled.

'The poor man could have been there hours, yelling for help.'

'I don't think so. A few seconds of pain, then he was gone.'

'It's still an awful way to die.'

When I put my arm round her shoulders, she leans in, accepting the comfort.

'Louis was isolated, since Faith died, last year.'

'His wife was the quiet type, wasn't she? I hardly remember her.'

'That's because he came down on his own from London, for years. She was very involved in charity work in London. Faith started coming down with him about twenty years ago, for long holidays. They did almost everything together after that.'

'Losing her must have hurt.'

'I know he came over as arrogant, but he was generous, Ben. He paid for some of the island kids' college fees, but never bragged about it.'

'How come you were bringing him food?'

'We've given him meals to put in his freezer every week since Faith's funeral.' Her voice crackles with sadness. 'He hated eating alone.'

'Did you see anyone come up here today? You're his nearest neighbour.'

'Not a soul.' Maggie's eyes are glassy. 'Kids flocked here years ago, didn't they? You all wanted a ride in his helicopter, or on his yacht, until he lost everything. I think most of it went when the stock market bombed in 2008. That's what made him bitter.' Her gaze clears again. 'Sorry, the past's irrelevant, is it? I was inside yesterday, doing the books, but Billy may have spotted someone. You don't think Louis threw himself down those stairs on purpose, do you?'

'We'll find out.' I give her hand a squeeze. 'Don't tell anyone until I make an announcement, not even Billy.'

She gives a solemn nod. 'My lips are sealed.'

'There's another thing, Maggie. No need to worry, but I've got a tricky situation.'

'I knew it, you've been preoccupied for days. What's up?'

Horror spreads across her face as I explain about past violence encroaching on the present, even when I offer reassurance.

'It's me he's after, Maggie. No one else.'

'You need specialist protection. No one should have to face this alone.'

'Six officers are flying over tomorrow. Have you got space for them at the pub?'

'Of course. We're empty while the island's locked down.'

'It may not come to anything.'

She narrows her eyes. 'I can tell you're rattled, Benesek Kitto. Remember, I've known you from birth. You'd be with Nina if things were okay.'

'This'll keep me here tonight, and I can't abandon the investigation yet. A man's died, Maggie, on our island. No one's safe here till we know why.'

I can see my godmother biting her tongue to avoid giving me a lecture on personal safety, but the situation calls for immediate action. The whole community's in danger if Hayle's death turns out to be murder. The sky is darkening when I look downhill to New Grimsby

Sound. A white yacht is sailing by at such a slow pace it leaves no wash at all, the water unblemished. I can't explain why such an innocent sight sends a chill down my backbone, like I've seen a ghost.

48

Ruby is curled up on a window seat at the Atlantic Hotel as night falls, admiring the view. Lights are twinkling in the slate-roofed cottages beside the harbour. Hugh Town is small and traditional, with its lifeboat moored in the distance, ready to protect mariners from danger. There's nothing to disturb her except a hum of conversation from the bar below, and the wound on her ribcage. She's pleased that the cut looks clean, even though it's deep enough to hurt every time she breathes. It's lucky that she met Joe Trescothick. The hotel manager reduced the price of her room without hesitation when she claimed to be his friend.

She glances round her room. The owners have renovated the old building tastefully; there's a flat-screen TV, soft carpet underfoot, and silk cushions piled on the king-size bed. It's the kind of place her dad would love for its discreet luxury. The memory of Craig Travis dying in pain, still manacled to his bed, tightens the knot in Ruby's stomach. She gets out her purse and studies her photo of him, taken in the days when life seemed perfect.

'One more, Dad,' she whispers. 'I'll wipe out his family too, then you can rest easy.'

She checks her phone, but there's no news of his condition. Journalists will fall over themselves to get the full scoop when he dies, paying prison wardens for illegal photos. She screws her eyes shut to avoid picturing her father in agony, and when they reopen, the view has lost its magic. There's a sudden noise from the bar below. It's a scream of electrical feedback, followed by a crash of drums.

'Fucking brilliant,' Ruby mutters.

She enjoys music most of the time, but she'd prefer silence tonight. The melody is cluttering her mind: first a guitar, then a fiddle playing a rapid tune too loudly to ignore. She marches out of her room in a bad temper.

The bar downstairs is full, and she orders a drink, keeping her back turned to the stage. At least the crowd will help her go unnoticed. The bartender smiles as she pours a glass of Chardonnay, and Ruby perches on a stool to drink it. The place is buzzing with energy, people chatting and laughing at high volume. The sea announces itself everywhere she goes. Crab, lobster, and mackerel are all on the menu, and she can smell the ocean's saline breath with every door standing open. She lingers over her meal, enjoying her seafood pasta undisturbed. She's still in the same spot when a young black-haired woman queues for drinks at her side. There are only two bartenders on duty, serving customers at a leisurely pace, like there's all the time in the world.

'I'll die of thirst at this rate,' the woman says.

'Patience is a virtue, isn't it?' Ruby smiles. She needs to

keep a low profile, but in a community this small, any contact could be useful.

'It's never been my strong point.'

Ruby notices that the woman is downplaying her attractiveness. Her angular features are framed by a cap of black hair, no make-up or jewellery. Her direct gaze is unsettling, like she's memorising her features.

'My name's Isla. You're new here, aren't you?'

'Yes, just visiting – I've wanted to see the islands for years. I'm Chloe.'

'What's your surname, Chloe?'

'Moore. Why do you ask?'

'No reason. You look like a student to me.'

Ruby smiles. 'Is it that obvious? I'm at art college, hoping to do some painting on my trip.'

'The light's good here, but be warned, the night life's rubbish.' The woman leans forward to catch the bartender's attention, finally ordering some drinks.

'I've fallen for the place already. Do you know if there's any summer work going?'

'Try the Island Deli, I think there's a vacancy.'

'What do you do, Isla?'

'I'm with the police.'

Ruby strengthens her smile. 'You don't look anything like a cop.'

'I'll take that as a compliment.'

'This place seems too peaceful for crime.'

'People still get up to mischief. We've only got five officers to cover all the inhabited islands, so it keeps us busy.'

Ruby is pleased by the new information. If the cops are scattered far and wide, Kitto must spend plenty of time alone.

'Enjoy your stay, Chloe. Nice to meet you.' Isla gives her a parting smile and disappears into the crowd.

Ruby's heart rate slows. The cop's dark brown gaze was hard to avoid, like her father's when she was a child. He would sing her to sleep, crooning Elvis songs and old lullabies, but his stare was terrifying if she broke his rules. It felt like being trapped in a long tunnel, with no light to help her escape.

She finishes her glass of wine. The place is even more packed now, standing room only as a new tune echoes from the walls. A fiddle is playing a hectic reel, coaxing drinkers onto their feet. When she looks up at the stage, she's surprised to see Joe Trescothick. He's strumming a guitar, while an old man beside him echoes the melody with his flute, six musicians filling the stage. He grins when he spots her in the crowd, and she waves back. Joe could be her ticket to ride. Her mind is full of strategies as she settles back on her stool then orders another Chardonnay.

49

Liz Gannick appears ten minutes after Maggie leaves, riding a golf buggy from the hotel loaded with equipment. She listens to my account of finding the man's body, her anger erupting when she sees the food scattered across the hallway.

'What's all that gunk?'

'Maggie spilled some soup; I didn't want to do any more damage.'

'Clear it up, for fuck's sake, but wear protective gear.'

Gannick is unrolling metres of clear plastic, like she's planning to wrap the entire house in cellophane. Her approach fascinates me. The woman's like a grenade, primed to explode. I can tell she's glad to arrive before the pathologist, but she's barely glanced at Louis Hayle's body. She casts her crutches aside, then climbs the stairs, crawling on hands and knees. Once fresh plastic is laid on each tread, she considers the victim at last.

'Is this the complainer, Ben?'

'That's him. He didn't have many close friends here, but no serious enemies either, as far as I can tell. I can't see why anyone would target him, apart from his arrogance.'

Gannick raises her hand, like she's stopping traffic. 'That's enough speculation to last me a lifetime. Give me some breathing space, for fuck's sake.'

I keep my mouth shut as she circles the body, remembering my uncle describing the dead man as a bully.

'It's rare to fall backwards downstairs,' she mutters. 'Trip-hazard injuries are normally face first: a broken back or neck. Facial wounds are rare. People normally raise their arms instinctively to protect their heads.'

I look at Hayle's damaged face; there's crimson swelling around a dark red line on his forehead that's still oozing blood.

Gannick is already too immersed to remember my presence. By the time I'm kitted out in a white sterile suit and overshoes, she's spraying luminol on surfaces, clutching a UV torch that turns the air blue. When she runs it over the stairs, its glare travels at the slowest pace imaginable as she checks for blood spatter.

My phone is buzzing with messages when I step back outside. Gareth Keillor says he can't get here until tomorrow morning, unable to find a boatman willing to ferry him over so late at night. He'll arrive bright and early on the police launch. Then DCI Madron calls to tell me to remain at Hayle's property until morning, with all doors locked, in case the killer returns. He reminds me that Travis's hit man might already be on the island, and offers to send Lawrie Deane over to stand guard, but I refuse. One unarmed cop with no experience of conflict would be no match for a professional killer. I hiss out expletives when the call ends. I could easily secure the place and return at first light, but now I'm forced to stay put. The case has picked the worst moment to consume my energy.

My only option is to tell Nina that I can't be with her tonight, or at the airport tomorrow. Her tone is muted when I ring the hospital, but there's relief in her voice too. I wanted our child's life to begin on the islands like mine, but now I don't care so long as they're both safe. She ends our conversation with another warning.

'Remember your promise, Ben.'

'How could I forget?'

She hangs up before I can give any more reassurances.

My thoughts are still with Nina and the baby as I check Louis Hayle's Victorian kitchen, with its range and butler sink. The room is so immaculate, he must have had a cleaner, or enjoyed buffing every surface to such a high shine, I can see my reflection in the chrome surface of his coffee machine. The man's loneliness shows in the content of his freezer. Maggie and Billy's meals are stacked in piles, their generosity bigger than his appetite. It reminds me of when I lived alone. I used to stand by the window studying the world outside while eating pizza from a box, instead of facing an empty table.

The pictures on Hayle's walls hark back to happier

times. One shows him hanging off the side of a yacht as it cuts through high waves, the photo bleached with age. The next is of him in his forties, full of swagger on Hell Bay beach, his skin deeply tanned, surrounded by grinning children, including me and my brother at the edge of the pack. He looks like a stand-in for James Bond, his glittering smile a fraction too white. There are hardly any pictures of his pretty, diminutive wife. Maybe he kept her in the background, too self-absorbed to notice her needs. The couple's daughter only appears in a few graduation and wedding photos. I can't recall her visiting the islands at all since her mother died.

Louis Hayle appears to have led a prosperous life, with homes in London and Scilly, until age overtook him. His desk is stacked with correspondence about the activities centre, including copies of letters he sent to the island council, English Heritage and Greenpeace. He urged numerous charities and ecology groups to fight the development, without success. It's possible that he reached the end of his tether, with no family to support him. I check his filing system, but can't find any evidence that he was under threat. His tax returns show that he lived on a handsome pension, but there's no sign of the huge wealth he accrued during his heyday. I'm still ploughing through his filing cabinet when Gannick calls me from the hallway.

'The stairs are clean, Ben.' There's a victory smile on her face.

'Meaning what?'

'There'd be blood marks from that cut on his forehead if it happened on the way down, but the wall and skirting are spotless. Those facial injuries were inflicted after the fall.'

'How do you know?'

'Check out the blood spatter by his head.' Her blue light shows a spray of droplets on the floor that are invisible to the naked eye.

'Someone kicked or bashed him in the face as he lay dying?'

'It looks that way, then they cleared up most of the blood. Keillor can tell you more. I'm going back to the hotel for food, alcohol and sleep. I'll run detailed checks tomorrow.'

'Thanks for your help, Liz.'

'I don't do it to please you. It's my job, remember?' She offers a grudging smile, then swings outside, her crutches tapping over the cobbled path.

It's only after she's gone that the reality of staying here alone till morning hits home, but it makes sense. I made the mistake of leaving one murder victim unguarded, with disastrous results. It can't happen again, even though my situation has grown more vulnerable. I take a final look outside, using a torch from the hallway; Hayle's back garden appears orderly, his recycling boxes stacked by the door, yet something is out of kilter. The man did something that left the killer so incensed he experienced a violent death.

I've taken a dozen pictures for the pathologist, but

I'd rather not spend the night next to the corpse, so I return inside to find a place to rest. The drawing room has a long view down Badplace Hill. I pick a sofa facing the window, but when I stretch out, sleep is a distant fantasy. I can see a handful of house lights glowing in the valley below, and a white thread spools across the western horizon every few minutes. The lighthouse on Round Island was automated decades ago, but it's still pulsing out warnings, reminding every man, woman and child that the sea cannot be trusted.

50

Ruby is with Joe on the deck behind the hotel, overlooking the harbour; the sea breeze is cooler now, sending other punters drifting indoors. They stand side by side, with elbows on the rail. Ruby's still surprised that Joe is such easy company. The boys she met in care wanted sex and nothing else, but he's different. Maybe that's because he's older, and the only challenge he's ever faced is his parents' divorce. He speaks about being an only child, with a mother who dotes on him, then leaving the island to study in Portsmouth. His expression is gentle when he turns to her again.

'You've had my whole life story, now it's your turn.'

She keeps her gaze on the boats bobbing in the harbour. 'It's too dull to mention.'

'Come on, everyone's got a past.'

'I should go, it's past my bedtime.' She's already backing away.

'Sorry, Chloe. I didn't mean to pry.'

'You didn't. I'm tired from the journey, that's all.'

Joe is studying her more closely, his gaze exploring her face. 'I could kiss you goodnight, but I hate being predictable.'

'You said that on the ferry, so you already are.'

'Meet me on the quay tomorrow, nine a.m. sharp.'

She looks up at him. 'Why should I?'

'You'll get a deluxe boat tour round the islands.'

'What if I've got more important stuff to do?'

'I'm your best option.' His hand skims her arm before he turns away. 'See you tomorrow.'

The bartender announces closing time, and Ruby glances over her shoulder. Joe walks with his head up, looking the world in the eye, like every stranger is a potential friend. She waits until the bar empties, then slips outside. People are disappearing into houses as she sets out to explore the town, the wine she's drunk making her dizzy.

Ruby stands in the shadows between two buildings, taking her measure of the place. The houses are crowded together, rubbing shoulders with no sign of discomfort, like family members packed inside a lift. The island's history is apparent everywhere she looks, with a huge stone archway above the lane to the garrison. She discovers the police headquarters easily, having memorised Hugh Town's layout from a map online. The small grey building is closed for the night, with no CCTV. The only vehicle outside is a dilapidated van, with *Island Police* written in faded letters on the bonnet. DI Benesek Kitto may be twice her size, but she's certain he will have grown complacent in this sleepy place. He'll be at home now, feet up, watching TV. It may be easier than she expected to complete the last stage. The police force is small, with no idea who she is, and Bryher is just two miles away.

She walks at a slow pace, letting the islands' pure air

cleanse her lungs. It's only when she reaches the edge of the settlement that panic bubbles to the surface. Once the street light fades, the dark is so complete it's like swimming through a bottomless sea. It's a different story when she looks up at the night sky. The North Star is bright enough to sear her retinas, millions of stars glittering like a circuit board. She remembers her father's words ever since she was small: *we're the moon and stars, you and me, looking down on the world.* She blinks her eyes shut to block out the light, preferring to remain in darkness.

51

Tuesday 6 May

I'm still half awake at 2 a.m. Shadow appeared a while back, howling outside the French windows; now he's curled up by my feet on Hayle's sofa, clearly hoping for a good night's sleep. It's lucky I'm not superstitious. The downs look ghost-ridden tonight, the land rinsed by starlight. It's still so calm out there; the landscape appears to be holding its breath. Hayles's determination to protect his view enters my mind, along with his belief that Maeve and Danny were building their activity centre out of spite.

I've only just fallen asleep when Shadow releases a whine and my eyes snap open. The dog is pleading to be let out. When I stumble to my feet, he puts his head back and howls at top volume.

'What now, for God's sake?'

Shadow streaks outside when I open the French windows, making my eyes strain to see where he's going. There's a light flickering at the cliff edge below, and instinct makes me grab my torch. I need to get there before it vanishes. I'm running so fast I almost trip over a rabbit hole, but manage to stay upright. The figure at the cliff edge is white-faced and dishevelled, wild eyes staring back at me. I can't guess why Danny Trenwith is out here in the middle of the night. Shadow is standing at his side, blocking his path to the cliff edge.

'What are you doing here?' I call out. The man's face is expressionless, like a sleepwalker. 'Come away from the cliff.' Adrenaline rushes through me when he takes a step backwards, almost overbalancing.

'I was taking a walk,' he says. 'I need time alone.'

'It's the middle of the night, Danny. You should be at home.'

Instinct tells me to grab his arm and drag him back to safety, but it could make matters worse. If he's set to jump, one wrong move might send him plummeting.

'Come this way, please, so we can talk.'

Shadow is still blocking his path, trying to shepherd him back to safety.

'Did you have a fight with Maeve?'

Trenwith makes a sudden movement, trying to dodge past the dog, so I lunge forward. My head spins as the rocks below loom up to greet us, their jagged edges bleached by moonlight. My feet are slipping as I grab his wrist and haul him onto safe terrain.

'Good work,' I mutter to Shadow. The creature's

nose for danger works overtime at night, like it's his job to safeguard the whole island.

Danny remains silent when I lead him to a boulder to sit down. I'm so concerned about his state of mind, I keep my hand on his shoulder in case he makes another run towards the cliff edge.

'Nothing will change,' he whispers. 'There's no point in talking.'

'Is this about the build?'

'Others are in the same boat as me.' His voice is sing-song, like he's reading a poem to a child.

'You're speaking in riddles, Danny.'

'Maeve can't help me now. We're past that stage.'

'You're worried about your marriage?'

'I thought we could sort this mess out together, but I was wrong.'

'You're not making sense. Let's get you home. Things will look better in the morning.'

He shakes his head vehemently. 'Maeve ought to move on; we were just kids when we fell in love. She's outgrown me.'

'Is she having an affair? Is that it?'

'Stop interrogating me, for fuck's sake.'

'Let's go, Danny. Maeve's waiting for you at home.'

He jumps to his feet, his movements jerky. 'I can't face her, Ben. I'm staying here.'

'Walk with me to the pub then; they'll find you a room for the night. Do you realise you almost fell to your death?'

Fresh tears leak from his eyes, but he doesn't reply.

'Talk to someone if you feel that bad again. Ring the Samaritans, or a friend, or me. There's plenty of support here if you hit rock bottom.'

Danny's gaze is so glassy, he seems beyond reach.

It doesn't take long to escort him to the pub, where Billy and Maggie answer my knock in their dressing gowns. Neither of them complain when I lead Danny inside. He looks frail, and Maggie is already offering him a hot drink as I say goodnight. I can't leave Louis Hayle's body unattended any longer. Shadow remains outside the pub even when I whistle; maybe I should be grateful he's guarding Danny, in case he runs back to the cliff.

The man's actions have left me shaken. No matter how bleak my life's felt at times, I've never been suicidal. It takes a big imaginative leap to empathise with his mindset as I trudge back up Badplace Hill, where the porch light is still shining outside Hayle's property. It seems too coincidental that Danny wanted to end his life so soon after his old mentor's murder, but questions won't reach him tonight. I feel sure he's only a danger to himself. He's spent so many years in his wife's shadow, maybe he's forgotten that his own life has value. I send Maeve a text, telling her he's safe and advising her not to disturb him until morning, so he can rest in a neutral environment.

Trenwith's desperation is still rattling around my head as I check the entrance to Hayle's property, where his body still lies prone at the bottom of the stairs, arms flung wide like he's expecting an embrace.

'Why you?' I mutter under my breath.

The house is so quiet I can hear myself exhale. I'm too wound up to sleep, so I watch the eastern skyline turning pink as I wait for backup to arrive.

52

Ruby wakes from a nightmare about her father. There were no mourners at his funeral when his fierce grip on life finally ended. No one bothered to pay their last respects. She sits up in bed, rubbing her eyes to erase the image. When she peers through the curtains, there's a fisherman on the sand below, unloading lobster creels. His movements are slow and deliberate as he clears the deck of his boat, like he's performing a dance he's practised all his life. The rest of the beach is empty. There's nothing marking the horizon except one matchbox-sized freighter, far out in the shipping lane, as dawn arrives.

She can feel her heartbeat slowing as her stress fades, but it would be a mistake to let down her guard. She pulls her Isles of Scilly guidebook from her rucksack and scans the largest map. The islands are a cluster of dark fragments afloat on the Atlantic's green surface, and the territory is forcing her to adapt. She'll need an escape route after killing Ben Kitto – *if* she can reach his house on Bryher. Anxiety about the future clouds her thoughts, so she looks out of the window again and tries to imagine an alternative life. Now that her past has been erased, she could relax here, with no one to cast blame. It only takes her a moment to snap out of it and remember that her own future is unimportant. She's still her father's handmaid, with no intention of going to jail. His suffering has proved that life inside is unbearable. She's spent years watching the light in his eyes fade to a dull glow of anger, and his suffering must be avenged.

She's studying her map of Bryher when a text arrives from Joe telling her not to be late. She smiles before deleting the message; it's lucky that she's met someone with good local knowledge. He could be the key to her final hit.

53

It's 8 a.m. when the police launch finally arrives, my system flagging from lack of sleep. I can see Lawrie Deane steering the boat from my high vantage point. Madron, Keillor and Eddie look like a sombre funeral party, all dressed in black. Deane remains on the boat, which is no surprise. The sergeant has a weak stomach and I'm starting to feel the same, but only from lack of food. The drawback of having a carthorse build like mine is the need for maximum calories to keep the machine running. Low blood sugar makes my head swim when I stand up, but my vision soon clears.

My colleagues are toiling up Badplace Hill when I look out of the window again. The spring in Eddie's stride shows that his zest for life is undimmed, with Keillor strolling at a slower pace, prepared for whatever life throws at him. Madron is the odd man out. He's lagging behind, tension evident in his posture. His shoulders are raised high, like an attack could arrive from any direction.

'Why didn't you call?' Eddie mutters so Madron can't hear. 'I'd have sailed over from Tresco.'

'A dead man only needs one guard, but something else happened. I had to stop Danny Trenwith chucking himself off the cliff.'

'Seriously?'

'I made him stay at the pub last night. He shouldn't be left alone till we've questioned him.'

DCI Madron remains on the path outside, as if the crime scene might sully his immaculate uniform, while the other two put on overalls and overshoes. I know my boss will find something to criticise, despite my all-night vigil. He's gazing with distaste at the acres of plastic sheeting Gannick laid down, his lips set in a hard line.

Gareth Keillor takes his time putting on his Tyvek suit, to avoid contaminating the scene, then drops to his knees to examine Louis Hayle's face and upper body, talking softly like he's reassuring the victim that he's in safe hands. 'You've been in the wars, old man, haven't you?'

I'm still observing the pathologist at work when my boss summons me outside.

'This is a mess, Kitto,' he barks at me. 'The timing couldn't be worse. Don't forget your security officers are arriving at noon. Focus on personal safety; there's no shame in stepping aside, especially with your baby due.'

'I want to close this case, before going to Penzance.'

'You'll follow my orders.' The DCI's grey gaze is cooling by the minute. 'Your old boss thinks Craig Travis's man may already be here, in hiding. He hasn't put a foot wrong until now.'

'I know, sir. That's why I'm glad Nina's out of his reach.'

'But you want to stay and face down a professional killer?' He huffs out a sigh.

'This is my community, I'm not deserting them.'

'Stay at the Rock then, surrounded by guards, and keep that bloody dog with you at all times. That's an order.'

'Yes, sir.'

'You're only being compliant because you've got your way. I'm not thrilled, Kitto. I won't rest easy if you get hurt.'

Madron's speech leaves me stunned. The man has shown genuine concern, which is a rarity. The house is buzzing with activity when I go back inside. Eddie is taking a fresh set of photos for the coroner's report, and Keillor is scribbling notes in his pocketbook, his face tense with concentration.

'Hayle was killed yesterday afternoon,' he says. 'I can't say if he was pushed or tripped down the stairs, but those facial injuries are posthumous.'

'Liz Gannick thought the same. How did he die?'

'Fast. Once the neck's broken, the victim blacks out; it takes around ten minutes for the major organs to shut down. He fell backwards, head-first, judging by the bruises on his back. Someone used a crowbar or heavy-duty hammer on his face.'

'So the killer's physically strong?'

'Or driven by pent-up rage. It takes serious anger to smack a dying man in the face with a crowbar. I'll leave psychology to the experts, but the attack broke his nose and fractured his skull. It happened somewhere between three and six p.m.'

I stay silent while the information registers. Hayle irritated me, but no one deserves such a brutal end. The killer must have hated his guts to lash out with such force.

Keillor sounds regretful when he speaks again. 'Louis Hayle mentored my son for a whole summer, one afternoon a week, when he was driving me and my wife mad. The boy applied himself at school after that, determined to be a success.'

'He helped a lot of young people.'

'Hayle seemed passionate about it, until his money ran out, which must have hurt. All those status symbols seemed to be his *raison d'être*.' Keillor faces me again. 'I need the body over on St Mary's. Get Gannick to finish her work soon, can you?'

'She did everything last night.'

'Does the woman ever sleep?' he asks, shaking his head. 'Let's move him now then.'

'Eddie and I will carry him down to the boat. The ambulance can collect the body from the quay in Hugh Town.'

301

We lift Hayle's corpse into a body bag, and place it on a stretcher brought over from St Mary's. I'm still unable to see a link between the two crimes. The killer who ended the man's life on Badplace Hill may have waited decades to strike again, or another islander has turned violent.

I hear a shrill mechanical noise buzzing in the distance when we step outside. The 8.45a.m. flight is taking off from St Mary's. Something shifts inside my chest like a piece of furniture being dragged over floorboards. I'm in the wrong place, at the wrong time. I should be on that plane, holding Nina's hand, but I can't place her in danger. My gaze stays fixed on the aircraft as I lead the way downhill, with Hayle's body swaying on the flimsy stretcher.

54

Ruby checks her appearance in the hotel mirror. She's wearing white jeans, espadrilles, a pink top and a dash of lip gloss. She looks like a schoolgirl ready for her first date as she picks up her handbag. It contains her purse and her key, but no trace of her old life. Her father's knife is hidden inside her denim jacket, away from the prying eyes of any cleaner who might tidy her room.

She knows this hit could take time to achieve, so a long-term plan is needed. Ruby stops at the Island Deli near to the hotel, but the manager says the job vacancy was filled yesterday. She leaves her phone number, in case more work comes up, then sets off for the quay ten minutes late, hoping Joe will wait for the pleasure of her company. There's no sign of him when she reaches the ticket kiosk. The quay is thronging with day trippers: open-decked ferries are queuing to deliver them to outlying islands. The scene looks like an illustration from a tourist brochure. Sunlight glints on the water, kids are building sandcastles in the distance, while the long mooring lines of fishing boats tether them to land.

Joe's boat is the last vessel on the quay, moored at the bottom of concrete steps that are slimy with seaweed, the acrid smell reminding Ruby of the night she abandoned her old identity by the Thames. When Joe raises his hand to wave, happiness shows on his face. Ruby has never met anyone who wears his heart so openly on his sleeve. Guilt washes over her, for using someone so innocent, but it soon passes. Her goal matters more than hurting someone's feelings, and enjoying herself along the way isn't a crime.

'I was about to find another passenger,' Joe calls out.

'Is that really your boat?'

He grins. 'I converted it so it goes like the clappers.'

'Is it seaworthy?'

'You bet. It's got an outsized engine; I've even sailed it to the mainland a few times.'

'I just want to know it won't sink.'

'Don't worry, everyone sails out here. It goes with the territory.'

When Ruby steps aboard, the boat rocks, then rebalances. There's an odd feeling inside her chest, like she's gulped down too much lemonade. Joe touches her shoulder, then shows her where to sit, beside him at the stern. It feels like she's stepped into a parallel world. Her old life in London was hemmed in by grey skies, traffic and pollution, but this landscape glitters with colour. Sea and sky are contrasting shades of blue, the horizon connecting them by a single thread.

Joe casts off and Ruby feels the outboard motor vibrating through her backbone, the environment suddenly real again. When she looks down, there's a holdall lying at her feet.

'What's in the bag, Joe?'

'Towels, so we can swim.'

'I didn't bring a costume.'

His smile widens. 'There are plenty of empty beaches for skinny-dipping. I brought a picnic too. I can't take you to Bryher, but how about Tresco?'

'Sounds good to me.'

Ruby is glad to have an excuse not to swim, because her knife wound is still wadded with plasters and bandage, but she ignores the discomfort. Joe uses his foot to push the boat's prow away from the quay, and the journey starts. She watches the harbour wall recede as they head for deeper water. The islands ahead are black and low-lying, like thoughts best avoided. Joe is already steering towards the largest one, the boat scudding over shallow waves, through a landscape that looks too pure for danger.

55

Eddie helps me load Louis Hayle's corpse onto the police boat. Lawrie Deane's reluctance to transport it back to St Mary's shows, even though it's wrapped in a body bag, but the journey will only take twenty minutes under such calm conditions. He avoids meeting my eye as the boat retreats, like the fatality's my fault alone.

'You look pale, boss,' Eddie says. 'Are you okay?'

I drop onto a bench, staring out at New Grimsby Sound. We've become friends, despite the ten-year age gap between us and the way his boundless enthusiasm grated on me at first.

'An old man's had a lonely death. Do you know how he looked when I found him?'

'I can't imagine.'

'Shocked rigid. I think it was someone he trusted. So he allowed them to come inside, but he didn't stand a chance. We're talking about an islander, Eddie. Let's go to the pub; I want to know exactly how Danny

306

Trenwith spent yesterday. Attacking his old mentor could have led to suicidal thoughts.'

'I can't imagine him hurting anyone.'

'Me neither, but that doesn't make him innocent. The whole investigation's a fucking mess.'

Eddie's watching me with a curious gaze. I've never vented my frustration so openly in his presence before. It's taken four years of working as partners for me to spit out my thoughts unedited.

'You should eat before we question Danny; you must be starving,' he says. 'But I've got news first. The body on Badplace Hill wasn't Jakob Bazyli. I finally tracked him down, in Gdansk. The bloke travelled round Europe for a few months, then went back to Poland to be a carpenter. His English isn't fluent, but he could answer most of my questions. He felt bad about running off. Apparently he couldn't face telling Ray he was leaving, so he cadged a lift over to St Mary's at the crack of dawn on a fishing boat. It sounds like an argument with Louis Hayle triggered it.'

'Good work, Eddie, we can cross him off our list of potential victims. Why did he fall out with Hayle?'

'It happened when him and Ray were refitting the yacht. I struggled to understand some of what he said, but it sounded like Hayle complained about his workmanship.'

'I'll try and find out more. We should get the DNA result from Liz's bone sample today at least.'

I mull the idea over as we take the ten-minute walk

to the pub. The news seems to put Nathan Kernow in the clear. He may have been telling the truth all along about holding a vigil to honour a stranger's life. I think of him veering from one religion to another for most of his adult life, a lost soul seeking shelter, but no one goes to prison for seeking comfort from the supernatural.

Billy is indulging his passion for Bruce Springsteen again when we reach the pub, with 'Born to Run' blasting out of the kitchen doors at top volume as he chops carrots at lightning speed. The man looks more like a pirate than a chef. He's dressed in ancient Levi's, a black T-shirt, and gold hoops in each ear, his grey hair tied in a ponytail. When he turns the music down, there's no smile on his time-worn face.

'Maggie's not here, Ben. I'm too busy to chat.'

I ignore his statement. 'We need to know how Danny Trenwith's doing, but give me some food first, before I keel over.'

He glances at me again, then grabs a frying pan, his surliness vanishing instantly. Billy sets to work, preparing his trademark full English in minutes. I'm too preoccupied by hunger to ask questions until he presents us with identical plates full of sausages, eggs and bacon, even though Eddie never requested food. Our breakfast might not be the healthiest choice, but it does the trick. I feel better at once, with saturated fat flooding my bloodstream.

'You're a lifesaver. How does Danny seem now?'

'He'd calmed down a bit by the time we got him to

bed, but when I came down this morning at seven, he'd scarpered, leaving the front door open. Maggie's so worried she's out looking for him.'

'Go and help her, please, Eddie. I want him back here before he hurts himself.' I'm increasingly concerned that Danny's behaviour may be linked to Hayle's murder.

My deputy hurries away, leaving his meal half eaten. Billy takes a seat opposite, watching me drink my coffee. 'What happened yesterday, Ben?'

'I can't say till we've made a formal announcement.'

'Maggie was shaking like a leaf when she got back.' He gives me a questioning look. 'I saw you carrying that body bag. It was Louis Hayle, wasn't it?'

I give a reluctant nod. It won't be long before the death is common knowledge. I remember that Billy visited Hayle once a week, to drop off food or play chess, simply because the old man was lonely. The chef's bluff manner often masks his kindness, but it's not working today. His eyes are glistening when he speaks again.

'Louis had a terrible year, losing his wife, then the row about the activities centre. I was concerned about his mental state. Was it suicide?'

'Why do you ask?'

'He was so depressed, I half expected it.'

'Did you see anyone go up there yesterday evening, after six?'

Billy shakes his head. 'I was slaving in here alone. Youngsters these days won't do an honest day's work.'

'Think, Billy, please. Are you sure no one came by?'

'Just Penny Cadgwith. She takes a daily walk all year round, to help her asthma.'

I'm about to ask another question when Gannick sends me a text. The lab has sent through the results on the shard of bone from Badplace Hill. The DNA profile is a fifty per cent match with Jamie Porthcawl's, which stops me in my tracks. It proves that the skeleton he uncovered belonged to his brother, even though his parents convinced the whole island Hugh was still alive. If they genuinely believed it, someone worked hard to fake his handwriting on the letters from America Bella said they'd found. It's still possible that Jamie is the killer. He may have lost his temper with his brother all those years ago, if their relationship was full of conflict, as Penny claimed. I make myself focus.

'Louis Hayle was murdered,' I tell Billy. 'We have to know why. It's my best chance of catching his killer.'

The chef's bravado deflates like a pricked balloon, draining his rock-and-roll spirit. The news of his friend's death has reduced him to an old man, the lines carved into his face suddenly deeper than before.

56

Ruby is reluctant to go ashore when Joe moors on Tresco. They've spent an hour anchored in New Grimsby Sound, lying on the deck with the sun beating down. She's glad of a break from the relentless pressure she's been under, and it's easy to ignore her duty while they're afloat. Setting foot on land will return her to reality.

'Wait till you see the gardens, Chloe. They're gorgeous this time of year.'

Joe is holding out his hand to help her disembark. When she hesitates, he grabs her waist and swings her onto the jetty; she feels weightless and carefree for an instant, but the sensation soon passes.

'You're built like a ballet dancer,' he says.

'I'm stronger than I look.'

'Race me then, tough girl.'

He sets off down an undulating path that leads through stands of reeds, and dunes covered in marram grass, towards the island's centre. Ruby's wound aches when they reach the Abbey Gardens, but at least she won. Joe is bent double, laughing at her with wheezing breaths.

'I bet you can run your way out of trouble.'

'Always.'

She barely notices when he takes her hand, distracted by the lush gardens. Huge trees overhang the path, too many varieties to name, the air heady with the vanilla scent of flowers.

'Let's go to the Valhalla Museum first. I loved it as a kid.'

When they reach a wooden-framed building Ruby sees dozens of brightly painted figures. A life-sized woman gazes down from the wall, her scarlet lips set in a wooden smile, turquoise eyes staring straight ahead.

'Where do they come from, Joe?'

'They're mastheads from local shipwrecks. Sailors thought they guaranteed good luck on long voyages, but divers had to bring all these to the surface.'

'They're beautiful, but creepy too.' She touches the woman's painted cheek. It's cold, despite the day's heat, and she can't help shivering. 'Can we get out of here?'

He stops in front of her, hands settling on her shoulders. 'The figures won't hurt you. Something else is wrong, isn't it?'

'It's nothing, Joe.'

'I'm a good listener, if you want to talk.'

'Thanks, but I just need some caffeine.'

'Follow me. The café's five minutes away.'

He leads her to an enclosed garden full of birdsong. Sparrows descend and peck at crumbs on the table where Ruby sits; even the wildlife is tamer than any she's seen before. London's pigeons are wily enough to scatter at the sound of footsteps. She shuts her eyes and blocks out her surroundings. Nothing matters except her dad's plan: she'll follow it whatever that takes. The thought is still in her mind when Joe crosses the lawn with two cups of coffee. He's so good-looking, it requires little effort to keep her smile bright when he sets them on the table.

57

Eddie had no luck finding Danny Trenwith, so I give him the task of phoning the Porthcawls when he returns to our incident room at 11 a.m. I want them here by noon, bringing the letters from America with them. I'll assess how Jamie reacts to the news that it was Hugh's bones lying on Badplace Hill. Eddie will do a general call-round afterwards, informing island families of Hayle's death and the need to stay safe in groups, as well as asking for sightings of Danny. It takes a leap of imagination to imagine a calm man like Jamie hurting anyone, but no one on Bryher seems a likely killer of an eighteen-year-old boy. I know that Travis's hired man may be close by, but I have to focus on immediate tasks. We'll hold another public meeting tonight, after the plain-clothes officers arrive, but the news of Hayle's death is already in the public domain. We'll need to stem the tide of panic.

Maggie appears with grey curls flying while I'm scribbling a list of things to announce. Words spill from her mouth almost too fast to hear.

'We couldn't find Danny anywhere, Ben. Maeve's still hunting for him, she won't go home till he's safe.'

'Slow down and tell me step by step.'

'I've walked the whole coastline.' My godmother drags in a breath. 'I'm so bloody cross with myself.'

'Why?'

'I thought he'd calmed down. The poor guy was beside himself last night, though he never said why.'

'None of this is your fault, Maggie.'

'What put him in that state?'

'I don't know yet. I found him by the cliff edge, then brought him here after he refused to go home.'

'Maeve says he had a breakdown last year, from overwork. He's been tense for days. Coming back here unsettles him, apparently.'

'I need to do a final check on Louis Hayle's house; I'll look for Danny on my way.'

'Want me to come along?'

'Stay safe here, and call me if he comes back. Keep him indoors, will you? I need to ask some more questions.'

My heart is beating too fast as I walk back up Badplace Hill. A new text arrives from Nina as I set off. She's arrived at the hospital in Penzance already, yet it fails to set my mind at rest. An odd feeling travels up my spine. It feels like I'm being watched, but when I swing round, the coastal path is empty. I can see Tresco's sandy beaches across the water, and the off-islands pale in the distance, but I'm out of step with the landscape's beauty. There's a mismatch between the vivid wildflowers woven through the dry-stone walls and the darkness of Hayle's murder. The last few days have felt like a bad dream, with one fatality heralding the next on the mainland. Danny's misery might be connected to Louis Hayle's death, but I still can't imagine why he'd kill his mentor.

I could have overlooked something at Hayle's property to explain the link. But when I return, all I find is silence. The place feels sterile, with every room tidy, as if the man forecast his own death and left his home in perfect order. I'll have a long wait while his computer is sent to the mainland so the hard drive can be checked for evidence.

I step out of the back door and study his well-kept garden, where the island's native agapanthus displays dozens of tall purple blossoms. There's an outbuilding, but all it contains is a lawnmower and gardening tools. It's only when I spot the recycling boxes again that I realise something Hayle threw away could provide a clue. I pull on sterile gloves to root through old newspapers, but find nothing incriminating. The next box rattles when I try to open the lid, but it's sealed by tape. When I finally prise it open, sunlight pours down on a jumble of bones. There's no denying they're from Badplace Hill, the fractured skull shattered into pieces I recognise.

My thoughts spin like a gyroscope. I can't tell whether Louis Hayle removed the skeleton himself, or the killer brought it here as a tribute. All I know for certain is that someone collected Hugh Porthcawl's remains and placed them inside this box. The boy's ribs jostle for space beside his broken skull. A wave of nausea hits me, and I have to concentrate hard to hang onto my breakfast. I'll need Liz Gannick's help for the second time today. I'm still staring into the box when I call her. The bones are bleached white, like ancient relics.

58

Ruby is impressed when Joe's boat reaches Pentle Bay on Tresco. The long beach is free of litter, its gentle curve hugging the land, no people in sight. It's a far cry from the endless queues outside Southend's cafés and packed amusement arcades when her father treated her to a day out. She loved those adventures, sitting in deckchairs on the beach eating fish and chips with him, but this is another world. The bay is a bare strip of gold, the air tinged with the sour odour of seaweed.

'It looks so calm,' she says.

'You should see it in July. Have you done much travelling?'

'Not really. How about you?'

'I did the whole gap-year cliché: Vietnam, Laos, Cambodia, Bali.'

'That sounds amazing. Did it take long?'

'Ten months, working whenever I could.' Joe lays down a blanket, then unloads their picnic. Next he kicks off his tennis shoes and walks into the sea, wedging a bottle of wine in the sand to cool in the shallows.

'I see you're an expert picnicker,' Ruby says, laughing. 'I bet you've brought every girl in Scilly here.'

He shakes his head. 'Only Sharon Reid, in Year 9, which was a disaster. She sent a Valentine's card to another boy. It put me off outdoor meals for a whole year.'

'What a bitch. Want me to kill her for you?'

'I'm over it, thanks, but it's good to know you're an assassin. I thought you were a poker player, from that game face of yours.'

'What do you mean?'

'You're a closed book, Chloe.' He leans over to tap her arm. 'Give me just one fact about yourself. Please.'

'I was born in Brighton.'

'Great, I love southern girls. Any brothers or sisters?'

'That's my limit. One fact, you said.'

'How about parents? Are you close to them?'

'Mum died giving birth to me.' The truth slips from Ruby's mouth before she can stop it, another reminder not to let her guard down.

'That's awful.' The sympathy in Joe's eyes looks a hundred percent genuine. 'Your dad must have been heartbroken.'

'He's the strongest man I know, but I hate thinking about it.'

'Let me distract you then.' He pulls her close, his lips warm on hers.

The kiss wipes Ruby's mind clean. The moment spins out, until Joe pulls her to her feet, dragging her towards the tideline.

'Come on, lazybones,' he says. 'I'll chuck you in the sea, then we'll have lunch.'

They fool around in the shallows until their clothes are soaked, with the ocean behind them azure blue. Ruby glimpses how life might have been if she was another man's daughter, but the image is fleeting, like fragments of sunlight glinting on the water's surface.

59

Jamie and Bella Porthcawl are waiting when I return to the Rock. It's lucky they don't know about the box I've left at Louis Hayle's house. I speak to Eddie outside. My deputy's jaw drops when I explain about finding the bones abandoned like household rubbish. I'm certain it's the skeleton from Badplace Hill, but Gannick will have to check the box for fingerprints so we can work out who placed them there. Eddie hurries away to phone her, leaving me to conduct the first part of the interview alone.

The Porthcawls appear to be expecting good news; I'll have to walk a fine line between speaking to Jamie as a bereaved relative and treating him as a suspect. Bella grips her husband's hand while he searches my face for clues.

'That can't be right,' Jamie says. 'I know Hugh's still alive.'

'There's a fifty per cent genetic match between your DNA and the bone sample from Badplace Hill. I'm afraid the skeleton is definitely your brother's.'

Bella presses her fingers to her lips like she's suppressing a scream, but Jamie's speech is a dry whisper.

'We've brought Hugh's letters with us. He's in the States, like I said. These were franked in New York.' He pulls two worn envelopes from his pocket, brandishing them like they're cast-iron proof.

'Anyone could have copied his handwriting and posted them from the USA.'

'It doesn't make sense.'

'I need to interview you formally, please, Jamie. Would you mind waiting at home, Bella?'

'No way, I can't leave Jamie when he's had such awful news.'

Bella's expression sours when I insist she goes. We've always been on friendly terms, and I'm still grateful she took care of Nina, but that's meaningless now. Her gaze cuts through me like cheese wire before she marches away.

Jamie is blank-faced when Eddie joins us for the formal interview. Disbelief resonates in his voice as I record our conversation on the laptop. He repeats his speech about his brother abandoning his past to start a new life, but that story has changed since his bones were found.

'You and your brother fought sometimes, didn't you? Was there ever physical violence?'

'It was just words. You must argue with your brother sometimes?'

'Not often. How about your father? Did he ever strike either of you?'

He shakes his head. 'Dad showed his disappointment if we let him down, but he wasn't the type to
hit anyone.'

'Where do you think Hugh went after their big row?'

'His closest friend was Danny Trenwith, but he had
other mates. Any of them would have welcomed him.
Penny's mum and dad never let him stay over at their
place. They didn't believe in sex before marriage.'

Eddie is taking notes, even though the computer
is recording every word, leaving me to ask awkward
questions.

'You'll have heard the stats about violent crime,
Jamie. Ninety per cent of murders happen within fam-
ilies, or the killer is from the victim's intimate circle.
Can you think who might have targeted Hugh?'

'Not me, if that's what you're saying. He was my kid
brother; I loved him, even though we were so different,
we drove each nuts sometimes.' Jamie is staring at the
surface of the old bar-room table, as if the answer lies
among the beer stains. 'I still miss him, even now.'

'His death may be connected to Louis Hayle's.'

'My brother saw him as a guru. Do you remember
Hayle saying that all we needed was self-belief, a brilliant idea and a strong work ethic? Hugh took that to
heart; he recited those words like a mantra.'

'Do you think Hayle influenced any other kids
that deeply?'

'Bella respected him a lot. He was the reason she
started her greeting card business, and she stayed loyal

to the old boy. She took him a cake just last week to cheer him up.'

Jamie provides little fresh information. The only clear link between the dead boy and Hayle is that the older man mentored him, just like numerous other children. His main message was simple enough for any teenager to memorise: hard work, a unique business idea and confidence lead to success.

I turn possibilities over in my mind as Jamie speaks. He could have fallen out with his brother badly enough to go on the attack, then discard his body, or his father may have killed the prodigal son for rejecting his life-style. Jamie's smart enough to realise that our only hard proof is the bone fragment from the scene, the copper nail that ended Hugh's life and my uncle's tool bag in his hand. I may have to accept that two different islanders are guilty of murder. I can't prove who killed Hugh Porthcawl, because the crime turned cold twenty years ago, but Louis Hayle was murdered yesterday, and even Ray is implicated.

The cause of the teenager's death almost three decades ago could be right under my nose, and I won't let his brother out of my sight until he can prove his innocence. My only option is to arrest him for Hugh's murder, based on his return visit to the crime scene and his denial that their relationship was antagonistic. There's a slow fire burning in Jamie's eyes when I read him his rights, but I've got no other choice.

60

Jamie Porthcawl's anger bubbles to the surface when I lead him upstairs to one of the vacant guest rooms at the pub, which will have to serve as a temporary holding cell.

'You've known me all my life, for fuck's sake. Do I look like a murderer to you?'

'I have to do my job. You said your relationship with your brother was good, but others say it was full of conflict, and you trespassed on a crime scene when his body was found. You may have tampered with evidence.'

He gives me a long stare. 'Don't waste your time, please. Get on and find my brother's killer.'

'You're entitled to a lawyer at this stage, Jamie.'

'Why? I've done nothing wrong.'

I feel uncomfortable locking him inside the guest room, even though it's luxurious compared to the bare holding cells we have on St Mary's, which contain nothing apart from a narrow bed. Jamie's response is cold anger; he could be in shock about his brother's death, or keeping his guilt hidden, if he played a part in the murder.

I take a quick look at the letters Jamie claims his brother sent, back in the incident room, then I email photos of them to a police graphologist. The penmanship could help us find the killer. The words on the envelopes are a misshapen scrawl, which could be someone trying to disguise their writing style, but there's no time to read them now. Six officers from the mainland will arrive soon. It could make life easier, provided they keep a low profile.

When I hurry down to the quay, two middle-aged holidaymakers appear to have persuaded Arthur Penwithick to ferry them here despite the lockdown. Then reality hits home. The two men must be all the Cornish force can offer. One of them is already hurrying towards me.

'Would you be Inspector Kitto? Your colleague just dropped us here.' His West Country accent is as thick as clotted cream. He's carrying a hefty spare tyre, his smile eager-to-please.

'I was expecting more of you.'

'The chief could only release us two; there are staff shortages. I should never have volunteered, to be honest. The plane made me sick as a dog.'

'What are your names?'

'I'm Constable Ken Ellis, and that's Tom Kinsella.'

'He's the same rank?'

'That's right, sir. I'm traffic patrol, and Tom's been on security jobs since his back trouble started.'

My heart sinks as he provides more details. I was hoping for young bloods, fit enough to patrol the coastline and help me find Danny, but this guy doesn't look fit enough to defend anyone if Craig Travis's hired killer arrives by sea. The second officer is a marginally better prospect. He's got a wiry build, with grey hair shaved close to his skull, pockmarked skin and a forthright stare. Constable Ellis may have spent the past twenty years doling out motoring fines, but Kinsella appears to be cut from different cloth. There's a deep groove between his eyebrows from constant frowning, but the curiosity in his expression gives me hope.

'I'll walk you to the incident room,' I say. 'My deputy can bring you up to speed.' Eddie can give out tasks while I look for Danny Trenwith.

'I thought we were here to guard you, sir?' Ellis looks confused.

'There's been a murder. If you're following me around, you may as well help us solve it.'

Ellis proves that he's a talker before we've covered ten yards. He describes every part of their journey from Truro, by train, taxi, then plane from Land's End, while Kinsella remains silent. He appears to be scanning the horizon, observing the landscape for clues.

'Are you ex-army, Tom?'

He turns in my direction at last. 'How did you guess, sir?'

'From your posture. What unit?'

'EOD, till I got injured.'

'That's unlucky,' I reply.

'Not in my case, sir. It was human error.'

His gaze returns to Badplace Hill, and my hopes dwindle. The Cornish force has sent me a wounded hero from the Explosive Ordnance Disposal unit, and a traffic cop. I doubt either man could identify a killer who's bold enough to hide in plain sight. Ellis's monologue rumbles on as we approach the pub, and my certainty that only I can save myself from Travis's hitman grows stronger all the time.

Eddie rises to the challenge when I leave our new recruits at the Rock. My deputy has a higher pain threshold when it comes to small talk, but Ken Ellis is likely to wear even his patience thin by the end of the day. I leave them discussing how to find out which islander could have approached Hayle's house yesterday and who will keep an eye on Jamie Porthcawl. Liz Gannick is checking the box I found for fingerprints, to see if they match Porthcawl's.

I'm followed by Constable Kinsella and a blast of hardcore American rock when I cross Billy's kitchen to the fire escape. The chef is bent over his steel table, gutting salmon, the fish's pink flesh splayed across the board. His surly expression vanishes when he's at work, replaced by pleasure he rarely shows in public. He must enjoy his craft, but there's no time to stay and watch. Danny Trenwith is still missing, and it will be my fault if he's never found. I can imagine him casting himself off the cliff all too easily after his behaviour last night, which quickens my pace. It's a relief that Kinsella doesn't feel the need to communicate, following behind while he scans the landscape, as if the fields contain snipers with me in their sights.

I take a circular route west towards Gweal Hill. Trenwith might be sheltering in one of the island's bays, trying to calm himself. But when I drop down to Great Par beach, the long horseshoe of sand is empty. I'm about to move on when Maeve emerges from the dunes. The architect is wearing a black sundress, pale shoulders scorched pink by the day's sun. I gesture for her to join me on a boulder overlooking the sea while Kinsella loiters in the distance.

'I can't stop for a minute,' she says. 'I need to keep looking.'

'How long has Danny been depressed?'

'Years, but he's always denied it, until his breakdown six months ago. He hates taking his medication. I should have spotted the warning signs.' She's clutching her hands so tightly her knuckles are turning white.

'Where do you think he is now?'

'God knows, but it's me he's avoiding.'

'How do you mean?'

Maeve is staring at the seascape ahead, but it doesn't seem to bring her peace. Her hands flutter in her lap, burdened by silverware. The rings draw my attention again, each one with its distinctive pattern.

'We've reached a turning point. The pair of us got together at sixteen. It wasn't easy, going through uni then setting up our practice together, but I can't imagine life without him. That's why we're struggling. I'd like to stay on Bryher, even though he finds it suffocating. I should probably just agree and keep on travelling, but it's not what I want.'

'You're splitting up?'

'I hope not, but he thinks we should abandon the activities centre and go to Spain.' Maeve looks embarrassed, as if she regrets blurting out her troubles.

'I need to ask something else, Maeve. Were you mentored by Louis Hayle too?'

She looks surprised by my sudden change of tack. 'Dan was his favourite; he taught him to sail, along with a few other kids, until his wife made him slow down.' Her gaze is still riveted to the horizon. 'I was never anything special at school, but Louis' advice gave me focus, at least. I've grafted for everything we have, but I'd trade it all to see Dan happy.'

'Do you remember who else Hayle mentored?'

Maeve gives a slow nod. 'Lucy and Christian Boston, which made sense. They were both so painfully shy, they needed encouragement.'

'Did you know them well at school?'

'Lucy was in our year, but it was a bad environment for her.'

'How do you mean?'

'She's sensitive, isn't she? Everything wounds

her.' The sadness in Maeve's voice makes me keep pushing.

'Give me the full story, please.'

'Lucy was pretty, a real English rose, but vulnerable. The boys taunted her. They started yelling names at her in the playground, calling her easy, until her brother sorted them out. Kids made stupid judgements back then. I'm sure that doesn't happen now, thank God.'

I don't share her certainty; the same ugly double standards applied when I was at school, five or six years later. If a girl had several boyfriends, she was seen as fair game. Those taunts must have dented Lucy's confidence. Maeve's explanation reveals why she chose to remain in her brother's protection long after her schooldays ended.

'I'll keep looking for Danny. Wait for him at home, please.'

Maeve looks solemn when I say goodbye, her long hair bronzed by the sun as it plummets towards the horizon. Bryher's western beaches all have a fine view of the Atlantic, but that will be little comfort to Danny Trenwith, who sounds even more fragile than I realised. Kinsella is still standing sentry as I glance back at the sea. The rocky outlines of Gweal, Maiden Bower and Seal Island are turning orange, and Maeve's black dress stands out against the colourful background, her shoulders hunched with tension as sunset ignites the sky.

61

Ruby is still with Joe as the day ends. Gold discs are scattered across the water, like dying fireworks, the sight peaceful enough to make her drowsy. The charade she's playing has sapped her energy. She's spent the whole day pretending it's the start of a light summer romance. It was easy to get Joe to text his contacts about a summer job, which would allow her to blend into the island's fabric. He's sitting opposite her now, studying his phone.

'Message from your girlfriend?'

'I didn't have one till you came.' He carries on checking messages. 'There's work going at the Rock on Bryher, for a kitchen hand. Can you see yourself washing dishes and slaving for a tyrant?'

Ruby smiles. 'Sounds like my dream career, but you said strangers can't go there.'

'I'll sort it.' He leans down to kiss her again. 'The guy who runs the kitchen is a bit gruff, but he's a sweetheart really.'

'Why are helping me, Joe?'

'Because I fancy the heck out of you, obviously.'

She stares back at him. 'Do you always say exactly what you think?'

'It's the best way, isn't it? Unless the truth's hurtful.'

'That job on Bryher sounds okay. Can you really get me over there?'

'Let's try. It's only ten minutes away.'

Ruby keeps her smile concealed as Joe steers his boat into the sound. Bryher's dark outline lies directly ahead, growing bigger all the time, with house lights scattered across its central valley. Maybe seeing Joe will have extra benefits in the future. If she plays her cards right, he could be her escape route too.

The boat reaches the quay in less than ten minutes. An old man stands outside a boatyard with a big grey dog at his feet. The creature slinks towards Ruby when she steps off the boat, snarling, with teeth bared.

'Away, Shadow, get back here now,' the old man calls. 'Visitors aren't allowed, Joe. Haven't you heard?'

'This is Chloe, Ray. She wants a job at the Rock; we're going there now.'

'You'll still need to register with the police.'

'I will. Thanks for the advice,' Ruby calls back, smiling.

The dog slinks back up the jetty, but its vicious barking continues as they walk north along the bay, with the old man watching them leave. It's too dark to measure the island's scale, or look for hiding places. It feels like the air is smothering her, and her heart is beating too fast.

'You've tuned out, Chloe,' Joe says. 'What are you thinking?'

'Nothing. I'm just crap at interviews.'

'Don't worry, the people at the Rock are great. I've known them all my life.'

His arm settles round her shoulders as they follow a shingle path behind the dunes. The moon looks unnaturally wide overhead, its light turning the sea silver, the sand bleached pale. Instinct makes Ruby keep her head down, as her father's promises of immortality echo in her mind.

62

I walk the island's circumference in less than an hour, with Kinsella trailing a few metres behind. My guard's presence is so quiet I soon forget he's there. Bryher is just two miles long and half a mile wide, yet Danny Trenwith remains out of reach. I won't let myself believe that he's leapt into the sea until every other possibility has been exhausted. I still believe one of the island's elders may know the secret behind Hugh Porthcawl's death.

Shadow is waiting for me when I reach Ray's boat-yard, the sound of hammer blows resonating from the building. My dog jumps up to greet me as though we've been separated for years, desperate to lick my face.

'Down,' I tell him. 'Where are your manners?'

He stays close as I approach the yard. I can see my uncle through the half-open doors, applying varnish to the new dinghy. He takes a while to acknowledge me when I walk inside. I learnt long ago that Ray is unshockable; I could fire a starter pistol by his ear and he still wouldn't jump. Several minutes pass before he finally stops hammering and meets my eye.

'Is this social or police business?'

'Both, I suppose.'

'Your lockdown isn't working too well, by the way. Young Joe Trescothick just brought a girl over. She looked fresh out of school.'

'I'll make sure she's checked, but I doubt she'll cause trouble.'

'Why are you here? I've got this boat to finish.'

'I can help if you like.'

'Keeping me sweet?' Ray narrows his eyes. 'Varnish the port side if you want a job.'

I fetch a brush and a pot of varnish. 'I heard about your old apprentice, Jakob Bazyli, today. He lives in Gdansk now, with a wife, two kids and a successful carpentry business. He did a midnight flit because he was embarrassed about letting you down.'

Ray gives a slow nod. 'That makes sense. He was a decent lad, but I knew he was homesick.'

'How come you never told me he argued with Louis Hayle?'

'It didn't seem important. I left him working in the yard and went over to St Mary's for supplies. When I got back, Hayle had a face like thunder after inspecting our work. I asked Jakob why he'd stormed off. He said that Hayle was too critical, and the worst kind of man.'

'Why's that?'

'I don't know. A few days later, Jakob was gone.'

I'm hoping our shared labour will open Ray up. I loved working alongside him as a teenager during school holidays, watching boats emerge from raw lengths of wood. The process eases my tension as I apply varnish in long sweeps until the cedar glistens. Ten minutes pass in silence before I speak again.

'You know more, don't you, Ray? Louis Hayle may have died for keeping the same secret. You might be in danger too.'

'I can't solve your case for you.'

'Tell me why you disliked Hayle.'

'It was just a gut reaction.' He lays down his brush, frowning. 'He expected the youngsters to flatter his ego. The man loved being hero worshipped; he had his favourites too. Maybe some of those kids got bruised along the way.'

I stare back at him. 'Abused, you mean?'

'I'd never accuse a dead man of that.'

'Did you confront him at all?'

'It was just a suspicion; no one ever complained. I told him not to misuse his power. The island kids were dazzled by his Rolex watch and those fancy clothes.'

'I wasn't, and neither was Zoe.'

'You came from secure homes. Some were much more vulnerable.'

'How did Hayle react?'

'He denied any wrongdoing, then made threats to ruin my business. The bloke always had to be in control.'

Silence settles over us as I brush on more varnish, hiding every flaw. The picture is finally taking shape. Louis Hayle was a powerful man, and the islands' kids – including me – were innocent. It took me months to develop a tough shell after leaving Scilly's protection. I can imagine Hayle coming down here to steal the murder weapon and the tool bag to frame my uncle in case the remains were ever found.

'There's something else before you go,' Ray says.

'What's that?'

'Tell me why you let Nina go to hospital alone.'

'I want her out of harm's way, and don't preach to me about relationships. Why do you act like seeing Sandra's a dirty secret?'

'Neither of us likes gossip.' My uncle shrugs my comment away. 'Have you even phoned Nina today?'

'Don't guilt-trip me, Ray. I've got enough to handle.'

'You promised her to stay safe, but here you are, stirring up the past and looking for trouble.'

'That's my job, remember?'

He slams the lid back on his tin of varnish, terminating our conversation, which is just as well. I might get short-term relief from accusing him of withholding evidence, but it wouldn't solve anything.

My head's pounding with anger when I leave the boatyard, and Kinsella looks startled. He's been standing guard close enough to hear every word. My private life is no longer hidden from view, but that's a given until the threat passes. Ray is one of the few people who can shame me into action. Instinct tells me to rush back to the station to see my team before they quit for the night, but my conscience is troubling me, so I drop down on the jetty wall to make a phone call.

Nina sounds tired but relaxed. Her day has been uneventful, listening to the radio and gazing out of the window. I can hear a slow grumble of vehicles on the road outside the hospital. We're separated by forty-five kilometres of rough Atlantic, while Penzance carries on as normal, regardless of the dangers facing us. I promise her I'll take care, then tell her I love her and hang up. I bet she's laughing out loud. She didn't need to goad me into saying it, for once in my life.

The stars are out in force as I stuff my phone back into my pocket. Their cool light picks out details when I look north towards Badplace Hill, where traces of silver on the dry-stone walls have turned the scene monochrome. When I hear a sound behind us, Kinsella jumps to his feet, but it's only Shadow trotting across the gravel. He stands at my side, with ears pricked, like he's heard a warning sound.

'What's eating you, for God's sake?'

The dog gazes up at me, his eyes pale in the moon-light. His head's still cocked, his stance alert, but at least he's behaving himself. He ignores Kinsella's presence, staying glued to my heels as I head north along the coastal path.

63

Ruby feels uncomfortable when she and Joe arrive at the Rock. Through the pub's windows she can see a group of islanders laughing at someone's joke, and wishes she felt that relaxed. The wound on her ribcage hasn't troubled her for hours, but now it's smarting again, impossible to ignore, just when she needs to be at the top of her game.

'The chef's called Billy. He's a decent bloke, I promise. His bark's a lot worse than his bite.'

Ruby can feel butterflies in her stomach when she knocks on the fire door and a gruff voice summons her inside. She's greeted by a wall of steam and a man with a long grey beard, frowning as he hurls a rib-eye steak into a pan.

'What are you after, young lady?'

'A job, if you still need someone.'

He switches off the gas and swings round to face her. 'Ever done catering before?'

'Two years in a busy café.'

'I need proof, not references.' He places a chopping board in front of her with three onions, laying a knife on the table. 'Dice those for me, love, nice and fine. Show me what you can do.'

Ruby washes her hands in the sink, relieved to be thrown back onto familiar ground. Her nerves have steadied by the time she's finished chopping the onions, the test completed in moments.

'Good knife skills. What's your name?'

'Chloe Moore. I'm here on holiday, but I want to stay longer if I can.'

'I pay the living wage, plus bed and board.'

'And tips?'

'You strike a hard bargain.' He lets out a laugh. 'Just as well I like people who stand their ground. Staff all get an equal share. How does that sound?'

'Good. I could start tomorrow.'

'I'll pay you for a day's trial and see how you cope.'

'Do I need to register with the police first?'

'That's right. No one can stay on Bryher without their permission right now. You're in luck; most of them are here tonight. They're using our function room as their base.'

Ruby feels a surge of panic. If Kitto's here, she's inches away from being exposed. Her camouflage suddenly feels paper-thin. It's essential to hold her nerve; she no longer resembles Craig Travis's daughter, and her fragile blonde act has worked perfectly so far. She follows the chef to a back room, which must have been a bar years ago, with faded wallpaper peeling from the walls. Two old-timers are sorting

341

through reports, but it's a slim fair-haired man who rises to his feet. He looks too young to be a danger until his keen gaze scans her face. She listens while Billy explains the situation. If she takes the position, she'll stay in the accommodation block behind the pub.

'Got any ID on you?' the policeman asks.

She pulls her fake driving licence from her bag, keeping her movements small and gentle, like she wouldn't hurt a fly. The officer scans the barcode with his phone, then hands it back. 'You spoke to my colleague Isla Tremayne last night, didn't you? She mentioned your name.'

'Are you going to lock me up?'

'You've got three points for speeding, but that's okay. There are no cars here. I hear you're an art student?'

'The debt terrifies me, to be honest. I'd rather find a job.'

'Looks like you've got one. Welcome to Bryher, Chloe.'

Ruby's answering smile is genuine, for once. She's found work and a room without trying, even though the island's locked down. Maybe the rest of her mission will be just as easy to execute. All she needs now is to track down DI Benesek Kitto and his girlfriend. She feels like punching the air when she goes back outside.

'You got the job, didn't you?' Joe grabs her waist and swings her in a circle.

'Stop it, Joe, you're making me dizzy.' Her feet land on solid earth, but it still feels like she's flying.

'I could take you back to St Mary's tonight, or you can stay at mine. The decision's yours.' He studies her face as if her choice will determine his future.

She makes the moment last before replying. 'I'll stay, but only because I'm doing a trial shift at the pub tomorrow.'

When he lifts her off her feet again, excitement rises in her throat as the stars overhead spin in a wild circle.

64

I hear raised voices as I approach the pub, with Shadow racing ahead and my middle-aged body-guard ten paces behind. Tiredness keeps me on high alert, until laughter rings out. Whoever's coming this way is having too much fun to pose a threat. When I look down from the path, a young couple are cross-ing the sand in the opposite direction. It's Sandra Trescothick's son, Joe, with a slim blonde girl. They're too busy flirting to notice me, giving me time to study her more closely; that face looks familiar, but I can't place her. The lad's body language proves that he's fallen head over heels. His arm is tight around her shoulders, like he wants to shield her from danger. The sight fills me with envy. I'd like to do the same for Nina, even though she's proved capable of looking after herself time and again.

I can tell something's changed when I take a short-cut through the kitchen at the Rock. Billy doesn't complain about Shadow's presence, for once, and even manages a smile for Kinsella. His relaxed mood shows in his choice of music; Eric Clapton is whispering about angels crying tears in heaven, with the chef humming the tune. I send Kinsella up to unpack before entering the incident room, where Eddie is the last man standing. He runs me through the evening's events. He's gone house-to-house collecting samples of people's handwriting, but so far nothing matches the letters received by the Porthcawl family. Liz Gannick has requested an early meeting tomorrow, even though there have been few developments, apart from Jamie calming down since his arrest. When Eddie took him food earlier, he seemed keen to clear his name, then arrange a proper funeral for his brother.

I'm bleary-eyed with tiredness when our talk ends. Eddie's informed me that our new recruits will be staying in rooms either side of mine, and he's taken the one opposite. I'm not certain that two middle-aged constables and an inexperienced sergeant could stop a hired killer, but professional courtesy makes me go upstairs to make sure our newcomers have everything they need. Ken Ellis is on the phone, but he gives me a cheery thumbs-up. I can hear him babbling at high volume as I return to the corridor, informing his wife that his trip so far has been restful, like a seaside holiday.

There's a different reaction when I knock on Kinsella's door, then enter without further announcement. The man is standing by his bed, the contents of a gun case spread across the duvet, bringing me to a sudden halt.

'What the fuck are you doing?'

He jerks his shoulders back, like a squaddie on parade. 'Checking my firearm, sir. It's a daily requirement.'

'Stand down, Constable. You're not in the army now.'

'Didn't you know they were sending an armed officer?'

'I haven't read all my emails.' My gaze drifts to the hardware laid out in neat piles. 'What are you carrying?'

'Standard Glock 17, nine-millimetre.'

'I haven't touched one for years.'

He jerks the barrel open to show it's empty, then passes me the weapon. A prickle of tension crosses the back of my hand like an electric current. The gun is lightweight, its metal casing cool against my hand. It brings back memories of my training at the police firing range in London, before my first undercover job, when I was still green. I understand the statistics better now. Armed officers often fare badly in conflict situations, their weapons causing violence to escalate.

'You'll carry it concealed?'

'Of course.'

'I hear you're on guard first tonight.'

'That's right, sir. Six hours on, six hours off.'

'I appreciate it.'

Kinsella stares back at me. 'The chief super never told us why you're under threat.'

'I helped put a gang leader away for life.'

'So it's a contract killer?'

'It looks that way.'

He gives a curt nod. 'I've done protection work before, sir. You can sleep easy with me in the corridor.'

It's a relief to find the bar empty when I go back downstairs, apart from Maggie, preparing for tomorrow's regulars. She looks so at home behind the bar it makes me regret leaving here at eighteen. I could have worked for her or Ray, but I was desperate to experience life on the mainland.

'Fancy a nightcap, sweetheart?' she asks.

'More than life itself.'

I sit on a bar stool watching Maggie pour brandy into shot glasses, while the past blurs my vision. I've visited this pub since I was old enough to walk, my godmother finding tasks for me and my brother to keep us entertained. The place hasn't changed much since then, apart from fresh paint and newly sanded floorboards to replace threadbare carpet. Maggie clinks glasses with me, watching my reactions.

'Those two don't look much like bodyguards, Ben.'

'They're the best the Cornish constabulary can offer. Want me to help you secure this place tonight?'

'Shut the windows, can you? I normally leave them ajar, to air the place, but not with all this going on.'

I circle the room, locking each window, while

Maggie locks the doors. Her expression's tense when she returns from securing the kitchen exit, like she can't quite believe her island is in turmoil.

'Tell me your theory about why Louis Hayle was killed, Maggie. You were here in the days when he ran his summer schools. I never liked the atmosphere up there; two days of being patronised was enough. I had my own adventures after that, thank God.'

My godmother blinks rapidly. 'The other kids seemed to love visiting his world.'

'Maybe he misused his power.'

'What do you mean?'

'Victims are often too afraid to talk. If anyone was abused, they'd still have reason to want him dead. Scars like that don't go away.' It crosses my mind that I'll need to speak to Maeve, to find out if Danny could have been harmed.

'I don't believe it. Louis mentored my son; he loved every minute.'

'Abusers target quieter, less confident kids. If anything happened, Hayle's the only one to blame, but it still doesn't explain why Hugh Porthcawl was murdered.'

She looks thoughtful. 'I wonder if Faith had a sense that something was wrong. It seemed odd that she rarely visited, then about twenty years ago, she started coming down here too, like she was keeping an eye on him. I thought he might be ill, but she might have been worried about his behaviour.'

'That could be it.'

'Ask the ferryman about Hayle. Arthur went down to the Solent, to crew in a big race for him, and he sailed his boat sometimes, years ago.'

'He's been tight-lipped, but I'll try again in the morning.'

I may be grasping at straws, trying to understand a man who exerted too much power, until time stole it away. The brandy tastes sour while the truth hovers out of reach. My godmother busies herself polishing glasses and emptying the dishwasher, until I say goodnight.

Shadow is behaving oddly when we climb the stairs to my room at the back of the pub. He normally loves his independence, roaming across the island, bothering people for food, yet he's spent the past two hours glued to my side, which always means trouble. When I open the window to let in fresh air he whines at high volume until it's shut again.

'Stop fussing, there's no one out there.'

I scan the empty beach, but there's only white sand, ribboned with seaweed, and moonlight beating down from a sky full of stars. It's the silence that bothers me. There's no wind, the tide's barely moving and it's too quiet. I send Nina a text, then go to bed, so tired that sleep arrives straight away.

Shadow wakes me a few hours later. He's whining again, and this time he's standing with his paws on the window ledge, like someone's climbed a ladder to peer through the glass. I drift back into sleep, but nightmares come thick and fast. I dream of falling head-first down a well, struggling to stay above water, even though it's a hopeless fight. The glass walls enclosing me are too sheer to climb.

65

Ruby is naked on Joe's bed, lying on top of the covers. She wasn't planning to sleep with him so soon, but it happened anyway. When she studies him again, his face is relaxed in sleep, one arm flung back against the pillows, the other around her waist. Joe is nothing like the boys she met in care; sex with them only deepened her loneliness. They would dress quickly afterwards, unwilling to meet her eye. Joe is the opposite. He touches her gently, like she's made of porcelain.

Joe pulls her closer, his body wrapped round hers. There's contentment on his face as starlight streams through the window, yet Ruby can't relax. She scans his studio again. The simple wooden building has its own shower and kitchenette. He seemed embarrassed by its compact size, but Ruby is envious. The place feels like a home. His sports trophies are lined up on a shelf, books stacked on the desk, his wetsuit hanging behind the door. There's an ache at the centre of her chest that doesn't make sense. Her dad always said you don't have to belong somewhere to be happy; all you need is to stay in control. It feels like power is slipping from her hands to Joe's, even though he's never even raised his voice.

He turns to her sleepily. 'How did you get that cut on your ribs?' The bandage has fallen away, leaving her wound exposed.

'You wouldn't believe me.'

'No?'

'Just a stupid accident.'

'You ought to get a doctor to look at it.'

'There's no need.'

'Are you in some kind of trouble?'

'Don't push me, please.'

'I'll keep you safe, Chloe. I've been waiting for someone like you.'

He touches her with the same gentleness as before. Ruby tries to pull away, but it's impossible. She's slipping into a world that doesn't make sense. They move together like dancers, blindfolded but keeping time. A different future opens in front of her when she rises over him, setting the pace. She doesn't even notice when her father's plan slips from her mind for the first time, as she lets herself fall.

66

Wednesday 7 May

When I step into the corridor, Ken Ellis is fast asleep in his chair, snoring loudly. Anyone could have snuck past him to pick the lock on my door last night. He only wakes up when I call his name three times: my new protection may have no effect at all, apart from slowing me down.

Liz Gannick is waiting when I go down for breakfast. She looks as sour as the black coffee she's drinking, her lips pursed into a thin line. The forensics specialist resembles a sulky teenager from a distance, but morning light filtering through the pub's windows exposes circles under her eyes and the depth of her frown.

'This case is a nightmare,' she says in a stage whisper. 'First the skeleton goes missing, then the bones show up in a recycling bin. Someone's baiting us, aren't they?'

'Or laying the guilt at Hayle's door. Did you find any prints?'

'That box was scoured with bleach, inside and out.'

'And the bones?'

'Soaked in ammonia too. Your man loves cleaning fluids.'

'Can you take another look at Louis Hayle's house? He may have let the killer in, but I want every window checked for forced entry, just in case.'

'I did a thorough job the first time.'

'Please, Liz. I'll buy you dinner at the hotel and a decent bottle of wine.'

Gannick snarls something toxic before clipping away, her crutches battering the wooden floor, but her act doesn't convince me. I worked out years ago that she only pretends to be angry; she relishes any task that could deliver a positive result.

The reality of my situation dawns when Eddie arrives. He's followed DCI Madron's safety advice to the letter, wearing a stab-proof vest, a taser and baton clipped to his belt. Our two new colleagues are dressed the same, making me stand out like a sore thumb in jeans, trainers and a black shirt. I accepted my post on the islands on the proviso that I continue working in plain clothes. It would feel strange to don police uniform after almost twenty years, but I'll have to wear a stab vest to honour my promise to Nina. Steve Pullen died from a knife wound to the heart, so it can't be avoided.

My decade of work as an undercover officer taught me how to read body language in order to identify potential threats. I can see that Eddie has formed a bond with Ken Ellis already, the two talkers in the group hunched over the breakfast menu discussing their options. Tom Kinsella remains separate at the end of the table. His face looks battle-worn in the morning light, bumpy with scar tissue. I can't tell whether his aloofness comes from his army days or is second nature. The man seems like a highly tuned instrument, vibrating to any change in frequency. I watch him reposition himself as the kitchen door swings open, his gaze shifting to the window, scanning the room for entry points.

'Ready to order, gents?' Billy looks happy for once in his life.

We all choose a full English, except Kinsella, who requests water, fruit and dry toast. He seems determined to treat his body like a temple, while the rest of us consume maximum fuel. The chef asks how we like our rooms, then announces that the weather forecast predicts a fine day ahead.

'Why are you so cheery, Billy?'

'I've got a new kitchen hand. Shy little thing, but she's got skills.'

'I've heard about her. Local, is she?'

'Joe Trescothick's girlfriend, Chloe Moore.' Eddie leans forward to catch my eye. 'I ran her through the system, boss, and so did Isla. She's an art student, but she told Billy she might quit her course if things go well here. Her record's clean as a whistle, apart from a speeding fine.'

'Chloe's doing a trial for me today, but she won't last five minutes if she's workshy,' Billy says.

'I bet she does well,' Eddie replies. 'She wants to be with her bloke.'

My deputy's world view is simpler than mine. A inevitably leads to B in Eddie's mind, but life has taught me that human psychology is more complex. I'm curious about why a student would abandon her course for a menial kitchen job, but it has no relevance to the case. Trescothick's girlfriend fades from my mind as I give my new team duties. I must have at least one guard with me to satisfy Madron's requirements, but at least they can lend a hand. Eddie will stay with Gannick in case the killer returns to Louis Hayle's house. My most pressing task is to find Danny Trenwith, who's still missing, and I need to follow Maggie's advice and speak to Arthur Penwithick again.

I'm putting final arrangements in place with the team when I realise that Shadow is missing. He must have slipped out unnoticed, which fills me with relief after his behaviour last night. I've got enough guards without dealing with a paranoid wolfdog. When I rise to my feet, though, he slinks out from under the table. I order him to stay behind as the four of us head for the door, but he's not playing ball. He gives a bark of protest, then exits the building a few millimetres behind me, determined to live up to his name.

67

Ruby feels relaxed when she wakes, with sunlight pouring through the open window. This place is far better than her gloomy home in London. It takes her a moment to remember that she's on Bryher, stretched out across Joe Trescothick's bed. She only comes round fully when she hears someone moving nearby, and panic floods her system. It was stupid of her to stray from the plan last night.

Joe is crouched over her belongings with her father's knife in his hands, a shocked look on his face. Ruby snaps at him before she can stop herself.

'What the fuck are you doing?'

'It fell out when I moved your jacket. That's one hell of a knife, Chloe. Why do you carry it?'

'Sentimental reasons.'

'Tell the truth.'

'I am. It belonged to my father.'

She's wide awake now, buzzing with adrenaline. It would be easy to grab the knife from Joe's hands and finish him before he asks another stupid question, but she needs him alive. He's too useful to let go.

'Something's scared you, Chloe. That wound on your ribs looks serious.'

'It's mending fine.' A plan to regain control is already forming in her mind.

Joe tests the knife's sharpness with his thumb. 'These kind of blades aren't even legal. You're scared someone'll find you here.'

'How did you know?'

'A girl like you wouldn't carry it unless you're afraid.' He kneels at her feet, leaving the knife on the floor. 'Tell me who hurt you, then we'll go to the police.'

'I can't.' She covers her face with her hands. 'It's my ex. He'd kill me for ratting on him. I'm so scared, Joe. He's bound to track me down.'

'Whatever happened, we'll fix it. Give me the whole story first.'

'I trusted him, like an idiot. We were together six months.'

Joe puts his arm round her shoulders. 'Keep going, it's okay.'

'He was so paranoid about other blokes looking at me, he started throwing his fists around. I ended it, but he broke into my flat with a knife. He's crazy, Joe. If he comes here, he'll kill me for leaving him, and hurt you too.'

'That explains why you ran away.'

Ruby stares down at her clasped hands. 'Why didn't I see he was a psycho?'

'You're trusting, that's why. I bet you only see the good in people. Does your father know about it?'

'Dad's sick in hospital; it's keeping us apart. That's the worst thing, Joe. He's all I've got. I miss him so much.'

'We're together now, Chloe, you're not alone.'

He pulls her into his arms, like he's soothing a child. Ruby finds it easy to release more tears. She only has to remember her dad, sick and alone as death approaches. A seed of guilt has been planted in her mind too, because Joe has shown her nothing but kindness.

'You have to promise me something, please.'

'I'll do my best.'

'Take me to the mainland on your boat if things get bad. Will you do it, the minute I ask?'

'Of course, if it keeps you safe.'

She touches his face, grateful that he's such a willing stepping stone. Joe finding the knife may turn out to be positive; it's given her a guaranteed escape route from the islands. She might have to kill him in the end, but with luck that won't be necessary. A new emotion is growing inside her chest. It's so unfamiliar, she can't even give it a name.

68

I'm beginning to fear the worst about Danny Trenwith. We've searched the whole island, without a sighting. It's possible he killed his old mentor, then returned to the cliff and threw himself off, but if that's what happened, I need to know why.

Kinsella maintains a discreet distance as I head back to Church Quay. He seems glad to stay in the background; if he's concerned about his latest assignment, there's no outward sign. He keeps his gaze fixed on me like I might vanish in a blink. I'm keen to speak to the ferryman again. Plenty of the island's elders may have suspected Louis Hayle of wrongdoing but feared his power too much to speak out. Arthur Penwithick is likely to remain silent, but I'm hoping to be proved wrong. He knew Hayle well enough to act as his crewman, so the man must have trusted him.

The ferryman is pouring oil into his boat's engine when we reach the quay, even though the lockdown is still in place. He's wearing the dark blue sailor's cap he rarely takes off, and gives me a buck-toothed smile, which fades when he spots my companion. Arthur's shyness is so deep the presence of a stranger is a disadvantage, but I have to find out what he knows. A line of sweat erupts on his upper lip when I request another chat. Shadow helps out by approaching to lick his hand; my dog often eases social situations, provided he behaves.

Arthur and I sit on a bench overlooking the jetty, with Shadow curled at our feet. I can see Kinsella waiting by the boatyard's entrance from the corner of my eye.

'You were on good terms with Louis Hayle, Arthur. Is that right?'

'I was his employee.' He shifts awkwardly on his seat. 'I sailed his boat round the islands at the weekends, years ago.'

'Didn't you crew his racing yacht as well?'

'One time, that's all.'

'I need to know more about him.'

The man's shoulders jerk with tension. 'My memory's bad.'

'Can we start with how he treated you?'

'Hayle paid decent wages, that's all I cared about.'

'He could be flash with his money, to impress the youngsters, I've heard.'

'Most admired him anyway; they didn't need bribes.' The ferryman gazes down at his bitten nails.

'How come you stopped working for him, if the pay was good?'

'The ferry's my living. He wanted me to drop everything whenever he snapped his fingers.'

'Tell me more about the children.'

Penwithick's face is flushed, his voice quiet. 'Those kids were blinded by all that glitter.'

'Why did you resign, exactly?'

'Hayle was a bloody liar, that's why.' His gaze finally meets mine, his small eyes hard with anger. 'Someone should have finished him years ago.'

He suddenly jumps to his feet and marches back up the jetty, leaving me stunned. Arthur never speaks ill of anyone, mildness engrained in his DNA. Whatever he knows about Louis Hayle must have left a scar. It's obvious he wants to be left alone, but finding the truth matters more than reviving painful memories.

Penwithick doesn't reply when I knock on his front door, but I go in anyway. His living room is in semi-darkness, despite the brightness outside, the curtains closed. The air smells of mildew and stale coffee. The place has gone unchanged since his parents died, with lace doilies on the table, dark wooden furniture, and damp blossoming on the ceiling. Arthur is in the kitchen, with shoulders hunched and eyes closed, like he's fighting to stay calm.

'Tell me the truth, Arthur. It'll be a relief. You've been carrying it too long.'

'He made me keep his secret.'

'Did Hayle threaten you?'

'That man said he'd break my business. I still refused to work for him again.'

'He's gone now. You're perfectly safe.'

'I didn't care what he told anyone, it was the kid I wanted to help. He made me promise not to say anything to anyone, so I kept my word.' He drags in a deep breath. 'Hayle picked out the quiet ones; they would have done anything for him, if he snapped his fingers.'

'Keep going, please, I need all the details.'

The ferryman's arms are wrapped around his chest, like he's holding himself together. 'Hayle asked me to sail his boat one summer day so he could teach a lad to navigate. I heard the boy cry out below decks, so I ran down. Hayle had him on a bed, in the cabin ...' His voice peters into silence.

'Who was it?'

'The lad begged me to keep quiet, to protect his family.'

'Give me his name, please, or I'll have to arrest you for obstruction. You should have told me all this before.' I feel like shaking the information out of him, but keep my hands clenched at my sides. I'm almost certain the child was Danny Trenwith. 'Say his name, Arthur.'

'Nathan Kernow,' he blurts out. 'He'd just finished at primary school. I pulled that monster off him, but the lad was sobbing. His father had only died a few months before. He came to see me that evening. He knew the truth would break his mother, so he begged me not to report it. How could I refuse?'

I mumble my thanks as the facts register. It explains why Kernow has retreated into fantasy games and religion, his trauma increased by grief for his dad. I can see why he prefers house plants to people. But it doesn't mean that he caused his abuser's death, unless I find absolute proof.

69

Ruby thinks of Joe while she prepares salad at the Rock. She had to think fast to avoid exposure, but it helps that he believes she's vulnerable. Joe's kindness can be included in her plan. Her hands fly as she washes a mound of lettuce then moves on to scrubbing new potatoes; it's important she passes her trial. Billy's stereo is playing a random selection of music, from rock and roll to jazz. Most of the songs are unfamiliar, but she sings along to 'That Old Devil Called Love'. When she looks up, Billy's grinning.

'You can carry a tune. Ever done karaoke, Chloe?'

'I could never stand up in front of a crowd.'

'Why not? You sound like Amy Winehouse.'

'I prefer peeling spuds with you.'

'Thank God. The last lad was a proper misery-guts.'

'I like keeping busy.'

'We'll get along famously then, won't we?'

Billy shunts more vegetables her way, then carries on stirring a vat of pasta sauce, the smells of garlic and oregano filling the air. Ruby lets her gaze stray to the window. Tresco's outline keeps changing with the shifting light; the island's hills waver, then turn solid again. She's never seen anywhere so beautiful. The castle perched high above the beach makes the scene like a fairy-tale illustration, full of mystery. There's no sign of Joe's boat now that he's gone to work. He could be miles away, ferrying birdwatchers out to Gweal or Samson, unaware of what lies ahead.

Ruby's still working hard when she hears footsteps. There's no time to catch her breath before the grey dog that barked at her yesterday bounds through the fire doors. The creature approaches her workstation, growling and baring its teeth. She flinches but stands her ground. If she was alone, she'd slit the creature's throat without hesitation, then leave its body on the beach for birds to pick over.

'Shadow won't bite you, love,' Billy says. 'No need to be scared.'

Ben Kitto appears on the threshold before she can reply. He's so tall and broad, his form blocks out the light, but she keeps her chin up, determined not to look away. That would only draw his attention, and she knows how observant he is. He hasn't changed much since the days when he exploited her father's trust. He's still got handsome features, but there are threads of grey in his black hair now, his build like a heavyweight boxer. He'll be hard to kill unless she catches him unawares. His green-eyed gaze is strong enough to burn through her camouflage.

'You must be the mysterious Chloe,' he says. 'Poor you, working for Billy. That can't be easy.'

'It's just a trial. I may not get the job.'

'You're doing fine so far,' says Billy.

'Good luck putting up with his moods,' Kitto says.

'His music's the only problem; I prefer rap.'

'You'll have to live with it, sweetheart,' Billy mutters. 'My kitchen, my tunes.'

Kitto looks at her again. 'We've met before, haven't we? Your face is familiar.'

Her heart rate quickens. 'I'd remember being arrested by a giant like you. This is my first time in Scilly, and I love it already. I can imagine settling here for good.'

He finally cracks a smile as two more men appear, the middle-aged cops in plain clothes that she saw last night. The bodyguards will be easy to defeat, but she's glad when the trio finally go to their base room.

Ruby doesn't blink when Billy asks her to make coffee and carry it through on a tray. Playing the role of Kitto's server will keep her close until his guard drops. If she can build his trust, she'll be invisible when the right moment comes.

70

Billy's assistant appears with coffee and sandwiches, blushing when she sets down the tray. I've got a good memory for faces, but with so many other distractions, her familiarity could just be my imagination playing tricks. My thoughts are pulling in three directions at once. Nina is top of my list, followed by Hayle's murder. I'm trying not to consider the hired killer who's heading my way, but the threat stays at the back of my mind.

I wait until Chloe leaves the room before explaining what I've learnt: how Arthur Penwithick witnessed Hayle's attack on Nathan Kernow as a child. There's a bemused look on Ken Ellis's face when I explain that he may have harmed other kids too, under the guise of mentorship. Tom Kinsella seems to be taking events in his stride, proving that he's cool under pressure.

Eddie is the first to speak after my update. 'Most people saw Hayle as a force for good, boss. No one's claimed he was a predator until now.'

'That's how it works, isn't it? High-profile abusers create a smokescreen of respectability, then choose their victims. Confident kids never get picked in case they squeal. We still need to find out why Hayle died, whatever his crimes, but this is compelling as a motive. Ray sensed there was something sinister behind Hayle's regime too.'

'Sounds like the bloke had it coming,' Gannick mutters, but her professionalism soon returns. 'There's no sign of forced entry on the external doors and windows of his house. I've lifted fingerprints from internal surfaces too, but they're all his so far. The killer did a tidy job cleaning up after themselves.'

'We're looking for someone meticulous then. The only reason we know the skeleton was Hugh Porthcawl is because you found a minute bone fragment. They must have gone over the burial site with a toothcomb. But it's possible Louis Hayle killed him, isn't it? The lad had just reached adulthood, and might have been a victim as a child. If he threatened to tell the authorities, Hayle's world would have crumbled.'

'Jamie's complaining about being locked up, boss,' Eddie says.

'We can keep him until tomorrow morning. I need to be sure he's innocent, before releasing him.'

'It wasn't Nathan Kernow who killed Hayle. I've checked alibis for the time of death, and his is cast-iron. He was helping old Mrs Wood in the Town; he rigged up an outdoor light, mowed her lawn, then stayed for dinner. Apparently he's given her loads of support since her husband died.'

The news interests me. Kernow endured more trauma than any child should face, yet he's made a life for himself here. Why would he return to a place where his abuser lived in a hilltop mansion, staring down at the rest of us like a king? Shame or embarrassment about the attacks, as well as horrifying memories, might have silenced other victims too.

'We can work out the exact timescale. Nathan Kernow is forty now, which means that Hayle was abusing kids twenty-nine years ago. Maggie says his wife started accompanying him on his trips here about twenty years ago. Eddie, can you find out the names and ages of all the kids and teenagers on the island during that nine-year window? One of his victims may have taken revenge at last. We also have to find Danny Trenwith. Can you get a party of volunteers together to scour the island again?'

When I cast my gaze round the room, my team are reacting differently to the news that Hayle was a child abuser. The expression on Liz Gannick's face is the most memorable. Her scowl has drawn a hard vertical line between her eyebrows that looks too deep ever to be erased.

I let everyone return to their tasks after the meeting then check my phone messages. The first is from my old boss in London. Local police and the murder squad have had no luck yet in finding out who killed Annie

Hardwick. Commander Goldman sounds convinced that the killer will have got here before the ferry's last crossing.

'Stay safe, Kitto. Take every imaginable precaution,' she says. Her message ends abruptly, leaving nothing behind except white noise.

71

Ruby enjoys the lunchtime rush. The Rock is different to the café in London, where she kept her head down, to avoid attention. Billy makes her feel welcome. He shows her how to pan-fry freshly caught fish, offering praise when she masters a new skill. His personality reminds her of her dad; she can't help warming to him.

'You're a natural, Chloe. Maybe you should take over? I'll do the prepping, you can run the show.'

'In a million years,' she says, laughing.

'You've passed the trial with flying colours.' Billy's standing by the window, wiping his hands on a kitchen towel. 'Here's lover boy, come to distract you.'

When Ruby sees Joe carrying her rucksack, her face breaks into a grin.

'The lad's nuts about you. Don't hurt him, will you?'

'Do I look like a heartbreaker, Billy?'

'No, but the sweet ones are always the worst. Now scarper and get your room sorted. Mind you're back here by six.'

'I won't let you down.'

She can't explain why a rush of excitement hits her when she leaves the pub. The feeling is deeper than gratitude that Joe has carried out his promise to collect her things from the hotel on St Mary's. It's the first time a man has treated her so kindly since her dad. They're holding hands when they climb the outdoor stairs to the accommodation block behind the pub. The air in the corridor smells stale, and the carpet is covered in ugly red swirls, but Ruby's new room is spacious, with a modern en suite. The sea view is its best feature, the water littered with distant islands as the sun beats down.

'This is perfect,' she says.

'You'll be safe on Bryher, I promise.' Joe puts his arm round her shoulders.

'I hope you're right. I feel at home here already.'

'Has Billy introduced you to some of the locals?'

She nods. 'Maggie's lovely, and so's Ben Kitto, with his scary wolfdog.'

'Shadow's fine once he knows you. Ben's about to become a dad. I heard his girlfriend's in Penzance hospital.'

Ruby doesn't reply, her thoughts clouded by the news that Kitto's girlfriend is out of reach on the mainland. She'll have to travel there to finish her, and their baby too. The gesture would please her father, but it brings her little genuine comfort. She has no regrets about taking the lives of adults that caused his downfall, but a newborn child will be a harder matter.

'It doesn't feel right.' The words slip from her mouth in a whisper.

'How do you mean?'

373

She pushes the thought aside. 'I was thinking about you and me. I've never been great at relationships, Joe, and my last was a disaster. I wasn't planning on meeting anyone here.'

'Me neither, but I got goosebumps when I saw you on the ferry.'

'I struggle to trust people. Don't let me down, will you?'

'Never.'

His gaze is steady when he makes his promise. Ruby lets a few seconds pass before reaching up to kiss him, controlling the situation again, then turning away. She feels certain he'll comply with every request if she keeps him sweet. She unpacks her few possessions, then follows him back out into the sunshine.

72

Eddie is out leading a search party for Danny Trenwith when Nathan Kernow arrives. The beauty of island life is that no one is ever far away when you need them. The games designer seems wary. His face is deadpan, and his second-hand clothes appear to have time-travelled from the summer of love; he's wearing a faded yellow T-shirt, flared jeans, and Birkenstocks. His image seems to fluctuate constantly, his identity never fixed.

'Come in, Nathan, thanks for being so prompt.'

I nod at my bodyguards to leave us alone, but feel certain Tom Kinsella will remain outside, watching for intruders with his gun at hand. Shadow raises his head to growl at Kernow until I give him a firm rebuke.

'Sorry about that, his manners are lousy.'

Kernow gives me a nervous smile. 'I left Elsa at home, just in case.'

Words fail me when he takes a seat. There's no easy way to ask an abuse survivor about the past, but his information might unveil Louis Hayle's killer.

'I've got to ask you about a delicate subject, I'm afraid. I had a conversation with Arthur Penwithick.' I can see the penny dropping already, his expression startled. 'He told me about Louis Hayle hurting you.'

'Arthur kept quiet for decades. I suppose I should be grateful.'

'I know you weren't involved in Hayle's murder, but maybe you heard about other victims with reason to harm him.'

Kernow looks down at his hands. 'Louis said I was the only one. He told me I'd brought it on myself. If there are other survivors, I bet they got the same message.'

'You never told anyone?'

'I felt complicit, I suppose. Louis showered me with attention after Dad died. Mum was thrilled; she thought I needed a male role model.'

'I'm sorry, Nathan.'

'My beliefs help me keep going. Humanity's screwed up, but at least nature's pure.'

'Did you ever confront him?'

'Of course.' His gaze is suddenly hot enough to burn. 'I walked up to his house days after it happened and made him promise to pay my boarding school fees or I'd tell my mother and the police.'

'That was brave, for such a young boy. I thought your relatives covered the cost?'

He gives a slow laugh. 'None of them had money. Louis agreed immediately, and Mum was overjoyed.

She thought it would unlock a brilliant future for me, but all I wanted was to escape from Bryher.'

'Was it hard coming back?'

'Easier than I expected. The power balance had shifted by then; Louis knew I could send him to prison, but my mental health mattered more than revenge. I couldn't face a trial. They'd have questioned me about every violation, and the rape itself.'

'You preferred to keep the anger inside?'

'I had counselling in the States to help me release it. Rage just keeps the wound open; it's best to let it go.'

'There's someone on the island who can't move on, Nathan. Did any other kids spend a lot of time with Hayle?'

'Christian Boston was another favourite. Maybe he got the same treatment.'

I think of Lucy's much-loved brother, dying at fifty from a sudden heart attack. It seems tragic that he may have carried Hayle's abuse to the grave.

'Anyone else?'

'You must remember how it worked, Ben. Louis held an open house every Saturday, the summer I turned eleven. He preferred boys, but he focused on a few girls too, like Penny Cadgwith and Maeve Trenwith.'

'That's useful, thanks.'

'I don't remember anyone else.'

'Is this linked to your vigil on Badplace Hill?'

Emotions flow across Kernow's face. 'Hayle

threatened to kill me if I told anyone. It terrified me, because it felt like more than an idle threat. I thought that skeleton might have been another of his victims.'

'You think he killed Hugh Porthcawl?'

'He would have done anything to stay out of jail.'

Hayle's paranoid world is starting to make sense. I'm still amazed that Kernow lived with such a heavy secret, but I might have done the same, after the worst type of violation.

'Thanks for being so honest,' I say, rising to my feet.

My head is still pulsing with information when Kernow leaves, so I step outside with Shadow at my heels, Kinsella and Ellis keeping their distance. Danny Trenwith may have experienced the same abuse as Nathan, the secret breaking him at last. Coming home to Bryher might have triggered his childhood pain.

The scene ahead is far more innocent when I look out at the beach. Two kids are frolicking in the sea, the girl in a red bathing suit, the boy in dark blue shorts. When I look closer, I see that they're actually young adults. It's Joe Trescothick and his girlfriend; he keeps dragging her under the calm water, the girl laughing and splashing him when she resurfaces. It helps to put Kernow's terrible experience in perspective: island life is continuing as normal, with young lovers having fun. They're oblivious to my presence a hundred metres away, until Shadow streaks past me, barking at full volume. My loudest whistle brings him back a minute later, with his tail between his legs.

'One more howl and you're going home.'

He gazes up at me, whining, his pale blue eyes impossible to read.

73

Ruby and Joe are back in her room after their swim. They're lying on the single bed, her skin fizzing with pleasure. She's forgotten about duty for the time being, but Joe's eyes are full of questions.

'What was your childhood like?'

'Perfect till I hit thirteen. How about you?'

'My parents divorced when I was six, but Mum's been great. I don't see much of my father. He's a teacher, on the mainland, with a new family.'

'But it must have been peaceful growing up here.'

'Those defences of yours are still way high, aren't they?'

'What do you want to know?'

'Tell me about your dad. He matters to you big time, doesn't he?'

'He was my world as a kid. I'd love to be with him now.'

'I'll go with you, if it helps.'

She gives him a smile of gratitude. 'Thanks, but I have to stay here for now. I think my ex is keeping an eye on the hospital.'

'Is your dad very ill?'

'It's stage four pancreatic cancer. I hate seeing him in pain.' She shuts her eyes, real emotions flooding her mind for once. Joe makes a hushing sound as she cries on his shoulder.

'It's okay, Chloe,' he whispers. 'I'll help you, I promise.'

'I may have to drop everything to go to him.'

'We can take the boat, I promise.' He kisses her forehead. 'I'd better go and tell Mum about you, before someone else does. Be warned, she'll want to meet you soon. I'll be back tonight, okay?'

He gives her a long kiss before leaving. Ruby can hear her dad's voice, reminding her that emotional ties only cause trouble, but she's dangerously close to riding that roller coaster for the first time. It's a relief when Joe's gone, even though she misses him straight after the door closes.

She checks for news of her father on her phone, but there's no signal. The vital connection between them has been severed like an umbilical cord. Panic rises in her throat, but she forces it back under control. Her happiness is already drifting away, like steam evaporating.

74

It's 6 p.m. when I get back to the pub. I'm still buzzing with nervous energy from so many revelations, but my trio of security guards look tired. Shadow curls up in the corner to sleep, and Ken Ellis retreats upstairs with a migraine, leaving Tom Kinsella in the corner. There's something odd about his unblinking stare, making me glad we're on the same side. My day has been so busy, I've almost forgotten the terrible deaths of my old colleagues, but maybe that's just as well. I can't afford distractions with so much work to complete.

Eddie is alone in the incident room, after having no luck finding Danny Trenwith. There are several frantic messages from Maeve on my phone, but when I call to ask for information about Danny's relationship with Hayle, she doesn't pick up. I've got a feeling she's outside, scouring the island for signs of her husband's presence. The worst outcome would be a phone call from the coastguard reporting his body washed up on the shore. I can tell my deputy's nerves are paying the price for our lack of progress, his movements jittery as I update him on Nathan Kernow's revelation. He looks frustrated when I remind him that Kernow can't have killed his abuser; his alibi is watertight.

'Two people were spotted on Badplace Hill yesterday afternoon, boss. Lucy Boston and Penny Cadgwith. They both took walks there alone, between four and six p.m. I've got no other sightings.'

'Thanks for checking, we need to keep a close eye on both women. It's possible they were abused by Hayle too. What's Liz doing now?'

'Dusting surfaces at Hayle's place.'

'Alone?'

'Maggie's keeping a lookout.'

'Good. I don't want anyone left isolated till the killer's found. Let's go through the evidence again.'

My deputy collects a mound of paper covered in Post-it notes. He likes to document every detail, while I file a single daily report in the operations tracker, our approaches complementing each other well. Three days have passed since Jamie Porthcawl exposed his brother's skeleton on Badplace Hill. There's no categorical proof that Louis Hayle killed the eighteen-year-old. All we know for certain is that someone tried to frame my uncle. Nathan Kernow's words make me believe that Hayle may have killed Porthcawl to avoid facing justice, if the lad threatened to blow the whistle. A man with an ego that size couldn't have coped with public hatred and a long jail sentence, after so much adulation.

'Hayle's finances are complicated,' Eddie says.

'How come?'

'He didn't go broke in 2008, like people say. He piled huge sums into a business called New Venture.' Eddie peers at a computer printout. 'He shelled out millions, starting twenty years ago. The holdings were on the Isle of Man.'

'Let me see.'

The figures prove that Hayle slowly emptied his wealth into New Venture, leaving less than fifty thousand in his deposit account. 'Maybe it was a tax scam.'

'But where did it go? New Venture was registered with Companies House, but it's got no media presence at all. That money's vanished into thin air.'

'It's out of character for Hayle to make a professional mistake. He kept tight control of everything he touched. If it was him who attacked Porthcawl, he even buried his body close to home, to keep an eye on it. That explains why he fought so hard to stop the activities centre being built, and why he wanted people to believe the bones were ancient.'

My phone buzzes on the table, the message filling me with relief. 'Danny Trenwith's safe. Maeve says he came home exhausted; she's made him go to bed.'

'Do you think *he* killed Hayle, boss?'

'He could be another victim, but that doesn't make him a killer. Someone removed those bones from the ground with care. Maybe it was Hayle himself, but why keep them, when he could have chucked them in the sea?'

'It was a professional job, that's for sure.'

Eddie is already leafing through documents, but his words have sparked a fresh idea. Only one person on Bryher could have removed the bones with such skill, yet her background is beyond reproach. It may be a wild goose chase, but I have to find out.

'I'm going to see Penny Cadgwith. Stay here, Eddie. I won't be long.'

He's too busy figuring out how Louis Hayle lost his money to look up, but my two remaining guards, canine and human, won't leave me alone. Shadow noses out of the door once it opens, with Kinsella close behind.

Dusk has fallen already. Tresco's smooth curves look like a woman dressed in green, lying supine, waiting for nightfall. The water is already shiny with starlight. My gaze scans the beach, but Bryher's minute scale is deceiving. There are dozens of caves, barns and coves where a killer could hide.

75

Ruby is washing strawberries as night falls, the kitchen windows misted with steam. Billy is too busy for conversation as he prepares fish stew with saffron, the pungent odour making her hungry. His stereo is tuned to local radio, which plays the shipping news and weather forecasts interspersed with old pop songs. She lets herself daydream as she prepares desserts.

What if she allowed the last man on her dad's list to survive? Kitto's child could grow up with two parents, and she could stay on Bryher with Joe. Billy would teach her to cook every dish in his repertoire, and the loneliness of her childhood might be replaced by friendships. She remembers Denny Lang telling her to make a fresh start; his words infuriated her at the time, but perhaps the old bastard was right. She's never done anything for herself alone; Bryher could give her the type of freedom she dreamed of as a child.

She jerks out of her reverie when Billy calls her name.

'How are you at boning fish?'

'Not too bad.'

'There's some cod in the fridge. Can you prep it for me?'

'Will you let me make a call first?'

He rolls his eyes. 'Not lover boy again.'

'I need to check my dad's okay. He's not been well.'

'Okay, love. The fish'll still be there you get back.'

Ruby rinses her hands, then slips outside. She stands with her back to the wall, keeping the sea in view. There's no signal at first, but the internet finally delivers a horrifying message: Craig Travis died today, bringing peace to his victims' families, according to the headlines.

She wants to scream, but bites her lip instead, trying to quell her grief. It feels impossible to keep up her pretence. If she stays outside too long, Billy will find her crying and she'll have to find an excuse. Ruby screws her eyes shut. It takes effort to summon the self-discipline her father instilled in her from the start. Personal happiness is irrelevant now; her dad deserves a final tribute. She must kill the last man on his list, then hunt his girlfriend down.

76

Shadow dashes ahead, chasing my torch beam, loving his night-time adventure. Tom Kinsella is far more subdued. His silence feels oppressive until I ask how he's adapted to the change from army to police duties.

'It wasn't my first choice,' he says, keeping his eyes on the path. 'But it beats sitting at home drinking all day.'

'Did you see much active service?'

'Fourteen years, but EOD isn't always front-line.'

'How do you mean?'

'We cleared old battlegrounds. Landmines, chemical devices, and dirty bombs full of shrapnel. It's easy to get hurt in that environment.'

'Tread on a bomb, you mean?'

'We'd emptied a whole field the day I got hurt. My commanding officer tripped and fell. If he'd stayed on his feet, it would have been a different story, but the device killed him instantly. The fallout hit me and two colleagues. My chest and torso took the worst of it, plus a few facial wounds, but I was lucky. One of the guys was blinded.' Kinsella comes to a sudden halt, then listens to the night air, his voice lowering. 'Someone's following us, sir. Take cover down here.'

He shunts me off the path, dropping behind some bushes. His hearing must be sharper than mine. A minute passes before footsteps, light and rapid, tap along the path. Kinsella's face looks white in the moonlight, his expression fixed as he clutches his gun. I only draw breath again when I spot Bella Porthcawl hurrying along, her face solemn. She's sure-footed despite the dark, relying on her knowledge of the landscape and the moon's glitter to find her way home.

There's no embarrassment on Kinsella's face as we rise to our feet, his gun back in its holster, but I can see he's unsettled. I let the last five minutes of our journey pass in silence, instead of forcing conversation. As we follow the path down to Penny Cadgwith's home by the beach, it's so quiet I can hear her bees collecting pollen, even though the air's cooling.

'Wait here, please, Kinsella. I won't be long.'

He comes to a halt, shoulders back like a sentinel, but Shadow stays at my heels as I approach the back door. No one bothers to pull their curtains in Scilly during the warmest months of the year, with few neighbours around to play peeping Tom. I can see directly into Penny's kitchen. She's standing by the table, rooted to the spot, her fingers pressed against her lips. I wait for a moment, but her posture doesn't change. When I tap on the door, she jumps out of her skin.

'Sorry to startle you, Penny. You looked deep in thought.'

Her eyes are puffy with tears. 'Bella's just given me the news.'

'She told you about Hugh Porthcawl?'

Penny manages a smile. 'Maybe his promises were genuine after all. I feel bad for doubting him.'

'Did you guess it was him on Badplace Hill? Is that why you were so upset at seeing the skeleton?'

'I tried to ignore my doubts. He was so young, Ben. We talked about all the adventures we'd have together, but then I saw those letters sent from abroad years ago. The handwriting looked different, but his mum was convinced they were from him. It hurt to believe he'd walked away.'

'It must have broken your heart when he vanished.'

She looks away. 'I didn't tell the whole truth about never hearing from him again.'

'You got something in the post?'

'The envelope was typewritten, franked in America, six months after he'd gone. It was the words of a song we both loved, after seeing a live performance in Penzance.'

'Do you still have it?'

She hands me a worn envelope from the table. I can see it's been read often, the page inside refolded carefully every time. It contains the typed words to 'Elusive', by Scott Matthews, and I suppress a smile. Matthews is one of my favourites too. The song

390

describes the pleasure and pain of young love in a few poetic words.

'How did you feel getting this, Penny?'

'Devastated, but it seemed like an apology of sorts.'

'Who else knew that you and Hugh liked Scott Matthews?'

'All my friends and family.'

'What about Louis Hayle?'

She looks uncomfortable. 'Hugh was so close to him, maybe he mentioned it.'

'It's time to level with me, Penny. There's no shame in admitting the truth.'

'I don't understand, Ben. I've never lied to you.' Her voice has risen by half an octave, high and breathless. 'Things improved after the letter came. I was able to move on, but it affected my choice of career. I wanted to reunite victims' families with their loved ones, because I knew how much separation hurt.'

'Do you know why Hugh spent time with Louis Hayle?'

'Louis was successful, rich and charismatic. We were just kids, looking for role models.'

'Hayle sexually abused one of his protégés. I'm certain there were more.'

My words make her flinch. 'Not me, thank God, but I've wondered over the years. There was something predatory about him. The vulnerable ones got most of his time; he called it individual coaching.' Her gaze is fixed on the blank wall, picturing things I can't see.

'If Hugh found out there was abuse, he'd have challenged Louis straight away. He hated cruelty more than anything.'

'I think he faced him down, on Badplace Hill. It may have cost him his life.'

Tears well in her eyes. 'That monster got what he deserved then, didn't he?'

'I have to ask this, Penny. Did you take the bones from Badplace Hill and leave them at Hayle's house?'

'Of course not. Why would I?' The astonishment on her face would be hard to fake.

'They were placed in a box by his back door.'

'Someone wanted him to suffer for his past,' she says quietly.

'Another of his victims, maybe?'

'Vulnerable kids become vulnerable adults, Ben. They wouldn't have the strength to face him down.'

'Some have got plenty of guts, believe me.' I'm thinking of Nathan Kernow. At eleven he was brave enough to plan his escape route and force his rapist to make amends.

Penny's hands are shaking, even though she's one of the toughest people on Bryher. I know she's got the technical expertise to remove Hugh Porthcawl's bones from the crime scene, without leaving evidence, yet her reaction seems genuine. Who else could have done such a thorough job of removing a skeleton from a haunted piece of land?

77

Ruby completes her duties on autopilot, hardly looking up as the last dinner orders arrive. Billy seems concerned, but she hates sympathy.

'Are you okay, Chloe? You've gone quiet on me.'

'It was a tough phone call, that's all.'

'Your old man's in a bad way?'

'Cancer's a cruel illness, Billy.'

The chef pats her shoulder. 'Go outside for a bit, love. Breathe some sea air.'

'I'm better off keeping busy.'

'Fair enough, but take breaks whenever.'

'Thanks, Billy. I appreciate it.'

The man's kindness lingers as Ruby prepares ice cream sundaes. She hasn't eaten since lunch, but the sight of so much food makes her nauseous. Half an hour passes before she looks out of the window again. Kitto is returning with one of his guards, and her grief turns to anger. That man turned her dad's last years into a living hell; he deserves the worst death imaginable. She forces herself to concentrate, clearing plates and stacking the dishwasher, until Billy calls to her.

'Can you carry this tray to the back bar for me, love?'

It's loaded with cheese, ham and French bread, plus a flask of coffee. Kitto appears when she taps on the door. The man towers over her, his hulking frame blocking the opening. Ruby wishes she'd brought her knife, to finish him now, yet he seems oblivious. Only his dog has guessed her true motives. It bares its teeth again, issuing a low growl.

'Behave,' Kitto hisses at the creature, then leans down to take the tray. 'Thanks, Chloe. That's just what we need.'

The door clicks shut in her face, filling her with frustration. She was hoping to overhear details, but the men are talking so quietly she can't make out a single word.

78

The girl's expression lingers in my mind. She looked so young and innocent earlier, playing on the beach, but up close her face is troubled. I don't know why that bothers me. Plenty of people come to Scilly for a new life, far from the mainland, but the past can be hard to shake off. She's still in my head while Eddie grabs a sandwich from the tray.

'Food at last, boss. I'm starving.' My deputy has been busy, scribbling reams of notes on his A4 pad.

I watch Tom Kinsella loading his black coffee with sugar and feel a twinge of relief. Perhaps my chaperone is human after all.

'At least we've learned the truth about Louis Hayle. He left at least one victim and a witness too scared to talk, until his death. There could be others on Bryher who are too afraid to blow the whistle even now he's dead. They might be unwilling to rake up the past.' I glance at my phone, but no new messages have arrived. 'Did you find anything else on New Venture, Eddie?'

'The company shifted their account to New York, but it closed years ago. I can't see who withdrew Hayle's money.'

'It could have been a tax fiddle he set up. He travelled the world when his company was at its height. Maybe he copied a sample of Hugh Porthcawl's handwriting to fake those letters home to his family then.'

'That doesn't explain where his money went. The only thing I found is New Venture's company logo.' He points at the letters NV in Gothic script on his computer. It looks familiar, but I can't place it. 'The financial records have been wiped away.'

'Hayle was great at sweeping things under the carpet.'

'It's unbelievable,' Eddie says. 'If he abused more than one kid, surely someone would have guessed?'

'No one expects a Jimmy Savile in such a tiny community. They thought he was a hero.'

'The fucking scumbag,' Kinsella mutters.

My bodyguard appears to be settling in nicely, swearing and polluting his system with caffeine, like the rest of us. When I glance at Eddie again, his fresh-faced choirboy image has taken a pounding. He looks his age for once, his eyes red from screen-gazing.

'Go to bed, Eddie. You've done twelve hours straight.'

He objects, but not for long, before heading for his room.

'And you, Kinsella. I need to check one more thing before I hit the sack.'

'I'll stay, thanks,' he insists. 'I'm on guard duty till morning. Ken's migraine's knocked him out.'

'You can't skip a whole night's sleep.'

'Watch me. I just loaded up on caffeine and carbs.'

'No one's going to storm the building tonight.'

'Better safe than sorry.' His cool stare carries a warning. I suspect he'd happily sit by my door all week to prevent any more bloodshed; he's seen enough human suffering to know that mistakes can be fatal.

I'd like to call Nina in private, but he'd only follow me outside. Her voice sounds tired but calm as she lets slip that the consultant's keeping an eye on her blood pressure, which rose again today. If it goes any higher, they'll induce her before the due date. I promise again to be at her side for the birth.

Anger wells up inside me when I drop my phone back into my pocket. I need to close this case fast and get over to the mainland, but the last piece of the jigsaw puzzle is missing.

'I'm going up, Kinsella. You should rest too. This place is like Fort Knox; every door and window is locked.'

'I'll sleep when my shift ends, sir.'

'Thanks for your hard work.'

Shadow follows me to my room, and my guard stations himself in the corridor on a folding chair. Kinsella's eyes are wide open when I say goodnight, and I'm grateful for a break from invisible threats. I take off my shoes and lie down, falling asleep fully dressed.

Shadow wakes me after a few hours. He's pawing at my arm, giving a high-pitched whine.

'Shut up, you hell hound.' The dog runs to the window and releases a howl. 'There's nothing out there.'

My brain is too overloaded for sleep to return. The New Venture logo enters my mind; an N entwined with a V. I've seen it somewhere before, then the truth clicks into place. It's identical to one of the rings on Maeve Trenwith's hand, the letters cast in silver.

79

Ruby is with Joe in her room, sitting on the bed, his fingers laced through hers. His presence gives her pleasure, but it's her father she remembers. He deserves to be honoured. Once Ben Kitto and his girlfriend are dead, Ruby will spend the rest of her life on the run. Joe will have to die if he lets her down, even though he's shown so much kindness. It's time to finish what she started.

'I can't stop thinking about you,' he whispers.

'Me too. I never expected to feel like this.'

'Why not?'

She shrugs. 'Maybe I don't deserve it.'

He ruffles her hair. 'You need more self-esteem.'

'I'm not safe here, Joe, that's the problem. My ex has reached Bryher; he must have paid someone to bring him over. I saw him hiding in the dunes.'

'Why didn't you say before?'

'What's the point? I can't call the police. If he found out, he'd hurt me even more.'

'He won't get anywhere near you while I'm around. The police can help us.'

'It's too late for that.'

'Why?'

'I have to get away.'

'It's safer to go at first light.'

'My dad needs me now. You promised, Joe.' Her gaze settles on his face, preventing him from looking away.

'I'd never break my word, Chloe. We'll go together, whatever happens.'

She showers kisses on his face, then asks him to wait for her in his boat. Her heart pounds with relief when he finally leaves.

Ruby slips on her jacket with the knife concealed inside, then skirts round the side of the pub, counting windows to locate Kitto's room. There's no point in using the stairs. She's memorised the building's layout, but none of the access points on the ground floor would work. His guard will spot her, and he must be armed. Her only chance is to shin up the drainpipe, then jemmy the locked window. She's about to start climbing when the fire escape flies open, forcing her to duck behind a wall as Kitto marches out with his guard behind. She hears him say that he needs to see someone named Maeve. The dog is with them, releasing its high-pitched whine.

'Vicious mongrel,' she whispers under her breath.

Fate has delivered another lucky break, but the dog could slow her down. She'll have to kill it before Kitto's name can be wiped from her father's list.

80

'Where does Maeve Trenwith live, sir?' Kinsella is marching to keep up.

'In the Town, it's not far.'

'Stop for a minute, please.' He comes to a sudden halt on the path. 'We're being followed again.'

All I can hear is a gull shrieking as it wings inland. 'Are you sure?'

'There were footsteps, sir. My hearing's a hundred per cent.'

'We have to keep moving, this is urgent.'

The ex-serviceman looks set to argue, but Shadow is sprinting ahead and Kinsella has no choice but to follow.

It takes us five minutes to complete our journey to the Trenwiths' house. Lights glow through the downstairs curtains, which are not fully drawn. I can see Maeve in her living room, fully dressed and peering at her computer screen, even though it's past midnight.

There's no smile on her face when she greets me at the door, her voice a hoarse whisper.

'Danny's asleep, Ben. He needs rest. I can't wake him.'

'I'll keep my voice down, don't worry.'

I leave Kinsella on guard in the porch. Shadow noses his way inside, but Maeve doesn't seem to notice. She flicks her laptop shut when we enter the lounge, like she's concealing something private. Some of her glamour has vanished since the build ground to a halt. She's removed her heavy silver rings, and her black eye make-up is smudged.

'It's late to be working, Maeve.'

'I'm sorting stuff out for the Spanish developers, to take the stress off Dan.'

'How's he doing?'

'Better, I think, but he needs time to recover. I've been so worried.' Her gaze drifts towards the open door.

'Sit down, please, I've got a few questions.'

Her hands jitter in her lap when she follows my instruction. I keep thinking of ways to frame my question, but there's no gentle way to raise the issue.

'How long have you known that your husband was abused as a child?'

There's a pause before she speaks. 'What are you talking about?'

'Finding that skeleton broke him, didn't it? Hugh Porthcawl was a pushy, ambitious lad, but they were best mates. Danny confided in him about Hayle's abuse, and Hugh marched up Badplace Hill to confront him.'

'That's just guesswork.'

'I'm right, Maeve, aren't I?'

'We thought Hugh had started a new life abroad, like we planned for ourselves.' She rubs her hands across her face, her expression bleak with exhaustion, as if she's fought a long battle.

'You keep saying "we". Did Hayle hurt you too? Is that why you and Danny stuck together, the same as Lucy and Christian Boston?'

'It happened once for me, but it went on years with Danny.' She pulls in a ragged breath. 'Louis Hayle was a paedophile, as you've worked out. He was indiscriminate, too. He didn't care if his victims were male or female, so long as they were young. We should have reported him, but who would have believed us? We dreamed up a better way to get even.'

'Explain for me, please.'

'Hayle cared more about money than life itself. I set up a limited company when we were still in our teens, to bleed him dry.'

'It's called New Venture, isn't it? One of your rings is cast in the shape of the company logo.'

She gives a weak smile. 'You're too observant, Ben.'

'Hayle's cash helped you establish your architecture practice, but the anger and pain never went away. Maybe I'd feel the same. You decided to erect a building in his back yard as a kind of torment. What else did you do to him, Maeve?'

'I told his wife about the abuse, giving her every detail. She never let him come to the islands alone after that. It was one of my conditions.' Her head has dropped now; she's unwilling to meet my eye. 'I regret involving Faith now; it was cruel of me. The bastard had managed to hide everything from her.'

'How many more kids did he hurt?'

She hesitates before replying. 'Nathan Kernow, Christian and Lucy Boston. I can't be sure how many more.'

'He should have gone to jail instead of you punishing him. You could spend years inside for shoving him down those stairs.'

'I didn't kill him.' When she leans closer, violence simmers in her voice. 'Hayle treated us all like rubbish. That's why I put those bones in his recycling box and delivered them to his door.'

'I don't see why you came back to Bryher. You're successful, and you'd stolen his cash. There was no need to risk it.'

'These islands are our home. I still love it here, no matter what happened. The landscape's not to blame.' There's sadness in her eyes as well as fury. 'Danny's always been the sensitive one, keeping everything locked inside. Watching him suffer has been the worst part.'

'Why did you go to Hayle's house the night he died?'

'For an apology.' Her face hardens again, but she's talking faster now, finally ready to tell the truth. 'Louis was such a coward, he tried to escape, but I followed him upstairs.'

'You pushed him, didn't you?'

'He tripped. All I did was turn him over to check if he was alive after he fell. He died without ever facing his guilt; that's what made me lash out. I couldn't help myself.' She's on her feet now, backing away, her eyes darting towards the door.

'I think you took a weapon up there, a hammer or a crowbar, after realising Danny was suicidal. You chased Hayle up those stairs so you could push him down then watch him die.'

'He was a monster, for fuck's sake. You're lucky he never touched you or your brother.'

'I pity everyone he hurt, but the law will settle this now.'

Reality appears to be hitting home. She'll be dragged through a long murder trial. It seems unfair that she and Danny will pay dearly for getting even, while Louis Hayle's reputation never suffered during his lifetime. It's possible that both the Trenwiths will go to jail as a consequence of his terrible crimes.

Eddie barges through the door while I'm deciding where to keep Maeve locked up for the night. He's panting for breath as he delivers his message.

'The hospital's been ringing you, boss.'

'I left my phone at the pub. What's wrong?'

'Nina's in labour. She needs you there right now.'

I tell him to guard Maeve and Danny until morning, then rush outside, where Kinsella is still keeping watch. Shadow chases ahead as I take a shortcut through the woods. My head is empty of thoughts, except how to reach the mainland fast.

81

Ruby is hiding when Kitto runs out of Maeve Trenwith's house, followed by his guard. The older man is slower, already struggling to keep up. Her father's blood pulses in her veins as she gives chase, and Kitto's torch beam is easy to follow. She keeps pace with him until she meets an obstacle. The dog has doubled back to find her. It blocks her path, its muzzle gaping in an ugly snarl. She backs away, but it jumps up at her face, jaws snapping. When she pulls out her knife, the blade slices deep into its flesh. The creature yelps as a spurt of blood soaks her sleeve.

'That'll shut you up,' she hisses as it limps away.

There's no need to chase the dog through the bracken – such a deep wound will soon kill it – but the encounter has left her shaken. Kitto is further ahead now, and she's lost track of his sidekick. She'll have to run fast to overtake them, and the wind is picking up from the sea, blowing hard in her face. Her father's voice whispers in her ears, still calling for revenge, which gives her an idea. Kitto's instinct to protect could be his downfall.

She lets out a wild scream, and the effect is instant. The cop's torch beam wavers in the distance. When she cries out again, the streak of light arcs back to find her, shining brighter through the trees.

82

Instinct tells me to keep running, even though I heard Shadow yelp in pain. If he's caught himself on barbed wire, any of the islanders will help him, but that shrill female voice can't be ignored. I should head for the quay, yet my legs aren't following my instructions. Trees surround me as I retrace my steps; there's no sign of a victim anywhere.

The next cry comes from directly ahead, making me tear through high brambles into a clearing. A woman is lying between tree stumps, so petite she looks more child than adult. It's Billy's new kitchen hand, cowering on the ground, eyes terrified. One sleeve of her denim jacket is dark with blood.

'You're safe now, Chloe. Tell me what happened.'

'Help me, please. It won't stop bleeding.'

Her face contorts when I lean down to take her hand. I only see the knife a moment before she lashes out. Its blade skims my jaw, triggering a lightning flash of pain.

'What the fuck are you doing?'

The knife glints in the moonlight as she lunges at me again. When she kicks the torch from my hand, I'm in trouble. Whoever she is, she's used to the darkness, while I'm night-blind. Instinct makes me spin round: she's two metres away, just a thin silhouette, laughing at me.

'Who the hell are you?'

'Take a guess.' She moves fast, her blade slicing through my jacket.

I grab her wrist to shake the knife from her hand. When moonlight floods the clearing, I realise why she looked familiar. I see a glimpse of the innocent child that used to play video games while I waited for her father's next command, but it's buried under a new facade. Her features are pinched by misery and spite, her hair blonde instead of black.

'Craig sent you, didn't he, Ruby? He's gone now, you don't have to follow his orders.'

'Lying bastard, you betrayed both of us.'

Somehow she slides from my grasp. When she lands a drop kick on my chest I reel back, winded. Now she's scrabbling for her knife among fallen leaves, until I stand on her wrist, making her release a piercing scream, but I'm dealing with an expert fighter. Ruby frees herself in moments. The blade glitters in her hand, inches from my chest.

'Never forget my father, will you?' she hisses.

A shot rings past my face, the sound deafening. It

misses me by inches, but Kinsella has missed his target too. Ruby is already sprinting through the trees, at a pace neither of us can match.

83

Ruby heads for the quay. Her father's disappointment floods her mind, even though he's left this world, she can feel his spirit guiding her. Escape is her only option. She can't reach Kitto with a gunman at his side, and next time she might not be so lucky.

Joe is waiting on his boat, about to start the motor. He looks concerned by the blood on her sleeve, but she reaches for his hand.

'He's armed, Joe. We have to leave.'

'Let me check you're okay first.'

'Cast off, please, before it's too late.'

The boat powers through the sound. Ruby can see the compass pointing due east, towards the mainland.

'It'll be a bumpy ride, Chloe. The weather's turning.'

When she looks back at Bryher, the boat's wash leaves a ragged trail. Kitto is on the jetty, with his guard doubled over at his side, catching his breath. She hoped her last knife blow had finished Kitto, but she missed her mark. At least he can't touch her now. It's only when she faces the open sea again that fear enters her mind. The ocean's immensity unrolls for miles. She's beyond the sound's protection, with waves peaking in high crests.

Craig Travis's voice echoes through her thoughts. *Kill their families if you can't reach your target.* She'll get to Penzance hospital before Kitto, to kill the woman he loves, and their unborn child. It will be the cruellest punishment imaginable. Her father would be ecstatic.

84

Kinsella is catching his breath as I jump aboard my uncle's boat. My bowrider wouldn't cope with waves like this. Ray has left the keys in the ignition as usual, thank God, but the engine won't start. It gives a sick cough before fading into silence. I try again, still with no result. The powerful motor only kicks into life as Kinsella climbs on board. The lights of Joe Trescothick's converted fishing boat are pinpricks in the dark, already far ahead. The boy must have swallowed Ruby Travis's charade. He's taking a big risk carrying her to the mainland when the gale could overwhelm his small vessel.

'Take the wheel, can you?' I yell at Kinsella as the wind gathers force. 'Give me your phone, and keep the compass pointing east.'

When I glance back at the jetty, there's no sign of Shadow. He's been glued to my side for days, but I can't help him now, if he's hurt. I use Kinsella's phone to call the hospital, telling them I'm on my way. The signal fades as we leave the islands. The line's even worse when I ask Eddie to alert the coastguard and let them know we're chasing a converted fishing boat that's heading for Land's End, with a killer on board. I tell him to call Joe Trescothick as well, to warn him that his girlfriend is dangerous. My last instruction is to keep a lookout for Shadow.

I should have checked how much diesel was in the tank before setting out. The gauge shows it's half empty. That's not enough for the three-hour journey to Penzance, but at least we're narrowing the gap. Kinsella is struggling to keep us on course, so I take the wheel again. His face is so full of tension he's a liability.

'Don't shoot again,' I tell him. 'I want her alive.'

'What else could I do? That bitch would have killed you, you're covered in blood.'

'It's only a scratch.' I'd forgotten the cut on my jaw, blood still dripping down my neck. It must be deeper than I thought. 'She's just a teenager.'

'What difference does that make?'

The heat in his eyes worries me. He seems to have a score to settle with the past, after witnessing too much violence, like Ruby. The waves are higher now, slowing our progress, and Trescothick's boat is pitching to starboard with breakers smashing over its prow. Everything I care about hangs in the balance: Nina, the baby, my job. I've put all three in danger, but there's no turning back.

85

Ruby can feel the storm winning, the boat's engine straining under her feet. There are no lights on the pitching sea, except from Kitto's boat, which is drawing closer all the time. If only she'd managed to kill him, her work would be complete. It doesn't matter what happens to her now. The wind screams as it passes overhead. Rain falls in hard pellets that batter her face whenever she glances back, and Joe is wrestling the wheel.

'That crazy bastard shot at me,' she says. 'I had to run through the woods.'

'He won't hurt you now, I promise.'

'Go faster, Joe, please.'

'This is top speed. My boat's not built for water this rough.'

Ruby's feelings overwhelm her when she looks at him again. There's determination as well as naked fear on his face. He's risking his life to save hers. They might have stayed together for years if things had been different.

'I'm sorry, Joe. You don't deserve this.'

He shakes his head. 'Don't apologise. We're in it together.'

'You'll hear about my past. It'll change how you feel.'

'Nothing could.'

'You won't believe it at first. Then you'll grow to hate me.'

'How could I, Chloe? It was love at first sight.'

The other boat's lamps look brighter as a huge wave lifts them above the breakers, like they're riding a roller coaster. Ruby presses her lips to his, taking comfort from his words, but her enemy is so close, they'll soon be overtaken. She's not prepared to languish in jail, her decision made in a split second. Before Joe can stop her, she dives overboard.

The shock of freezing cold water is followed by terror. A wave crashes over her head as the sea's raw symphony throbs in her ears. When she resurfaces, Joe's boat looks tiny as the current drags her away. She can hear his voice in the distance, yelling her name. The next wave knocks her under again, yet instinct makes her keep on fighting back to the surface.

A breaker rolls her onto her back and she's granted a last moment of peace. The sky's glitter seems endless, and her father's words reach her again. *We're the stars and the moon, Ruby, looking down on them all.* But what if he was wrong? She could have loved someone and been loved in return. The question haunts her as currents swirl in a vortex, dragging her under, into water that's far blacker than the sky.

86

I see her leap overboard, then Trescothick's frantic attempts to throw her a safety ring. I can tell he's about to dive after her, stripping off his waterproofs as our boats draw level.

'Stay on deck, Joe,' I yell. 'You won't make it. Let the coastguard find her.'

He's on the prow as the boat pitches, clinging to the handrail. He looks terrified, too afraid of losing his girlfriend to value his own life. His boat should be facing the oncoming waves, but with no one steering, it's spinning like a cork in a whirlpool. My only chance of saving him is to get on board, before it capsizes.

I have to wait until we're alongside before making the leap. I steer as close as possible, then let Kinsella take the wheel. There's a deep gulf between the vessels as I stand on the bow, waiting for the right moment. If I fall, I'll be crushed like a butterfly, the two boats grinding together with the next high wave. It's a leap of faith when I take my chance, overbalancing as I hit the deck. I try to guide Joe's boat into the oncoming sea, but he's still in danger. His waterproofs have washed overboard, rain soaking him to the skin as he yells for a girl who never really existed.

Relief floods my system when I hear the rescue helicopter's engine, until it dawns on me that their first duty is to find the killer, despite the lives she's claimed. They won't carry me to Nina. The symbol Ruby carved into her victims' skin has a different meaning now. Craig Travis used it as a warning to his gang: three strikes and you're out. But the square slashed through with vertical lines looks like a cell window too, covered in bars. Ruby's father died behind them, but she never intended to suffer the same fate.

I only start to relax when the lights of a second helicopter arrive. Eddie must have scrambled the Cornish police to send their only chopper. The RNLI are on their way too; the lifeboatmen will sail both boats back to harbour safely. Joe Trescothick is in no state to get home alone. I can't imagine how he'll feel when he learns the truth about his girlfriend, whether she's dragged from the sea dead or alive.

I'd enjoy the adventure of being winched into a helicopter, on a normal day, but Nina's my only thought as I dangle from the rope, with the sea sprawling below me. Even the revelation that Maeve killed Louis Hayle as revenge for his abuse drifts from my head. The medic's face is compassionate when he puts a silver blanket round my shoulders, even though I'm too numb to register the cold. I tell him not to bother dressing my wounds, but he does it anyway, swiping iodine into the cuts on my jaw and shoulder, then covering them with bandages.

'We'll get you sorted properly at the hospital,' he yells over the engine's scream.

The sea's still churning fifty metres below us as Land's End comes into sight, but I may already have missed the birth. Over an hour has passed since Eddie told me to go to Penzance. My hands are shaking with delayed shock.

When the helicopter lands on the hospital's roof, I run under the spinning rotor blades towards a nurse who's beckoning me. The chopper's engine is deafening as we rush down the emergency stairs, then through brightly lit corridors and wards reeking of bleach. Then I hear a woman's scream, the sound low and guttural.

Nina is surrounded by monitors, yelling at full blast, when I crash through the doors of the delivery room. The sight of her makes the skeleton on Badplace Hill and Ruby Travis's killing spree vanish like mist. I feel calmer when she screams at me. Anyone who can curse that loudly can't be in danger.

'You bastard. You almost missed the whole fucking thing.'

'I'll never leave you again, I promise.'

'Get me an epidural, before I kill you.'

A consultant appears in the doorway, looking

concerned. I watch as she checks the monitors then turns to Nina.

'Your blood pressure's still a little too high. I'll give you some more pain relief then take you to theatre for your C-section. Everything's set up.'

Nina barely responds while she battles the next contraction, and a wave of panic hits me. She must have signed consent forms already if they're doing a Caesarean.

'You got here just in time,' the medic says. 'Scrub up now, please, if you want to see your baby born.'

'He does,' Nina says through gritted teeth.

When I catch sight of myself in the mirror above the hospital sink I see a giant with wild eyes, sea-blown hair, and a bandage on his jaw that's saturated with blood. I look more like a Cornish pirate than an expectant dad, but I'm determined to see our kid arrive, so I pull on the blue scrubs the doctor hands me.

Calmness settles over us once Nina gets her epidural, but her exhaustion shows. Her olive skin is grey with tiredness. It takes ten more minutes of grovelling until I'm forgiven. My feelings for her slip from my mouth unedited for once.

'You're all I want. We're getting married this summer, whether you like it or not.'

My announcement seems to amuse Nina, but her smile fades when she's wheeled into theatre. I focus on her instead of the surgeons working behind their screen. Something about her reactions worries me. Her eyes are glassy; she barely responds to the nurse who stands opposite telling her how well she's doing.

I only transfer my attention to the birth in the final moments. Our baby emerges from Nina's belly blue-faced and furious, with a cap of black hair, and white streaks of grease marking his skin. He's punching his small fists at the air like he's won his first prize fight, and the knot in my stomach releases at last. I reach for him, but a nurse carries him away. When she returns, he's wrapped in a blanket, his face wiped clean.

'Congratulations, he's a healthy eight-pound boy. No one would guess he's a week or two premature.'

'Let me hold him, please,' Nina says.

The surgeons are still stitching her wound when a nurse places the baby on her chest, and my relief is bone deep. The joy of seeing our son for the first time wipes the exhaustion from Nina's face. She touches his tiny fingers, cooing at him, then beams up at me. I've been gripping her hand so hard through the procedure my knuckles ache, but I'm too elated to care.

It's only now that something changes. Nina's eyes are rolling back, her jaw suddenly rigid. One of the monitors releases a high-pitched alarm, then they all ring at once, filling the room with their electronic scream. A nurse reaches out to seize our baby.

'Her pressure's down,' the anaesthetist calls out. 'She's flatlining.'

The nurse dumps the baby in my arms, then hustles me towards the exit. I'm so busy looking over my shoulder, watching the medics caring for Nina, that the experience of holding my son for the first time barely registers. The kid is gurgling to himself as the nurse grabs my sleeve.

'Wait in the corridor, please. Your wife needs our help.'

'I'm not leaving.'

When I stand my ground, she soon rushes back to the circle of blue-coated medics, all working fast, trying to rouse Nina. Her eyes are still closed, and my gut tells me that our son is losing his mother already, just like Ruby Travis did. The sensation feels like water flowing down a drain, taking me and the baby with it.

'Stay with us, for fuck's sake.'

The words hiss from my mouth unnoticed. But the second time, my plea is loud enough for a nurse to spin round and stare. The doctors' faces tell me that she's already gone. One of them looks close to tears as they place the pads on her chest. When they shock her again, my own body is rigid with tension. The heart rate monitor is silent when a sound leaves my mouth. I couldn't stop it if I tried. It's like Shadow's loudest howl, raw and ugly, but it has an effect. The monitor clicks back into life, its bleep fast but regular. When two of the doctors step away from the table, there's relief on their faces. Nina's eyes open slowly, and I witness the ghost of a smile on her face as she sees me clutching our baby, who is now fifteen minutes old.

My system is still flooded with adrenaline and relief,

but the drama hasn't affected our son at all. He is observing me through hazy blue eyes. His skin smells of honey, his minute fingers grasping the air, and I realise he needs a different name than any we planned. He's risen into the world triumphant, while Ruby Travis sinks to the ocean's depths.

'It's good to meet you, Noah,' I whisper.

He lies still in my arms, warm and sleepy, oblivious to any type of danger.

87

It takes the medics all night to find out why Nina's heart stopped then restarted with a sudden jolt. She's fast asleep when a consultant calls me into the corridor with the test results.

'Pre-eclampsia's a nasty condition, because it's unpredictable,' she says, gazing down at Nina's latest heart tracing. 'If blood pressure spikes repeatedly, it can cause an arrythmia.'

'Will it happen again?'

'Unlikely.' She shakes her head. 'Nina's heartbeat's normalised, but we'll keep a close eye on her. If you have a second child, we'll monitor the pregnancy from day one.'

'There's no way she's going through that again.'

'You may feel different in time. Get some sleep if you can. I hear your boy looks like a rugby player already.'

The medic disappears before I can ask another question. I'll never know whether it was my yelling that brought Nina round, or a well-timed shot of adrenaline.

She's still sleeping, so I take a walk down to the neonatal unit to see our son. His cot is closest to the window, and I watch him sleep, his black hair unmistakable. Something shifts in my gut, like all my major organs are being rearranged. I'll need to make changes, and grow up at last. I've got no religious faith at all, but I remember the stories we heard at Sunday School. Our kid strikes me as a miracle, spat from his mother's belly onto dry land, like Noah stepping from the ark.

I get a few hours' sleep in an armchair before Nina's parents arrive from Bristol. Her larger-than-life Italian mother never stops talking, while her English dad rolls his eyes. Noah's grandmother insists on taking hundreds of photos, then carries him out into the corridor so nurses, patients and visitors can all admire him.

I've been ignoring the texts that keep on arriving, but the room's so packed with visitors I slip outside to check my phone. The coastguard searched all night for Ruby Travis, but she's still missing, presumed drowned. Joe Trescothick is traumatised; he can't yet accept that his girlfriend was a ruthless killer. The next email proves that Liz Gannick never sleeps. She tested all of Maeve Trenwith's shoes overnight, finding bloodstains on a pair of boots. If it belongs to Louis Hayle, Maeve will face a murder trial, and Danny will be seen as complicit. She may regret giving me so many details last night, even though it was off the record, but the blood proves she was at the scene. The couple will be placed in holding cells at Penzance jail. It still strikes me as tragic that they may pay a high price for Louis Hayle's abuse.

I assume it's a friend calling to congratulate us when my phone rings, but my old boss's face appears on the screen. DCI Goldman looks relaxed for once, her brittle features forming a smile.

'What an extraordinary case, Kitto.'

'It certainly was, ma'am.'

'Ruby Travis took four lives in a single week. Malcolm Pierce, Denny Lang and two of your fellow officers, which I deeply regret.'

'She was following her dad's orders.'

'Or she was evil to the core. We can't escape our genes.'

Goldman congratulates me on wrapping up the case on Bryher, but my thoughts are still on parenthood when we say goodbye. Ruby Travis never stood a chance. There was fear as well as hatred on her face when she lunged at me. She had no mother to guide her, and a father fuelled by psychotic violence. Little wonder she couldn't tell right from wrong.

I'm about to go back into the room when I remember Shadow, and a ripple of panic runs through me. There was no sign of him when I jumped onto the boat after hearing his cry. My hands are shaking when I call Eddie, but there's no reply. Pictures are forming in my mind. Why was there so much blood on Ruby's sleeve when she had no visible injury? The station's not answering either, the line busy, so I call Ray instead. He announces that he's booked a flight this afternoon to come and see Noah, our argument already forgotten. There's a long pause after I ask about Shadow.

'He got hurt, Ben. I'm with him now, at the vet's.'

'What happened?'

'He was smart enough to crawl to my yard; he'd lost a lot of blood. There's one hell of a knife wound on his chest. It's lucky he survived the ride to St Mary's.'

'But he'll be okay?'

'He's too stubborn to die.' My uncle's laugh echoes at the end of the line. 'But he's agitated. Your voice might calm him; he'll hear you, if you speak loudly.'

'You did well, you scruffy hound,' I say. 'Rest now, and get some sleep.'

I hear him whine a quiet reply, and my head drops, a few tears hitting the lino at my feet. I don't know why the idea of almost losing Shadow finally undoes me, after so much danger. It's the thought of him risking his life to defend me again, even though we annoy the hell out of each other most days. Ruby Travis did her best to kill us both, but at least he's safe now. He'll be comfortable at the vet's until we're home, then he'll get plenty of rewards.

When I return to Nina, the room is still full, so I stand in the corridor and peer through the doorway. I want my son in my arms, but last night's nurses have dropped by, so I'll have to wait my turn. Nina is telling them his full name will be Noah Simon Mark Kitto, which is a bit long-winded, but who cares? He will be surrounded by admirers on Bryher, with me and Nina always in the background, keeping him safe and sound.

Acknowledgements

Many thanks to my friends and supporters in Scilly, including Linda Thomas and Rachel Greenlaw. Your kind welcome makes the islands an even greater pleasure to visit. I'm also grateful to Judy Logan, Amanda Grunfeld and Penny Hancock for listening to me bang on about this book's plot and characters. Dave Pescod, my long-suffering husband, thanks for the tea, advice and chocolate biscuits. Who knew that during the COVID lockdown you would not only master the art of breadmaking, but also write your own brilliant novel? I am well and truly proud of you.

I owe a big debt to Bethan Jones, my new editor. The relationship between author and editor can be a tense one, but you have been so kind and supportive from day one it's been a pleasure working with you. Your notes help hugely at every stage of writing these books. Jess Barratt, thanks so much for being such a committed and talented publicist. Many thanks for all your support on the Locked Island series. Knowing that the lovely sales team at Simon & Schuster also work so hard to promote my books is a huge encouragement.

My Twitter pals are too many to thank individually, but I'm so grateful for the wonderful support of Polly Dymock, Jennie Blackwell, Janet Fearnley, Anna Tink, Joanna Blatchley, Richard Purser, Peggy Breckin, Elaine Cook, Rachel Ward, Ian Dixon, Hazel Wright, Joanna Beesley, Angela Barnes and many more.

Thanks again to Vicki, Clive and Avril at Mumford's in Hugh Town, St Mary's, for requesting signed copies every year for your customers. I love seeing my books on your shelves!

Don't miss the other atmospheric locked-island thrillers featuring DI Ben Kitto from highly-acclaimed author, Kate Rhodes

'An absolute master of pace, plotting and character'
ELLY GRIFFITHS

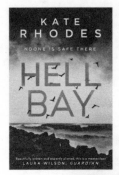
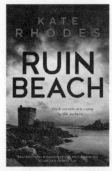
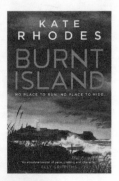

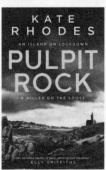
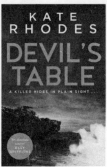

'Gripping, clever and impossible to put down' **ERIN KELLY**

'Beautifully written and expertly plotted;
this is a masterclass' *GUARDIAN*

**SIMON &
SCHUSTER**